The Last Note of Warning

Also by Katharine Schellman

THE NIGHTINGALE MYSTERIES
Last Call at the Nightingale
The Last Drop of Hemlock

THE LILY ADLER MYSTERIES
The Body in the Garden
Silence in the Library
Death at the Manor
Murder at Midnight

The Last Note of Warning

of Warning

KATHARINE SCHELLMAN

MINOTAUR BOOKS
NEW YORK

First published in the United States by Minotaur Books, an imprint of St. Martin's Publishing Group

THE LAST NOTE OF WARNING. Copyright 2024 by Katharine Schellman Paljug. All rights reserved. Printed in the United States of America. For information, address St. Martin's Publishing Group, 120 Broadway, New York, NY 10271.

www.minotaurbooks.com

Designed by Gabriel Guma

The Library of Congress Cataloging-in-Publication Data is available upon request.

ISBN 978-1-250-32579-2 (hardcover)
ISBN 978-1-250-32580-8 (ebook)

Our books may be purchased in bulk for promotional, educational, or business use. Please contact your local bookseller or the Macmillan Corporate and Premium Sales Department at 1-800-221-7945, extension 5442, or by email at MacmillanSpecialMarkets@macmillan.com.

First Edition: 2024

10 9 8 7 6 5 4 3 2 1

For Nettie and Whitney, who put this series in your hands
And for Brian, just because

The Last Note
of Warning

ONE

Manhattan, 1925

The champagne was flowing in the Nightingale, poured out for the dancers who crowded around the bar.

Don't tell, they agreed, toasting each other with sultry voices and bold laughter. *Don't tell. You never saw me here.*

You couldn't see the stars if you went outside. The city lights were too bright, the dingy clouds too thick. But inside, champagne stars fizzed in cut-crystal glasses, dancing like the couples who found their way through the back alleys and down the stairs each night.

I'll dance 'til last call, they whispered at the door, all hoping to escape something. The monotony of wealth. The needs of a lover. The demands of family and work and sometimes just scraping by. The drudgery of a city where you would never see the stars at night.

Vivian Kelly knew what it was like to wish for those stars. She had learned not to look up, to find her freedom in the rhythm of the music, in champagne bubbles and dances with strangers, in the secrets they kept for each other. She could tell, just by looking, who was there on a whim or a dare, money flashing bright as the spangles on a dress, cares light as a whisper of silk. They kept the liquor flowing, the dance floor busy, the laughter loud.

And she could tell who was there for the same reasons she was. The ones whose shoulders relaxed as they came down the stairs, who slipped into their true selves like coming home. The ones who knew that freedom came with a price, that freedom wasn't safe, and still decided it was worth the cost.

Don't tell, they agreed when they heard what they weren't supposed to know.

Don't tell, they whispered when they saw someone they shouldn't.

Don't tell, they begged. *Oh, please, don't tell.*

You never saw me here.

TWO

"Mrs. Buchanan's not here."

Vivian Kelly, twenty-four years old and feeling three times her age, her feet aching from trudging twenty blocks between deliveries and her arms limp from the weight of three dress boxes, bit the inside of her cheek. The housekeeper didn't deserve her impatience or her anger. And the woman who did—the one who had *insisted* that her gowns be completed and delivered a week early—wouldn't see anything but a polite shopgirl when she finally arrived, either. Not if Vivian wanted to keep her job.

She arranged her face into a smile. "Does she want me to leave the dresses? The hem and shoulders need to be checked, but if she wants her own maid to do that—"

"I don't know," the housekeeper said, already distracted by the sound of an argument in the next room.

Vivian stood in the tradesmen's entrance, shivering from the wind that snaked around her ankles and crept up her stockinged legs. It could snow tonight, judging by that wind. She didn't want to trudge back here in the snow.

"Just come in. You can wait a bit, can't you? God willing she'll be back soon." The housekeeper cast a glance over her shoulder as the sound of the argument grew louder. "You, with the red hair! What's your name, Lena? Take this girl to the upstairs parlor. And tell me the minute Mrs. Buchanan is back. She needs to—"

The shouting grew, along with something that sounded like a whole stack of pots toppling to the ground. "Lord almighty, I hate opening a new house," the housekeeper muttered. "Go with Lena, young lady. I can't be bothered figuring out what to do with you just now."

Lena, a maid with brilliant red hair and the expected number of freckles scattered across her nose to go with it, pulled a face as the housekeeper disappeared. "Sounds like the new cook won't last any longer than the first one," she said, shrugging. "Hurry up, will you? I've got better things to do than play nursemaid."

Quiet descended as they made their way upstairs, the sound of servants concealed, like their presence, behind closed doors. Vivian hid a yawn behind her hand as she followed.

Delivering dresses instead of making them meant she no longer spent hours hunched over a sewing machine or a tray of beads. But her days still started early, and her nights often didn't end until two or three in the morning. She stumbled a little as her feet sank into the plush carpet that ran up the stairs, and she blinked rapidly, looking around to keep herself alert.

The Fifth Avenue mansion was like so many she had visited, deliveries in hand: sweeping ceilings, marble floors, glass windows like works of art. Most of them were gilded, decorated, and filled to within an inch of their lives, temples to success and excess both. But this one felt half-finished, its tables bare of ornaments, paintings leaning against the walls instead of hung on them.

Lena caught her glancing around. "New house," she said, by way of explanation as they made their way to the second floor. "Well, old house, but new family in it. They're still settling in."

"Did you come with them?" Vivian asked, glad the other girl was willing to make conversation. She hated walking through big houses in silence. It reminded her too much of life in the orphan home.

Lena shook her head as she swung open a heavy, paneled door. "Most of us are new, too. Which is why they're all shouting at each other downstairs."

"Are they at it again?" a mild voice asked from inside the room.

Both girls jumped, and a stricken look crossed Lena's face as she dropped a quick curtsy. "Beg your pardon, Mr. Buchanan. I didn't mean—"

"That's all right." The older gentleman didn't move from the wing-back chair where he was installed, legs propped on a footstool and a cigar between two fingers, the window behind him cracked to let fresh air in and smoke out. But there was a smile on his face as he winked at the maid. "God knows we've been a mess since the house was opened, and we likely will be for several weeks yet. D'you think the new cook will last?"

Lena giggled, her blush nearly as bright as her hair. "Not if Mrs. Mulligan has anything to say about it, sir."

"And even I don't dare cross Mrs. Mulligan." He made a little shooing motion with his free hand. "Off you go. I'll keep our guest company."

"Yessir." Lena curtsied. There was something sly in her sideways glance, something that made the back of Vivian's neck prickle warily. Lena smiled. "I'll tell Mrs. Buchanan you're waiting when she arrives."

"Thank you," Vivian said. But she only glanced at the maid briefly as she said it, not wanting to take her eyes off Mr. Buchanan after seeing Lena's smile. There was a tray on the table in front of him, with a silver carafe that was still steaming and a cut-glass decanter of some amber liquid. The smell of strong, good coffee filled the air, and

Vivian had to hold back another yawn. Buchanan set down his cigar long enough to take a drink from his cup as he looked her over.

Judging by appearances alone, he was the sort of man she often saw at the Nightingale, the kind who waited for an old-fashioned waltz to ask pretty girls onto the dance floor. Their shoulders were still broad, and their gray hair made them look distinguished instead of stooped and tired like the men where Vivian lived. They wore expertly tailored clothes, the fabrics so luxurious that she wanted to rub her cheek against them like a cat while they danced. They threw a little money around because it made them feel important, drank and danced because it made them feel young.

Buchanan smiled, beckoning her forward with a hooked finger as he took a puff from his cigar. Vivian stepped farther into the room.

Plenty of men like him were polite—harmless, even—gallantly trying to recapture the feel of their youth.

And some of them she wouldn't trust farther than a Charleston kick.

"You're very kind, sir, but I'm not a guest. I'm the dressmaker."

"I can see that," he said, still smiling as he nodded toward the boxes she held. "You can put those down if you like and take a seat. I promise I won't think you're shirking. I've no idea when Mrs. Buchanan will return." He shook his head, looking a little embarrassed, as he stood and glanced out the window.

Vivian set the boxes on the table, then perched on the edge of the velvety sofa. She clasped her hands in her lap to keep from stroking the soft nap of the fabric and shivered a little.

He noticed. "Oh, my apologies, my dear." Stubbing out the cigar in a crystal ashtray, he closed the window against the cold air before turning back to her with another smile. "There, that's better, isn't it? Shall I pour you something against the chill? Coffee, perhaps? Or . . ." He smiled, almost like a mischievous boy. "Something stronger?"

"No, thank you." She liked a good time as much as the next girl, but she preferred it on her own terms.

Buchanan chuckled as he refilled his own cup. "Really? I wouldn't have expected a girl with hair like yours to say no to a drink."

Vivian resisted the urge to reach up and touch her bobbed hair, which fell like a straight black curtain to just below her jaw. "No, thank you," she repeated. "Sir." He sounded like he meant it as a joke, but she had to go in and out of too many houses like this one to risk word getting around that the delivery girl from Miss Ethel's shop was fast.

Buchanan gave her a shrewd glance, then sighed as he returned to his chair. "My apologies, again. I've made you uncomfortable. But I promise, my philandering days are long behind me, if you'll forgive my bluntness." This time, the smile he gave her was self-deprecating. "I'm just an old man hoping to enjoy a little conversation to pass the time."

"You're not that old," Vivian said without thinking, though she regretted it right away. She didn't want him to think she was flirting.

But he only laughed before taking another drink. If she took a deep breath, she could smell the whiskey in it, floating just under the scent of the coffee itself.

"Thank you, but age is a fact we must all face eventually." His expression grew distant as he stared down at the cup in his hand. "If we are fortunate. Not everyone lives to face it." He cleared his throat, then looked her over with a critical eye. "Your coat is too skimpy for a girl who must be out in this weather. Allow me to provide you with coffee, at least, while you wait. It would be a great kindness to me, so I don't have to worry about you."

He spoke politely enough, and his smile was disarming—fatherly, almost, as if he had sensed that his tone needed to shift to something less playful. It made Vivian wary, that he could read her so clearly and change so quickly. But the coffee did smell good, and she was already fighting back another yawn. "Well, all right then. For your sake."

He chuckled as he poured her a cup. "What have you brought for my wife, then?"

Here she was on safer ground. Vivian glanced down at the boxes. "Three very pretty dresses for the spring."

"And very expensive, I don't doubt," he said, smiling as he handed the cup over. He wasn't wrong, but Vivian wasn't about to agree with him out loud. A man could make fun of himself for spending too much money if he wanted, but the girl delivering his wife's dresses would keep her mouth shut if she was smart. "Did you make them yourself?"

Vivian shook her head as she accepted the coffee. "I used to do the dressmaking. Now I just handle deliveries. But I know the girls who did the sewing. One gown has over a thousand beads stitched onto it."

She took a sip. It tasted even better than it had smelled—rich and sweet, which her coffee at home almost never was because sugar was an expense she could live without. The heat was a welcome pain against her chilled hands, and she took another sip, her eyes closing for a moment in pleasure.

"Thank you," she said as she opened them.

Buchanan was looking at the door, a frown pulling down his brows. "Well, I am sorry Evangeline is keeping you waiting." He stood, his own cup in hand, and paced toward the window once more. "She's new money, I'm afraid, and still likes to make people wait for her. She'll move past such games eventually." He shrugged, crossing to the sofa where Vivian perched. To her relief, he sat at the other end, so most of the expanse of velvet was between them. "Or not. Many do not."

It was an odd comment to make about his own wife, and not entirely kind. Vivian wondered whether their marriage was as new as the house. It was on the tip of her tongue to say he, at least, didn't seem like new money, but she stopped herself just in time. Being tired was no reason to get careless and say something he might take as an insult to his wife.

"I don't mind the wait," she said instead, giving him a smile that was friendly but not too familiar—the sort of smile she employed on the dance floor at least once a night. Buchanan seemed decent enough, but she knew the assumptions he might make about a girl like her. Still, she didn't want to offend him. Miss Ethel would throw a fit if she lost his wife's business. It was a delicate balancing act. "The company and the coffee both are nothing to sneeze at."

He lifted his cup to her in a small toast, the slight wobble in the gesture making her think that he had been sitting there enjoying his whiskey-laced drink for longer than was typical on a Monday morning. She thought there was something sad, though, in the look he gave her. But whatever he might have said next was interrupted by a knock at the door. Vivian started to her feet, quickly setting her cup down on the side table.

It wasn't Lena this time, but an older woman—closer to Buchanan's age, her cheeks and shoulders both beginning to sag with time and fatigue, with the sandy-gray hair of someone who had probably been a fiery redhead in her younger days. She kept her eyes turned toward the floor, and Vivian felt a lurch of sympathy in her chest. Working in service was an endless carousel of early mornings, late nights, and few rests, and most folks didn't stick it out after forty unless they had moved up in the ranks. To still be running your feet off as you spun toward sixty was a rough life for sure.

The maid barely glanced at Vivian as she stepped into the room, her face still turned toward the ground. "Begging your pardon, Mr. Buchanan, but there's someone in your office asking to see you." Her voice dropped, as though she was nervous to pass on the visitor's message. "Said it was a business matter, and that you'd know what it was about."

"Hmm. Yes, thank you." Buchanan barely spared her a glance, lifting one finger in careless acknowledgment as he refilled his cup with a splash of coffee and a large pour of whiskey. "Tell him I'll be there in just a moment, please." He turned to Vivian, and she wondered but didn't ask what sort of business he was in. "Here," he said, leaning over to refill her cup. He gave her a little wink as she met his eyes. "Have to keep off that chill, young lady."

Vivian cast a quick, worried look toward the maid, hoping she wouldn't get the wrong idea. But the woman had already hurried out to deliver her employer's message. Just when Vivian was about to breathe a sigh of relief, Buchanan caught her chin, lifting her gaze toward him.

She froze, anxiety prickling down her spine like a warning. But the paternal look was still there as he looked her over, a sad smile on his lips. "You know, you remind me of my daughter. She's a bit of a hellion, from what I've heard. I wouldn't be surprised if you are, too."

Vivian leaned back, unnerved by the casual assumption of his touch. To her relief, he didn't stop her, his hand dropping and sliding into his pocket. He even looked a little embarrassed, clearing his throat as he bent to retrieve his coffee cup.

"Don't you know if she is or not?" Vivian asked, surprised at herself.

"I would if I'd been a better father," he said, the self-deprecating edge back in his smile. "Take care, young lady. I hope Mrs. Buchanan doesn't keep you waiting much longer."

"Thanks," Vivian said, a little uncertainly, as he departed.

She sank against the velvety sofa as soon as the door closed behind him, relieved to be alone for the moment. She tipped her head back before she thought better of the casual pose and sat up abruptly. No sense risking someone coming in to find her lounging like she owned the place.

The pretty glass clock on the mantel began to chime eleven, and Vivian fought down another yawn. She'd been running her feet off at the Nightingale last night, delivering contraband drinks and catching dances on her breaks until two in the morning, and she hadn't made it home until three. Once her deliveries were done for the day, she could stumble home and catch a little shut-eye. But until then . . .

Maybe she should have that second cup of coffee. Or open the window again so the cold air could keep her awake. Just one more minute, she told herself, and she'd stand up.

Vivian's next yawn stretched her jaw wide enough that she could hear it pop. The motion tipped her head back, and once it was resting against the sofa, picking it up suddenly felt like too much work. She rubbed her eyes, trying to wake them up, but they were too heavy, and the cushions were too soft. She yawned again, not bothering to open her eyes this time. The coffee would kick in at any moment, and then she'd feel more awake. She'd hear someone opening the door in time to get up.

—·—

The clock on the mantel began to chime, and Vivian was on her feet before she remembered where she was or why she was there. She glanced around the room a little frantically, trying to shake off her drowsiness.

It was noon. Vivian let out a loud sigh of relief. Mrs. Buchanan hadn't come home to find her asleep on the sofa, and apparently the whole household was such a mess that no one else had remembered she was there either. It was a lucky break—and she didn't often get those.

But she couldn't hang around waiting much longer, or Miss Ethel at the dress shop would start wondering where she was. Vivian gathered up her delivery kit—a black satchel shaped like a doctor's bag but filled with everything a seamstress might need on the go. Then she hesitated over the boxes that held Mrs. Buchanan's gowns.

On the one hand, if she left them there, they might get damaged or mislaid, and then she'd be blamed. On the other, if she was just going to return for fittings the next day, she could save her arms the extra hours of carting them around the city.

Stumbling over an embroidered footstool, still groggy from her unexpected nap and sudden wake-up, Vivian finished gathering her things and looked around the room.

There was no desk and nothing to write with that she could see. But she had passed what looked like an office when Lena led her upstairs, more than an hour ago. Likely that was where Mr. Buchanan had gone. If his meeting was done—there was no way she would risk interrupting that—maybe she could just poke her head in and grab a piece of paper and write a note to say she'd be back at the same time tomorrow.

Leaving her things for the moment, Vivian peeked out the sitting room door.

The hallway was empty and silent. It made her shiver—she was used to houses like this being full of servants and families. But if it was noon, likely folks were polishing off a meal downstairs and enjoying a break before they got back to work.

The thick carpet muffled her footsteps as she hurried down the hall. The door she thought was an office had been left ajar, so the odds of her interrupting some important or confidential business deal were slim. Still, she knocked.

"Mr. Buchanan?" Vivian called. "Are you in there? It's me—the delivery girl."

When there was no answer, she hesitated only a moment before pushing the door open.

The smell hit her first—a deep, animal smell, the taste of metal and filth. Vivian knew it, had smelled it once before, and the fear that followed only a moment later felt like iron in the back of her throat.

She would have fled if she hadn't seen him right away, slumped on the floor against his desk, his body curled on itself as it had collapsed to the ground, helpless and childlike. The coffee cup lay next to him, the fragile handle snapped off and the coffee already soaked into the deep red carpet.

"Mr. Buchanan?" Vivian croaked.

He didn't move, and for a moment she didn't either. But she couldn't leave him there.

"Mr. Buchanan!" She knelt beside him to grab his shoulders. He wasn't a small man, but she was wiry and determined, and he didn't resist as she turned him over, planning to check for a pulse, to call for help, to do what she could.

Her hands slipped against him as he rolled onto his back. Vivian lurched away, stumbling to her feet. She felt frozen, unable to move, unable to do anything except stare at the wide-eyed look of disbelief still on his face, at the blood that had soaked through his clothes and into the carpet, at the handle of the knife that had been plunged into his neck, right where it met the edge of his open collar.

THREE

S he needed to run.

She needed to get out of there as fast as possible, before someone came looking for her, or him, or just found them there, him
with a knife sticking out of his neck and her . . .

Vivian stared at her hands, covered with his blood.

Even if she ran, even if she made it out the front door, someone
would see her hurrying down the street. She had already talked to the
servants—had left her purse and her deliveries upstairs—they knew
her name and where she worked.

She couldn't run.

Vivian's heart beat so frantically she thought she would choke on it.
And Mr. Buchanan's wasn't beating at all. She could see his face, pale
above his soaked collar, his lips blue where they weren't streaked with
blood.

She could see that he wasn't breathing, not anymore.

She didn't know a thing about him, didn't even know if he was a good man. But he had cared whether she was out in the cold in a skimpy coat, and he had a daughter she might be a little bit like. He had talked to her like she was a real person, and then he had bled to death alone on the floor.

She couldn't leave him like that. She couldn't run.

Vivian took one slow step backward, then another, until she was at the door. She had left it open when she came in. As if from miles away, she could hear a murmur of voices, servants returning to their work downstairs.

Vivian took a deep breath. She screamed for help as loud as she could.

———

A nd you claim you just found him there?"

Vivian hunched her shoulders, as if that could shield her against the disbelief in the officer's voice. "I don't claim I just found him there, I did find him there. Sir," she added, not wanting to make things worse.

She was sitting on the house's grand staircase, a blanket wrapped around her shoulders. Her hands had left bloody prints on the faded cotton, and she kept trying to move them, trying to shift the stains out of her sight, but it didn't seem to work. If she glanced up, toward the floor where Mr. Buchanan's body was still waiting for the coroner to arrive, the carved wood of the banister and its supports cut across her view like the bars of a cage.

"Tell me again."

She shivered. "I was looking for a piece of paper, and no one answered when I knocked. So I went in and . . ."

She hadn't expected good things when she yelled for help. But it had been so much worse than she had imagined. Mrs. Buchanan, just arrived home, had screamed when she saw Vivian smeared in blood.

The servants had grabbed her and pinned her against the wall. Everyone was yelling for the police, the doctor, some kind of help.

Then the officers had arrived, faster than she'd ever seen police turn up to help folks where she lived. They had asked the housekeeper for a blanket, sat her on the steps, asked for a statement. For a few brief moments, she had thought they would listen. She waited for someone to suggest she wash her hands, to ask if she was all right.

But the questions kept coming. Who she was. When she had arrived. Why she had waited over an hour for a client who was clearly not coming, without going to find the housekeeper or anyone else. Why she had gone to Mr. Buchanan's study at all.

Why her hands were covered in his blood.

And when they got to the end of their questions, they started at the beginning again, pouncing on her stumbling words, the moments she didn't remember clearly, the things she couldn't explain in the first place.

"And who was this man you say he was meeting with?"

Vivian clenched her jaw to keep her teeth from chattering. Or maybe it was to stop herself from screaming. "I don't know." She closed her eyes for a moment, but all she saw behind her eyelids was the look of shock on Mr. Buchanan's face, the blood that had trickled across his lips while he was dying. She opened her eyes quickly. "The maid said someone was waiting for him. She didn't say a name, and Mr. Buchanan didn't ask, just said bye to me and went out after her."

There were footsteps on the parquet floor of the hall below them, then thumping up the stairs. The two officers stepped to the side as a man in a dapper suit, carrying a doctor's bag, nodded to them and continued toward Buchanan's study. He was followed by two young officers carrying a stretcher between them. The coroner didn't spare Vivian a glance, but the two with the stretcher gave her a quick look over. One of them couldn't hide his flinch as he caught sight of her bloody hands.

They were both young—Vivian thought the one who had flinched might even be younger than she was. She wondered if they liked to go out dancing or drinking on their nights off. She wondered how the flincher would feel when he saw Mr. Buchanan's body lying on the floor.

"Let me see her!"

There was someone else on the steps, a red-haired man in an elegant suit that was too rumpled, as though he'd been out all night in it and was finally coming home. He had his hat in his hand and he was glaring at another junior officer who was blocking his way.

"I'm very sorry, Mister . . ."

"Rokesby. Cornelius Rokesby," the young man said impatiently. "My mother is Mr. Buchanan's wife. Where is she?"

"Mrs. Buchanan isn't upstairs—"

"Then let me see her. Immediately. And tell me what happened to my stepfather."

"Sir, she isn't—"

"Dawes." The older officer had turned away from Vivian and was looking over the rail. "Go ahead and take him up. Let him talk to the coroner."

The junior officer barely had time to reply before Cornelius Rokesby was pushing his way up the stairs. Vivian shrank against the banister, her head turned down, her hands curled into the edges of the blanket once more. She didn't want Buchanan's stepson seeing her covered in his blood. But he didn't even glance at her as he went past.

"So, you claim the maid didn't say what the business matter was?" the younger officer asked, his voice snapping her back to the present.

Rokesby was gone, and they were looming over her again. "Why would she need to tell Mr. Buchanan his own business? Why would she even know?"

"We're the ones asking the questions, young lady," the older officer said. His voice was soft, softer than the bluster and brass of his partner. "How many times had you delivered dresses here before?"

"Never, sir," Vivian said, shifting her hands again. "Mrs. Buchanan's a new customer."

"And had you ever met Mr. Buchanan before?"

"No, sir."

"And yet he sat with you for some time, by your account. Shared a cup of coffee with you, even. Strange thing to do with a delivery girl he didn't know." The older officer's voice grew even quieter. "Tell me, do you often socialize with the husbands of your clients? Husbands you claim you never met before?"

"I don't claim it, sir. I never *had* met him before." Vivian clenched her fists hard enough that her nails bit into her palms, the discomfort reminding her to keep her temper in check. "Like I said, he was sitting in the room when I arrived, and he only spoke to me for a few minutes, including that cup of coffee. He was polite, nothing more. And I was polite, too, because that's how I am with customers. And their families. And everyone else." She met his eyes. "Sir."

"It pays to be *polite,* doesn't it?" The snide voice of the younger officer cut through the air, and Vivian turned in time to see his knowing smirk. "Girls like you don't make much money, isn't that so? Gotta make *friends* where you can if you need a little extra. And from what we heard, your conversation started out so *very* friendly."

Vivian felt as though someone had punched her in the stomach. "You heard from that redhead, you mean? That girl Lena?"

Something flickered between the two officers as they exchanged a glance. "Just answer the question," the older one said, sounding annoyed.

"It wasn't a question, it was a statement," Vivian snapped, knowing it was unwise. She wanted to jump up and shake them, to make a wild dash for the door. She wanted to lie down and sleep for a week, to pretend it had all been a dream. "That maid was in the room for all of thirty seconds, and I barely even opened my mouth until after she had walked out." She thought about mentioning that Lena had been more than happy to giggle and smile at Mr. Buchanan herself. But she wouldn't talk trash about someone she didn't know, not when it could get another girl in trouble. Not even if the other girl had done it to her first. "Like I said, he was polite, and I was polite, and then he left. That was it."

The two officers exchanged another glance. "All right, stand up." The younger one nudged her with his toe, and Vivian shot to her feet, mouth half-open to tell him not to touch her.

But before she could say anything, the older one added, "You're coming to the station with us."

The words echoed in Vivian's head. She wasn't surprised. But they had kept her waiting there so long, without saying anything about taking her away, that she had started to hope they would let her leave after all the questions were done. That hope vanished like a missed step that sent her careening down a staircase in the dark. "I'm under arrest?"

"What kind of dumb question is that?" the younger officer demanded. "Sitting there, covered with the dead guy's blood? Of course you're under arrest."

"But I didn't do anything. I called for *help* when I found him. Why would I do that if I was—"

"You were the last one to see him alive."

"But I wasn't. The fella he was meeting with—"

"We're not a jury, sweetheart," the older one interrupted coldly. Any protest that Vivian might have made got stuck in her throat, the word *jury* echoing through her head. "So you can save your begging for someone who cares. Now, you gonna be a good girl and come with us without arguing, or are we slapping cuffs on you and dragging you to the car?"

Vivian's breath was coming in such quick bursts that she felt dizzy. "Tell you what, *sir*," she said, knowing that she didn't have any leverage in that moment and taking the chance anyway, because she didn't have anything to lose either. When poor girls went to jail, they didn't usually come back out. "Tell you what. We all know I could make a big stink leaving this place. I could make you haul me out hollering and screaming and getting all kinds of attention from the neighbors that I'm pretty sure Mrs. Buchanan doesn't want. Or . . ." She took a deep breath. "Or you let me make one phone call, and then I come along quiet as you like."

"Listen here—" the younger officer began, but his partner cut him off.

"And who do you plan to call?" he asked. There was a hint of a smile in his voice, like an indulgent parent watching a child about to throw a tantrum and deciding to be amused instead of angry.

Vivian lifted her chin and met his eyes, hoping he couldn't tell how nervous she was. "The commissioner's nephew."

"Our commissioner?" The younger one scoffed. "Nice try, girl. But he doesn't have a nephew."

But his partner cut him off once more. "You know Mr. Green, then?" he asked softly.

Vivian wondered if there would be permanent marks on her palms from where her nails had been pressed into them so long. "Yeah. I do."

The younger guy was frowning, but he didn't say anything as the older cop gave her a considering look. At last, he tipped his head toward the downstairs. "Telephone's in the hall. I make the call so I know you're not trying to pull one over on me. And then you can have your say. For two minutes."

Vivian gave a short, sharp nod. "That'll do."

He glanced at his partner. "Don't take your eyes off her, Sully."

The younger one had been staring back and forth between them as he tried to make sense of the conversation. But he nodded anyway. "Sure thing, boss."

It seemed even loudmouth young cops knew when to ask questions and when to shut up. Vivian tried to keep her head up as she walked down the steps between them, imagining that she was someone important—a movie star, maybe, or one of the socialites that was always in the gossip columns—and that they were just her body-guards or escorts. She wondered how many servants were watching and what they thought of her. She wondered if they could tell how scared she was.

The Buchanans had a telephone in their front hall, in pride of place next to an overflowing urn of bloodred roses even though it was only March. Vivian took one look at the color and had to swallow down her nausea.

The older cop lifted the receiver and waited to connect. "What's the number?" he asked her impatiently.

Vivian swallowed. "Circle two-four-four-one."

Another pause after he gave the number. "Leo Green?" The cop let out a short breath of surprise. "Well, I'll be damned. It is you. Got a girl here who wants to speak to you."

Vivian's fingers felt cold and clumsy as she took the receiver. "Hey, pal," she whispered.

"Vivian?" Leo's voice crackled with concern, even across the telephone wires. "Sweetheart, what's going on? Who was that fella?"

"A cop," she whispered, hating the way her voice was trembling. The back of her eyes felt hot and prickly, and she took a deep breath, trying to hold herself together. "I'm in a real jam, Leo. I'm under arrest, and I don't know what to do."

"It's all right, Viv," he said immediately. "We'll fix it, whatever happened. If they're taking you in, I'll meet you at the station and get it all sorted out. Just don't tell them anything else until I get there, okay?"

"Okay."

"What're they arresting you for?" he asked, almost as an afterthought.

Vivian clutched the telephone with both hands, looking up to meet the eyes of the older officer, who was watching her impassively, with just that bare hint of amusement still showing. "Murder," she whispered into the receiver. "They're arresting me for murder."

The silence on the other end was so absolute that Vivian was afraid they'd been disconnected.

"Okay," Leo said at last. "Okay. You just sit tight, okay? And keep your mouth shut if you can do it without getting smacked around. It'll be a little while before I get there."

"Why?" Vivian asked, her voice shaking again. For a wild moment, she wondered if he was going to leave her on her own after all.

"Gotta track down some help. Put the cop back on, sweetheart. I need to know where they're taking you."

FOUR

The windowless room was cold, so cold that Vivian couldn't feel her toes. She wanted to draw her feet up and curl her body around itself like a cat. But if anyone came back, she refused to let them see her like that. She kept her spine straight, her gaze fixed on the opposite wall, her hands clasped in her lap.

They had at least let her wash those when they got to the station. Looking in the mirror above the sink, she had discovered that at some point she had touched her face, and Mr. Buchanan's blood was smeared across her cheek as well. She had stared at the blood for too long, re-membering his smile when he handed her the cup of coffee—or was she imagining it? Had he smiled? It had all happened so fast, and why would she have paid attention? And then she had stared at herself, dark eyes with darker circles under them, bobbed hair that she wished were longer. Maybe then she'd seem sweet and respectable, instead of looking like someone who folks assumed made *friends* with other women's husbands to pay her bills.

It wouldn't have made a difference. People thought whatever they wanted about poor girls who had to support themselves. And they'd think plenty more, if they ever found out she had no parents, no family at all except for a sister who had recently married a Chinese man. If they ever found out she worked at a speakeasy, or danced with other women as much as she danced with men . . .

Vivian had barely noticed how cold the water was as she scrubbed the blood away.

None of that needed to matter, she told herself. Leo was on his way. All she had to do was stay quiet for as long as she could.

The two cops that had brought her in had handed her over to the sergeant at the station. He'd been the one to let her wash up before she was brought to the windowless room and seated across from another officer whose name and rank she never learned. He had played nice at first, but that soon changed.

He hadn't liked her silence. He'd liked her one-word answers even less.

Alone, now, Vivian wondered if she should have called her sister instead of Leo. If Leo couldn't get her out, Florence would have no idea where she had gone, maybe not for weeks. But her sister couldn't help her right now. Even together, it wasn't like they could afford a lawyer.

The sergeant had taken her purse and work bag when they brought her into the station. Little wonder about that—the sewing kit had scissors in it, and pins and needles, things they weren't going to leave in the hands of a girl who might be guilty of murder. But she hoped that, one way or another, she could get it back. Those things weren't cheap, and she didn't want to be on the hook for replacing them on top of everything else.

It was easier to worry about money and work than to think about what might be coming next. She'd be sent to jail if she was lucky. Maybe in three or five years they'd let her out, if they thought she hadn't meant to kill him. Or maybe she'd end up at one of the state's workhouses, if they looked at her and saw a poor girl in danger of an immoral life, someone they needed to save from herself or save other people from.

And if they thought she'd killed him on purpose . . .

Vivian swallowed down a wave of nausea. If that was the case, at least Florence would know where she was, because it would for certain end up in the papers.

In the middle of that grim thought, the door banged open.

Vivian jumped, then tried to look like she hadn't. But there was no disguising her nervousness as she eyed the man who had just walked in.

He didn't look like a cop. He was wearing a suit instead of a uniform, and the up-and-down look he gave her didn't have the brittle edge of suspicion that she expected.

"Get your coat, young lady, and follow me."

"Who are you?" She didn't stand up.

"Jacob Dubinski. I'm your lawyer."

"I don't have a lawyer."

"You do today. Get your coat. We're leaving."

Vivian wanted to bound to her feet, to push past him and make a break for the door. She stood slowly. "They're just letting me walk out? Did something happen? Did they find who killed Mr. Buchanan?"

"No, and no, and I very much doubt it." He chuckled. He was older than she had first thought; his dark hair had only a sprinkling of gray in it, but the veins stood out in the back of his hands, and his eyes and cheeks folded up in creases when he laughed. It wasn't quite a friendly sound, and the look he gave her couldn't be called friendly either— curious, calculating, as though she were an odd-looking insect being examined under a magnifying glass. But there was no cruelty in it. "Your explanation is waiting out in the lobby, if you'd care to get a move on? Unless you've grown to like it in here." He glanced around the dim room, so small it felt like the walls were slowly inching toward them, and chuckled again at his own joke.

Vivian didn't ask any more questions. There was only one person who could have sent a lawyer for her. Grabbing her coat, she hurried after Dubinski.

She had lost track of time alone in that windowless room. The sun had begun to set, a single red ray snaking through between the buildings and hitting one of the station's windows in just the right spot to blind her for a moment as she came into the front lobby. She blinked rapidly, and when her vision cleared, her knees nearly gave out with relief.

In that sterile, uniformed building, the dark-haired man waiting for her stood out like a wolf in an alley full of city strays, sharp and handsome and dangerous if you knew how to recognize his type. A red plaid scarf was draped around his neck and his coat hung open as if he'd been waiting for a while. He would have looked relaxed as he leaned one elbow against the sergeant's desk, chatting with the young man on duty like they were friends out for a drink. But he was spinning his hat on one finger, over and over, a sure sign that he was more keyed up than he wanted to let on.

He turned when he heard the click of her heels on the cold tile floor. His posture didn't change, but the relief in his eyes was plain, and his lips curved up in a smile.

"Hey there," he said, slowly standing up straight.

Vivian didn't move. She didn't know what he had told them, didn't know what was actually happening, and she didn't want to risk revealing something he had kept hidden. It was dangerous enough that she had called him in the first place. "Hello."

Leo turned back to the sergeant on duty. "We all square? She have any bags when they brought her in?"

The sergeant frowned. "I don't think I'm supposed to hand those back over to her. It's evidence, isn't it?"

"Of what?" Leo said, leaning his elbow back on the desk. "She's walking out of here, right?"

The sergeant shrugged. "Guess that's fine then. But I'm blaming you if anyone comes after me for it."

"You do that, my friend," Leo said with a smile. But for all he looked and sounded relaxed, the hat was still spinning on his finger.

Dubinski was holding Vivian's coat, and he helped her into it. She felt like she was in a dream, like she was floating inches above a fast current of water that would pull her back down at any second, as Leo buttoned up his own coat and perched his hat on his head.

"Thanks for your help," he said, nodding to the young officer as he accepted her purse and workbag. Turning to where Vivian and the lawyer waited—was he even a real lawyer, or just someone pulled in to play a part?—Leo gave them a friendly nod. "Shall we?"

Vivian walked out the door between them, still not knowing what had happened, sure that at any second, she would hear the shriek of a police whistle and be dragged back inside.

They walked in silence until they were ten blocks away. Vivian had no idea where they were taking her, but the last place she expected them to stop was in front of a little diner, the placard in the window advertising a three-course dinner plus coffee for twenty-five cents.

"What are we doing?" Vivian asked warily.

"When was the last time you ate today?" Leo replied.

"I . . . I don't think I did," Vivian admitted. The morning seemed so long ago that she couldn't remember if she had grabbed breakfast or not.

"I figured," Leo said. When he saw her shiver, he pulled the scarf off his own neck and draped it around hers, his hands gentle. "You need to eat on a day like this."

The concern in his eyes made her feel warmer than she had in hours. But it also made her wary. What he meant—what he wasn't saying—was that her trouble wasn't over. She had a reprieve. But she didn't know for how long. Vivian took a shaking breath and nodded.

Leo's hand crept around hers, their fingers locking together, and she wished he would do more than that, wished he would wrap his whole body around hers until she could feel safe again at last. But then he glanced over her shoulder, and she remembered that they weren't alone. "Plus, I promised Dubinski dinner. So let's see what's on the menu tonight."

———•———

Leo was right: dinner helped.

It didn't make her nerves go away. But they were a hell of a lot easier to handle when she didn't feel like she was about to keel over from hunger.

Leo barely touched more than the coffee. But Dubinski—who, she learned, was indeed a real lawyer, or had been before he retired—ate twice as much as either of them and looked like he was thoroughly enjoying himself. "Not as good as dinner at home would have been," he said, giving them a stern look, though the lift of his eyebrows said he might have been teasing. "But good enough for now."

"We appreciate you coming, anyway," Leo said.

Vivian nodded as the waitress placed three slices of cake in front of them and began to clear the dinner plates. "So what did you actually do?" she asked when they were alone again. "What happens next?"

"Oh, the usual," Dubinski said, giving the cake a slightly wary look before trying a nibble. "Hmm. That's not too bad. Show up, throw some fancy legal terms around, give the sergeant on duty a bit of a scare. Helps to have someone like Leo here pulling a few strings behind the scenes. As for what happens next . . ." He raised his eyebrows at her. "I assumed you planned to disappear. A murder charge is a serious thing."

Vivian had just put a bite in her mouth, and she had to swallow quickly, making herself cough. Her eyes darted to Leo. "You mean the charge isn't gone?"

He shook his head. "You're not officially charged with anything. Not yet. But the case isn't going away."

The taste of the cake on her tongue suddenly felt sickly. Vivian dropped her fork with a clatter and pushed the plate away. "Then why'd they let me out?"

"We'll get to that," he said quietly.

Vivian stared at him, waiting for him to say more, then turned to the lawyer. "What d'you mean, disappear?"

"If they can't find you, they can't arrest you again, right?" Dubinski said, looking unconcerned as he dug into his own dessert. "I assume you gave them a fake name?" When Vivian shook her head, he rolled his eyes in exasperation. "Well, why the hell not?"

She flinched. "I was there working. The housekeeper already knew who I was, and she told the cops. So they know who I am, they know who I work for, if they talk to my boss they can find out who my sister is . . ." She turned to Leo. "Plus, I called you. And you got me out, which I'm guessing means you had to drop your uncle's name. And he . . ." She shuddered. "He probably remembers me."

She'd had one run-in with Leo's uncle before—a cold, manipulative man who, along with the rest of his family, had cut off Leo's mother for marrying a Jewish man. She never wanted to be in his sights again. The commissioner was happy to take advantage of Leo's connections to the bootlegging world when he needed someone who could work off the books and outside the law. But there was nothing like love or even affection between them. There was barely even respect. And a man like the commissioner of police always had an agenda.

"I did," Leo said quietly. "And he does. And they're probably tailing us right now to see where I take you," he added with a grimace.

"Oh, they certainly are, no question about that," the lawyer said cheerfully, having finished his cake and moved on to Leo's slice. He paused only to take a long drink of coffee. Vivian could smell the whiskey in it, and she wondered when he had added it. She'd been too wrapped up in her own thoughts to notice a flask come out. "Bit of a pickle for you, my dear."

"You don't sound too broken up about it," Leo said dryly.

Dubinski shrugged, returning to his plate. "You asked me to show up and promised me dinner. No one said anything about getting all worked up."

Vivian found her voice again, and there was an edge to it that she didn't bother trying to hide. "And you don't care that someone who doesn't deserve it might go to jail for murder?"

Dubinski gave her a sideways glance. For a moment Vivian caught a glimpse of something under his veneer of unconcern, something hard and sad and tired. "I spent decades caring, young lady, losing sleep and cases and friends, and sometimes losing my mind. It wears you down. I'm not going to let myself be dragged back into it, not even for a pretty girl and the son of an old friend."

Vivian flinched and looked away.

Leo let out a heavy breath, then nodded. "All right. Don't look so scared, Viv. It's going to be hard, but it's not impossible."

"But it won't matter for long, right? Once they find out who really did it, I'll be in the clear," Vivian said hopefully.

"Not to burst your bubble, young lady," Dubinski said dryly. His mask was back in place as he took another drink of coffee. "But the odds of them doing that are nothing to bet on. Your best chance is to present them with some evidence that shows it couldn't have been you."

"What kind of evidence?" she asked in a small voice.

He raised an eyebrow. "I don't know. But either you come up with something, or you need to hire one hell of a lawyer. One who's *not* retired, by the way," he added. "I, meanwhile, need to catch my train, or my wife will be very cross."

"Okay." Vivian nodded. "Okay. Swell. Thanks for getting me out, anyway." She hesitated, then asked the dreaded question. "How much do I owe you?"

The lawyer chuckled. "Oh, your young man knows that's already taken care of." He tossed his napkin onto the table as he stood. "Leo, tell your father after next week's game, *he* will be the one who owes me." He nodded to them. "Good luck, kids. I'll be hoping for the best for you."

Leo waited until Dubinski was gone before answering Vivian's unspoken question. "He plays poker with my dad. And I got his brother out of a jam last month, when his supplier stiffed him on half an order, and he was afraid he wouldn't be able to open for the week."

"You do get around," Vivian said faintly, looking back down into her own coffee mug so she wouldn't have to meet his eyes. "I guess you had to cash in a lot of favors to get me out of there. I owe you big time."

"Hey." Leo slipped a finger under her chin and lifted it gently. His hand slid sideways, the other one rising, and he cupped both her cheeks. Vivian found herself leaning into the gentle touch. "Whether I did or not, there's no favors between us, Viv. You know that, right? We're always square." He grinned. "What kind of fella wouldn't help his girl beat a murder charge?"

"Ha," Vivian said weakly, not quite ready for that joke. She hadn't beaten it. Not yet.

But his hands were warm and strong, and his confidence was catching. She found herself nodding. "Okay, then. First thing is to get home, because I have work tonight, and I can't afford to miss a shift."

"Hey, and that's a good starting place," Leo pointed out, standing and pulling out her chair for her. "Plenty of gossip at the Nightingale. Find the right person and they might know a thing or two about the Buchanans."

He wasn't wrong. Places like the Nightingale attracted all types, including the ones that lived on the Upper East Side. Normally, folks like that wouldn't give the time of day to a girl who wore catalog shoes and considered the Automat a pricey meal, never mind answer a question or spill a secret. But the rules were different when you wandered into back-alley dance halls.

Plenty of times, Vivian had found out secrets she didn't want to know and wished she hadn't learned. This time, hopefully, she'd find the ones she needed.

"Okay, then," she said again, taking a deep breath, gathering her confidence around her like a shield. She had no idea how, but she would find something. She knew people, she had friends who knew people, and she'd always managed to land on her feet before. She would this time too. "Let's get ready to go to work."

FIVE

The sun had set by the time they hopped off the streetcar, disappearing between buildings that crowded too close together and leaned on each other like drunks stumbling home at the end of the night. The streetlights were pools of molten gold, but all they lit up was piles of slush and trash, the icy pavement in between sparkling like a warning.

Vivian lived on the second floor now. The two tenement rooms she had shared with her sister had been too much to afford on her own after Florence married and moved downtown. But she couldn't leave her building or her neighborhood, ugly and unloved though they were.

As they turned the corner, she could hear music drifting through the frosty evening, a window left improbably open in the cold air. Will Freeman had recently bought a radio, and even when it was freezing, he threw his windows open to share the music with the world. It cut across the sound of voices raised in an argument, of children shrieking in a way that could mean joy or rage. When she opened the front door of her building and a dog launched into a volley of fierce barking, she could tell it belonged to Mr. Brown. When a baby began crying in response, she recognized Mrs. Gonzales's newborn.

She knew each sound without thought. And as much as she longed to leave behind every run-down, desperate inch of her home, she couldn't bring herself to.

Maybe someday. But not yet.

Vivian shivered as the wind chased them inside before Leo slammed the front door closed. Her feet climbed the stairs without her needing to tell them to.

The thought of a shift at the Nightingale made her shake with fatigue. Usually, it was the place she loved the most in the world, the place she most felt like herself. But tonight, all she wanted to do was curl up like a child, to try and forget everything that had happened.

But there was no forgetting, not yet. If she closed her eyes, she would just see Buchanan's face again, that vacant, shocked stare, the trickle of blood that curved over his chin.

So she might as well go work, sneak a glass of champagne from the bar. Might as well lose herself in the music, wear out her body and her mind until she felt like herself again. Maybe then, she'd sleep without dreaming.

"What the hell are you doing here?"

Leo's question, his sudden grab at her arm, brought her thoughts tumbling back into her body. There was a man standing in front of her door, arms crossed as he stared at her, his hat casting shadows over half his face so that she couldn't see his expression. But she could hear the amusement in his voice as he spoke, and it was colder than the air outside.

"I don't think you really need to ask me that, Mr. Green. Not after what happened today." He glanced at Vivian, and she felt the look like a physical touch on her skin.

A movement at the end of the hall, half-seen out of the corner of her eye. Vivian turned as the second man stepped forward, blocking their path back to the stairs. Even in the dim light, she could see the buttons shining on his uniform. She turned back; the man by the door smiled. "Invite me in, Miss Kelly. We have a few things to discuss."

"Sure thing," she said hoarsely, pulling out her keys and stepping past him, the back of her neck prickling under his gaze. She unlocked the door and pushed it open, then stepped out of his way. "Come on in, Commissioner."

SIX

V ivian kept her eyes on the commissioner as she turned up the lamp, watching him take in the details of the room: the rickety table and two chairs that took up most of the floor, the bed with its rumpled quilt, only half-made in her haste to get to work that morning. The radiator hissed and shuddered as it tried to heat the little room, and if she pulled aside the curtains she had sewn, the only view out the window would be the trash piled in the street.

Vivian had been to the commissioner's house once before, escorted in through the back door to wait in his study, battered and bruised from one of the worst nights of her life. She could only imagine what her home looked like to him as he compared it to the warmth and so-phistication of his own. But she wasn't ashamed of where she lived. If he was uncomfortable there, it didn't bother her. At least that way he wouldn't linger.

"Have a seat, if you like," she said. The police officer who had come with the commissioner followed them in, shutting the door and taking up a post in front of it. Vivian tried not to look at him. "I'd offer to make you coffee, but I'm fresh out."

His eyebrows rose as he pulled out one of the chairs for himself. In the half-hearted light, she could see the amusement in his expression. "Nothing stronger to offer?"

"I don't keep liquor in my house," Vivian said softly. "You might not have heard of it, but there's a thing called Prohibition."

That made him chuckle, though the sound was not a friendly one. "And why would you need to? You can drink much better quality at work than you could ever buy for yourself."

Vivian didn't answer, and he smiled, clearly not expecting her to. It had been a reminder, nothing more: he knew details of her life that she might have wanted to keep hidden. They weren't on equal footing in this chat, and she had better watch her step and her mouth if she wanted to make it through in one piece.

She swallowed and, hesitating only a heartbeat, took the seat across from him. There was nowhere else to sit except her bed, so Leo leaned against one wall, his face in shadow as he nodded to the officer by the door. "Evening, Levinsky. How's the new baby?"

"Green." The man, Levinsky, nodded. "Good to see you're staying in one piece. She's nearly six months old now."

"Mazel tov," Leo said quietly, before turning back to his uncle, whose lip was curling in distaste. "All right if I stick around for your chat, Commissioner?" Leo asked, ignoring the expression. There was very little emotion in his voice, but his weight was planted, his stance wide and solid. He looked ready for a fight; Vivian wondered nervously if he knew something she didn't, or if he was just on edge from his uncle's presence.

"By all means," the commissioner said, his face unreadable once more. He sounded unsurprised by the request. "What I came here to say concerns you as well."

"And that is?" Leo asked. In spite of his tense posture, there was something polite, even deferential, to his tone that Vivian wasn't used to hearing. It sent a shiver down her back, though she tried to hide it. Leo was worried.

The commissioner glanced at the officer by the door. "That'll be all for now. Wait for me downstairs."

Levinsky looked at Leo, a quick flicker of his eyelids, before nodding. "Yes, sir."

When the door had closed behind him, the commissioner turned to examine Vivian. Whatever he was thinking, he hid it well. Vivian tried to stare back without any of her nerves showing, but she wasn't sure she was succeeding.

He wasn't a large man; Vivian thought he was shorter than Leo, and he didn't have the muscled build of a man who worked with his hands or knew how to hold his own in a street fight. But those kinds of men would take one look at him and give him wide berth anyway. His clothes were polished, his hair pomaded, and a silver mustache curled above his mouth. But his expression was cold as he looked her over, as though she was an interesting, even irritating problem, but nothing as important as a person. Vivian wanted to shiver, but she wouldn't give him that satisfaction.

At last, the commissioner spoke. "Let's not waste time with pleasantries none of us care about. You're in a difficult situation, Miss Kelly."

She nodded. "That's a hell of an understatement. Sir."

"Well said." Her agreement seemed to amuse him. "I'm glad you're not inclined to argue." He settled back in his chair, fingers steepling under his chin. "I let you walk out of that station today, Miss Kelly. Give me a good reason why I shouldn't have Levinsky haul you back."

Vivian swallowed. She clenched her hands in her lap so he wouldn't see them shaking. "Because I didn't kill him," she said, as firmly as she could manage. "I think that should count for something."

"Perhaps for something," the commissioner said, still studying her. His finger dropped to drum briefly on the table before one side of his mouth lifted in a cynical smile, nearly hidden under his luxurious mustache. "But not for much, especially if you can't prove it. Buchanan was a well-known man, and well-connected. There are people who will be clamoring for answers. For accountability. The sort of people I'd hate to disappoint. And the press will have a field day with it if I can't give them a killer."

"So you just offer her up, is that it?" Leo said. He spoke evenly, almost conversationally. But Vivian could hear the controlled anger in his voice. She wondered if his uncle could hear it, too. "I thought your fine officers could do better than that."

The commissioner gave him a look that was almost pitying. "Mr. Green, your friend"—he gave the word a twist that Vivian didn't like, though she couldn't blame him for it—"was found with Buchanan's dead body. She was the last person to see him alive, and the state she was in . . . Well. There's isn't a bleeding-heart do-gooder in this city—in the entire damn country—who would blame me for arresting her. And you know it."

"Then what am I doing here?" Vivian asked quietly, wanting to insert herself back in the conversation before Leo was provoked into saying something unwise.

The commissioner gave her another emotionless glance. "You're here out of the goodness of my heart, Miss Kelly."

"You're here because he likes it when folks on his payroll owe him favors," Leo said softly, his eyes fixed on the man who would never acknowledge him as family. "And I haven't owed him one this big in a long time."

"But like any reprieve, yours won't last forever," the commissioner continued, ignoring his nephew. "You have one week of freedom, and you can do with it what you wish. But make no mistake, we will be keeping an eye on you." He pointed at Leo, carelessly, dismissively, without even turning his head. "On both of you. And at the end of that week, if we don't have another suspect in our custody, you'll be under arrest once more." He leaned forward, his elbows propped up on the table and his fingers laced together in front of him. When he spoke, the menace in his soft, uncaring voice made her feel sick. "And the second time, Miss Kelly, it will be far more difficult for you to gain your freedom."

He meant that she wouldn't, of course. If she was arrested again, that would be it. Vivian swallowed against the fear in her stomach. "A lot can happen in a week," she said defiantly, refusing to look away from him.

He smiled. "True. And if one of those things that happens is you skipping town, or if anyone helps you disappear, then I won't have qualms paying a visit to, let's say, a sister. Or a friend. Or a father." He glanced at Leo again before turning back to Vivian. "There are all sorts of crimes happening in this city, you understand, just waiting for the perpetrators to be found."

The sick feeling in Vivian's stomach tightened into a knot. Of course he knew about Florence. Of course. She bit the inside of her cheek, the pain bringing some strength into her voice. "I understand," she said, glad the words didn't shake.

"Good girl," he said.

The patronizing curl of his voice made Vivian grit her teeth. But she didn't argue; they both knew he held all the cards in this game. He stood, looking satisfied, and Vivian climbed to her feet too. God, she was tired.

"You do good work when I need you to, Mr. Green," the commissioner added as he crossed to the door. "So I don't mind you asking for an occasional favor. But I'd hate for one of those favors to cause trouble between us." He met Leo's eyes, his hand on the doorknob. "Do *you* understand?"

Vivian could see the muscles clench in Leo's jaw. "I do, sir. Here's hoping we can all be pleasantly surprised by the end of the week."

"I do enjoy your optimism, young man." The commissioner gave them both one final considering look before turning to open the door, as though they were already dismissed from his thoughts. "You'll hear from me if I need you."

And then he was gone, though the chill of his presence lingered, and silence filled the room where he had been. Leo was staring at the door, though by the rigid set of his neck and shoulders, Vivian suspected he wasn't seeing it at all.

The silence continued to stretch between them, and Vivian wasn't sure how to break it. "Real charmer, your uncle," she said at last.

That made Leo laugh shortly. "Don't let him hear you calling him that," he said as he turned away from the door.

Vivian hesitated a moment, then went to him, laying a hand on his arm. "You're better off, you know," she said gently. "Without him. Without any of them. It's a hell of a raw deal, having family that doesn't want you. But imagine if you'd grown up into someone like that."

Leo wrapped his arms around her, and Vivian burrowed against his warmth, her eyes closed. He rested his chin on top of her head. He didn't reply, and she could still feel the tension in him, but he didn't push her away either. At last he sighed. "Well, sweetheart, what do you want to do?"

"With my one week?" Vivian pulled away, walking three jittery steps into the room. "If running away isn't an option, I guess it's time to start calling in some favors." She glanced out the window. "And if I'm going to be asking for favors, that probably means I shouldn't be late for my shift."

He nodded, his eyes back on the door as she collected her shoes, her dancing dress, her treasured pair of silk stockings, tossing them on the bed one by one. Then she hesitated. She and Leo had gotten a bit frisky a time or two, enough that she shouldn't feel so strange changing her dress with him there. But tonight, she felt raw and exposed, even with all her clothes still on. One week. Only one week.

Snatching up the pitcher from the washstand, she thrust it toward Leo. "Will you get fresh water? The washroom's up one flight."

He frowned as he took it, still looking distracted. "You sure you're up for it tonight? You're all right?"

"Of course," Vivian said, giving her head a little toss to settle her hair and beginning to hunt for her lipstick. "All things considered, I'm swell."

She didn't look back toward him, and after a moment, she heard him go out into the hall, closing the door behind him.

Her hands were shaking as she reached for her dress. She clenched them into tight fists until the tremors stopped. Then she yanked the pretty gown—she had raised the hem and sewn the fringe on herself—over her step-in, shimmying her hips until it fell into place. When she glanced in the mirror, her cheeks were pale against the stark black frame of her hair, her eyes wide and scared. She took a deep breath and smiled at her reflection until the expression felt right.

If she didn't think about the future, if she just kept moving forward, she could get through it. She had one week. And, as she had said to the commissioner, a lot could happen in a week.

By the time Leo came back with the wash water, Vivian was able to take the pitcher from him with hands that were steady. "Thanks, pal," she said, pouring out just enough to wet her hairbrush and slick down her bob. When every sleek hair was in place, she twisted it back on one side, sliding in a pin decorated with feathers and glass pearls. Tilting her head as she considered her reflection, she met Leo's eyes in the mirror. "Ready to get to work?"

For a moment, she thought he would say something that she would have to ignore, something that matched the worry in his eyes. But instead, he nodded and held out his hand. "Let's see what we can find."

SEVEN

Seven Days Left

There were half a dozen doors into the Nightingale. They led into alleys, snaked through tunnels, opened up in trapdoors and closets and the storeroom where bathtub gin from Chicago kept company with cases of French champagne.

That was where the employees entered these days; they were expected to change it up every few weeks so no one could track their comings and goings too closely. But Vivian sent Leo around to the front before she ducked into the alley that wound its way to the basement door. He knew a lot of the Nightingale's secrets by now, but Vivian didn't want to get caught breaking the rules right before she started asking for favors.

After everything that had happened that day, she was running late, and she could already hear the band. The music, a joyful Charleston beat, unknotted something inside her chest, and Vivian took a deep breath as she headed up the stairs. The night was young, but the scent of wildness lingered in the air from the countless nights that had come before, smoke and Shalimar, promises and secrets. Already there was laughter echoing through the air.

The Nightingale was home. It wouldn't let her down.

But before she reached the top, she heard footsteps coming down. Vivian pulled against the wall, pushing down a burst of panic. Anyone coming down here worked at the Nightingale. There was no danger.

Vivian straightened her spine just as her boss came around the corner.

"Vivian." Honor Huxley paused, her surprise, for once, not hidden. "I was wondering where you were."

Vivian's eyes drank in the familiar sight: the curly blond hair pinned back around Honor's head, the bright slash of red lipstick visible even in the dim light. Her long legs in dark trousers, her white shirt open at the neck, the sharp lines of her suspenders. If she let herself, Vivian could remember the smell of Honor's skin, the vanilla and vetiver scent of her perfume.

But she wouldn't let herself. Not anymore. Vivian dragged her gaze up.

There was a frown between Honor's brown eyes. "Is everything all right?" she asked, and the real worry in her voice soothed some of the raw places in Vivian's heart.

Honor of the sometimes-criminal childhood, who had built a back-alley kingdom for herself at the Nightingale in defiance of the outside world, who ruled over it with fierce pride . . . Honor would know what to do. She collected information and favors like a child gathering candy. If she doled them out sparingly, she had also made it clear, to many curious players in her underground world, that her employees were under her protection.

Vivian had been hoping to see her. She took a step forward. "I need your help."

"Oh, pet." Honor's voice was soft as she replied. "It's bad this time, isn't it?"

"Yes."

Honor glanced upward, in the direction she had come, then nodded. "You know I'll do what I can," she said. Her words gave away none of her thoughts, but her voice was gentle. She put her hands on Vivian's shoulders, turning her back toward the basement. "Let's talk in private, and you can tell me what you need."

The music was a distant brass wail, and Vivian paced to its rhythm without realizing it as she told Honor what had happened that day. She didn't think about the slip of Buchanan's blood against her hands or the commissioner's cold gaze as she spoke. None of that mattered. Favors needed confidence, and she could put on plenty of confidence when she had to.

"He gave me one week," she said at last. Her voice shook a little, but she pushed that tremor down. "So I'm hoping—" Vivian turned back to her boss at last but fell silent instead of continuing.

Honor had been watching her without speaking, her body held perfectly still, but there was something painful in that stillness. Exposed by the glare of the electric lights, there was a glittering in her eyes that Vivian thought might have even been tears.

Was Honor, who usually showed as much emotion as a statue, crying for her?

But a moment later that was blinked away, and Honor's mouth pulled to one side thoughtfully. "You're hoping," she prompted, her voice soft and impossible to read once more.

"A week isn't much time, but there's plenty of secrets to be unearthed in this city, right? It just depends on who you talk to and who owes . . ." She trailed off. Honor was still watching her, saying nothing. Vivian lifted her chin. "I don't even know where to start. But sometimes it feels like you know everyone. You've got ways to find things out. And I could sure as hell use that right now. So can you help me find out what happened to this Buchanan fella?"

In the silence, Vivian could hear the song changing upstairs, the rush of feet as dancers scattered to find new partners, the shouts from the bar. She could tell just by the noise that it was a crowded night. Someone would be coming down to restock the bar soon; they wouldn't have privacy for much longer.

Then Honor stepped forward, and for a moment everything else fell away. She laid her hands against either side of Vivian's face, thumbs brushing lightly, soothingly, over her cheekbones.

"I'm sorry, Vivian," she murmured. "I'm so sorry for what you've gone through, and for what you'll have to face next."

The warmth of the touch melted some of the bravado that was keeping Vivian going. She didn't want to let it go—she needed it—but she also wanted to lean into Honor's hands, to believe that someone else could solve the mess she was in. Her eyes fluttered closed when Honor leaned forward. She felt the brush of lips against her forehead, a kiss like a sister, like a mother.

A kiss like an apology.

Vivian's eyes snapped open, meeting Honor's, her breath coming faster when she saw the regret there.

"I wish I could help you. But I can't. Not this time."

Honor let her hands fall, her smile like heartbreak. Vivian watched, too stunned to speak, as her boss stepped away. At the foot of the stairs Honor paused, her hand on the railing, and half turned back. But it wasn't far enough to meet Vivian's eyes.

"I'm sorry."

EIGHT

Vivian didn't know how long she stood there after Honor left. It didn't make sense. None of it made sense.

Whatever history there was between them—and there was plenty—Honor had never hesitated to help her before. Hell, she had volunteered for it, even when it was downright illegal. And she had to know what a thing like a murder charge would mean to a girl like Vivian. There was no way she would let that happen.

Can't, she had said. Not *won't.* Vivian clung to that word, desperate for it to mean something. Honor never said anything without a reason. So what was the reason this time? Who was she afraid to cross?

It didn't matter, not now. Maybe she'd find out later. But if Honor wouldn't help her, all right then. She would help herself. She'd been doing that her whole life. She'd do it now, too.

And she wasn't getting any closer to answers standing in a cold cellar. Vivian took a deep breath, checked the pin in her hair and the cinch of her garters, and made her way upstairs for her shift.

She scanned the dance floor when she arrived. A few regulars, plenty of strangers. No one yet whose help she wanted to seek out. That was all right. There was time. Vivian made her way to the bar to scope out the patrons there and get her marching orders for the night.

Danny Chin was the Nightingale's head bartender and, unknown to most of its patrons, Honor's second-in-command. Right now, he was watching her as she stepped up to the bar. Once upon a time, he had been the dance hall's biggest flirt as well, infamous for the killer smiles and soulful eyes that could make women of any age blush and stammer. These days, though, he saved his most decadent smiles for the woman waiting for him on Spring Street, in the cozy, cluttered rooms they shared above his parents' restaurant.

Danny had married that fall. And his new wife was Vivian's older sister, Florence, now expecting their first child.

The thought of her sister made Vivian's throat grow tight. How the hell was she going to tell Florence what had happened? Did she even want to? Florence had always been the worrier between them, feet firmly planted on the pavement of New York's ugliest streets while Vivian dreamed of freedom, one dance at a time. Now that Florence was happy, could Vivian bear to take that away from her?

Vivian bit the inside of her cheek. Of course she had to tell her sister, there was no way around that. But she'd wait until she had good news to share, something that would show Florence she didn't need to worry.

There had to be something like that, she told herself firmly. There had to be, and she'd find it.

It took Vivian, lost in her thoughts, a moment to realize Danny had been speaking to her, his quiet voice nearly lost in the bright rhythm of the music.

"What?" Vivian asked, stepping toward the bar.

"I said, are you all right?" Danny repeated, frowning as he looked her over. "I can't remember the last time you came in late, and Bea didn't know where you were. We were worried."

Vivian glanced up at the bandstand, where Beatrice Henry was singing, and winced. Of course they had been worried—she had been so caught off guard by the commissioner's visit that she hadn't even remembered Bea would be waiting for her.

Beatrice Bluebird, she was called these days. She had become one of the main draws at the Nightingale ever since she moved up from waitress to chanteuse. But she and Vivian still walked to work together most nights; cabs were expensive. And there was safety in numbers, even when those numbers were just two, if you had to navigate the dark streets and alleys of Manhattan.

The thought made Vivian shiver. Daytime had proved plenty dangerous for her. Though maybe if she hadn't been alone, it would have been different.

"Viv?"

The concern in Danny's voice called her back to the present moment. Vivian managed to find a smile somewhere, though it took some effort. "I was talking to Honor," she said by way of explanation as she lifted the tray he had set out for her. But she couldn't entirely hide the tension that knotted her shoulders and stomach, and the glasses trembled against each other before she steadied them. He'd find out, eventually. But if she told him what had happened, he'd tell Florence. And her sister deserved to hear it from her. "You never need to worry about me, Danny-boy, you know that."

The look he gave her was frankly skeptical. "Did you and Leo have a falling-out?"

"'Course not," Vivian said, too quickly. There were people who worked at the Nightingale who might have suspected her history with Honor, but Danny was one of the few who knew. "Not that kind of talk. All business. Where's this one going?"

He looked like he wanted to say more, but it was a busy night, and he couldn't afford to keep his customers calling for their drinks. He tipped his head in the direction she needed to go. "Across from the bandstand. Crowd of fellas in the black suits. They look like they could shake up some trouble if they wanted, so let's not keep 'em waiting any longer than we have to." He caught her arm. "We're not done. You'll level with me later, yeah?"

Vivian gave him a wide smile, as fake as it was dazzling. Danny could probably tell the difference, but the customers who swarmed the Nightingale never could. They came for the party. They didn't want reality. "Absolutely, boss."

"Be careful, Viv," he murmured as she turned away. "Whatever it is, be careful."

It was too late for that. Vivian didn't answer as she threaded her way around the edge of the dance floor.

The young men who crowded the table where Danny had sent her were a familiar sight. She didn't recognize a single one of them individually, but they were the sort who always found their way to the Nightingale. Everything about them—the tailoring of their suits, the scent of hair pomade, the confident smiles and loud laughter—shouted money. If they had been just a little older, it would have whispered. But boys their ages hadn't yet learned about whispering. Vivian shared her smiles with them, brushing aside flirtatious glances and suggestions that she join them for a drink. But they were polite enough. Either they had been to the Nightingale before and learned that Honor Huxley expected a certain level of respect for her staff, or they were good kids in spite of their money. One of them even slipped Vivian a dollar and a wink when she handed over their gin cocktails.

"Bring us another, will you, baby? Not gin, something with whiskey this time," he said with a smile that could have been splashed across a screen at the Paramount. "We've got a pal coming who can't stand gin, and he's going to need some cheering up after the day he's had."

"Sure thing, mister," Vivian said, tucking the dollar into her palm and giving one of her smiles just to him. The extra cash would go into the tip jar and be shared out at the end of the night. "You're a sweet fella to look out for your friend."

"How sweet?" he asked, grinning and leaning forward before one of his friends pounded him in the shoulder to get his attention.

"So what did Corny tell you about his stepdad?" the friend asked. "What happened?"

Vivian slipped away while they were distracted. She didn't want to deal with Danny's worried looks again, so she headed to the other end of the bar.

She spotted Leo on the dance floor as she waited for her order. Seeing him there made her heartbeat slow for the first time since Honor had walked away. Leo would help her out, and between them, they could unearth a whole mess of secrets. Vivian dodged around a man in a blue suit who seemed to want to stand right in her way, the single drink balanced on her tray as she made her way back to the table. The band was just sliding through the intro of an Argentine tango, and the music sent a shiver up Vivian's spine as she stood aside to let an eager-looking couple go past.

Leo had just finished a dance with a cheerful brunette; as she went spinning away in the arms of a new partner, he paused at the edge of the dance floor, his eyes locked on Vivian. One of their first dances together had been a tango. She had been worried that he was the sort of fella who used a dance as an excuse to get handsy. Instead, she had discovered that he loved it as much as she did, that moving across the floor in his arms barely required thinking.

She wanted to be on that dance floor again, not thinking about anything but her partner and the music. But that would have to wait. She turned back in the direction of the table full of young men.

Only to stop before she could move a step, nearly losing her grip on her tray before she caught herself. Their missing friend had joined them, somber and handsome in his own black suit, his red curls standing out in the crowd.

The Corny they had been talking about was none other than Cornelius Rokesby, Buchanan's stepson.

Vivian took a quick sideways step, putting a group of chattering men and women between her and Rokesby, turning away quickly so he wouldn't see her face. She didn't know if he would recognize her. He wouldn't. He couldn't. They had crossed paths so briefly that morning. He'd barely seen her leaving with the police, and as far as he knew, that's where she still was. There was no reason he'd expect to run into her at a place like the Nightingale.

But she didn't want to take that chance.

"Ellie!" she hissed at another waitress heading toward the bar. Shoving her tray into Ellie's hands, she whispered quick directions as she took Ellie's own empty tray.

"What's wrong?" Ellie asked, frowning in confusion. "You look all balled up."

"Nothing. Nothing at all. They tip real good."

"Then what—"

Vivian didn't wait for Ellie to finish. She didn't think about Leo watching her from across the room or whether Danny would notice her ducking out on her already interrupted shift. She had to get out of there.

She made a beeline for the back hall, dropping her tray onto the end of the bar without letting anyone catch her eye. Out in the hall, the air was cooler than the sweaty heat of the dance floor, but the music still flowed out in a dark, sultry tumble of notes. The door of the ladies' powder room swung open as a crowd of laughing girls spilled into the hall, shoulders bare and lipstick freshly painted in bright, challenging flourishes of color. They barely noticed her; Vivian dodged around them, head ducked down, and hurried toward the back door.

It wasn't locked; it rarely was during business hours, since it opened only onto a cramped trash-pile of an alley. You could leave—or enter—that way if you were determined to find your way through the maze of streets that it joined. But mostly the Nightingale's patrons came there for a breath of air on a sweaty night.

The cold sent goose bumps chasing across Vivian's skin, and the light from inside skittered ahead of her. But she didn't want light just then any more than she wanted company. She let the door slam shut, leaving her in the slinking, moonlit shadows. It was heavy on purpose, cutting off the sound of the Nightingale from anyone who wasn't supposed to know it was there. But the city itself was never silent. Vivian closed her eyes, arms wrapped around herself as she listened to the distant sounds of animals fighting, a baby wailing, the tinny strains of a jazz record spilling from someone's open window.

The city didn't care that a man had been stabbed to death that morning. It wouldn't care if she was arrested for his murder and was never part of its endless noise again.

Good thing she was used to looking after herself.

At last, Vivian took a deep breath, her smiling mask ready to slide back into place for the rest of her shift. But before she could turn the knob, the door swung open. Vivian had to skip back, nearly turning an ankle, so it wouldn't hit her.

"Careful!" she gasped, one hand out to catch her balance on the alley wall as the dark silhouette of a man filled the doorway. "Watch where you're . . ."

She trailed off as he stepped forward, the shadows growing less severe and the dim light of the alley sliding across his face like a warning.

"Watch where I'm going?" Cornelius Rokesby asked. When he let the door fall closed, the sound of the latch catching was the loudest thing Vivian had ever heard. Without meaning to, she took another step back. "Golly, that's good advice, sweetheart. Shame someone didn't give it to you before you ran out here." He glanced around the alley, then turned back to her. The smile that pulled at one corner of his mouth made her stomach drop. "All by yourself."

NINE

Vivian swallowed, eyes darting around. He was between her and the door, and while the alley wasn't a dead end, it was narrow and crowded. If she tried to run, odds were he'd be on her before she went more than a few steps. And with how loud it was inside, no one would hear her if she called for help. Besides, for all she knew, his friends were waiting on the other side of that door. She was as good as cornered, and they both knew it.

Vivian swallowed down a wave of fear. She'd been in tighter jams before. She had to keep her head. And she couldn't let him know how afraid she was. She was just fixing a soothing smile on her face when he reached into his jacket. Vivian flinched away, then stared in confusion as he held out a dollar bill.

"I've got some questions for you, doll. So stop twitching and don't think about trying to run. I'm not budging, okay?"

It took Vivian a moment to find her voice. "What kind of questions?"

"This is that Huxley woman's place, right? And you work for her."

There was a curl to his lip as he looked her over, dismissive and superior. But he spoke a little too fast, the edges of his words sharp and his eyes darting around. He wasn't quite as sure of himself as he wanted to seem.

"Looks that way," Vivian said slowly. "But I don't have anything to say—"

"Look, I don't know who you are, but you're a dumb bird if you're going to turn down cold cash," he said impatiently. "So—"

"You don't know me?" Vivian demanded, unable to stop herself. She wanted to sag against the wall with relief. If he wasn't there for her, had he just stumbled into the Nightingale by accident? But then what kind of questions could he have? And how did he know who Honor was? "Then why are we out here?"

"I already said, I've got some questions for you," he said, snapping his fingers at her. "Keep up, I haven't got all night. Are you going to answer them or not?"

"That depends." Vivian took another step back as he moved forward, wanting some distance between them. But she didn't take her eyes off him. He was still between her and the door. He still had half a foot of height on her, and he was jumpy as a drunk flea. She wasn't out of the woods yet. "Corny, right? That's what your pals called you."

"You're not my pal."

"I could be," Vivian said, giving him a smile. "What could a girl like me tell a fella like you that he doesn't already know? We might as well go back inside and see about getting you another drink, on the house. You're wasting your time with me."

He laughed, crossing his arms. "You think I'm dumb enough to just believe whatever a pretty girl tells me?"

"Trying to sweet-talk me, Corny?" Vivian asked, giving him a smile. She was shaking all over, but maybe he wouldn't see that in the dim light.

"I don't need to sweet-talk you," he said softly, stepping forward again. Her back was against the alley wall now, and he was only a few inches away from her. Vivian's heart was beating like her chest was a jail cell and it was trying to break free. But she had to hope that if he'd wanted to hurt her, he would have done it by now. "I've got questions, and you're going to answer them."

"And if I don't feel like talking to you?" she asked, her hands sliding over the wall behind her back, looking for a loose brick, the edge of a crate, anything she could use if she needed to defend herself.

One of his hands shot out, gripping her chin. "Don't play games with me, little girl. My stepfather was murdered today, and I'm all out of patience. So you'll tell me what I want to know or—"

"Or what?"

The cool voice, the coiled menace of it, caught them both by surprise. Light scattered across the alley, and Vivian's eyes, which had been locked on Rokesby's, darted over his shoulder.

Rokesby dropped her chin and spun around, stepping quickly away from her when he saw Honor in the doorway. And she hadn't come alone. Benny, one of the hulking bruisers who kept the clientele in line—and whatever other tasks Honor needed him to take care of—stood at her shoulder. Behind them, still half in the doorway, hovered Bea. Her eyes were wide with worry when they landed on Vivian, but her gaze shifted to Corny Rokesby, her mouth set in a fierce, protective line, and the worry turned into a snapping glare.

Rokesby held up his hands. "We were just having a friendly chat."

"Not that friendly," Vivian said sharply, giving him a shove that sent him stumbling away from her. "I told you, you're wasting your time here."

But he wasn't paying attention to her anymore. Instead, he was staring at Honor. "You're Miss Huxley?"

"Ms. Huxley," Benny growled.

The correction made Honor smile; Vivian might have joined her if her heart hadn't still been jumping with nerves. "I am."

"I'm—" Corny Rokesby began.

But Honor cut him off, her smile fading. "I know who you are. Is there something I can do for you, Mr. Rokesby? Or will you be heading on your way now that you've made . . ." She looked him up and down. "Some kind of point, I suppose?"

"I didn't come here to cause trouble," he said, raising his hands. "I wanted to talk to you."

Vivian stared at him, then at Honor, not bothering to hide her confusion. She glanced at Bea, who looked equally surprised, her sharp brows drawn into a frown as she silently watched the drama unfold.

Why in God's name would Rokesby be looking for Honor?

"Oh?" One of Honor's brows arched upward, but she didn't sound surprised. "Well, you sure as hell went about it the wrong way. I might have been available to talk . . ." Her lip curled. "If you hadn't started out your night by threatening my staff."

Rokesby blinked at her, then scowled, a petulant mix of confusion and irritation. "But—"

"Unfortunately, you did. So I've got nothing to say. Benny, escort our guest out," Honor said softly. "Gently, please—I hear Mr. Rokesby's already had a rough day."

"But—" Rokesby swallowed down the rest of his protest when Benny stepped forward, lightly cracking the knuckles on one hand. "Fine," he bit off. "But you know we're not done here, right? I know all sorts of interesting things now."

"You know nothing." Looking unconcerned by his threat—and what exactly had it meant?—Honor stepped aside, gesturing him toward the door. "Have a good rest of your evening, Mr. Rokesby. And my condolences for your loss."

As soon as the men were gone, she nodded at Bea. "Thank you for coming to get me, Beatrice," she said. Vivian let out a shaky sigh. She had wondered if Honor was watching her. But Bea must have been just coming off her set and seen Rokesby follow her outside. She'd have run to get Honor in case he was the sort of man who liked to cause trouble for girls on their own.

Vivian didn't know if she was relieved or angry that Honor hadn't been keeping an eye on her after their earlier conversation. But she was damned lucky Bea had found her in time.

"Who was he?" Bea demanded.

But Honor shook her head. "Give me a moment to talk with Vivian, please. I'm sure she'll fill you in later."

Bea glanced between them nervously. Honor might have built the Nightingale into a refuge for plenty of people who wouldn't be so welcome in other places, but she was still Bea's boss. And no matter how curious or worried she was, Bea was still a poor Black girl working an illegal job in a city full of trouble. She had learned plenty of times that it was safest to keep her head down.

"Sure thing," she said at last, though there was still a question in her voice. "See you in there, Viv?"

"Bea—" Vivian swallowed as her friend turned back. "Thanks," she said, her voice shaking. "I'm lucky I got you looking out for me."

"You sure are," Bea said with a little lift of her chin. There would be questions later, Vivian knew. But for now, she settled for giving them both one more wary look before disappearing inside, letting the door swing closed behind her.

Honor watched her go, then turned back to Vivian. "You're all right? He didn't hurt you, did he?"

"No, just talked a big game. I think. I'm not sure what all he was getting at." Vivian bit her lip, hesitating. "You gonna fill me in? How did you know who he was? How did he know who *you* were?"

"Like you said before." Honor shrugged, looking away. "Seems like I know everyone."

"*Honor,*" Vivian said sharply. She wasn't in the mood for games.

"Honestly, pet . . ." Honor gave a short laugh, closing her eyes. "You'll probably know soon enough."

"What does that mean?" Vivian demanded, suddenly worried for an entirely different reason. Honor looked tired—no, she looked *sad.* Her normal cool expression was drawn, tight lines curving around her mouth like she was in pain. "What's going on?"

"Like I said." Honor opened her eyes. "You'll know soon enough." She hesitated, then reached out to brush her fingers down one side of Vivian's hair. "Got a bit mussed there." Her smile was bittersweet as she dropped her hand. "Time to get back to work."

Vivian caught Honor's hand when the other woman would have turned away. The feel of it, of smooth skin and strong calluses, was like a wave of memory—when was the last time they had touched like that?—but she didn't let it pull her eyes from Honor's. "If there's something going on, you can tell me. You know that, right?"

"Because you care about the Nightingale?" Honor asked softly.

"Because I care about you," Vivian snapped, dropping her hand. "God knows why. You don't make it easy."

That made Honor laugh, though there was no humor in the sound. "You're not the first to say so, pet," she said. "You don't need to worry about me. I'm fine. I'm swell. You keep your mind on taking care of yourself, okay?" As she turned away, Vivian heard her add quietly, "We both know you're going to need it."

The sting of those words went through Vivian like an electric shock. "You know, sometimes I wish I hated you," she bit off as she pushed roughly past, beating Honor through the doorway. They'd had the door open long enough that the hallway was cool from the night air, though Vivian could feel the heat spilling out of the dance hall along with the music. "It would make my life a lot easier."

"You might yet," Honor whispered behind her. "And I might deserve it."

Vivian didn't know what she meant. She didn't want to know. Fixing her smile like armor, she strode down the hall toward the bar. She didn't look back.

———•——

It only took a quick look around, once she was back in the dance hall, to see that Corny Rokesby and his friends were gone. The band was playing a jaunty Charleston, and the dance floor was a whirl of bodies, a mix of strangers and regulars. There was Miss Rose, the best dancer at the Nightingale, dancing with a woman Vivian had never seen before; she could barely keep up, but Miss Rose made her look good anyway. Mr. Lawrence almost never got on the floor for a Charleston, he was too old-fashioned for that, but someone had persuaded him out there, and he was holding his own, though his forehead gleamed with sweat. Mags Crawford, only seventeen years old though she would never admit it, had diamonds flashing in her hair as she twirled in the arms of her newest fella.

Vivian watched as if from a distance. The Nightingale had been her haven ever since she first stepped foot in it, trembling in Bea's shadow and hoping no one noticed that she had no idea what she was doing there. The thought made her glance at the bandstand, but Bea was on her break, probably smoking and laughing in the female employees' dressing room with her heels off and her feet kicked up. Most nights, Vivian would be in there with her.

But even the Nightingale couldn't protect her right now.

Vivian took a deep breath and squared her shoulders. She'd been caught up in police raids and trailed by a mob boss's bruisers. She'd seen dead bodies and dirty cops and the barrel of a gun pointed right at her. She'd unearthed more than one secret and kept her fair share too.

She wasn't going down without a fight.

When she turned back to the bar, she nearly jumped out of her skin. Leo was sitting there, watching her, and he wasn't alone. Danny leaned on the bar next to him.

"One of you gonna tell me what's up now?" Danny asked, glancing from her to Leo, who he had known since they were kids. They had met on opposite sides of a street brawl, packs of Jewish and Chinese boys fighting over who had the right to a few grimy city blocks. They had fought each other growing up as much as they had fought anyone else, a rivalry that grew into respect and eventual friendship, even after Leo lit out for Chicago.

Vivian had tensed when she saw them together, shoulders creeping up defensively as she waited to find out what Leo had told his friend. At Danny's question, though, she relaxed, if only just barely. Her news was still safe.

Leo hesitated, looking at Vivian. "Anything going on you want to share, Viv?"

"I—" Vivian bit her lip. "Will you tell Flo something for me, Danny? When you get home tonight?"

"I can," he said slowly. "Though maybe it's something you should come by and tell her yourself? You know she's going to blow her top if she finds out you're keeping something important from her."

That made Vivian laugh, though the sound came out tense and short. It was an understatement if there ever was one. Florence had a lifetime's worth of good reasons to dislike it when Vivian kept secrets. "I'm not keeping anything—I mean, I'm not going to. I'll come by and see her soon. But will you tell her it'll be a little bit?" Vivian swallowed down her nerves and smiled, hoping the expression was less shaky than it felt. "I've got a few things to take care of, and I don't want to bring any trouble her way right now."

"Viv—"

"You won't say anything that'll make her worry, right, Danny-boy?" she insisted. "I know you don't want her to. She's got enough to deal with right now."

That made Danny sigh. He and Florence were both thrilled to pieces to have a baby on the way. But her pregnancy hadn't been easy so far. Vivian knew the last thing he'd want was Florence worrying over her little sister—her little sister who was always in some kind of trouble—when she should be taking care of herself.

Danny nodded, though he didn't look happy about it. "If you say so, Viv." He looked like he might say something else, and Vivian braced herself for more questions. But a group of men and women came laughing up to the bar, debating whether they wanted gin or champagne, and he had to get back to work. "What's your poison, folks? The Nightingale's got it all . . ."

Leo was watching Vivian when she let out a sigh of relief. "How much are you actually working tonight?" he asked, one hand spinning his hat in restless circles on top of the bar.

"I'm supposed to be . . ." Vivian let out a breathy, humorless laugh, shaking her head. "I'm supposed to be working a regular shift. But I've managed all of one drink order. My head's up in the clouds tonight." Her head was back at the station, back in that office with Buchanan, but she didn't want to say that out loud.

Leo was still studying her. "Can you just go ahead and make this a break now?" he asked. "You look like you could use a dance."

Vivian wanted to throw herself into the music, to get lost in the sway of a dance, air heated by too many bodies against her bare arms. She knew if she pressed her cheek against the curve of Leo's shoulder, her nose would fill with the scent of shirt starch, the tang of the whiskey he'd been drinking, the spicy warmth of his cologne. She could pretend, just for a moment, that nothing else in the world mattered.

But tonight, she didn't need pretend. She needed a plan. "Can you get me in to talk to your pal at Bellevue?" she asked abruptly.

It took him a moment to catch up. "The medical examiner? What do you think he can—"

"I want to know if there was any kind of . . . what do you call it? When they look at dead bodies?"

"Autopsy?" He kept his voice low, not wanting anyone to overhear. "That one, yeah."

Leo grimaced. "From what you said, it seemed pretty straightforward, how he died. I'm not sure they could tell you anything new."

"Please?" Vivian begged in a whisper. "I've gotta start somewhere. That's a reasonable place, right?"

He sighed. "Sure, yeah. Of course. I'll see what I can do. But . . ."

"But what?" Vivian asked at last, when it seemed like he wasn't going to continue.

He didn't answer for several counts of the music. "I'm all out of favors at Bellevue," he said at last. "They don't owe me a damn thing right now, and the medical examiner's not going to risk getting on my uncle's bad side for nothing."

"What does that mean?" Vivian asked. "He'll say no?"

"Not necessarily," Leo admitted. "But you'll be on the hook for a favor yourself."

"Oh." Vivian let out a slow breath. What could someone from the coroner's office want from her anyway? "Well, that's how it goes, right? Can't get something for nothing. You'll do it?"

"I will." Leo gave her a gentle smile. "But we can't do anything about it just now, right? So we might as well enjoy a dance."

Vivian wanted to say yes more than anything. But the slow, melancholy drift of the music caught in her chest and her throat. It made her feel vulnerable, and scared, and she couldn't handle that tonight.

Vivian shook her head. "I don't think I can," she said, trying to smile as she took a step back. "I'm sorry. I should get back to work."

"Viv—" Leo caught her hand as she turned away. "You know it's going to be all right, don't you? We'll figure it out. Just tell me what you need."

She didn't look back at him. "Just that meeting, okay? And once I know something more . . ."

He squeezed her hand. "I'll do whatever I can. I promise."

"I know," she said quietly, turning back to him at last. "And you've got no idea how glad I am about that. Because I think I'm going to need a lot of help."

He tipped up her chin, then, and pressed his lips gently against hers. And even though they were in the middle of the dance hall, even though Vivian liked to keep her private life private and didn't want her regular customers to know she had something like a fella of her own, she kissed him back, fingers tight on the lapels of his coat. *It's going to be all right,* he had said. She wanted so badly to believe him.

Leo pulled back before she let herself get carried away, though, his eyes never leaving hers as he brushed the curtain of her hair back behind her ear. "You know I'm crazy about you, Viv, don't you?" he whispered, and for a moment Vivian felt like they were the only two people in the world. "There's not a chance in hell I'm letting anyone take you anywhere." Still smiling, he gave her hip a little nudge with his. "Now get back to work, sweetheart, or Danny's going to kick me out for distracting you."

TEN

Six Days Left

The sound of the factory bell down by the river woke her, as it did every morning. Vivian shivered, feeling like it had only been minutes since she had crawled into bed. Yawning, she pulled the quilt that she had restlessly kicked aside back up to her chin, burrowing into its warmth for a few more minutes. She sighed, her eyes drifting over the meager furnishings that made up her home, almost beautiful in the pale dawn light that trickled through the window.

She missed Florence the most in the morning, when she had to wake up alone and persuade herself out of bed for the day. She would miss her second-most when she walked into the dressmaker's shop and saw a new girl sitting in Florence's old spot, head bent over rows of tiny stitches or trays of glass beads. Miss Ethel, the shop's tyrant of an owner, had always told her workers that there were hundreds of girls in the city who'd be grateful for their jobs if they put a toe out of line. It wasn't an idle threat—it had taken her less than three days to find a replacement after Florence gave her notice.

Before her pregnancy had put an end to it, Florence had helped out in the kitchen of the Chins' restaurant, eager to become part of the family business as a sign that she was part of the family itself. Vivian had been invited to move in when Florence did. But the house on Spring Street was already crowded, and it would have been a challenge to squeeze her in there too.

Sometimes Vivian wished she had someone waking up next to her—that when she woke up shivering, she could bury her cold nose against warm skin and slowly drift into the morning. She had thought a time or two about asking Leo to stay. But the neighborhood was filled with cautionary tales: women who started having babies when they were too young and too poor, and who kept having them, their lives narrowed to survival and hope that one day, at least one kid would manage to escape.

Vivian still dreamed of her own escape. She still believed there was more to life than a cold morning, a cramped home, and long hours of work. She wasn't willing to risk that dream.

Gritting her teeth, Vivian threw off the quilt and staggered out of bed, teeth chattering as she fumbled for a second pair of socks and pulled Florence's tattered old dressing gown around her shoulders.

When Florence had been there, their days had begun with breakfast, silent and brittle for years, quiet and comfortable at last. On her own now, it was hard to summon the energy to eat anything so early in the morning. But there was a can of peaches at the back of the pantry and a little water left in the kettle from the night before, ready to be heated and turned into a cup of coffee.

She should buy more fruit after work, Vivian decided as she stuck her fork directly in the can, the syrupy sweetness a shock after the bitter taste of the coffee. Who knew how many days of peaches she had left.

Setting aside the grim thought and the empty can, Vivian squared her shoulders and pulled out her clothes for work. She hesitated when she was dressed, then pulled out the locked cashbox that she kept under her bed. There wasn't much in it—money saved up for next month's rent payment, a handful of nickels that could become subway fare if she needed them, a little extra from tips. She pulled out enough for a few groceries, then, hesitating, grabbed an extra quarter before she could talk herself out of it.

She needed the money. And she might need more of it than she planned for if she found herself with bribes to pay over the next week. But she had a thank-you to deliver after work, and she wanted to do it right.

Vivian could hear a baby fussing before she knocked. Before she could knock a second time, not sure whether anyone had heard over the noise, the door was yanked open.

"Don't you dare," Bea hissed, her eyes shadowed with weariness. "Nathaniel's stupid dog has been yapping all day, so the baby hasn't slept. He finally got home from work and took it out, so Alba's trying to get the baby down. She'll murder us both if we make any noise."

"When did Nathaniel get a dog?" Vivian whispered. Bea's family didn't live in the same building as Vivian did—the landlord refused to rent to Black folks—but they were only a few blocks away. It was bigger than the single room where Vivian lived, but the heat was just as unreliable, the gas sputtered, and the common tap was out in the hall washroom.

Not long ago, Bea and her mother had shared one bedroom, while her younger sister and two brothers had taken the second. But Bea's uncle, who had been working at the Nightingale, had died the previous summer, leaving his girl Alba pregnant and with nowhere to go. Now, she and the baby had one room to themselves, while half the Henrys crowded into the other and the boys slept on the floor in the main room.

Bea rolled her eyes as they slipped out into the hall, pulling the door shut behind them and sitting on the top stair. "He found it last week. Poor thing was half-starved, and some boys were throwing rocks or trash or something at it. He gave them a walloping and brought it home. I can't blame him for that, though it's ugly as sin, even now it's cleaned up and fed."

"Nice that your mom didn't make him get rid of it."

"You know she can't say no to anyone who needs help. Turns out dogs count, too." Bea rolled her eyes again, though she couldn't hide her proud smile as she did. Bea admired her mother, and the way she'd held her family together since her husband's death, more than anyone in the world. "And it's mostly behaving. But not today." Sighing, she rolled her shoulders and glanced at Vivian out of the corner of her eye. "You here for some explaining?"

Things had been too busy at the Nightingale last night for them to talk, and then Bea's fella Abraham had showed up to give her a ride home before Vivian's shift was done. She owed her friend an explanation for the scene in the alley. She also owed a thank-you.

"First, this." Vivian handed over the paper-wrapped package she had been carrying under one arm.

Bea gave her a suspicious frown, then carefully unfolded the paper, staring in surprise at the book of poems inside. "Countee Cullen?" she asked, sounding delighted. "Abraham says everyone's talking about him up in Harlem." Then her eyes narrowed. "Since when did you start reading poetry?"

Vivian snorted. "You know I don't," she said. Books were Bea's thing—she and Abraham had fallen head over heels for each other talking about poetry and Claude McKay. Vivian could count on one hand the number of times she had walked into a bookshop, and that number was one. "Once my deliveries were done, I went to ask a bookseller what was new, and he handed over this one. He said it had just come out, so I figured you wouldn't have read it yet."

Bea ran one hand over the cover, then shook her head. "I know you can't afford this."

"Keep it," Vivian said. "It's a thank-you for running to get Honor last night. I don't think that fella was going to play nice if we'd been out there alone much longer."

"Don't be dumb, Viv," Bea said, trying to push the book back into Vivian's hands. "We look out for each other, you know that."

"I want to," Vivian insisted. Her voice caught in her throat a little—less than a week until the commissioner's deadline—but she pushed that feeling aside and gave Bea a smile. "Can't a girl just want to do something nice for her pal?"

Bea's hands tightened around the slim cover of the book. "You gonna tell me what's going on?"

"Yeah," Vivian said, staring down at her lap. "It ain't good." Taking a deep breath, not meeting Bea's eyes, she told her what had happened at the Buchanan mansion. Her words stumbled over each other more than once, as she hurried past what she had found in Buchanan's study and tried to explain what the police had said and thought. She kept her voice quiet, not wanting to risk the neighbors overhearing. But she still felt exposed, as though at any moment someone would swoop in and haul her away.

When she got to the commissioner's surprise visit, Bea sucked in a sharp breath. "God almighty," she breathed. "Girl, you are in so much trouble."

Vivian glared at her friend. "You think I don't know that?"

"What are you going to do?"

"I don't know." Vivian's gaze dropped back to her hands. "Honor said she can't help me—not won't, *can't,* and she seemed real upset about it. Any idea what she . . ." Vivian swallowed. But Bea knew all about her history with Honor. "Why she would say that?"

Bea was quiet. "No," she said at last. "Honor's done plenty of hard things to help her people out before."

The silence between them grew heavy, neither wanting to meet the other's eyes. They were both thinking of the last time Bea had asked Honor for help—her and Alba both. Vivian didn't know what Honor had said, or what exactly had happened. But they all knew it had ended up with a man dead.

Vivian hadn't asked for details, too scared to find out who was to blame. If she didn't know, she could believe it hadn't been any of them, not really—or at least, not either of the people who mattered to her. And Bea had never shared.

It was one of the few things they never talked about.

Vivian swallowed. "Anyway, she came when you got her, at least. And I'm sure as hell grateful that you did. I don't know what that Rokesby fella was going to do next, but I doubt he was planning to ask me for a waltz."

Bea snorted. "He sure seemed like a piece of—" She broke off abruptly. "Wait, the dead guy. He had a different name, what did you say it was?"

"The dead . . . His name was Buchanan. Why?"

But Bea was already up and off, slipping back into the apartment and easing the door silently closed behind her. The baby's fussing had stopped, so Vivian stayed where she was, not wanting to risk waking him up. She didn't have to wait long; Bea was back in the hall less than a minute later, a newspaper under one arm.

"Abraham brought it this morning," she said absently, already leafing through the pages. "Mama wanted to find Everett a job, and I saw . . ." She flipped open a page, folding it back to stab at one of the posted advertisements with a triumphant finger. "Is that the same family?"

Vivian scanned the notice. *Mrs. E. Buchanan . . . 800 Fifth Avenue . . . Seeking a maid of all work . . .* "I think that's the same address," she said, frowning. "But why does it matter?"

"You said you didn't know what to do next," Bea whispered, looking pleased with herself. "*That's* what you do next. They're looking for a new maid, right? If you can get that job, you can probably find out what's really going on in that house. Because if you didn't kill him—"

"If?" Vivian demanded, forgetting for a moment to whisper.

"Keep your voice down," Bea hissed. "You know what I meant. The point is *someone* did. So why not get a job there, keep an eye on everyone, and see if you can find out something helpful?"

Vivian stared at her. "You're joking, right?"

"Why would I be?"

"Well, because in the first place, I don't know anything about that kind of work. I'm a dressmaker, not a maid."

"You think some Fifth Avenue lady won't snap you up for that exact reason? I bet she'd *love* to have her own seamstress on staff."

Vivian paused. "Sure, that's probably true," she admitted while Bea gave her a satisfied smirk, one finger still tapping the ad. "But in the second place, if I did get the job, I couldn't work at the shop too. What happens when this whole mess with Buchanan is over and done and I'm down a job and can't pay my rent?"

"You'd still be better off than if you went to prison for murder," Bea pointed out.

"Okay," Vivian said, gritting her teeth. Her head was starting to pound, and she wished she'd made time to eat after her deliveries were done. "But half the people in that house saw me, including the housekeeper *and* Mrs. Buchanan. I doubt they're going to hire me to dust the windowsills, seeing as they all think I—" She broke off, shaking. Her voice had risen as she spoke, and she didn't want to yell. "They'd probably just call the cops on me, and I'd be thrown in jail again. And I don't think I'm lucky enough to be released twice," she mumbled, pressing the palms of her hands against her eyes.

Once they were closed, her eyes felt so heavy that it was a struggle to open them again. When she did, she found Bea watching her.

"I could get the job," Bea said slowly, looking back at the paper.

"What?" It took Vivian a second to catch up with what her friend had said. "No, you don't want to put yourself through that. You can't."

"Why not?"

"Because," Vivian said, the word coming out strangled.

"I only sing at night," Bea insisted, her voice growing firmer. "And Alba's around days now, so I don't have to worry about the kids being alone while Mama's at the restaurant."

"Bea, working as a maid in some Fifth Avenue mansion would be bad enough. But someone was *murdered* in this one." Vivian shook her head. "I won't ask you to do that."

"You helped me out when Uncle Pearlie—" Bea broke off, and the two of them stared at each other without speaking. That was too close to the things they were careful not to talk about. Bea cleared her throat. "I don't hear you asking," she pointed out. "So that's fine, then."

Vivian wanted to reply, but she was interrupted by the sound of voices coming up the stairs. She and Bea jumped to their feet—both of them with smiles stretching wide and reassuring—as one of Bea's brothers and her sister stomped up the steps, schoolbooks under their arms, bickering cheerfully as they came.

"Hey there, troublemakers," Bea sang out, arms open wide for hugs. Baby threw herself into the hug gladly; sixteen-year-old Everett leaned against Bea with one shoulder, happy for the embrace but reluctant to show it. "Quiet when we go inside, yeah? Georgie's down for a nap after yowling his head off all day, so if you wake him up you're risking a walloping from Alba."

"Bea," Vivian said, quiet and urgent, as her friend began to usher the kids inside. Bea paused, her sharp glance a clear warning not to say anything that might scare them.

She didn't need to worry. Vivian knew better than that. "Don't do anything without talking to me first?" was all she said.

Expecting an agreement that was at most reluctant, Vivian was caught off guard by the sly lift to Bea's brows. "You don't get to tell me what to do, Vivian Kelly."

Before Vivian could say anything else, Bea had shut the door behind her.

Vivian's heart was thumping against her ribs as she walked slowly down the stairs. She needed to hear back from Leo's guy at Bellevue, and it needed to happen soon, before anyone else ended up in danger because of her.

God willing, he'd tell her something useful about how Buchanan died. Otherwise, she didn't know what she was going to do next.

Vivian stepped into the cutting afternoon wind. The sky was growing dimmer, but it wouldn't be dark for at least another hour. She glanced at the coins in her purse. Buying the book for Bea had taken most of what she had brought with her for the day, but one of her deliveries had ended with a ten-cent tip. That was enough to get her downtown and back home, if not guilt-free, then at least with less worry than she would have otherwise felt.

Vivian snapped her purse closed and headed toward the subway before she could talk herself out of it.

ELEVEN

The wind caught Vivian again as she climbed up the steps from the subway, twining around her legs like an angry cat. It caught up trash and dirt and the shouts of an angry motorist before it spun up toward the purple clouds that bruised the sky.

A man in a blue suit pushed past her, then stopped at the edge of the street to light a cigarette. Around her, shops were starting to wind down for the day, young men fetching in the bolts of fabric or carts of books that had been displayed outside. In the window of a butcher's shop, someone was just pasting a sign that declared what she assumed was *half off until closing* in multiple languages, though she could only read the line in English. Restaurants were starting to turn on their lights, windows glowing as the early diners inside received their bowls of soup or mugs of tea. Two cats darted out of an alley in front of her, spitting and hissing as they chased each other into the street. And all around her, voices called and shouted and laughed and complained in a comforting, undecipherable babble.

She couldn't understand most of it. There was some English mixed in, and two men arguing in what she thought might be Hebrew or Yiddish, not surprising with the Jewish neighborhood just on the other side of Bowery. But mostly the voices around her spoke Chinese.

No, not Chinese. What folks like her lazily called Chinese, Danny had told her sternly, was dozens of different languages and dialects. Vivian felt her cheeks grow hot with remembered embarrassment as she thought of how he had rolled his eyes at her ignorance. But that didn't stop her feet from moving.

The first time that she had ever come downtown, she had been overwhelmed trying to make sense of everything unfamiliar in the Chinese neighborhood. But now, after Florence and Danny's whirlwind romance and the first few months of their marriage had brought her there more and more, she mostly saw what was the same.

The buildings, old and shoddy and packed with tenants. A spindly tree, defiant and alone, waiting hopefully for a spring that was taking its sweet time arriving this year. The smell of food from chimneys and doorways, reminding her how long it had been since she'd eaten.

Plenty was different. But winter in New York was bitter no matter what part of the city you lived in. And people were people, no matter where you went.

Well, maybe not everyone. Vivian paused to watch a crowd of young men make their way down the street. There was nothing threadbare about *their* coats, and their shoes shone as if the mud of the city had never touched them.

Their sort wasn't an uncommon sight these days, wealthy young men coming downtown for what they called an adventure, away from manicured streets and stately stone walls.

Vivian hugged the shadow of a doorway as they went past. People weren't all the same. Not everywhere. And she needed to remember that if she wanted to have any chance of escaping this mess.

TWELVE

Vivian ducked into the kitchen door, propped open despite the chill outside, smoke and the scent of good food trickling out into the evening air. Inside, Danny's mother was busy at the stove; one of his cousins helped her, another washed dishes. All three of them turned as Vivian came. The two young men gave her unreadable looks—she hadn't yet discovered exactly what they thought of Florence's entry into the family, or the way Vivian herself came tagging along from time to time—before turning back to their work. But Danny's mother set down the wooden spoon she was using and brushed her hands briskly against her apron.

"Vivian. Good, make yourself useful. That tray needs to go up to your sister. She has not eaten enough today."

"Yes, Auntie," Vivian said, nodding as she went to pour a pot of tea and fetch a little ceramic cup, adding both to the tray on the counter.

The word still felt awkward on her tongue. She still thought of Danny's mother as Mrs. Chin, though she knew now that wasn't quite right either, because Chin wasn't actually her last name. Vivian had spent her whole life wanting a family, someone she *could* call auntie. But she was included in this one only because of Florence. She felt tacked on, an afterthought, part of the deal but not wanted in her own right. And she suspected they felt the same way about her.

But not using the honorific would be rude—or worse, ungrateful. "Has Florence been sick again?"

Mrs. Chin pursed her lips as she turned back to the stove, scooping up a second plate of rice and vegetables and eggs from the large pan there. "Not sick, just not enough appetite. You make sure she eats. For the baby, yes, but also for herself." Her smile, as she handed Vivian the plate, was unexpected. "And this is for you. I know you don't eat enough either."

Vivian wanted to cry from the kindness of the gesture. For a moment, she felt like something other than an afterthought, and the sensation burrowed comfortingly into her chest. "Thank you," she said quietly as she accepted the plate.

"Of course." Mrs. Chin nodded. "You'll never find a man to marry you if you are too skinny."

Vivian felt her cheeks growing hot. "Yes, Auntie," she said again, glancing at Danny's cousins in time to see them both smirking, though they tried to hide it. No doubt they'd been the recipients of Mrs. Chin's blunt instructions more than once, too. Vivian dropped her voice. "Is Danny upstairs?"

Mrs. Chin's expression closed off, and she turned back to the stove. "No, he has gone out for the evening," she said over her shoulder, her tone making it clear that she didn't want to discuss it any further.

Vivian understood. The Nightingale made Danny's parents nervous, and they didn't want word of his illegal second job spreading to their neighbors. Vivian knew that his cousin Lucky, at least, was aware of Danny's work. But she had no idea about the two that were currently in the kitchen. And given Mrs. Chin's clear reluctance to say more, she could guess which it might be.

"I'll make sure Florence eats," Vivian said again, adding her plate to the tray. "Thank you again, Auntie."

The restaurant was beginning to fill up with diners, bustling and noisy. Vivian slid between the dozens of small tables set out in neat rows as she headed for the stairs, which were roped off with a sign telling customers that the upper floors were off-limits. It would have taken some juggling to balance the tray and unhook the rope both, but Danny's father spotted her and left the table he was chatting with to come help.

"Thank you, Uncle," Vivian said after a quick exchange of greetings. That felt even stranger than calling Mrs. Chin *auntie*—Mr. Chin was more reserved than his wife. But he always had a smile for her, and tonight was no exception as he shooed her upstairs to see her sister.

The Chins, including the various cousins who stayed with them while they worked in the restaurant, lived upstairs in a series of rooms that felt more precarious the higher you climbed. They were small and cluttered but immaculately clean, their walls painted in cheerful shades of red and green and yellow, with hand-sewn curtains at the windows and photographs of relatives back in China proudly framed and displayed.

Danny and Florence shared a bedroom by the fire escape, where Vivian and her sister had once stayed. It was barely big enough for a bed and chest of drawers, but Florence had brought her own quilt and curtains. And the Chins, as a wedding present, had surprised Florence with a trip to a photographer, who had taken pictures not only of the newlyweds but of Florence and Vivian together.

Florence had told Vivian just before the wedding that she wasn't sure she knew how to be part of a family, she'd been without one for so long. But now those photos sat on the chest of drawers, Florence's new life and her old side by side.

She was in the sitting room today, not in her bedroom, humming quietly to herself as she flicked a duster over the furniture. She had to move slowly, one hand frequently on the small of her back or pressing against her hip, the growing curve of her belly pulling at her tiny frame in a way that was starting to look unbalanced. She and Vivian had always looked alike, though Florence's curly hair was a lighter shade of brown, and she, always proper, kept it far longer than Vivian's sleek black bob. But looking at her was so much like looking in a mirror that Vivian was startled by her pregnancy every time.

She wanted to be there when the baby came, to hold her sister's hand and remind her how strong she was. She wouldn't let anything get in the way of that.

"Vivi." Florence smiled. "Did I know you were coming?"

Vivian shook her head, putting her tray down on the table in the center of the room. "Surprise," she said. "Auntie has instructed me to make sure you eat something."

Florence rolled her eyes, but she was smiling as she set aside her duster. "I hope I'm not responsible for both those plates." She lowered herself gently into a seated position, wincing slightly. "Sit down?"

"Is your hip still bad?" Vivian asked, frowning as she tried to settle her chopsticks into the correct position, glad that none of Danny's cousins were there to witness her still-clumsy attempts. "Should someone look at it?"

"Someone did. But the cure is giving birth, so it'll be a while yet. Are you working tonight?" Florence asked as she handled her own chopsticks with practiced dexterity. Once, the question would have been an accusation. Florence hadn't approved of drinking, or dancing with strangers, or anything else that happened at the Nightingale. Now, it was simple curiosity.

"Not tonight. I just wanted . . ." Vivian bit her lip, not sure where to start or what to say.

"Vivian, what is it?" Florence asked. "And don't say nothing. You know I can always tell when you have something on your mind."

"It's . . ." Vivian hesitated. Florence watched her without saying anything, refusing to look away while she waited for an answer.

Florence always knew when Vivian had something on her mind, but that didn't mean Vivian had always told her what it was. For most of their lives, she'd refused to. They had been so different—Vivian convinced that they could have something, anything, more than the narrow life they had been given, Florence afraid that Vivian was waltzing headlong into danger.

They had both been right.

Even when the walls between them came down, Vivian had kept her secrets, determined to protect her sister.

She had failed at that, too.

Now, even knowing that, Vivian's instinct was to look away, to pretend that all was well. There was nothing Florence could do to help. Vivian was going to handle it on her own. All she could do if she said anything was make Florence worry. And her sister didn't need any more worries in her life.

Florence set down her chopsticks. "You and your secrets. Even now, when . . ." She shook her head, but there was no bitterness in the gesture, no anger.

Once, there might have been. But in spite of her uncomfortable pregnancy, she practically glowed with happiness. While Vivian had never known exactly what she wanted out of life, Florence always had: a husband, a family, a home. Her dream had been simple, but she had never let herself imagine she could have it. And now she did. It was hard to be bitter and angry when you were living a life you wanted.

"I hope one day that you don't have to keep them anymore," Florence said gently.

Vivian didn't want any more secrets, either. She pushed her plate away. "Flo," she said, taking a deep breath. "There's something you need to know."

———————

Florence hadn't wanted her to leave, after that. Vivian had lingered, until finally the light had faded and it was time to head home.

Vivian nearly slipped on the folded paper as she stepped through her own door at last, one heel catching on its smooth surface as she turned to close the door behind her. She caught the doorknob to steady herself, remembering at the last moment to keep the sharp profanity that slipped out to a whisper that wouldn't wake up any sleeping neighbors—or more importantly, neighbors' kids. She locked the door—she never forgot to do that first—before she turned around to see what she had stepped on.

There was only one window in her room, a dismal, rickety thing with a cracked pane. It looked out toward a streetlight, which could be a pain when she was sleeping but was helpful on nights when she got home late and didn't want to risk staggering around with a lit lamp while she yawned her head off. Tonight, the streetlight was flickering, golden light shaking as it flooded through the window, but it was enough for her to read the note when she unfolded it.

She recognized Bea's handwriting right away.

Viv, I know you said don't do anything, but you don't get to tell a pal to sit on her hands when you're in trouble. I got the job today. I start tomorrow morning, but guess what everyone was already whispering about? Some fancy pants lawyer will be coming by with Buchanan's will at three in the afternoon, and from what I overheard the wife and stepson aren't too happy about it. Might be worth you finding out what gets said and where the money's going—see you behind the garage at two thirty?

Vivian clenched her jaw and her fist both, crumpling the note in her hand. Bea could get fired if they found her sneaking someone into the house like that. Forget fired, she could end up arrested. Vivian couldn't ask her to do that.

And if someone found Vivian herself sneaking around . . . the commissioner had offered her a week. But that wouldn't be worth much if she got herself into trouble in Buchanan's own house again. It'd be back to jail for sure, and no chance of Leo bailing her out this time.

But that week was already slipping away.

She tossed the note into the rubbish bin and got ready for bed, her movements sharp and agitated as she kicked off her shoes and shrugged her coat from her shoulders.

By the time she had crammed another rag under the window's loose sash and was shivering under her quilt, knees pulled up nearly to her chin and arms wrapped around herself, Vivian had made up her mind.

She'd just have to keep her head down and pray they didn't get caught. Because if Bea was willing to take the risk, Vivian wouldn't say no.

She'd take whatever chance she could to find out more.

THIRTEEN

Five Days Left

"Quiet and quick," Bea said, glancing around as she gestured Vivian through the door.

The afternoon wind was still for once, and the air almost felt like spring—a promise or a taunt. The sharp, biting cold would return, but for the moment, there was no draft to give the open door away. As Vivian dashed from her hiding place behind the stone garage—it had probably once held a carriage, but now housed a gleaming black Rolls—and ducked into the Buchanans' Fifth Avenue mansion, she wanted to believe that was a sign. But she was too practical for that. It was good luck, and it probably wouldn't last.

That didn't stop her from following Bea up the back stairs, both of them nearly silent on feet that were used to the fast pace of a quickstep or the light breath of a waltz. The tradesmen's entrance, where she had come in before, opened into the main downstairs corridor, near the kitchen. This one had clearly once been meant to sequester the smell of horses and their handlers from the rest of the house. The passage from it was long, and it went straight to the narrowest set of stairs Vivian had ever seen.

"How'd you manage to get hired so quickly?" Vivian whispered as they crept up. "You don't know any more about being a maid than I do."

The quiet sound Bea made might have been a snort of laughter if it had been louder. "Seems like their applicants disappeared once girls put two and two together and realized someone here had just been murdered. And then another maid up and quit yesterday. Mrs. Buchanan was desperate. Now stop talking. Coast should be clear, but I'm not taking more chances than I need to."

Vivian held her breath as they went around each corner, but their good luck stayed with them—or maybe it was just that Bea had, in her usual practical way, planned everything with fierce caution. They didn't see anyone else, and soon they were upstairs.

Bea peered out into the hall, then beckoned for Vivian to follow. The hall itself—carved and gilded and tiled in crisp squares of black and white marble—was open on one side, overlooking the grand entryway below. Vivian hesitated, not wanting to risk being seen. But she followed Bea, and soon they were around the corner and out of sight.

The room Bea led her to was cramped with furniture and knick-knacks, many things still in boxes or crammed into crates. Against one wall, half a dozen large paintings were stacked carelessly one against the other. In another corner, leather-bound books were piled in a tower that looked like it was about to topple over at any second. Glancing around, Vivian pushed them toward the wall, nervous that someone might come to investigate the sound if they fell over.

"A storage room?" she asked, confused. Half of her wanted to tell Bea she'd changed her mind, that she wanted to leave. But she couldn't do that. She was just as likely to get spotted leaving as she was to be caught eavesdropping. Better to learn something first, if there was anything to learn, than risk getting caught for nothing. "Why—"

"No one's bothering with unpacking today, given everything that's happened," Bea whispered, glancing around. "There's a staircase behind that door. I figure you can—"

"Oh dear."

The quiet, faintly amused voice made them both jump, and Vivian grabbed Bea's arm as she spun toward the door.

The woman waiting there smiled at them. "Call it a hunch, but something tells me you girls aren't supposed to be here." She made a *tsk*ing sound with her tongue. "Now, what shall we do about that?"

FOURTEEN

Vivian stared at the woman, who had closed the door behind her, as stunned as if the floor had disappeared beneath her feet. "Mrs. Wilson," she said, her voice little more than a croak. "What the hell are you doing here?"

Hattie Wilson *tsk*ed again, resettling the fur stole that she wore draped around her shoulders. She was dressed for mourning, Vivian noticed, in black lace and silk, with pearls draped around her neck and hanging from her ears. It was a dress Vivian recognized. She had watched the seamstress who sewed it after Mrs. Wilson's husband had died. Her hat was perched stylishly on one side of her head, and the netted veil that draped across its brim hid half her face, making it nearly impossible to read her expression.

China-doll pretty, wearing her long hair pinned demurely back and with just enough cosmetics on to make her look as winsome as possible without opening her up to an accusation of being fast, Hattie Wilson wasn't much older than Vivian. But she had enough poise and confidence to make Vivian feel like a child around her. It was the sort of polish that came from years of living in wealth and comfort, confident that whatever you wished to happen, could and likely would.

And in Hattie Wilson's case, it came from being at the head of the small but thriving criminal empire she had taken over after her husband's death.

"I thought you had better manners than that," Hattie continued, turning just enough to glance at Bea. "At least one of you knows when to keep your mouth shut. Though it's a pity, really. You sing so beautifully when you open it."

Bea took a step back. "How . . ."

"I've seen you perform, Bluebird," Hattie said with a smile, beautiful and cold as a diamond. Whatever she was thinking, she hid it well. But at least she hadn't turned them in. Not yet. "Which is why you caught my eye when I was coming upstairs. Honor Huxley's star chanteuse, sneaking around here of all places, today of all days?" Hattie drifted, unhurried or maybe just tormenting them, toward one side of the room, pulling the top book from the stack and rolling her eyes at it. "*The Odyssey*? Really? How predictable. And I bet he never opened it once after he bought it." She glanced toward Bea and Vivian again as she tossed the book carelessly back down. "To answer your question, I was invited, Miss Kelly. Can you say the same?" When neither of them answered, she smiled again. "I thought not."

"Invited?" Vivian asked before she thought better of the question.

"To hear my uncle's will read, of course," Hattie said. "Well, Mr. Wilson's uncle. So I don't expect there to be anything in there attached to my name." She shrugged, but in spite of her careless attitude, she was clearly staying between them and the door. And her smile hadn't faltered. "Now let me think. A little bird told me that a *dressmaker*, of all people, is the prime suspect in Uncle's murder. And here you are, with your friend pretending to be a maid while she helps you creep around. You have a knack for finding trouble, Miss Kelly." Her gaze grew sharp. "You may choose, girls. You tell me what you're up to, or I start shouting that someone broke into the house."

"What's to stop you doing that anyway?" Bea asked defiantly, crossing her arms. She looked cool and composed, and even though Vivian knew she must be close to panicking, her voice never wavered.

"Absolutely nothing." The careless lift of Hattie's shoulders was so delicate it could barely be called a shrug, but her eyes glittered menacingly behind her veil as she watched them. "So I suggest you give me a good reason not to."

Vivian glanced at Bea as she tried to decide what to do. But Bea, sharp as ever, got there first. "Vivian didn't have anything to do with that guy getting bumped off. She was just in the wrong place at the wrong time."

"A bad habit of yours, that," Hattie Wilson said, looking amused when Vivian glared at her. "And you're here to prove your innocence?"

"I'm here to listen in while his will is being read and see if there's a good reason someone *else* might've wanted him dead," Vivian bit off. "I don't expect it'll turn up anything. But when a girl's feeling desperate . . ." She shrugged.

"Hmm." It was impossible to tell what Hattie was thinking. "And how exactly do you plan to gather this information? Hanging out a window, perhaps?"

Bea jerked her head toward a corner that held a second door. "Through there's a staircase going down—servants' stair, I think, it's pretty darn narrow. There's another door at the bottom, and it opens into the family parlor where they—" She gave Hattie a suspicious glance. "—you, I suppose, are meeting with the lawyer."

"And you know it's the right spot?" Vivian asked when Hattie said nothing.

"It had better be," Bea said with a scowl. "I had to spend over an hour dusting it this morning."

"All right." They both turned back to Hattie to find her smiling. "I'll agree not to tell anyone you're here because, to be quite honest, I'm curious to see what you make of our little gathering. Whether anyone surprises you . . . or not."

"More of a surprise than just seeing you here?" Vivian asked nervously. Hattie Wilson never did anything without a reason. This time Vivian didn't have any idea what that reason might be, but she couldn't imagine it was good.

Hattie's expression grew sly, almost smug, and Vivian wished she could see her eyes more clearly. But that delicate little veil was still in the way. "You might be surprised by who else you know here today, Miss Kelly. You aren't the only one who turns up in unexpected places."

"What is that supposed to mean?" Vivian demanded. Hattie Wilson terrified her, and she knew she didn't have a hope of hiding it. But she refused to be played with.

But Hattie shook her head. "I'd hate to spoil it for you." She gestured toward the stairs, and when she spoke again, there was a taunting edge to her voice. "Time passes, Miss Kelly. Will you take me up on my offer, or shall I summon Uncle Huxley's dreadful wife and tell her she has rats creeping about?"

Vivian knew the offer to stay quiet wasn't out of the goodness of her heart. Hattie Wilson had said it herself, more than once—she didn't have a heart.

Though that wasn't entirely true. Vivian had met Mrs. Wilson's sister, and she knew the woman had a son. Hattie was fiercely protective of both of them. But otherwise, she made her choices based on a very simple logic: what was going to be best for her and her business. In some ways that made her more reliable than most people. And if she was willing to help . . .

Vivian glanced at Bea, who grimaced but nodded. "All right," Vivian said. "Though it's not like we have much of a choice."

"There's always a choice, Miss Kelly," Hattie said. She turned to Bea, giving her maid's uniform a dismissive look. "Get along, Bluebird—I'm sure you have work to do. You can fetch your friend once the lawyer is gone."

Bea didn't look happy about it, but she wasn't in a position to protest. She gave Vivian a smile that would have been encouraging if her worry hadn't been so plain. Bea knew what she was risking here, too. "Remember, not a peep on the stairs, okay? You don't want anyone in that room hearing you."

"Got it," Vivian said, trying to sound confident. "Now get going before you get canned on your first day."

That made Bea roll her eyes. "Good luck, Viv." She gave Hattie Wilson a wary look as she slipped past her and out the door, closing it silently behind her.

As soon as she was gone, Hattie gestured toward the staircase. "Head on down, then."

But Vivian was frowning at her, something Hattie had said just moments before sticking in her mind. "What did you say your uncle's name was?"

"Not my uncle," Hattie reminded her.

"Sure, okay, but what did you call him? Did you say Uncle Huxley?"

"Uncle Huxley?" Hattie raised her brows, though her look of surprise seemed almost deliberate. "Don't tell me you found his bloody corpse but didn't know his given name."

"Why would I?" Vivian snapped. It was a stupid thought anyway. She pushed it out of her mind. "It isn't as if people like you introduce themselves to the folks doing their deliveries."

"I suppose not." Hattie shrugged again. "Are you going to stand there all day? I have to get downstairs myself."

Vivian still hesitated. "You're planning to double-cross me."

"Likely someday, but not just yet." Hattie held up one hand, though

Vivian knew better than to trust her solemn expression. "On my honor. I'll even sit in front of the door so you can open it a crack if you'd like to risk it." She turned to leave, calling softly over her shoulder, "Enjoy the show."

Vivian stayed rooted to the spot after the door closed. For a moment, she thought about locking the door or putting something in front of it so that no one could come into the room behind her. But locking it might attract attention from someone who knew it was supposed to be open. And any sort of ruckus wouldn't just tell her someone was up there. It would probably carry to the Buchanans and their lawyer, and what if they came barreling up the staircase to investigate? Besides which, anything she did was as likely to get in Bea's way as it was anyone else's.

No, she'd just have to take her chances that someone might come into the room, or that Hattie Wilson might give her away in spite of her promise. She'd have to be quiet, was all. Quiet and careful. She could do that.

The staircase was as narrow as Bea had promised, and with no windows it was nearly dark. From the top, Vivian could see a single electric bulb hanging above the steps. But if she turned it on, someone might see the light where it shouldn't be. No sense taking that risk.

The still air made her shiver as she eased the door closed behind her and crept down. The passage had plunged into darkness when she pulled the door shut, and she had to feel her way carefully down each step, one hand outstretched so she wouldn't run into the door. When she reached it, she hesitated, then pressed her ear against the wood. There was no sound from the other side. Taking a deep breath, she turned the knob, opening the door just a bare crack and praying it wouldn't swing any wider. She didn't want to risk poking her head in; all she could do was hope that no one had been in there early to see the door move.

Settling down a few steps from the bottom, Vivian drew her legs under her chin, wrapped her arms around herself, and waited.

———•——

H er legs had just started to go numb from being in one position too long when she heard the sound of a door opening. Startled, Vivian just managed to catch herself before she sprang up. The sound had come from the next room, and it was immediately followed by a hushed babble of voices.

Vivian sat up straighter, breathing as quietly as possible while she strained toward the door without actually moving. It was starting.

"Are we waiting on anyone else, Mrs. Buchanan?" a man's voice asked, accompanied by the quick tapping sound of papers being shuffled into order. The lawyer, maybe?

"No." The woman's voice was trembling, with a hint of tears. Vivian could picture her dabbing at her eyes with a handkerchief. "I believe this is . . . everyone." There was a hint of malice in those words that caught Vivian's attention. Unhappiness with the lawyer? Or dislike of someone else there?

"Very well." The lawyer's voice was businesslike and solemn, with just the right hint of kindness for a grieving family. "Shall we all take our seats? Mr. Whitcomb, Mr. Morris, there are places over here. Mrs. Buchanan, you and your . . ." He trailed off, sounding uncertain.

"Sister-in-law," said a brisk voice that reminded Vivian of the nuns who had raised her in the orphan home. It was the sort of voice that was not used to being argued with. "Miss Edith Rokesby, how do you do, I'm Mr. Rokesby's aunt as well. I'm here to support them in this trying time. And to see that their interests are protected."

There was silence in the room except for several clearing throats, as though no one was sure how to respond. "Pleased to meet you, Miss Rokesby," the lawyer replied at last.

"Mrs. Wilson, may I offer you this seat?" That was Corny Rokesby, and the sound of his voice made Vivian shiver. She wrapped her arms more tightly around herself.

"No, thank you. I believe I'll be comfortable right where I am." Hattie Wilson's voice was cool as always, no grief or even a pretense of it for her audience. It was also the closest one to Vivian yet. Apparently, Hattie was making good on her promise to place herself in front of the door. "Ms. Huxley, would you care to sit?"

Vivian had just started to relax a little, but Hattie's question—asked with too-obvious innocence—made her sit up sharply, eyes wide in the darkness of the staircase. There was no chance—she'd have known—

"I'm fine where I am, thanks. Don't draw things out on my account; I'm sure everyone wants to get this over with."

For a moment, Vivian felt like she couldn't breathe. She started to her feet without realizing what she was doing, her whole body shaking.

That had been Honor Huxley's voice.

FIFTEEN

still don't understand why *she* needs to be here." That was Mrs. Buchanan again.

"Mr. Buchanan's will concerns his daughter as much as it concerns
you, madam," the lawyer said, gentle but firm. "More, in fact, as we'll
see. Now, if everyone would take their seats, we can get started . . ."

Vivian pressed her hands against her mouth. Buchanan's daughter?
Honor was the dead guy's *daughter*? She couldn't even wrap her head
around what that might mean. What was it Honor had said, the day
he died? Had she given some hint that Vivian should have picked up
on? Why wouldn't she have said? When she said she couldn't help, was
that because—

The bite of Vivian's nails against her palms reminded her where she
was. Slowly, she took her seat on the steps once more. She didn't know
how long she had been standing there, but they were still talking, and
she might have already missed something important. She needed to
pay attention if she was going to make this worthwhile.

"—control of Buchanan, Morris, and Whitcomb passing equally to the remaining two partners, except for a ten percent stake each going to—"

"Equally?" rumbled an irritated, masculine voice. "Did he not say which of us would have controlling interest after him?"

"He . . . it seems he did not," the lawyer said, sounding a little nervous. "The will indicates equal control is to be held between you both."

"But that's outrageous," the man insisted, his voice rising. "He should have named one of us to—"

"One of you could always buy the other out," Hattie Wilson put in. "Isn't that how these things work? So one person has that controlling interest."

"Mrs. Wilson, I do not mean to offend," the man replied, his voice dripping condescension. "But I believe we can handle matters of our business on our own."

"Well, in point of fact, she's quite right," the lawyer put in. "The option is there, of course, if you wish to—"

"But what about Cornelius?" Mrs. Buchanan interrupted, her voice growing shrill. "Huxley was teaching Cornelius the ins and outs of—"

"Oh, yes, indeed, Mr. Rokesby was not forgotten," the lawyer said, soothing but firm. "Mr. Cornelius Rokesby and Mrs. Willard Wilson both receive a ten percent stake in Buchanan, Morris, and Whitcomb, with the proportionate level of control and profit. Mrs. Wilson's share is, naturally, to pass to her own son when he comes of age."

"Ten percent?" Even through the door, Vivian could hear Mrs. Buchanan's outrage. "That's hardly anything—"

"Hardly anything we would have expected, you're very right, Aunt Evangeline," Hattie Wilson broke in smoothly. "How generous of Uncle Huxley to think of us, who are not even his blood relatives. Don't you agree, Corny?"

Vivian couldn't hear what he mumbled in response, but she didn't much care what was happening with Buchanan's business. There was only one voice she really cared about in that room, and it was the one that was staying silent.

"—thousand each to Evangeline Rokesby Buchanan and Cornelius Francis Rokesby. The remainder of his estate is willed in its entirety to his daughter, Honor Margaret Huxley."

For a moment, Vivian thought something had exploded in the room. The sudden burst of voices was so loud, so outraged, that it seemed impossible for it to have come from so few people.

"—cannot be serious!"

"You expect us to believe—"

"—favor his *bastard* over his family?"

The word hung in the air. For a moment, no one spoke.

"No need to look so shocked on my account, everyone." Honor's voice was amused, though there was bitterness underneath it, too. "Miss Rokesby, you look like you expect me to slug you in the face. Which I've no doubt some folks would, for calling them a bastard. But I came to terms with what I am long ago."

"Then you admit that it's inappropriate," Miss Rokesby's voice quivered, though Vivian couldn't tell if that was from worry or outrage.

"I didn't say that."

"So you intend to claim this bequest?" That was Mrs. Buchanan, sounding as indignant as her sister. "We can challenge it, you know. We don't have to let this stand!"

"Out of curiosity, Mr. Hatch, did my father warn you that this was likely to happen when you and he drew up his will?" Honor's voice was even drier than usual, and Vivian had to strain to hear it. She wondered what Honor was thinking.

She wondered what Honor had known.

The lawyer cleared his throat. "He did. He predicted that Mrs. Buchanan or her son—perhaps at the urging of his aunt—would attempt to issue a legal challenge to the terms of his will. He had me draft a separate clause . . ." The room was deadly quiet, quiet enough that Vivian could hear the sound of shuffling papers. "Ah, here it is. A separate clause, which he signed six months ago, stating that, should such a legal challenge be registered with the courts, the party issuing it would forfeit their own inheritance." The lawyer cleared his throat again. "I hope I need not explain to anyone here that the presence of such a document would make winning a court case highly unlikely for anyone intending to challenge Ms. Huxley's inheritance."

Vivian had leaned forward without realizing it, and one of her feet slipped off the stair where it was resting and landed with a *thump* on the uncarpeted floor.

"Did someone knock at the door?" Mrs. Buchanan asked, sounding nervous.

Vivian froze. They wouldn't think of looking in the staircase, would they? Slowly, she stood, ready to bolt back up toward the storage room.

"Only my chair shifting, Aunt Evangeline." That calm voice was Hattie. "My apologies for interrupting. Mr. Hatch, do continue."

"Oh yes, certainly. Um . . ." There was the sound of shuffling papers once more, and Vivian sat down, her heart pounding, while the lawyer continued. "Now, as I was saying . . . where was I?"

"You were saying that . . . that . . . *creature* is just going to walk away with most of Huxley's money." That was a masculine voice, deep and cultured. Vivian could practically hear the cigars and whiskey in it, right alongside his obvious distaste. The second partner, likely. Had he been the business associate Buchanan had met with that day? Was it the other man in there? Or someone else entirely?

"And both houses," the lawyer put in, sounding apologetic.

"*Both* houses?" Miss Rokesby's screech made Vivian wince, even from the other side of the door. Mrs. Buchanan started crying.

There was an instant flurry in the room, concerned masculine voices and the scraping of chairs quickly pushed back.

"Please, madam, there's no need—" The lawyer sounded like he was wringing his hands. "Mr. Buchanan specified in his will that Ms.

Huxley may not take possession of this home for twelve months following his death. You are not being evicted, I promise."

"You did this." That was Miss Rokesby again, while a flurry of male voices urged her to calm down. "How did you convince him to abandon his family like this? To abandon his wife?"

"I had nothing to do with it," Honor replied. It was the first time she had raised her voice, but there was still no hint of what she was feeling in it. "I'm as surprised as the rest of you. But I do have to point out, Miss Rokesby, that it's hardly strange for a man to leave his money to his child." Honor paused, and Vivian could almost picture the ironic smile hovering on her lips. "Which I am, however much of a bastard I may be."

"She's right, Aunt Edith." That was Corny Rokesby, sounding exhausted. Or maybe just disappointed. "She has more claim to his money than either Mother or I do, and we all know it."

"Corny, don't you dare!" Miss Rokesby snapped, while Mr. Buchanan's business partners chimed in with their own protests and outrage.

The babble continued while Mrs. Buchanan cried. Apparently, whatever Corny Rokesby thought, the rest of the room could not bear the idea of Buchanan's low-class daughter walking away with his fortune. Throughout it all, Honor stayed silent.

Was she standing there in her men's trousers and perfect cosmetics, determined as always to do things her own way? Vivian could picture it, could picture the confident, defiant smile on Honor's face.

Or was she angry at these people? Was she actually sad about her father's death? Had she cared about him at all? Vivian didn't know, because Honor had kept it all from her. She had stood there while Vivian told her what had happened and said nothing.

The thought made Vivian angry all over again. The arguing in the next room was continuing unabated, and meanwhile she could only sit there wondering when one of them would say something that mattered, something that would help her. A week had seemed like a long time when the commissioner first set his deadline.

But it was no time at all. Vivian wondered if she should take the opportunity to leave. There'd be less of a risk that they'd hear her going upstairs if she did it while they were all still yelling at each other anyway. And maybe there was still time for her to head to Bellevue before the medical examiners went home for the night. Maybe one of them could tell her something, *anything,* that would help. Because she was running out of time, and the folks on the other side of that door were too busy yelling about money to care that someone had stabbed a man to death, and the only suspect the police had was just a poor Irish girl afraid for her life.

Vivian discovered that her hands were shaking. She balled them into fists and pressed her knuckles against the unyielding wood of the stairs.

She'd stay until they were done, because she couldn't afford to miss anything that might be important. Even if listening to them did make her want to scream with frustration.

Vivian pulled her knees against her chest, wrapped her arms around them, and stayed.

———————

Did you learn anything helpful?" Bea asked as she held open the door beside the garage.

She had come for Vivian once the meeting was done, wanting to get her out while the rest of the staff were occupied with the other guests. Vivian had waited only a few minutes at the top of the stairs with the door just barely cracked open, wanting to be out of sight in case anyone who wasn't Bea happened to come into the storage room.

When she had heard a familiar voice whisper, "I'll dance 'til last call," Vivian had darted out, not needing Bea's gestured reminder to stay silent.

They only had a brief moment to talk at the door by the garage before Bea had to duck back inside; her question made Vivian hesitate. "I might have," she said, thinking of Honor's presence, the business partners with their condescension and complaints about controlling interest, Mrs. Buchanan's sister-in-law so determined that her relatives would make a profit from Mr. Buchanan's death. She shuddered. "Sounds like everyone in his life was a nasty piece of work. Or at least . . ." She trailed off, her mind turning to Honor once more.

"Look, I've gotta run. We'll talk tonight, okay? I'm on with the band at nine."

"Sure thing." Vivian nodded. "Get back in there. I'll sneak around front without anyone seeing me. And Bea?"

"Yeah?" Bea paused with the door half-closed.

"Thanks. You didn't have to do this, but I—"

"Get out of here," Bea said, rolling her eyes. "Before someone sees you and I do get canned."

"You don't even care about this job," Vivian pointed out. Clearly Bea didn't want her getting sentimental. And that was just fine. Vivian wasn't sure she'd be able to hold it together if she did.

"Maybe not, but I don't want to give them any excuse not to pay me. I'll make it at least through the full day, thanks."

"Ha," Vivian said dryly. "See you tonight."

She wanted to get out of there as quickly as possible, but she forced herself to walk slowly, not wanting to draw any attention if someone happened to look outside. The alley that went behind the house connected to several others on the block, and she kept her head down, hoping that if anyone did spot her, they'd assume she was there for one of the neighbors. But just as she was about to step out of the alley, she drew back into the shadows, staring at the street, where Honor Huxley was climbing into a cab.

But it was too risky to linger in the alley. As soon as Honor's back was turned, Vivian started walking. She thought she was heading downtown, but all she really knew was that she was getting away from that house. Away from anyone who might recognize her.

Away from Honor Huxley.

She had said she couldn't help. And that look in her eyes when Vivian had told her what happened . . . had she been sad for Vivian or her father? Vivian didn't know why she hadn't admitted who he was to her, or why the fact that he was her father meant she couldn't help. Was there some other reason, something else she was hiding?

Had that moment in the Nightingale's basement been the moment she found out that her father had died?

Vivian's feet slowed to a stop, the thought making her feel sick. She stood in the shadow of another looming house, arms wrapped around herself as she stared at the people passing by. None of them gave her a second glance.

Honor had sounded cool as ever in that room, but Vivian couldn't blame her for that. She wouldn't have shown any grief herself, not in front of those Fifth Avenue bloodsuckers, with Mrs. Buchanan sobbing about how it all wasn't fair and that Miss Rokesby probably looking like she wanted to murder someone herself.

Had Honor known she was going to inherit all that?

And anyway, if he was her father, why was her last name the same as his first? Vivian didn't know much about how being a bastard worked. As far as she knew, her mother had been married to her father before he died or ran off, or at least Mae Kelly had pretended that was the case. The one neighbor in Vivian's building who had known Mae, and who had kept Vivian and Florence from being split up before they were sent to the orphan home, had always said she went by Mrs. Kelly.

Vivian's head hurt just thinking about it. She'd just have to ask Honor, was all. Even if she didn't want to share . . . well, after all that, after knowing what she had kept from Vivian when she refused to help, Honor owed her that much.

The sound of a car horn honking made Vivian jump. At the corner in front of her, a sleek black motorcar had just pulled up, its sides so freshly polished that Vivian could practically see every hair on her head reflected in its side. The driver unfolded himself from the front seat and walked around to meet her.

Vivian stared at him. He returned the look with as much emotion as a boulder might show—fitting, as he was the size of a small, hulking mountain. Vivian recognized him.

"What're you doing here, Eddie?" she snapped. "Gonna spend your day beating on girls half your size?" She didn't quite flinch away from him, but she did take a step back.

The first time she had ever seen Eddie, he was doing his best to beat the hell out of Danny in a back alley, though Danny had been the one to come out of that fight still standing.

The second time, he and a friend had cornered her, threatening to rough her up unless she told them what they wanted to know until someone else showed up and scared them off.

It was impossible to stare up at his broad-shouldered bulk without feeling something like terror. Vivian didn't think he'd do anything here, in broad daylight on the Upper East Side. But the people streaming past gave him wide berth, and they didn't give her a second look. If he hustled her off somewhere more private, no one would stop him.

"Boss wants a word," Eddie rumbled, looking unbothered by her accusation.

Vivian took another step back. "I've got nothing else to say to her."

Eddie ignored her, turning to open the car's back door and stepping to the side.

"Please don't waste my time, Miss Kelly," Hattie Wilson said, looking bored as she examined her nails. "You may get in on your own, or Eddie will put you in. Your choice."

Vivian thought about pointing out that, once again, it wasn't actually a choice. But there was no point. Eyeing Eddie warily, she scooted into the car. When the door slammed shut behind her, she pressed her back against it, trying to keep as much of the wide back seat between her and Hattie as possible.

Hattie watched her with a small smile on her face, as if enjoying Vivian's obvious discomfort. Her fur stole was laid across her lap, rather than around her shoulders, and a black portfolio rested on it. But she hadn't taken off her hat, and in the inconsistent light that flickered in through the windows, the veil cast eerie shadows across her face.

"Well. Did you listen in?" Hattie asked as the car pulled away from the curb.

Vivian wanted to watch where they were going, but it seemed more important to keep her eyes on the woman sitting across the seat from her. "I did," she said, trying to sound flippant and failing, even to her own ears. "Sounded like an interesting bunch. Hope you don't all get together for Christmas or anything."

Hattie made a soft *hmm* of laughter, but it didn't seem like it was Vivian's attempt at a joke that amused her. "You didn't know she'd be there, did you?"

Vivian thought about pretending she didn't know what Hattie meant. But there was no point, really: both of them knew exactly who she was talking about. "No, I didn't." She let out a shaking breath. "You recognized her last summer, didn't you?"

"I did," Hattie said, nodding. "She looks like her father. You were there, if I recall. But she didn't tell you then, did she? She forgot to mention that her father was an incredibly rich man, living right here in the city. I assume she also forgot to mention that he spent most of her life pretending she didn't exist?" Hattie sat back, the fingers of one hand drumming in a soft, persistent rhythm against the portfolio's leather cover. "Strange, that. Seems like it's the sort of thing she'd want you to know . . . what with you being a suspect in his murder and all. And, if what I've heard is correct, with you two being so *close*."

"She's my boss," Vivian said firmly, even as her stomach twisted into a knot of worry. Honor had made it clear that people like Hattie were one of the reasons she and Vivian couldn't be together. And it wasn't because they'd be scandalized or disapproving. Honor didn't care about things like that.

But romance was a weakness, one she couldn't afford to have in her line of work. Not when any day could put her at odds with folks like Hattie Wilson, who weren't above using other people as tools to get what they wanted.

Honor hadn't wanted to put Vivian in that position. Or maybe she just hadn't wanted to do it to herself. Vivian had never been sure, and she had been too afraid of the answer to ask.

Hattie gave another amused *hmm*. "If you say so."

Vivian clenched her jaw. "You don't care that someone killed him, do you? He was part of your family, and—"

"My husband's family," Hattie said, her voice icy, all her amusement suddenly gone.

Vivian fell silent. They both knew what kind of man Hattie's husband had been. And as much as Vivian disliked her, she couldn't blame Hattie for that grudge in the slightest. "They were similar, then?" she said, her voice catching as she remembered her brief conversation with Buchanan. He had seemed like a kind man. But she knew how people could lie.

So did the woman in front of her.

After a moment, though, Hattie shook her head. "Nothing alike, as far as I know," she said quietly. "Huxley was a decent sort of man." Then, as if she'd allowed too much humanity to show through, her smile grew mocking once more. "He remembered me in his will, so I can't complain about him that much, can I?" When Vivian didn't say anything in reply, she leaned forward. "And you're very much mistaken, Miss Kelly, if you think I don't care that he was murdered. But when you're in my line of work, you live in the present and the future, or you might end up dead yourself."

Vivian wished she could read the thoughts behind those glittering eyes. She'd feel a lot safer if she knew what Hattie Wilson was trying to get out of this conversation. But whatever Hattie was thinking, she had learned—long before she took over her growing empire—to keep it hidden behind a smile.

"You don't think I did it," Vivian said recklessly, trying to sound like she was certain.

"Of course not, Miss Kelly," Hattie Wilson said. Vivian wanted to sigh with relief, but there was nothing reassuring about Hattie's smile. "If I've learned anything about you during our strange acquaintance, it's that you don't have the stomach for that sort of messiness."

"Thanks," Vivian said dryly. They both knew it hadn't really been meant as a compliment.

"But you know who does. Don't you?" Hattie gave Vivian a pitying smile, then, as if the discussion was over, opened the portfolio in her lap, and started to look through its papers.

Vivian stared at her. "No," she said. But her voice shook as she said it. They both knew who Hattie meant.

Mrs. Wilson picked up a pen as the car stopped, waiting to make a turn, and leisurely signed two papers before it started again. "You know who gained the most from his death—you heard them all arguing about it," she said without looking at Vivian. "You know she has the stomach for it. And you know she's ruthless enough to set up someone else to take the fall for her. Someone she knows has an unfortunate habit of ending up in the wrong place at the wrong time. Someone she—and I'll admit, I'm speculating here, but I think I'm correct—has refused to help out?"

"No." The word came out in a whisper, and Vivian struggled to make her voice louder. "*No.* She wouldn't do that. Any of it. Not her father, and not . . ." The words got stuck again, and Vivian settled for shaking her head firmly while she glared at Hattie Wilson, who didn't bother to look up. "Your mind's twisted even to think of it."

"Then why hide it from you?" Hattie asked, sounding too reasonable.

Vivian wanted to press her hands against her ears to shut her out. "I'm doing you a favor here—another one, you may recall. Because it wasn't your Ms. Huxley who helped you spy on Buchanan's nearest and dearest, now, was it?"

"You only did that because you wanted me to find out about Honor," Vivian snapped.

Hattie shrugged as she pulled out one paper, looked over it, and tucked it back into the portfolio. "Like I said, a favor. You can believe me or not, suit yourself. But you'll be safer if you keep it in mind. Because it's family that profits from his death. And he didn't have any closer family than Honor Huxley."

"You're part of his family," Vivian said, her voice sharp.

Hattie looked up from the stack of papers at last, leaning comfortably back against the seat of the car as she did. "I am. And?"

"If someone in that room wanted him dead, why not you?" Vivian asked. It was a stupid thing to say, sitting in the car of one of the most dangerous people she knew, being driven by a man twice her size who liked to use his fists. But she didn't take back her words. "You're far more likely to bump off a family member than Ms. Huxley."

To her relief, Hattie looked amused more than offended. "Are you so sure about that?" she asked. "You should ask your Ms. Huxley about her late father. The answers might be . . ." Again that small laugh. "Illuminating. But in any case, no, I am not likely to have done in poor, dear Uncle Huxley."

"And why is that?"

"In the first place, because I liked him."

"That wouldn't stop you."

Hattie pursed her lips at the contradiction. "Not if I felt it was necessary, no," she admitted. "But it would give me pause. In the second place, I'm not inclined to, as you put it, bump people off left and right. It lacks finesse."

"And you do love finesse," Vivian said, her fear lending an edge of sarcasm to her voice.

"I do," Hattie agreed pleasantly. "Which brings us to the real reason you know I was not responsible for Huxley Buchanan's death." She leaned forward. "I'm sure you can tell me what it is, Miss Kelly."

Vivian met Hattie's gaze for as long as she could, which was not as long as she would have liked. She let out a breath and looked away. "Because it was sloppy."

"It was very sloppy," Hattie said, her voice soft and dangerous. "Which is something I never am. If it had been I who had my uncle killed, the police wouldn't have even known it was a murder. There'd be no questions, no suspicions. Just him dead and me getting whatever I wanted." She leaned back again, her red lips a smiling pout below the shadow of her veil. "Do you believe me?"

Vivian swallowed. "I do," she whispered as the car slowed to a halt. "Are you saying you think Honor Huxley is sloppy?"

Hattie shrugged. "Not as a general rule, no. But people tend to have a lot of feelings about their parents. And feelings make things messy." She smiled. "That's why I do my best to avoid them."

They stared at each other, listening to the sounds of Eddie stepping out, then coming around to open Vivian's door. He held it for her, and Vivian slid across the seat to leave. But at the last moment she paused. "But I think one day, Mrs. Wilson, you will be sloppy. You'll make a mistake, because as much as you want people to believe otherwise, you're human just like the rest of us." Her heart was thumping a warning that speaking to Hattie Wilson so bluntly was one of the stupider things she could be doing, but she still smiled as she spoke. "I wonder if I'll be there to see it?"

Hattie's jaw tightened, and for a moment Vivian thought she was struggling to control her temper. But she only nodded. "Perhaps you will," she said softly. "What an interesting day that would be." Looking bored, she turned back to her stack of papers. "It was a pleasure, as always, Miss Kelly. You'll be hearing from me, don't worry." She smiled, though she didn't look up. "I always collect on my favors."

Eddie slammed the door behind Vivian as soon as she was standing on the pavement, and the sound made her jump in spite of her attempt to seem poised and unworried. He gave her a single up-and-down look, smirking, then sauntered back to the driver's seat without a backward glance.

As she watched the car pull away, it suddenly struck Vivian that neither of them had asked her where she lived. And yet there she was, standing on the curb in front of her building.

She shivered. And then, because there was nothing else to do, she walked toward her door, resisting the urge to glance over her shoulder.

SIXTEEN

"Vivian!"

The sound of someone calling her name made her spin around.

Leo stopped a few steps away, his hands raised defensively. "Whoa there, sweetheart. You look ready for a fight."

"Where did you come from?" Vivian demanded, her heart still racing.

"I've been waiting for you to get home. I've got some news to share." He glanced back at the street. "Want to tell me the deal with the fancy car dropping you off? I thought you were doing deliveries today."

"I . . ." Vivian bit her lip, trying to decide what to tell him. Leo didn't entirely trust Honor as it was. What would he say if he learned she was Huxley Buchanan's daughter?

Or did he already know? Leo had some unexpected connections with folks in high places—along with low ones—courtesy of the commissioner. What if Hattie wasn't the only one who knew Honor Huxley had been keeping more secrets than usual?

"Viv?" Leo asked. "What is it? What's wrong?"

Vivian shook her head. "Sorry. Yes, it's fine. I'm fine," she said, thinking about Eddie driving straight to her front door without a word from her. "Let's go inside. I'm feeling jittery just standing out here."

"Tell you what," Leo said. He was watching her like he was worried she might bolt at any second. "How about I take you out to dinner? You've gotta eat at some point," he insisted when she was about to object. Vivian scowled at him, but she couldn't really argue with that. "And you can tell me what's got you looking so spooked."

"All right," Vivian agreed, trying not to sound too reluctant as he slid his arm around her waist. He was being sweet, there was no call to be acting surly in response, no matter how much she had to think over. "There's two things. One of them is Hattie Wilson."

She felt Leo's arm tense. He'd had his own encounters with Mrs. Wilson's bruisers. "What's she got to do with things?"

"I don't know, and that's part of the problem. The other thing . . ." She hesitated. "The other is Honor."

Leo's steps slowed long enough for him to turn and study her face. "Let's find somewhere to eat," he suggested. "And then you can tell me everything."

— · —

The Automat wasn't crowded, but Vivian still kept her voice down as she told him about her run-in with Hattie Wilson. He hadn't looked happy through that, his hands clenching and unclenching, as if he wanted to be swinging at someone instead of sitting there facing a problem he couldn't fix. But when she got to what Mrs. Wilson had said about Honor, he fell still, his expression growing stony.

Leo and Honor had crossed paths enough to develop a grudging respect, and they'd had to work together a couple of times in the past.

But Leo had never really trusted her. Maybe he had been right not to. Vivian didn't want to believe it, but suddenly, she wasn't so sure.

"Did you know?" she asked. "That Honor was his . . . had the commissioner said anything?"

"I had no idea." Leo shook his head. "Do you think Mrs. Wilson's right about her?"

"No," Vivian said too quickly. "I mean . . . I'm just all shaken up, you know? Those bruisers scare the hell out of me. And she's even worse. On top of everything else—I don't have that much time. And everything just keeps getting more confusing, not less . . ."

Leo's expression softened. "But you're okay," he said, leaning forward to take her hands. "And that's what matters, right? We'll figure the rest of it out."

"Yeah, I'm swell," Vivian said, smiling weakly. She wanted to believe him—they *would* figure the rest of it out, right? She couldn't bring herself to think about the alternative.

Vivian pulled her hands out of his, cupping them instead around the mug of coffee to try to warm them. But it was already cooling off, so she gulped it down quickly. It made her nearly empty stomach churn, but she had a long night ahead of her, and she needed whatever energy she could get. "Have you heard anything back from your pal at Bellevue?"

Leo had frowned when she pulled her hands away, but he didn't reach for them again. At her question, he perked up. "Hell, I can't believe I forgot to say. That's why I was waiting for you to get home. Norris gave me a call today." He glanced at his wristwatch, then gave her an encouraging smile. "What d'you say we hustle over there to hear what he has to say? You've got enough time, right?"

Vivian reached out to turn his wrist toward her and check the time for herself, feeling better at the thought of taking some kind of action. "Yeah. Yes, we should do that. I'll just need to change clothes after. I can't show up at the Nightingale like this."

"You'd look smashing even if you did," he said, looking relieved when she agreed. "I'm sorry I can't stay for your whole shift, though—I've actually got a job of my own to take care of."

Vivian couldn't help the sharp look she gave him. "For your uncle?"

"Nope," he said, holding one hand palm up. "It's strictly illegal, I promise."

That made her snort with laughter, in spite of how she was feeling. "That's what every girl wants to hear from her fella."

"I know what you like," he said with a wink. Vivian shook her head and went back to her coffee. "But I'll be able to meet up with you after and bring you home." He hesitated, then added firmly, "And then I'm staying the night."

Vivian's head shot up, her mug hitting the table with a thump. "Oh you are?"

"Don't look at me like that, Viv," he said quietly. "I'm not trying to get frisky, I'm trying to keep you safe. I'll sleep on the floor, if you like, but you shouldn't be alone. Not with Mrs. Wilson and her boys getting involved."

Vivian felt like a heel. Of course he just wanted to make sure she was safe. She wished he'd asked, instead of telling her what he was going to do. But he wasn't wrong about Mrs. Wilson and her bruisers. And now that she knew they had already tracked down where she lived . . . Vivian shivered.

"All right," she said, looking away. "But Bellevue first, yeah?"

"Absolutely," Leo agreed, standing and holding out his hand. "Let's shake a leg."

Vivian took it, giving him a sideways glance as they left the restaurant. "So you're saying you're *not* interested in getting frisky?" she said, trying to force a playful note into her voice.

Leo laughed. "I don't think that's what I said, was it?" he asked, pretending to frown like he couldn't remember.

"Just don't get your hopes up, pal," Vivian said, rolling her eyes at him, hoping he wouldn't notice that her heart wasn't quite in it.

As they paused at the edge of the sidewalk, waiting for traffic to clear so they could dash across to the streetcar stop, Leo glanced down, catching her eye. There was so much heat and tenderness in his that Vivian wanted to look away. "Any fella who knows you, Viv, has got nothing but hopes," he whispered. "But they'll keep until we're out of this mess."

Vivian gripped his fingers tightly, trying to anchor herself in the moment. They were heading to Bellevue. They were going to figure this out. "Five days now," she said with forced lightness, as though it was a hope and not a countdown. "Come on."

Pulling him after her, she dashed across the road, ignoring the drivers honking at them. They made it just before the streetcar pulled away.

<hr />

Well, so. You're back." The man across the desk from Vivian shook his head. "I thought the next time I saw you would be because I had good news about your mother."

"My . . ." Vivian let out a short laugh.

Last summer, she and Florence had discovered their mother was not, as they had always believed, buried with the other poor and unclaimed dead on Hart Island. She had asked, through Leo, whether the coroner's office had records that might help her uncover who had claimed her mother's body. The medical examiner had agreed to have his assistant look into it, when the young man wasn't busy with other work.

"To be honest, Doc, that's not much on my mind right now," Vivian said, trying to smile but not really succeeding. "Though I don't suppose your assistant has found anything?"

"Not yet." Dr. Norris cleared his throat. "I looked at the police report Mr. Green mentioned."

Vivian glanced over her shoulder to where Leo leaned against the door, arms crossed over his chest. He looked vaguely menacing standing there, though Vivian didn't think it was on purpose. He and the medical examiner had been trading favors back and forth ever since Leo came back to New York—though this time, Vivian knew the favor would be all on her shoulders, since Leo was fresh out.

And anyway, there was only one extra chair in the office, and she was sitting in it.

She turned back as the medical examiner added, "You live a dangerous life, young lady."

He had a habit, which Vivian appreciated, of not using names during their discussions. Not the names of the people they were talking about, and not her name either, even though he knew it ever since she asked for his help tracking down where her mother had been buried.

"Seems that way," she agreed. "I didn't do it."

He laced his fingers together, elbows resting on the desk and his chin tucked down as he eyed her. "I'm still not letting you anywhere near that report."

"I wasn't gonna ask you to," Vivian said sharply.

Leo shifted behind her, and Norris's eyebrows climbed toward his thinning hairline. The medical examiner made her nervous, with his office full of medical tools and dead bodies just down the hall. But he was upstanding as they came. She'd heard from Leo that he never touched a drop of alcohol, even before Prohibition. And judging by the political enemies he'd made during his investigations, he seemed to care about getting at the truth in his work.

Vivian took a deep breath. He was giving her the benefit of the doubt, just letting her be there without telling the police she was poking around. There was no reason not to be polite.

"I know you have to keep me out of it. But you know me and Leo, mister. Doctor, I mean." She grimaced at the slipup, but the medical examiner didn't look cross, so she barreled on. "And you know . . .

you know what can happen to a girl who's in the wrong place at the wrong time in a case like this." He nodded grimly, and Vivian felt something hopeful unfurling in her chest. "The commissioner let me go, at least for now. I just want to make sure I don't get snatched up again. If there's anything you can tell me, anything that might have been odd or . . ." She trailed off. "Well, honestly, I don't know what it would be. I don't know enough about folks getting killed to know what to ask about. But you do, Doc. You'd know if something was strange. Wouldn't you? That's all I'm asking about. Please. I'll owe you big."

She finished in a rush, cutting herself off before she could get too carried away. She glanced over her shoulder at Leo again and was relieved to see him nodding.

The medical examiner sighed, leaning back in his chair, his hands clasped across his stomach. "Well, here's the thing, young lady. I do believe that you had nothing to do with this man's death."

Vivian sucked in a sharp breath. "There was something strange about it."

It hadn't been a question, but Dr. Norris still nodded. Vivian could feel her heart speeding up, an ache of relief in the center of her chest. Strange was good. Strange could prove that the whole thing had nothing to do with her.

"He was stabbed in the neck with what seems to be one of the kitchen knives," the medical examiner said, grimacing with distaste. Vivian liked him better for it. He probably saw far worse than a stabbing in the course of his work; it said good things about his humanity that it still bothered him. "That itself isn't particularly strange. Lots of people come and go in that kitchen every day. I think you even did, according to the report, hmm?" Vivian nodded reluctantly. "And a knife is an easy thing to grab and carry with you without anyone noticing."

"But whoever it was would have had to plan on it," Leo pointed out. "No one's going to decide to murder a fella on the spur of the moment, run down to the kitchen, snatch up a knife, run back up, and stab him."

"Well, there you go," Vivian said, her voice rising in something that was half excitement, half outrage as she slapped her hands down on the desk. "Those damn cops were trying to make it out like I got so upset by him coming on to me—like any girl is going to be surprised by that sort of thing—and hauled off and stabbed him to death. That proves I couldn't have, right?" she said hopefully, looking between Leo and the doctor.

Her face fell when neither of them mirrored her eagerness. "If they need to, they're just going to say it was something else," Leo said quietly. "An affair gone wrong, or one of his enemies paying you to get close."

"He had them, of course," Dr. Norris said, nodding in agreement. "Men in his position always do." Seeing Vivian's face fall, though, he cleared his throat. "That wasn't all. The knife didn't narrow things down much, but I noticed a few . . . oddities about the body. So I performed some tests."

Vivian swallowed, trying not to look too nervous. She'd heard about the sort of tests he and his team did, grinding up organs like sausage meat and worse. It helped catch killers, sure, but it was gruesome to think about. "And you found something?" she said, more warily this time. She couldn't get her hopes up. She needed to think of the worst if she wanted to be prepared.

"I did." The medical examiner leaned forward. "Our victim had also been poisoned."

For a moment, the room was so silent that Vivian could hear the squeak of someone's shoes hurrying down the hall. "But then . . . what the hell does that mean? You're saying someone poisoned him, and then stabbed him for good measure? Just to, what, make sure he was really dead?" She shuddered at the thought.

"No." Dr. Norris shook his head. "The poison didn't kill him. It would have; those metals build up in the body over time. But if they're administered slowly, it doesn't look like a poisoning. It looks like someone getting gradually sicker, and then, after a long illness, dying."

"So . . ." Vivian glanced at Leo. "Someone was trying to kill him slowly. But they got impatient and killed him fast instead."

"Right now, that's how it looks." The medical examiner steepled his fingers under his chin, watching her.

"But that means it had to be someone close to him," Vivian said, sitting up straighter. "Someone who could get poison into, what, his dinner? His breakfast? Someone who could do it easily. Meaning *not* me." When the doctor opened his mouth to say something, Vivian held up her hand. "I know, I know. They could tie it to me still. Say I was hired, or something like that. If he liked pretty girls, it's easy to say I knew I'd be able to get close to him. But it's *something*."

"It is something," Dr. Norris agreed, standing up. "Do with it what you will."

Vivian, taking the hint, stood too. "Can I ask one more thing?"

The doctor raised his brows. "You can always ask."

"It's about . . . about my mother again." Vivian took a deep breath. She didn't want to think about what might happen to her. But she couldn't afford not to. "Would you send anything you find to my sister? I can give you her address. Just in case I . . ."

His expression had softened as she spoke. "I see. Yes, of course." He gestured to the pad of paper on his desk. "Would you like to write it down for me?"

Vivian quickly scribbled down Florence's name and the address of the restaurant on Spring Street, telling herself it wouldn't actually matter. When she straightened, she held out her hand. "Thanks for your help. With everything."

Dr. Norris smiled grimly. "Can't say it was a pleasure, young lady, but it certainly was interesting. And it will be even more interesting to see what you do with it," he said, shaking her hand. "And then next time you're in a position to do me a favor, you can be sure I'll be in touch."

Vivian swallowed, her stomach fluttering. She couldn't imagine what sort of favor she could do for someone like him. But that was how this worked—and he was a decent man, as far as she could tell. So she gave her hair a flip and him a smile that was only half bravado. "Anytime, Doc. You just let me know."

SEVENTEEN

The band was in a mellow mood that night. Mr. Smith, the bandleader, kept Bea crooning one love song after another, her rich voice filling every corner. More than once, Vivian worried whether her friend would be able to keep up after spending all day on her feet on Fifth Avenue. But Bea's voice never faltered. And the dancers were happy to keep their cheeks pressed close and hands clasped while their toes traced sweeping arcs across the floor.

Vivian longed to join them. As much as she loved the speed and wildness of a Charleston, there was nothing like the tingling electricity of finding a skillful partner for a tango. But she was waiting for one person in particular.

"Danny, where the hell is Honor?" she demanded, stretching out her aching shoulders as she deposited her tray on the bar. "Are you in charge tonight or something?"

"Aren't I always, kitten?" he asked, pushing aside the hair that fell across his eyes and grinning at her. He had abandoned his coat, and the sleeves of his shirt were rolled up over his forearms to keep them from getting splashed with each generous pour. Danny never stinted on the good booze; it was one reason the Nightingale had so many regulars.

The nickname made Vivian smile, since he so rarely used it with her anymore. Once he had flirted happily with nearly every woman at the bar. But he had left most of that behind when he and Florence married, even if he was still generous with what he knew all too well was a killer smile. Vivian approved—she'd have been angry if he gave her sister a kiss each night and left to make eyes at every pretty girl who crossed his path. But he had first called her kitten the night Bea brought her to the Nightingale, nervous and determined to pretend that she wasn't. It was still nice, from time to time, to remember that he had been her friend first.

But that didn't stop her from leaning closer and fixing him with a serious stare. "You know what I mean. I need to talk to her."

"About . . . ?"

Vivian raised her brows, and Danny grimaced. "It'll have to wait; she's chatting up one of our suppliers downstairs." He lowered his voice. "The guy who runs our whiskey got arrested last night. Stupid of him. Never skimp on your bribes."

"That's a problem, yeah?" Vivian asked.

Danny waved one hand as though waving away her concern. "He'll be out after the weekend. We just need to make sure we're not short until then. So you'll have to wait until—"

A sudden crash and a loud curse made them and everyone else crowding around jump, all of them turning to see what had happened.

"It's fine," the second bartender declared through gritted teeth, clutching a rag against one hand. Around him lay the shattered remains of the glasses he had tried too late to catch.

"Well, don't just stand there," Danny said, tossing a towel over his shoulder and striding down the bar. "No, I don't mean pick up the glass," he added impatiently. "Go get yourself cleaned up and make sure you don't need a doctor. If you do, Benny or Saul will take you. Go on." He gave the bartender a nudge toward the bar flap. "We're fine here, and we sure as hell don't need you bleeding all over the place. Nothing to see, folks," he added in a louder voice, smiling at the customers who were crowding around. "Give me half a sec to get things cleaned up and we'll make everyone's drink a double."

Vivian wasn't listening to him; her eyes were fixed on the rag wrapped around the bartender's hand as he scooted out of the room. It was slowly turning red from the cut on his hand, and the sight of it was too much like the memory of Huxley Buchanan lying on the floor. It took her a moment to snap herself back to the present and realize Danny was saying her name.

"Viv!" he said again as he finished dumping the dustpan full of shattered glass in the trash can and wiping down the bar. "Get back here."

"Me?"

"Yes, you." He lifted the bar flap and gestured at her impatiently. "I need an extra set of hands. Grab that bottle of gin and two coupes. French Seventy-Fives for that good-looking couple on your left." He winked at the customers as he said it, and they preened at the compliment even as he was turning toward the next man in line. "Now, sir, what's your poison?"

Vivian grabbed the bottle of champagne that was chilling under the bar and set it next to the glasses, then picked up the gin again. "How much—"

Danny didn't wait for her to finish. "Just count to three while you pour and top it off with as much champagne as will fit," he called. "It's an art, not a science."

"Make it five instead of three," one of the waiting men suggested, and the other people crowding around the bar laughed.

Vivian laughed along with them, even though her hands were

shaking with nerves and memory both. But she focused on the task in front of her, glad for the distraction and more than a little pleased to discover how much she had picked up from the other side of the bar as Danny called out instructions for the next round of drinks.

That was where Honor found her.

Vivian didn't see her at first; she didn't look up until a soft voice drawled, "I didn't know I hired a new bartender."

Vivian nearly dropped the bottle of rum she was holding; she caught herself just in time, sliding it across the bar to Danny. He stopped it with a flourish while Honor leaned against the bar with one elbow, watching them.

The other bartender had come with Honor, and he bumped Vivian's shoulder as he took his place behind the bar once more. "Thanks for the help, Viv," he said as he snagged a bottle of gin, the bandage wrapped around his hand not seeming to slow him down at all.

"You bet," Vivian said. But she kept her eyes fixed on Honor as she ducked out from behind the counter without bothering to lift the bar flap. "You got a minute?"

Honor studied her; from the wary look in her eyes, it was clear that she realized it wasn't a casual question. "You on a break, pet?"

The question felt like a slap, and Vivian sucked in an angry breath. Honor always had time for her employees, even on the busiest nights. It was one of the reasons they were so loyal to her. "No," Vivian said, trying to keep her voice calm. "But I need to talk to you."

Honor hesitated, then shook her head. "It's a busy night," she said, turning away.

Vivian caught her arm, pulling her a few steps away from the dance floor, closer to an out-of-the-way corner. She didn't want to make a scene—that would be bad for everyone—but she wasn't going to take no for an answer. "Seems I should have given my condolences last time we talked," she said, her voice low and sharp. "Funny you didn't mention it at the time. Any particular reason?"

Honor had gone completely still, her face at its most impassive and unreadable. "It wasn't your business," she said softly, easing her arm out of Vivian's grip. But there was an edge to her voice, like one instrument off-key in an otherwise perfect performance.

She was hiding something. And she was trying to warn Vivian away from asking more.

Vivian ignored the warning. "Like hell it wasn't. You gonna tell me what's going on?"

"Nothing is—"

"Or am I going to make a scene right here?"

"That would be unwise." The warning in Honor's voice was even sharper.

"Your call then," Vivian said. She didn't look away, and at last, Honor nodded, a barely perceptible jerk of her chin. She turned on her heel and walked toward the back hall.

Vivian glanced at Danny, who wasn't the only person at the bar watching the quiet confrontation. "Back in a jiff, pal," Vivian called, flashing him a smile that was all for show. He gave her a jaunty smile and a salute in return, and the small performance was enough to send the few curious onlookers back to their drinks and their dancing partners. But Vivian could see the worry in Danny's eyes as she hurried after her boss.

Honor was already vanishing from sight up the stairs. Vivian wasn't sure anymore whether she was supposed to follow. But she did anyway, her heart pounding with every step. The door to Honor's office was on the landing halfway up; a second door, which was usually locked, led to the apartment rooms upstairs where Honor often stayed. To Vivian's relief, the office door stood open for her.

She still paused at the threshold, a knot of anxiety clenching in her stomach. She didn't know what she was about to learn, but things were already strained with Honor. Was it worth making them even worse?

She didn't have much of a choice. Not if she wanted to find out what was going on. Not if she wanted to save her own skin.

Vivian closed the door behind her, watching as Honor, who was behind the desk and staring toward the room's one window, stiffened at the quiet sound. She wasn't admiring the view—the window faced the brick wall of the building next door, barely visible in the darkness. But she didn't turn around.

"You sure you want to do this?" Honor asked. There was an emotion in that honey-and-smoke voice that made Vivian pause. It was the sound of pain. But that could mean a hell of a lot of things, and Vivian wasn't the sort of girl to take anything for granted.

"I deserve answers, and you know it," Vivian said firmly. "Why didn't you tell me he was your dad?"

"We . . . weren't close," Honor said at last, each word sounding like it was carefully considered and turned over before being offered out loud. "How'd you find out?"

"Do I owe you anything here?" Vivian crossed her arms, glaring at Honor's back.

"No." Honor sighed as she turned around at last. She leaned back against the windowsill, her weight resting on her hands as she gave Vivian a regretful look. "You weren't supposed to find out." She shook her head. "Should have remembered you have a knack for digging up secrets."

"I was at the house yesterday," Vivian said quietly, almost resentfully. It was still hard for her to say no to Honor, even when she desperately wanted to. She didn't want to make trouble for Bea, so she settled on the other explanation that Honor would believe. "Hattie Wilson set me up to listen in. Seemed like an interesting group."

Honor had sucked in a sharp breath at Mrs. Wilson's name, coming forward half a step, her casual posture gone. "Vivian, she's not the sort of woman you want to be owing."

"I know that," Vivian snapped. "But right now, she's not the one who's lying to me."

"I didn't lie, pet. Not this time."

"It was a lie of omission, and you know it." Vivian clenched her hands into fists to steady herself. Lifting her chin, she met Honor's eyes. Once, she had thought she could drown in those eyes. But Honor had made it clear she'd never choose Vivian over anything else in her life. "You should have told me."

Honor didn't answer, either to agree or argue. Instead, she sighed again and bent down to open a drawer in her desk. Two heavy-bottomed glasses landed in front of her, followed by the bottle of whisky that she always kept on hand. It was good stuff, too, direct from Canada, no chance of it being watered-down homebrew or dyed moonshine. That wasn't how Honor did business.

Vivian accepted the glass Honor poured for her, glad to have something to do with her hands. But she didn't say anything, letting the silence stretch while Honor poured her own glass and turned it in slow circles on the polished wood of the desk.

Vivian took a fortifying gulp of her drink. "Tell me about your father." Then, a sudden thought occurring to her, she changed her question. "No, tell me about your sister first. Was he her father too?"

She could see the stillness that sank over Honor, shoulders tense beneath her crisp white shirt. "My sister?"

"You told me once that you had a sister," Vivian said. She half wanted to take back the question; instead, she barreled on recklessly. "She mattered to you. And I've got a feeling she matters now."

"She's dead now," Honor countered, her voice empty of emotion.

That bleakness tugged at Vivian's heart. What would it be like to say those words about Florence? She wanted to reach out, to lay her head against Honor's shoulder.

She steeled herself against the impulse. "So you mentioned," she said. "I was sorry to hear it then, and I'm sorry to hear it now. But you owe me more than that."

Honor took a drink from her own glass, her gaze going past Vivian. "Yes, Huxley Buchanan was her father too. And I'm sure you can guess he wasn't there while we were growing up. Or after. He wasn't interested in babies, so he didn't hang around once we were on the way. My sister and I were raised by our mother. He did send us money sometimes. But it was never enough."

"And your occasionally criminal childhood?"

The question surprised a short laugh out of Honor. "My what?"

"When you helped me break into the dressmaking shop last summer. You said you'd had an occasionally criminal childhood."

"I did." Honor stared into her glass as if she were seeing something else entirely. "Ma could never quite get by on her own, so she always had a fella around. They usually came and went like clockwork, but one of them stayed for a bit, and he took a shine to me. Got me to help on a job or two. Lookout, mostly. But he'd send me into a spot if they needed someone small. He was the one who taught me to pick locks."

"You ever get arrested?"

"Twice," Honor said, smiling wryly. "Second time, I was eighteen, and Ma couldn't afford to get me out. So I had them call my father."

Vivian sucked in a breath. "What did he do?"

"He bailed me out," Honor said quietly. "Or, his lawyer did. He wouldn't be seen coming down to a station in that part of town. But I think he'd softened toward us a bit by then." She hesitated, then added, "He'd had more kids with his first wife. Two boys. Made him rethink a few things, though it didn't change much."

They were both quiet for a moment. "And your sister?" Vivian asked, still certain that there was some connection there. "Did she have childhood criminal tendencies, too?"

"No." Honor shook her head firmly. "Not her. I wouldn't have allowed it."

"What was her name?" Vivian asked, unable to help her curiosity.

"My sister?" Honor asked, looking surprised by the question. When Vivian nodded, her face softened. "Stella. Her name was Stella."

"Was she younger than you?"

"Barely. We were twins."

"Twins?" Vivian stared at her. It was impossible to picture two women like Honor in the world. But maybe they'd been nothing alike. "You ever going to stop being full of surprises?"

Honor laughed, a short, humorless sound. "I would have liked to, for your sake," she said quietly. "Don't know if that's possible now."

Vivian felt her face growing hot and looked away, taking another sip to buy herself a moment. "So. Honor and Stella Huxley. As a reminder to him, I'm guessing? Or was your mother just trying to embarrass him?"

Honor shook her head, her expression wry and resigned. "Not just the Huxley part of it. My entire name was meant to make him feel guilty. Honor, right? As in, where is yours?"

"Oh." Vivian couldn't help her choked laugh. "That's . . . melodramatic."

"And then some."

For a moment they were smiling at each other, both forgetting or ignoring what had brought them there. But it didn't last. Honor looked away first, her expression growing shuttered once more. "Stella died in '19."

"Influenza?" Vivian said. She wasn't surprised when Honor nodded. Honor and her mother hadn't been the only ones to lose someone that awful year. Vivian shivered, remembering how the disease had torn through the close quarters of the orphan home, claiming young kids and aging nuns alike. "Did Buchanan try to help her then, at least?"

Honor shook her head. "He was traveling. I think he would have—he never came to see us, but I think for that, he would have. But Stella was gone before he could get back."

Vivian took a sharp breath. Was it as simple as that—a loved sister dead, the father who could have helped her gone? "What about your mother?"

"Ma got sick when Stella did," Honor said quietly, not looking away from Vivian's eyes. "She never recovered."

The pain that flashed across Honor's face was so stark it made Vivian catch her breath. "Did you think it was his fault?"

The stillness settled over Honor again, a moment of wariness that came and went so fast that Vivian wondered if she had imagined it. Her jaw tightened. "It was his fault. We were living in a miserable, crowded little place, and half our neighbors had it. It was no surprise that they caught it." She was looking past Vivian as she spoke, as though she were seeing something beyond the world she had built for herself, the office where she was always in control. "If he'd cared enough to raise us, we'd never have ended up stuck somewhere like that. Or we'd have at least had the money for a doctor." Her eyes focused on Vivian at last. "So yes, pet. It was his fault, and he knew it."

Vivian's hands shook. "So, you blamed him for your sister's death and—"

"No."

"No?" Vivian didn't bother hiding her skepticism. "You just said—"

"No," Honor repeated, closing her eyes on a sigh. "There's a difference between knowing it was his fault and blaming him for it. I was angry at him right after, sure. I'll probably never stop being angry at him. But I couldn't blame him. He had a good reason not to be there."

"A good reason not to come when his daughter was dying?" Vivian asked, her own anger tight in her chest. "Even if he didn't care much for you two, that's still—"

"He was overseas when it happened," Honor said quietly, opening her eyes. "Trying to find where his sons were buried in France."

Vivian's anger uncoiled like a load of bricks suddenly dropping into her stomach. Everyone knew someone who had died in the Great War, rich and poor alike. Everyone remembered the ache of that grief. "Both of them?"

The play of emotions across Honor's face, so different from her usual coolness, was hypnotic. Vivian couldn't tear her eyes away as Honor smiled sadly. "Both of them, poor bastard. Can you imagine being a father, knowing the boys you used to hold in your arms died scared and filthy in a trench, thousands of miles away from home?" She shook her head. "And then coming home to find your daughter—even if you weren't the one to raise her—had died too? For all his money, sometimes I think Buchanan's life was harder than mine. It had worse pain in it, at least." She sighed again, then shrugged. And with the gesture, it was as if she was tucking those emotions away, her expression calm and controlled once more. She turned to pour herself another finger of whisky. "So no, I didn't blame him. I still don't."

Vivian wanted so badly to believe her. But there had been that moment of stillness, of wariness, that she couldn't quite ignore. She thought Honor was being honest. But even when Honor told the truth, she didn't always tell all of it.

"Honor." She hesitated, fingers gripping her glass so tight it made them ache. "Did you want him dead?"

Honor looked up to meet her eyes. "What did Hattie Wilson say to you, after she made sure you knew I was in that room?"

The question caught Vivian off guard enough that she wasn't ready to hide her reaction. She could feel a hot blush rising to her cheeks even as she mentally scrambled for a reply. "Nothing," she said, too quickly. Then she lifted her chin. Maybe Honor wouldn't be honest, but she would. "She pointed out that you're the one getting the best deal out of his death. Sounds like he left a whole lot behind, and most of it coming to you."

"Vivian, pet." Honor shook her head. "You know someone like Hattie Wilson always has a game she's playing. You think she's, what? Helping you out of the goodness of her heart?"

It was as much as Vivian had said to Hattie herself, but coming from Honor, it made her angry. "Of course she had her own reasons.

That doesn't make her wrong. Or are you gonna tell me you didn't know he was leaving all that to you?"

Honor was silent so long Vivian didn't think she was going to answer. "I'd see him, from time to time, since Stella's death. He fronted me the money to open this place," she said, gesturing broadly and earning a surprised look from Vivian. A little proudly, Honor added, "It only took me a year to pay him back. He did tell me last year that he was leaving everything to me. But that was right after he married the new Mrs. Buchanan, and I knew he was planning on bringing her son into his business. So." Honor looked away to take a sip of her drink, then set it sharply down, as if she was eager to be done with the conversation. "I didn't think he was serious."

"You honestly expect me to believe that?" Vivian asked. Honor had sounded too composed, too sure of herself, in that meeting. She had known more than she was letting on.

"You honestly think I killed him?" Honor replied.

There was so much pain in the question that for a moment, Vivian felt like she couldn't breathe. She had to haul in a shuddering breath, and they could both hear the effort it took. "I don't want to," she said, her voice cracking. She cleared her throat. She didn't want to—but she hadn't missed the fact that Honor hadn't given her a clear *no*. "But God knows you've spent a long time giving me reasons not to trust you."

Honor took a step forward. Her lips trembled before she pulled them back into a tight line. "Haven't I given you reasons that you should, too?"

If she was acting, it was a damn good performance. But Vivian still took a step back toward the door. "You have," she whispered. "But I'm gambling with my life, this time. If you want me to trust you, then *help me*. Tell me what you know."

"I can't, pet." Honor's jaw clenched. "I don't know anything."

Vivian nodded slowly. "Then that's all there is to it." She tried to smile, giving her head a little toss to flip her hair back, wanting to look like she didn't care. "Guess it's time for me to get back to work, then."

"Vivian—"

But she was already out the door. No matter how much she wanted to believe Honor was telling her the truth, Vivian couldn't ignore Hattie Wilson's voice in the back of her mind.

You know who gained the most from his death. And you know she's ruthless enough to set up someone else to take the fall for her.

She was so caught up in her thoughts that she didn't see the person waiting for her at the bottom of the stairs until a hand shot out and grabbed her arm. Vivian stumbled, too surprised even to yell, as she was yanked backward.

"Get ready to run," Bea whispered, pulling Vivian into a corner and away from the door to the dance hall. "We're about to be raided."

EIGHTEEN

W hat?" Vivian demanded, her whisper as low as her friend's. "How do you know?"

The band was still playing, and Vivian could hear the laughter and stomping feet, the shouts from the bar. No one in there sounded like they expected a raid.

"There," Bea whispered, scooting closer to the doorway so she could peer in. Her dark eyes were wide and worried.

The risks of getting arrested were real, and if you didn't have money to pay off your bail and disappear from the system, they could be harsh. But the Nightingale had been raided before. The staff knew to bolt for the club's hidden exits and to take whoever they could with them. Honor, her bruisers, and whatever stacks of cash she had on hand would take care of the reasons behind the raid.

With her father's death, she'd have even more of that cash to draw on. Vivian shuddered, tucking that thought away to be examined later. She couldn't deal with it, not now.

She hesitated, then crept up behind Bea, who nodded her head toward the bar. "Plainclothes on the stool there," she murmured. "Three from the end."

The man was unremarkable, wearing a decent but unfussy suit, his hair slicked back and his hat on his lap. He had a glass of something in front of him, which he nursed without taking a drink, and from time to time he lifted his head to glance around, as though he was waiting for something or someone. "Danny spotted him. I'd just started my break, and he yanked me aside and sent me to get Honor." Bea took a deep breath. "He doesn't look like he's in a rush, but don't go back in there until—"

"Wait," Vivian said, putting a hand on her friend's elbow when Bea would have turned away. "I know him."

"You what?" Bea stared at her. "You palling around with cops now, Viv?"

"No, he . . ." Vivian swallowed. "He's the one who came with the commissioner." She racked her brain, trying to remember his name. "He knew Leo, too. I think there's a good chance he's not here for a raid."

"Viv, don't be an idiot, you don't—"

Vivian wasn't listening. She plunged back into the heat and noise of the dance hall, making a beeline for the police officer sitting uncomfortably on his stool. Behind her, she heard Bea growl something that didn't sound complimentary, then the quick tap of heeled shoes as her friend followed her.

Danny saw them coming toward him, and he shook his head sharply, his glare unmistakable. But Vivian ignored him as she slid onto the stool next to the man. His name came to her just as she sat down. "Levinsky."

He jumped, spinning around toward her, then relaxed when he saw who was there. "I'll be honest, I don't remember your name," he said. "Though maybe that's just as well. How are you enjoying your last week of freedom?"

It was said sympathetically, without any sarcasm or cruelty, but it still hit Vivian like a punch to the gut. Behind her, she heard Bea suck in a breath. On the other side of the bar, Danny looked like he was ready to leap over the counter and start swinging. He wasn't pouring drinks anymore, just watching to see what the cop would do, even though he kept his distance.

Vivian decided not to answer the question. "What are you drinking?"

Levinsky glanced down at his glass. "Honestly, I got no idea. I haven't even tried it yet, I just had to order something." He looked a little embarrassed. "I'm not much of . . . with the new baby, you know. I'm either working or at home."

Vivian gave him a smile, trying to pretend that her heart wasn't pounding. "Let me get you something good," she suggested, turning to Danny.

He was watching them; when Vivian caught his eye, he made the shape of a C with his hand against the counter, his eyebrows raised in question. Vivian nodded, but she crossed her fists low in front of her at the same time, pulling them apart in the club's sign for "safe." The exchange barely took half a second, and Vivian didn't think Levinsky had noticed. Then Danny was smiling too, friendly and unthreatening, as he gathered his ingredients with a flourish. A moment later, he was sliding a glass across the bar to Levinsky.

The cop gave it a wary glance. "What is it?"

"It's called a Corpse Reviver," Vivian said. "Just the thing to perk up a new dad." Over her shoulder, she heard Danny give a short laugh as he went back to work, though she knew that was mostly for show; he'd still be keeping an eye on Levinsky, even with Vivian letting him know that things were, at least for the moment, okay.

The cop took a tentative sip. "That's pretty good. Thanks."

"You're welcome." Vivian leaned one elbow against the bar. "Did the commissioner send you to check up on me?"

"Actually . . ." Levinsky glanced around, as if worried his boss might be lurking at the other end of the bar. "He doesn't know I'm here. I was hoping to run into your friend."

"Leo?" Vivian asked, trying not to look too surprised. They had seemed like they knew each other, but not well enough for Levinsky to seek him out on anything but orders. Unless they had a closer relationship than she realized . . . Over Levinsky's shoulder, Bea caught her eye, looking wary. "He's got a job tonight, so I'm not sure when he'll turn up. Need me to deliver a message?"

"No . . ." Levinsky hesitated, turning his glass in nervous circles on the bar. The band was playing a bright quickstep, loud enough that it would be difficult for anyone sitting even a couple seats away to overhear them. Still, he leaned toward her and lowered his voice. "Well, depends. I had news for him, about the Buchanan family. Which I guess means news for you, too."

Vivian took a slow breath. "And what's the cost of this news?"

Levinsky frowned, staring down into his glass. "I know how this game is supposed to work," he said quietly. "I've played it before when I have to. But it's not one I enjoy." He met her eyes. "I took this job for two reasons, you know. My family needed money. And I wanted to help people."

Vivian couldn't help the skeptical snort that escaped her, and she heard a similar scoff from Bea. Levinsky jumped, glanced back over his shoulder as if he'd just realized someone else was there. When he saw Bea, though, he relaxed.

"You got a nice set of pipes, kid," he said, giving her a quick smile.

"Thanks," she replied, taking the stool on his other side. "You got a naïve way of looking at the world."

"Maybe," he admitted. "But you think catching a murderer doesn't help people?"

"Depends on whether that's what you and your boys do," Bea pointed out. "How likely do you think it is?"

Levinsky grimaced, then took a sip of his drink to cover the expression. "That really is good," he said, sounding surprised.

"He's known for it," Vivian said, tilting her head toward Danny, who was still keeping an eye on them. Even if Levinsky wasn't there for a raid, he could still cause trouble.

"I've heard." Levinsky nodded, studying Danny, then turning his scrutiny on her. Vivian wanted to squirm, but she met his gaze steadily, waiting to see what he'd decide. The cop sighed. "Like I said, I've played it when I have to. But we're gonna say this is me paying back a favor I owe, okay? Let's say it's because Mr. Green helped my dad out when he was going to lose his shop a few years back. And you're Leo's girl, yeah?"

"Yeah, you could say that," Vivian said quietly.

Levinsky just shrugged. "I don't know him much myself; he ain't been around, but he doesn't seem like the easiest fella to trust. But his dad's good people. And you . . ." He looked her up and down, then shrugged again. "Well, just say those Buchanans don't seem like they're telling us everything they could."

"Like what?" Vivian asked. He seemed like a decent enough guy, but she had a hard time believing everything he said.

Levinsky hesitated again, taking another drink to buy time, then seemed to make up his mind all in a rush. "The wife, Mrs. Buchanan," he said, lowering his voice. "She's got nothing to say about where she was all day. Says that it's nonsense to ask her for an alibi, as if she'd kill her own husband. But if she was somewhere harmless, why not just say so?"

Her own husband hadn't known where she was, Vivian remembered. There were plenty of reasons a woman might be running late for an appointment, of course—especially an appointment with someone she didn't consider an equal, someone like a dressmaker. But Levinsky was right—why not just say so?

He wasn't done, though. "And that stepson, Rokesby? He seems like a sly piece of work and then some. Getting in on his stepdad's business like that, and after just a few years of him being married to his mom?" He leaned forward, looking eager to share what he knew at last. "Plus, he says he was with friends that day, but he's given us four or five different names and says he can't remember which of them were around. And all of them have told us different things about what they were up to, so it sounds like the lot of them are just making it up."

"And no one's following up on that?" Bea demanded.

Levinsky shrugged. "We're looking into it, sure. One of the maids in his house said he keeps an appointment book, so we asked to see it. And he got real angry." Levinsky rolled his eyes. "Said we had no business asking the staff about his personal papers—and what else are the police supposed to do? He claimed that he never kept any such thing as an appointment book in his life. And then my pal Connors said he overheard the housekeeper *sacking* that poor girl who had mentioned it. For indi—whatsit—indiscretion, which apparently means not doing a good enough job keeping your mouth shut—even when someone got himself bumped off." Levinsky took a long drink and shook his head. "Connors says that's just what some folks are like, think they can make us all dance around them like puppets. But it seems damn fishy to me. If they've got nothing to hide, they can say so. And now that poor girl's out of a job."

It took Vivian a moment to realize he had finished when the flood of words finally came to an end. "So what are you going to do about it?" she demanded, remembering Corny Rokesby cornering her in the alley—had it only been a couple nights ago? It felt like half a lifetime. It made all too much sense, now, why he had wanted to talk to Honor.

And it seemed damned suspicious that he had. To find out what she knew about the will? To try and scare her off of claiming whatever inheritance she had coming? And with him hiding things from the police . . .

Levinsky sighed and took another drink. "Just having suspicions isn't enough to pin anything on the Buchanans. We need proof, and we need time, and neither is looking likely right now. Not with reporters sniffing around, getting people riled up and clamoring for quick answers."

"I saw it in the papers," Bea said quietly. "They're making a real stink about it."

"It's the sort of thing that catches attention," Levinsky agreed.

"Haven't they found anything else?" Vivian asked. "Buchanan had a business meeting right before he died. What about his partners?"

Levinsky frowned. "That Whitcomb fella was at the office all day, half a dozen people saw him there. The other one . . ." He shook his head. "We're still looking into it."

Vivian wanted to ask him about the poison. But she didn't know how to bring it up without getting Dr. Norris in trouble. "What about anything . . . strange? About how he died? Do they think more than one person might've been involved?"

He gave her a dry look. "Right now they think you were involved. I don't know how much they'll look beyond that. So . . . good luck, I guess." He stood, tucking his hat under his arm. "I'm off. Baby's up at all hours still, and Maud'll be expecting me home soon to give her a break. Tell your fella I stopped by, will you? And . . ." He shrugged. "Whatever else you want to tell him. It's a hell of a mess you've got yourself in. Hope you can pull through."

"Thanks for your help," Vivian said quietly. "I know you didn't have to do that."

"Long as you don't go telling my boss, I should be okay." He gave her a tired smile, looking for a moment like a young, exhausted father who was just trying to do the right thing.

Vivian was starting to suspect that was exactly what he was. "Boy or girl?" she asked impulsively, putting a hand on his arm.

He gave her a surprised look. "Girl," he said, his eyes lighting up. "Rebecca Maud."

"Congrats," Vivian said, meaning it. "Hope she figures out her sleeping soon."

"Don't we all." But he was smiling as he headed for the stairs.

They watched him until he disappeared toward the front door, and then Bea let out a heavy sigh, dropping her chin into her cupped hands. "Lord almighty, Viv. You sure meet some interesting folks." Her dry tone said that *interesting* was the mildest word she could come up with. "How much you think you can trust him?"

"Enough," Vivian said. "I think. Leo seemed on . . . well, not friendly terms, but some kind of terms with him. And it was a decent thing for him to come here. God knows he didn't have to."

"It was decent if he was telling the truth," Bea said skeptically. "It was decent if he was here to help you and not because he was playing some other game for his boss. You don't know for sure."

"Gotta be some fellas on the police force that want to help people, right?" Vivian pointed out as Danny slid a tray onto the bar and started filling it up with drinks. "Stands to reason."

"Sure," Bea said, though she didn't sound convinced. She glanced over her shoulder and hopped to her feet. "Mr. Smith is sending his death glare my way. I've gotta scoot on up to the bandstand." She frowned. "You'll be all right?"

"Absolutely," Vivian said, giving her friend a sunny smile that didn't make Bea's frown go away. "See you after last call?"

"Count on it."

When Vivian turned back to the bar, Danny was watching her. "You making friends with cops now, Viv?" When she shrugged, he laughed. "It's not a bad idea, you know. Honor's on friendly terms with a lot of them. That one spooked me pretty bad, though, showing up on his own like that. I thought we were getting raided for sure."

"Not yet, anyway," Vivian said quietly, thinking of the commissioner casually revealing that he knew exactly where she worked.

Danny smiled comfortingly. "But if they like you, they look out for you."

"And in our line of work, we can use the looking out," Vivian said, taking the tray as he added the final drink, her mind darting back to Corny Rokesby. What was he trying to hide? "Where's this one going?"

"Pretty Jimmy and his pals in the corner," Danny said, nodding toward the cluster of well-dressed young men who were flashing smiles and cash in equal measure. "And then hop on back here. It's going to be a busy night."

He wasn't wrong, and Vivian was glad to spend the next few hours running her feet off. It didn't leave her much time for worrying about things like whether Levinsky was telling the truth or why Buchanan's family didn't want to talk to the police. She took her break right when they were playing a Charleston, and Pretty Jimmy Allen, whose friends were either making eyes at the girls on the dance floor or had disappeared into dark corners with them, snagged an arm around her waist and begged her for a dance. He had a smooth, easy lead, even if he wasn't the flashiest dancer, and Vivian was happy to lose herself in the music for as long as it lasted.

When the song ended, she and Jimmy were both breathless, and he grinned at her. "I'm glad your Ms. Huxley lets her girls take a spin on their breaks," he said, leaning over to brush a kiss against her cheek. "Dance floor wouldn't be the same without you, baby doll. I think someone else is hoping for a turn."

With a playful wink, he disappeared back into the crowd, looking for a new partner as the band started up a Baltimore beat. Vivian turned to see who he had been talking about and froze.

"George," she said, her voice flat and cold. "What do you want?"

Bruiser George grinned at her. It wasn't a pleasant smile. "Is that any way to greet an old friend, girlie?"

They weren't friends. Wiry and weaselly, with a mouth that was always twisted into a leer and hands that liked to hurt people, he didn't have any friends as far as Vivian could tell.

She didn't reply, just waited. His eyes narrowed, and he held out his hand. "Let's go for a spin, all nice and normal-like, and I'll tell you why the boss lady sent me."

"Not damned likely," Vivian said softly. She didn't want to attract any more attention by starting an argument in the middle of the dance floor. But she was even more certain that she didn't want to let him touch her. "I'll buy you a drink, and you're lucky to get that much here."

George scowled but followed her to the bar without argument.

Vivian led him to the side where Danny wasn't working. She wanted to find out what George was there to say and send him on his way, not risk someone starting a fight. When George ordered his drink and said with breezy confidence that she would be paying for it, she received a worried look from the bartender. He knew trouble when he saw it, even if he was too new to recognize it by name.

"I'm good for it," she said, giving him a nod. "And he won't be staying long." Up onstage, Bea was belting out "Everybody Loves My Baby," sweet and fast, with the trumpet playing counterpoint.

"What does Mrs. Wilson want?" Vivian asked quietly as George took a long, satisfied drink. Hattie Wilson was the only "boss lady" in Bruiser George's life. "It had better not be anything to do with this place or anyone in it."

George smirked. "No need to show your claws, little cat. I'm not here for anything too messy or nasty. Just a little favor is all. You'll be making a delivery tomorrow to a Mrs. Morris. Boss lady wants you to retrieve a letter of Mr. Morris's. It'll be somewhere in his bedroom— they keep separate ones, right next to each other with a sitting room in between—and not in his study or office. You'll know it because the stationery says *Swan's Point*."

Vivian didn't ask how he knew about another couple's bedrooms; it wasn't hard to picture Hattie gathering details about the lives and homes of the city's wealthy families. But at the rest of George's statement, Vivian felt the same sort of cold that she'd felt after Eddie drove straight to her front door. "And how does Mrs. Wilson know where I'll be making deliveries? Usually I don't even know that until I get to work."

George just laughed. "You think you're the only one who owes the boss a little favor?"

"That's not a little favor," Vivian said sharply. "I could get arrested for prowling around someone's house stealing their things. Not interested, thanks. Tell her to come up with something else."

She would have turned away, but Bruiser George caught her wrist. He was smaller than his buddy Eddie, but still bigger than Vivian. "Don't be stupid, girlie, or the boss'll get angry," he said, soft and menacing. "You owe her. Just do what you're told, nice and quiet and no one the wiser, and you won't need to worry about anything."

Vivian stared into George's eyes, hating every inch of him. "Fine," she said, deliberately even, and just as deliberately not pulling her hand away. She wouldn't let him see how scared he made her. "Swan's Point, you said?"

"There's a good girl," he said, smiling. "She'll be in touch once you've got—"

"Vivian."

The voice cut through their conversation, raised just enough above the music for them to hear it. Vivian whipped her head up to see Leo pushing his way across the dance floor, his eyes dark with fury and locked on where George's fingers still gripped her wrist.

George sighed, but he didn't stop smiling as he dropped her arm at last. "See you around, girlie." He nodded to her with exaggerated politeness and headed toward the back door.

Leo reached her only moments later. "Are you okay?" he demanded, catching her upper arms as he looked her over, head to toe. "Wasn't that one of Mrs. Wilson's boys?"

"I'm fine, and yes, but don't make a scene, okay? There's nothing too—"

She hissed as one of Leo's hands met her wrist. There were angry red marks where George had held her. Vivian grimaced, but it wasn't bad enough to leave bruises. She would have happily ignored it. But then a finger caught her under the chin, lifting her gaze until she was looking at Leo. He leaned forward and brushed a gentle kiss across her lips, one so at odds with the murderous look in his eyes that it made her feel cold all over.

"I'm going to kill him," Leo whispered, and turned to head for the back door.

"*No.*" Vivian lurched after him, catching his arm and leaning all her weight back to bring him to a stop.

"I'll send him back to his boss in goddamn *pieces*—"

"*Please,* Leo, just let him go, okay?"

Leo's head whipped around, the glare he gave her as fierce as the one he had directed at George's retreating back. It almost startled her into letting go of his arm—she'd seen Leo angry before, even seen him in a fight. But he'd rarely turned a look like that on her. "Like hell, Viv, you can't let a fella like him get away with—"

"No," she snapped, still barely above a whisper. "I know just as much about dealing with *a fella like him* as you do, thanks. And right now, what I know is that I've only got a few days to outrun a charge for murder, and his boss knows it. So what do you think she's going to do if I make her angry? If you send one of her boys back *in pieces*?"

"He hurt you," Leo said.

The anger in his expression hadn't disappeared, and his voice was hard as jagged glass. All around them, the dancers dipped and swayed their way across the floor while Bea crooned a love song from the bandstand. A group of men and women jostled past them to get to the bar, none of them giving Leo or Vivian a second glance. At the door, Bruiser George had stopped to look back through the crowd, and he smiled when he saw Vivian holding Leo back from following him.

Leo saw it, and his hands clenched into fists as though he were longing to throw a punch. "I'm not going to let him get away with that."

"Yes, you are," Vivian said. She didn't let go of his arm. "You're going to calm the hell down and stop trying to start a fight."

A muscle jumped in Leo's jaw. "I'm just trying to look out for you."

"You keep saying you want to help me, Leo, but you can't do that if you don't *listen,*" Vivian pleaded. She knew he meant well—Leo always meant well. But that wouldn't do her any good if he made an enemy of Hattie Wilson and her boys. Over Leo's shoulder, she nodded at Bruiser George, hoping he would get the message and leave. To her relief, he gave his hat a mocking tip and disappeared into the hall.

Vivian looked back at Leo. "I'm telling you right now what I need. Are you going to do it or not?"

At last, she felt him stop straining against her grip. "Whatever you say," Leo agreed through gritted teeth. Vivian could hear the anger still simmering below his words. She hoped none of it was directed at her. "What did he want?"

"I owe Mrs. Wilson a favor." She wanted to rub at her wrist but resisted. If Leo saw her do that, he would just get all riled up again. "And that you *can* help me out with, because I think it's going to be a two-person job."

That got his attention; Leo finally stopped glaring after George and turned to look at her. "What kind of job?"

Vivian glanced around, feeling exposed. Her break should have been long since finished, and someone might start looking around to see where she'd got to if she stayed tucked in the corner any longer. "I need to get back to work. But if you're still—" She swallowed, hating that she could feel her face heating, even though her embarrassment seemed stupid in the face of everything else. "If you're still planning to spend the night, I can tell you then, and we'll come up with a plan."

Leo sighed. "If I'm still welcome, then, yes. Count me in. But when all this is done," he added, "if I see Bruiser George again, I'm going to smash his face in."

Vivian let out a shaky laugh. "When all this is done, be my guest."

NINETEEN

Four Days Left

Vivian hesitated, then, before she could talk herself out of it, rang the bell on the house's lower door. The hulking gray stone of the mansion's front loomed over her, making her feel small and unimportant. But maybe that was a good thing, this time. Maybe everyone else there would think so too, and they wouldn't guess what she was planning.

Vivian hoped that if anyone saw her shaking, they would think it was just from the cold spring wind. Nervous, she rang the bell a second time.

"Jesus, Mary, and Joseph." The young maid who yanked the door open glared at her. "Ain't you got no patience? Took me all of five seconds to come trotting down the hall, and you're already clamorin' and complainin'—That must be the dress for Mrs. Morris, then, yes? It looks like a dress box."

The last question was said without pause for breath, and it took Vivian a moment to catch up. "Yes," she said at last, her voice coming out too loud. She cleared her throat. "Yes, that's right, dress delivery for Mrs. Morris."

"I'll take it." The maid held out her hands.

Vivian swallowed. "Is Mrs. Morris available? I'd like to check the shoulders and hips to make sure she's satisfied." It wasn't quite a lie— many customers wanted one last fitting before they accepted the delivery. But it hadn't been in Miss Ethel's instructions for this particular delivery. Vivian didn't know whether that was because Mrs. Morris didn't care for the practice or not.

Her question was met with a weary sigh. "Well then, don't just stand there, for goodness' sake. Might as well throw the coal out with the trash as keep the door open for every cold breeze to blow right through . . ." Still grumbling, the maid, who looked all of twenty but sounded like she had the soul of an eighty-year-old great-grandmother, led the way to the kitchen stairs. There was an old clock in the hall; Vivian glanced at it as they went past, noting the time.

And then she kept looking around as she was led up, the dress box still clutched in her hands and the black bag that held her seamstress's kit a heavy weight hanging from her arm. The house was not as large as some of the upper-class mansions where her deliveries had taken her, but what it lacked in size it made up for in gaudiness. Nearly everything that she could see was gilded, enameled, or hung with shivering crystal drops. Beneath her feet, the black-and-white marble tiles were nearly hidden under bright silk rugs, and if there wasn't a painting on a wall, there was a mirror instead.

The entire effect was horrible, and Vivian bit her lips to keep from smirking as they made their way up the stairs. She had been in houses so opulent that they felt like enormous jewel boxes, places where she longed to simply lie down on the carpets because they were so luxurious. But most of them had some taste to their furnishing. This house had none.

The Morrises, she suspected, were new money. She wondered if that had something to do with why Mrs. Wilson was targeting them and, if so, how.

Vivian realized she was falling behind the maid. Shaking her head, she hurried to catch up. It was none of her business why Hattie Wilson wanted something from these folks, and wasting time wondering about it would only get her in trouble, one way or another. All she needed to worry about was finding that letter and leaving without anyone the wiser.

And at least the house looked nothing like the Buchanans' home. Vivian had been shaking as she lugged the dress box uptown, unable to stop thinking about what had happened during the last delivery she had made. Even remembering the sight of Leo, sprawled out and sleeping deeply on the floor next to her bed after a late, anxious, excited night of planning, couldn't erase the memory of Huxley Buchanan, dead in his study, of the feel of his blood on her hands. Even now, the thought made her shudder.

"So it's true, he had a natural daughter tucked away somewhere?"

The voice drifted out of an open door ahead of them, followed by delighted laughter. The sound was jarring against the backdrop of her grim thoughts, but at least it shook the memories loose and helped her remember where she was.

"Not just one," a second voice said, making no more effort than the first to be quiet. "Apparently there used to be two of them, though the other one died or something. It was just the one he left the money to. Nearly *all* of it," the second voice added with relish. "Can you imagine Evangeline's fury?"

Vivian's steps slowed again before she remembered to act as though the gossip meant nothing to her. They were talking about Buchanan.

Of course they were. These people likely moved in the same circles, or similar ones. Why wouldn't they discuss the scandals of Huxley Buchanan's life and death?

Vivian glanced at the maid, but the girl's face was impassive. Either she didn't care about the gossip, or she was so used to it that she didn't bat an eye.

"And he always seemed so somber and buttoned up," the first voice said. "Who'd have thought he'd leave it all to his little bastard street-walker?"

"Well, be fair, Iris, we don't *know* she's a streetwalker," a second voice chortled.

"Oh, girls of that class always are," the first voice said, airy and dismissive. Vivian's hands clenched around the dress box so hard that the edges of it bit into her palms. "But how did he come to have two?"

"Apparently the mistress was a long-standing habit of his, years ago." The second voice lowered a bit, but by then Vivian and the maid were just outside the open door and could hear everything clearly. "A dancer, Mr. Morris says, and Huxley kept her in Brooklyn where—"

The maid knocked at the frame of the door, and the voices fell silent as their owners turned to stare at the interruption. Vivian held back a scowl—that was Honor's mother they were discussing, and she desperately wanted to hear more. But the two women currently looking down their noses at her didn't look like the sort whose information could be trusted, anyway. Not about someone like Honor.

"What is it, Mary?" one of the women asked. She was the second voice that had spoken, wearing a day dress that hadn't come from Miss Ethel's shop, not with those overdone layers of ruffles and bows. Vivian tried to keep her lip from curling in distaste.

"Begging your pardon, Mrs. Morris, but the dressmaker's girl is here. She says she would like to take a moment to check the fit of the gowns, if it suits you, ma'am."

Mrs. Morris scowled. "Well, Mary, as you can plainly see, I have a guest, and—"

"Oh, no need to fret about me, Dora," the other woman said as she stood. She was older than Mrs. Morris but dressed just as showily, with a cloud of expensive perfume floating around her. "It's high time

I head home to check on the little monsters anyway, or I might risk losing another nanny. But thank you for all the news!" she added, leaning down to drop a kiss in the air next to Mrs. Morris's cheek. "Lord, who knew a murder would be so entertaining?"

The two women giggled together while Vivian stood as still as possible, hoping none of her thoughts could be read on her face. She didn't even risk glancing at the maid, Mary, to see how she took such a statement. Her eyes darted to the clock over the mantelpiece.

"Mary, see Mrs. Hartford out," Mrs. Morris said, leaning back against her chair. The maid curtsied and obeyed silently, leaving Vivian alone behind. Mrs. Morris eyed her. "Why do the gowns need to be checked? Didn't you have my measurements when you made them?"

There was none of the bored, superior irritation that Vivian expected to hear in her voice. Instead, she sounded uncertain, like a woman at a party who didn't know how to behave. Maybe she'd never had dresses made for herself before. Or she'd had it done few enough times that she wasn't sure how it was supposed to go.

The thought lifted Vivian's confidence a notch. "Oh, yes, Mrs. Morris, no need to worry. I just need to double-check that the hem and hips and all fit properly. We want you to feel as beautiful as you deserve when you wear your new things."

Mrs. Morris blushed a little, looking pleased at the idea. But a moment later she frowned, her mouth twisting. "And how much extra will that cost me?"

Vivian had to bite the inside of her cheek. All this ugly wealth around her, and her already paying for custom-made gowns, and the woman was worried about the cost of having their fit checked? The muscles across her stomach quivered with held-back laughter. "There's no extra charge, ma'am."

"Oh!" Mrs. Morris went from suspicious to smug, as though she had somehow got the better of Vivian by getting a good bargain. Vivian pressed her lips together, stretching them into a wide smile to keep herself from saying anything else. "Well, in that case, absolutely. You may follow me upstairs."

Vivian's heart sped up as she remembered the real reason she was there. They didn't enter through the bedroom itself, but through a gaudy sitting room, its walls dressed in gold paper, chairs gathered before a marble fireplace, and a gleaming chandelier hung low over it all. Vivian tried not to be too obvious looking around. But there was a door immediately opposite and identical to the one where Mrs. Morris was leading her. That had to be Mr. Morris's bedroom, where the letter Hattie wanted was supposedly kept.

Vivian hoped he was the type to spend all day at his office.

Mrs. Morris led her into the connected bedroom and closed the door. "Well?" she asked, looking uncertain again.

Vivian smiled to put her at ease. "Do you have a—Oh, yes, I see the mirror there. Why don't you go stand in front of it? I'll just close the curtains to give you some privacy while you take off your dress. You may keep on whatever you have on underneath."

As Mrs. Morris stripped down to her silk-and-lace underthings—nothing cheap there either—Vivian kept up her easy chatter. It was a habit she fell into with most of her customers, to put them at ease during the often-intimate process. And it didn't hurt that folks were more likely to tip well if she acted as friendly as possible. But this time she was more pointed than usual in her questions. After commenting on the weather and some of the paintings while she helped Mrs. Morris slip on the first dress, Vivian knelt and pulled out her tailor's tape while asking, "And is Mr. Morris still with us?"

She already knew the answer, but it was a tactful question—Mrs. Morris was old enough that she could have been married either during the Great War or the influenza pandemic that followed.

"Oh yes," Mrs. Morris answered, preening at herself in the mirror. The gown was silk and chiffon, with beading on each layer to catch the light no matter how she moved. Luckily, the fit was already perfect—

her constant shifting would have made it almost impossible to check. But Vivian went through the motions to give her time to answer. "Mr. Morris is in excellent health. But rarely at home during the day." She frowned a little at her reflection, then shrugged. "Thank goodness. I cannot imagine being married to one of those men who is always underfoot."

"He must be wonderfully important, for you to live in a grand house like this," Vivian said, keeping her head down as she fiddled with the gown's hem, her eyes flicking up to the clock on Mrs. Morris's dressing table. Any minute now . . .

Mrs. Morris, distracted from whatever had preoccupied her a moment before, smiled smugly at the mention of her house. "Isn't it grand? Mr. Morris works in shipping and imports, so he's very busy. And very successful."

Vivian replied politely, not really paying attention to what she was saying while Mrs. Morris began to describe her furnishings in detail. She had just donned the second dress and launched into a recitation of the number of chandeliers in the house when the pounding came from downstairs. It sounded like someone was beating the front door with a battering ram. Mrs. Morris jumped so sharply that the dress's fragile hem would have torn if Vivian hadn't let go quickly.

"What on earth?" the woman demanded.

That was when the shouting began, a man's voice raised in what might have been anguish or anger or simple excitement.

"Marie!" he bellowed. "We don't have to hide anymore, I promise. I don't care what your parents think! Just come down, you'll see!"

Vivian didn't have to make herself look surprised; she stared just as wildly as Mrs. Morris at the bedroom door. But she clenched her jaw shut against a hysterical bubble of laughter. Leo was putting on a hell of a show down there.

"Marie!" he called again, and they could hear the clamor of servants' voices as they tried to calm him down and find out what he wanted. "Marie, my love, come down!"

"What on earth could it be, ma'am?" Vivian said, afraid that if she kept silent any longer she'd lose her nerve.

"I don't—I can't imagine—Who is Marie?" Mrs. Morris demanded. "I suppose I had better . . ." The shouting from downstairs grew louder. Mrs. Morris rushed to the bed to snatch up the dressing gown draped there. She clutched it to her chest for a moment like a shield, then threw it over her new dress and pelted from the room.

Vivian followed her into the sitting room but lingered as Mrs. Morris ran out the door. Vivian could hear her voice join the shouting as she hurried downstairs, the commotion only growing louder and more confusing. Leo's voice rose above it all, demanding that they let "Marie" come to him.

Vivian felt hysterical with laughter and panic, her feet frozen in place. Surely no one would believe such a wild performance. Surely at any moment, they'd come charging back up the steps and catch her in the act . . .

Before she could talk herself out of it, Vivian ran across the sitting room on a dancer's light feet and tried the door to Mr. Morris's room. To her relief, it swung open.

If she had expected a man's private space to be more restrained, she would have been disappointed. The room on the other side of the door was as gaudy as the rest of the house, an excess of heavy furnishings and dark upholstery. One whole wall had been turned into a liquor display, cut-crystal decanters full of amber and gold and clear liquids all sparkling in the sunlight that streamed through tall windows. Vivian shook her head. Some people really did have more money than brains.

There was no desk in the room, but there was a wardrobe and a tall chest of drawers, and she went to those first. She had just started searching the wardrobe when she heard the door open behind her.

Vivian spun around, her mouth dry with fear and her mind completely blank. There was no way to explain herself, so she said nothing, just stared at the maid who had walked in.

It was the same girl, Mary, who had shown her upstairs. Vivian wondered for a wild moment if she had come up specifically to check on the dressmaker's girl while everything was busy downstairs. But her arms were full of folded linens, and she stared with as much blank surprise as Vivian, neither of them speaking for a handful of heartbeats that seemed to last forever. From downstairs, Vivian could hear Mrs. Morris's voice raised in an exasperated shout. "Young man, you are mistaken, there is no Marie living in this house!"

Mary was the first to speak. "You robbin' them?"

Vivian swallowed. "No," she said, her voice hoarse. Her hand was still on the open wardrobe door. She dropped it as though the metal handle had burned her.

The maid laughed. "Yes, you are. And if you keep standin' there looking dumb as a rock with your jaw hangin' down, Mrs. Morris'll be back here and catch you doin' it."

"I'm not—"

"What are you tryin' to find? Because Mr. Morris don't keep his money in here."

"I'm not looking for money."

"Then what?" When Vivian only stared at her, Mary shrugged. "Make it worth my while, and I'll tell you where it is. I clean in here every day."

"What?" Vivian demanded, certain she had heard wrong.

Mary shrugged again. "They're a pain to work for."

Vivian had to decide quickly. The shouting was dying down; she probably didn't have much time left. But years at the Nightingale had taught her to read people and to trust her instincts. She made up her mind abruptly. Reaching into her pocket, she pulled out the quarter that would have bought her dinner and held it up between two fingers. "I'm looking for a letter."

The maid plucked it from her hand and made it vanish under her apron. "It's blackmail, then. Know which one you're looking for?"

"Any of them come from Swan's Point?" Vivian asked.

"Oh, that." Mary crossed to the nightstand and slid the drawer open. "He keeps it stashed inside the Bible here. Hysterical, that is." She held an envelope out, its flap open and its contents bulging, smirking a little as she looked Vivian up and down. "No girl like you is going to get mixed up in this sort of affair. Who's paying you?"

Vivian gave her a small smile. "Better for you not to know," she said, plucking the letter from Mary's hand before the girl could object.

The maid only shrugged. "Ain't that always the way. I'm off, then. Good luck, I guess. And if you try to say I was here, I'll call you a liar to God himself."

"Same," Vivian said in cheerful relief as the maid headed out the door at a quick trot. She pulled the letter out of its envelope, unfolding it just enough to see that the stationery was engraved with *Swan's Point* at the top in graceful lettering. She would have liked to read the whole thing, but she couldn't risk staying there any longer.

When Mrs. Morris returned a few minutes later, looking exhausted, Vivian was in the sitting room, wringing her hands together and hovering by the door as though trying to decide whether to go downstairs or not.

The letter was tucked into the bottom of her sewing bag, where Mrs. Morris would have no reason to look.

"What was all that commotion, ma'am?" Vivian asked, hoping she didn't sound too breathless from her dash across the rooms. "Is everyone okay?"

"Oh, yes. My goodness." Mrs. Morris dropped into a chair before the fireplace. "Yes, it was rather charming, really, once we got the mistake sorted out. Some young man looking for his sweetheart, hoping to convince her parents to let them marry. So romantic. I sent him on his way with some good advice." She shook her head, fanning herself with one hand. "Bring me a glass of lemonade from the sideboard."

Vivian bristled. She wasn't one of the woman's servants, and the

order had been given impatiently, as though Vivian should have already thought to provide her with a drink. But she needed to get out of
there with as little fuss as possible. Gritting her teeth, she poured the
glass of lemonade and brought it to Mrs. Morris.

"Is there anything else I can do for you?" she asked, stretching a
smile across her face.

"No, no, I think I need to lie down after all that excitement," Mrs.
Morris said, leaning back and closing her eyes. "Can you return tomorrow to finish?"

"I won't need to, everything fits just right," Vivian said, already
heading back to the bedroom to gather her things. Her hands were
shaking as she snapped her bag closed. "Thank you again for your
order," she added. Her feet itched to run out of the room, but she kept
them firmly in place. "We look forward to sewing for you again."

"Of course you do," Mrs. Morris said, sounding half-asleep already.
"So romantic," she added in a murmur.

Vivian didn't wait any longer. She managed to keep her steps to a
walk, but only just. In barely more than a minute, she was down the
stairs and heading to the kitchen.

She caught a glimpse of Mary in the hall as she went past and looked
resolutely away, not wanting to catch the other girl's eye. To her relief,
Mary didn't turn from her work. But Vivian didn't let out the breath
she was holding until she was on the street once more and heading
downtown, the black bag with Mr. Morris's letter inside clutched in
both hands.

———•—•———

An affair?" Leo asked, as Vivian spread the sheets of the letter
out on her kitchen table. "That sounds . . . I mean, I don't know
anything about the fella's home life. It could be disastrous, depending on whether their money is his or came with his wife—"

"And depending on who *E* is," Vivian added as she glanced at the last page of the letter. "That's the only signature."

"Sure. But that sounds so . . ." He shrugged. "Boring."

Vivian cradled a cup of coffee between her hands. It was bitter—she hadn't been able to afford sugar or milk that week—but the stress of the theft had left her exhausted. And she still had a shift at the Nightingale to get through, so she had made coffee as soon as she got home. At Leo's comment, she snorted. "Well, an affair might not be that creative a thing to blackmail someone over. But the letter itself is anything but boring. If any of it ended up in a gossip column . . ."

She had felt every inch of her body blushing with embarrassment while she read it while on the streetcar to meet up with Leo, and she had quickly stuffed it back in her bag in case anyone peered over her shoulder. Now, as Leo bent over to read it, Vivian watched his eyebrows climb toward his hairline. It was some satisfaction to see that he was embarrassed, or at least surprised, by the letter's contents.

"Well. Nope, that's definitely not boring." Leo glanced up, his cheeks red as he ran a hand through his hair. He took a sip from his coffee and coughed. "What kind of idiot puts that sort of thing in writing?"

"No idiots like rich idiots," Vivian said, shrugging as she folded the papers back up and stuffed them into their envelope. She hesitated, then tucked the whole packet into the purse she would take to work that night. There was no telling when Hattie or, more likely, one of her errand boys would show up, and Vivian wanted to be ready when they did. "And I for one don't intend to worry over what Mrs. Wilson plans to—"

She broke off, jumping as someone knocked at the door. Leo frowned at her.

"You expecting company?" he asked quietly, reaching toward the back of his waistband.

Vivian felt chilled. She knew he often carried a gun, and she didn't much care for it. "Probably just a neighbor," she hissed, grabbing his elbow. "Don't get jumpy when there's no cause."

"It pays to be prepared—"

"Not in my house," she snapped.

He looked like he wanted to argue, but she didn't give him a chance before she crossed to the door. Her own heart was hammering—the surprises lately hadn't exactly been good—but she didn't let Leo see that as she opened the door. "Who's—" She broke off, letting out a relieved breath. "Bea! What are you doing here?"

"Finished my shift at the Buchanans'," she said, breezing into the room, her coat fluttering open over her maid's uniform. "I'll say this for them, it's not a fun place to work, but they do pay decent. Sent me home with cash today. Mama's not too sore over the extra money this week, even if she knows I'm not telling her the truth about why I took the job."

"What did you tell her?" Vivian asked, closing the door and turning the lock. Just in case.

Bea shrugged as she pulled off her coat. "That I was helping out a friend. Which was the wrong thing to say, of course. It made her plenty nervous. But no help for that now." She glanced between Leo and Vivian. "What's got you two looking like you're exchanging secrets?"

"Mrs. Wilson's errand," Vivian said. She had told Bea all about her run-in with Bruiser George while they were heading home from work the night before. "Leo put on a hell of a show to distract them while I snatched the letter."

"Tell me all about it, but not quite yet," Bea said, taking a seat and helping herself to a swallow from Viv's coffee mug, recognizable by the ring of lipstick around one side of the rim. "First, I have a present for you. From that rotten Corny Rokesby. But really from me." She smiled, looking pleased with herself.

Vivian stared at her friend. "Bea, please tell me you didn't do something dumb or dangerous."

"Little bit of both," Bea said. Her tone was light, but her eyes were serious as they met Vivian's. Her coat was hanging over the back of her chair; she reached around to pull a small, leather-bound notebook from its pocket. "I told you I was going to help you out. And I meant it."

"And I told you not to put yourself in danger—"

"Just shut up and read it," Bea said, rolling her eyes with impatience as she held the book out.

Vivian took it with tingling fingers, half wondering what it was, half sure she already knew. She turned the pages slowly, even as her heart was pounding like a Charleston beat. "Bea," she said, looking up. "Did you steal Cornelius Rokesby's appointment book?"

"Something like that," she said, propping her feet up on the remaining chair and rubbing the small of her back with a sigh. "Lord almighty, but it's a hell of an achy business, being on your feet all day. I don't know how Mama stands it."

"Bea," Vivian said, her voice rising. "What were you thinking?"

Bea's expression grew serious at last. "I was thinking that my pal is in trouble and needs help. It wasn't all that hard to find. Don't you want to know what he's lying about?"

"But he could report you to the police," Vivian said, starting to feel frantic. "You could get arrested yourself, and then what—"

"No, he couldn't," Leo said suddenly, a grin spreading across his face. "He already told them he's never kept an appointment book. How's he going to report that someone stole it now, even if he figures out who it was? Hell, he might even think it was a cop who snuck in and snatched it." He shook his head admiringly. "Slick work there, Beatrice. Real slick."

"Thank you," she said smugly, returning his smile. It was the friendliest Vivian had ever seen them. "Now it's Vivian's turn to say thanks."

Vivian wanted to protest more. But it wouldn't do any good. Bea had already taken it. All Vivian could do was hope that Leo was right about Rokesby not being able to report the theft. Vivian swallowed.

"Thank you," she said, her voice coming out a little hoarse. "You're one in a million, you know that?"

"I sure do," Bea said. "So, what are you thinking? He bumped off his stepdad to get his inheritance? Bit of a letdown for him, then, how it all shook out."

"Maybe," Vivian said slowly as she turned the pages. She glanced up at her friend. "Both Mrs. Buchanan and Corny wouldn't give the police a straight answer about where they were, right? And being as they're his family, they'd probably have the best chance to be the ones slipping him poison. And then they got impatient, and . . ." She trailed off, pushing aside the memories of that morning, and glanced back at the book.

"Right," Bea agreed as she plonked her feet down on the floor and leaned forward. "So are you going to tell us what the hell is in there that was so important for him to keep secret?"

"Well, you're not going to like it." Vivian flipped through the pages until she found the week of Buchanan's death. "But I'm pretty sure half of it is written in code."

Bea's face fell. "What?"

Leo had stood to peer over Vivian's shoulder, and he grimaced at what he saw. "That's damned inconvenient."

"But also damned suspicious," Bea pointed out. "So maybe we're on the right track?"

"Maybe," Leo agreed, looking doubtful. "But not much help if we can't figure out what it means." He glanced at Vivian. "What are you thinking?"

Vivian drummed her fingers against the table, a syncopated *rat-a-tat* that jumped around with her thoughts. "Is there any chance we could take this to your pal Levinsky?" she asked, looking at Leo. "He's the one who mentioned it. Would he—"

But Leo was already shaking his head. "He'd have to stick his neck out pretty far to explain how he got it, and I don't think he'd risk that kind of trouble. Not with a new baby at home." One corner of his mouth lifted in a cynical smile. "And even if he did, if the damn thing is written in code, the odds of anyone trying to figure it out aren't great."

"So I still need something more solid to give your uncle," Vivian said, nodding as she let out a slow, anxious breath. "Okay. Then I need to find someone who knows what the Fifth Avenue folks have been up to recently." She glanced at her purse, where the letter for Hattie Wilson was tucked away. "And I think I know who might be able to help us."

TWENTY

Like hell you will," Bea snapped for what felt like the hundredth time as she fixed her lipstick in the dressing room mirror, wearing only her step-in, stockings, and the red velvet heels she always wore to perform. "Viv, you can't ask her for another favor. Look what she already had you do!"

Vivian, seated on one of the couches, kept her gaze fixed on her hands, not wanting to meet Bea's eyes in the mirror. She had a good reason for looking down—she was fixing a split seam on the back of Bea's dress before she returned to the bandstand. But they both knew it was an excuse.

"Maybe, but odds are she'll have our answers. Or she can find them out," Vivian said, keeping her voice low. It was just them in the dressing room for the moment, but there was no saying when someone else might pop in. "That's gotta be worth it, right?"

"Maybe," Bea said, setting aside her lipstick and lighting a cigarette. She blew out an anxious stream of smoke. "Or maybe not. Depends on what she asks you to do next."

"Might not matter tonight anyway," Vivian said, tying off the thread and snipping it close before handing the dress back to Bea and packing her sewing things up. "I don't know when she's going to send someone for the letter." She stood, stretching out her back, and plucked the cigarette from Bea's fingers, taking a quick drag before stubbing it out in the ashtray on the dressing table. "I've got to get back out there, and you do too."

"Don't do it, Viv," Bea warned one more time as they opened the door to a wave of music and heat.

Vivian pretended not to hear, lifting two fingers in the barest wave as she dodged toward the corner of the bar where Leo was waiting, nursing a glass of Canadian whisky and paging through Corny Rokesby's appointment book.

It was half appointment book, half diary, and many of the entries were straightforward: dinner receptions that lasted all night (*not enough Champagne* Corny had noted next to that one in a wobbly, drunken scrawl), a week with friends at Great Neck (*toasted Martin's last days of freedom with some excellent Scotch*), time in his stepfather's office (*boring but not too boring*), regular family dinners (*Mother complaining again*).

But every so often events would be noted in initials or codes. *Ds with GCBs* appeared every few weeks. And *XX* appeared at irregular intervals with no pattern that they could see, accompanied by the appointment time and what looked like a string of random words, all of them different each time.

The most recent *XX* (*rutabaga coat East River blue*) had been at nine o'clock in the morning the day Huxley Buchanan was killed. The next *XX* (*violet charmer snakebite gin*), along with an *HLMB,* was happening the next night.

"Any luck?" Vivian asked.

"No," Leo muttered, one cheek slouching in the palm of his hand as he glared at the leather-bound book. "Who does this fella think he is, Al Capone?"

That made Vivian laugh, though there wasn't much humor in it. "God, let's hope not. Put that away for now. I don't want to risk anyone seeing it." She smoothed a few strands of his hair back into place. "And get on the dance floor. People will start to wonder if they see you sitting around looking grumpy."

Leo grumbled, but he tucked the notebook back inside his jacket. When she next spotted him, he was on the dance floor with a girl she didn't recognize. And just beyond them, checking in with Benny, was Honor. Vivian hesitated, then made up her mind quickly. She wanted to know what Honor could tell her about Corny Rokesby and what he might have wanted that night.

She was halfway there when Honor caught sight of her. A moment before, her hands had been tucked in her pockets, her limbs loose and relaxed as she finished her chat with Benny and turned to survey the crowd. But as soon as her gaze fell on Vivian, she tensed.

Vivian took a step toward her. Honor turned and walked out of the room without looking back.

Vivian stared after her. Honor had every reason to be acting strange. Her father had just died. And she didn't, in fact, owe Vivian anything—even if Vivian had hoped for more. Even if she wanted at least a few answers that she didn't have to struggle for on her own.

Vivian turned back to the bar, trying not to let herself worry, and discovered that she wasn't the only one struggling that night.

"Everything okay?" Danny asked her as he handed a drink to a man in a blue suit and paused for a breather.

"Swell," Vivian said, not really paying attention to her answer. Instead, she looked him over, not liking what she saw. His usual friendly smile had been in place all night, and his hands moved as fast as always as he mixed drinks and managed people. But there were dark circles of fatigue under his eyes that weren't usually there, and he sighed as he leaned against the bar, as if he were too tired to stay upright. "What about you, Danny-boy? Everything okay?"

"Swell," he said, smiling as he echoed her. It was a tired smile, but Vivian was relieved to see that it was genuine. "Just been busy recently, between here and the restaurant and taking care of Florence."

Vivian's stomach twisted. "Anything I should worry about?"

He shook his head. "You're the one who needs worrying about right now," he said. "She's just not feeling her best, is all. Can't be on her feet too long without getting dizzy. But Ma says it's all normal." He smiled again. "And she promised us babies are worth it."

Vivian laughed at that, but his words left a pinching ache in her chest that she couldn't shake off. She trusted Danny, and Mrs. Chin would have pounced instantly if there was anything really worrisome with Florence's pregnancy. But Florence was *her* sister. They'd always taken care of each other, even if they'd glared and complained while they did it. They'd spent every day of their lives together until Danny swept Florence into a new life.

Vivian would see her. Soon. She just had a few things to take care of first.

"Anyway." Danny rolled his shoulders to stretch them out as he stood upright once more. "You've been running your feet off, kitten, and Ellie just arrived. Take a break."

"Thanks, boss," Vivian said, sliding her tray onto the bar and taking one of the open stools. "Any chance of some bubbles while I do that?"

He rolled his eyes. "I'll see if we have any bottles already open. I'm not opening a new one just for you."

"How about you open one for me, then?" a playful voice asked.

A pretty, pouting brunette dropped onto the stool next to Vivian, shimmying so that her fashionable dress scooted up a little more toward her knees. She gave them a smile as dazzling as the diamonds in her ears. "One glass for me and one for Viv, if you please."

Danny grinned back. "Coming right up, miss."

The girl turned to Vivian. "Well, hello, shellshock. You two were looking awful serious just a moment ago. Nothing that'll ruin the party, I hope?"

"Just talking shop," Vivian said, shrugging one shoulder. She smiled back. "Good to see you, Mags."

Behind the bar, Danny popped a cork on a new bottle of champagne, and Mags jumped a little, then laughed at herself. Her curly hair was pinned under to look like a fashionable bob, a style popular with girls who still wanted to look proper when they weren't out drinking and dancing. And Mags, Vivian knew, was every inch a well-behaved girl when she needed to be. Her parents were society folks, with their own uptown mansion and loads of servants. Vivian had delivered dresses there before; it had been a shock, the first time, to see Mags out of her glamorous nighttime persona and realize she was probably not more than seventeen years old. It had been even more of a shock for both of them to be confronted by the obvious gulf between their lives.

But they managed to forget that sort of thing when they were at the Nightingale. No one was being their real selves there—or they were being the real selves they couldn't show anywhere else. Pretending that Vivian didn't work with the girls who sewed Mags's expensive clothes was just how things were done. It irritated Vivian sometimes, but mostly she was grateful. She liked Mags, even if the girl was oblivious to the world outside her comfortable, wealthy cocoon. She was still a kid, she had time to learn.

"Cheers, doll," Mags said, lifting her glass and clinking it against Vivian's. "Here's to the party."

And in the meantime, she never minded buying a round.

She also never minded sharing a bit of gossip. Vivian's hands shook a little as the thought occurred to her, and she put her glass down quickly before Mags could notice. There was a decent chance she moved in the same circles Corny Rokesby did; she might have some idea what his strange notes meant.

And if Mags could help her out, Vivian wouldn't need to ask Hattie Wilson for another favor after all. It was worth a shot.

The band struck up a Charleston, and Mags cut a sideways look at Vivian. "You gonna ask me to dance?"

Vivian laughed, distracted for the moment from her nervous thoughts. It was well known in the Nightingale that Vivian could lead a Charleston as well as she could follow.

"Is that why you came over to say hi?" she asked. She was picky about her partners—a Charleston was no fun with someone who couldn't keep up—but Mags had light feet.

Mags shrugged, smiling. "I was hoping. Pickings of the male persuasion are slim on the ground tonight, so what's a girl to do?" When Vivian glanced around pointedly—there was no shortage of men that night—Mags laughed. "All right. What I mean is, you're a better dancer than most of them, and I know *you* won't get fresh. What do you say?"

"You got it, sweetheart," Vivian said, hopping down from her stool and holding out her hand. Mags downed the rest of her champagne with a quick gulp and took it, bouncing on her toes with anticipation. "Maybe when we're done kicking up our heels, you can help with a puzzle I've been trying to solve."

"Oh, I love a good brain-tickler," Mags said as they squirmed their way onto the crowded dance floor. "What's yours about?"

"Fella named Corny Rokesby. You know him?"

Mags's expression grew curious and a little sly. "I might. But first . . ."

Vivian gave Mags a spin with one hand, sliding the other around her waist in a loose hold and letting the movement pull them into the music. After that, they needed all their breath for dancing.

———————

Well, first, I just want you to appreciate that I'm not asking how you got this, because I am damn curious," Mags said, sipping a new glass of champagne as she leaned over Corny Rokesby's appointment book.

Showing it to her was a risk, and Leo hadn't hidden his disapproval when Vivian reclaimed the book from him. He hadn't protested, though Vivian suspected she'd get an earful from him if it turned out the girl couldn't help her after all. But Vivian trusted her instincts, and they were telling her that Mags wasn't the sort to rat out her friends. Especially when she turned a page and said, "He's not that nice, you know."

"Rokesby?" Vivian asked, scooting her chair closer. They were in a dark little corner where couples usually went to cuddle and drink if they weren't the sort to make their way to the back alley for more privacy. With the bandstand not far away, it was as private as a spot in the Nightingale could get.

"Mm-hmm." Mags nodded, head still bent over the book. She wrinkled her nose. "He's a cold fish, you know? He doesn't like talking to people. Awful secretive, too. He was at a party that Mother and Dad hosted last month, and I tried asking him about the night the Von Hilsens were robbed, but he didn't want to say a word about it!"

Vivian leaned forward. Had Corny Rokesby been involved in something illegal? "What's the story about this robbery?"

"You don't know?" Mags looked shocked. "Golly, I thought everyone in the city would have heard! The Von Hilsens were throwing a party that got robbed." She glanced up, eyes wide and excited. "You honestly didn't hear anything about it?"

"I mighta heard something," Vivian said slowly, frowning. "Everyone got knocked out with chloroform in the punch, right? And when they came to, all their jewelry and things were gone?"

"That's about the shape of it," Mags said, giggling. "Can you imagine? And they never found out who did it. Mr. Von Hilsen sacked all their servants, just to be safe."

"And you think Rokesby might have been involved?" Vivian asked, trying not to dwell on the thought of all those folks losing their jobs for a crime they probably had nothing to do with.

"Him?" Mags looked shocked. "Golly, no. I mean, he was robbed along with the rest of them! I just wanted to get the scoop on what happened. But Corny won't say anything if you ask him about himself, and who doesn't like talking about himself? He's a funny one. I wouldn't mind knowing what he gets up to." She looked up, smiling slyly again. "You never know when it'll be useful to know what people get up to."

Vivian snorted. She couldn't argue with that. But she gestured to the book, hoping to get Mags back on task. She didn't like sitting there with something stolen on the table right in front of them, even if there was almost no chance anyone else would guess what it was. "Anything catch your eye?"

Mags snorted. "Well, I can guess that one," she said, pointing to one instance of *Ds with GCBs*. She lowered her voice, eager once more to share her gossip. "The GCBs are probably the Gold Coast Boys. They throw the most amazing parties every few months, rotating between different houses. Usually whoever actually *owns* the house is abroad or something like that, because things get . . . Well, from what I've heard, they get awfully wild."

"And those nights were some of their parties?" Vivian asked.

"Might've been. I'm still too young to get invited." Mags shrugged. "But if Corny Rokesby was, he wouldn't turn that down. The Gold Coast Boys are connected to *everyone* who matters."

"How do you know that if you don't know for sure who they are?"

Mags smirked, shaking her head. "*Everyone* knows that," she said. There was an edge of pity to her voice that made Vivian's cheeks feel hot. "And even if it's not actually true, what matters is that everyone thinks it is."

"Sure, of course," Vivian said, trying not to sound too embarrassed. This was why she'd asked Mags for help. She didn't know that world, and Mags did. And anyway, there was nothing about the Gold Coast Boys the week that Huxley Buchanan had been killed. "What about those double exes?"

Mags wrinkled her nose and shrugged. "I've got no idea what those mean. Are those poems next to them? Odd, if they are. But I'm pretty sure . . ." She leaned forward, her voice dropping, even though the music more than covered their conversation. "I'm pretty sure that *HLMB* is a Hamilton Lodge masquerade ball. Because there's one tomorrow night."

"Hamilton Lodge?" Vivian asked in disbelief. "You're joking, right?"

Mags shrugged again. "I don't know what else it could be."

Hamilton Lodge was a fraternal lodge up in Harlem. Vivian didn't know much about it, but she had heard of the masquerade and civic balls thrown around the city. Glamorous and scandalous, they were attended by thousands of people and written up in all the papers.

And while it was hard to picture a man like Rokesby somewhere glamorous *or* scandalous, a civic ball would be the perfect spot for something shady and secret. Especially because, from what she knew about them, guests at the balls came from all walks of life, so long as they could afford a ticket—or knew someone who could afford it for them.

For a moment Vivian felt like she would lift out of her seat with excitement. Then her heart sank. If a ball was happening tomorrow night, tickets would have been sold weeks ago. And there was no chance of getting in without one.

"Mags," she said, not really hoping but needing to ask anyway. "I don't suppose you have tickets to the lodge ball tomorrow?"

Mags sighed, chin dropping into her palm. "Golly, don't I wish. I've never been, and I hear they're a smashing good time." She sat up straight suddenly. "Would you take me with you?"

"Mags, I just asked you for tickets," Vivian reminded her impatiently. "How'm I supposed to take you when I can't get in myself?"

"I can get us tickets," Mags said eagerly. "I know who always gets extras. It's just he's refused to take me with him. Says he doesn't want to be stuck babysitting all night." She made a face. "I'm not *that* much of a kid, you know."

"'Course not," Vivian said. She'd have said whatever she thought she needed to get those tickets. But it seemed true enough to her— she'd had no idea how old Mags really was when she first met her.

Though maybe that was just the confidence of someone who wore real diamonds and knew her daddy would always pay her bail money. "Do you really think your friend would help us out?" Vivian hesitated. "How much do tickets cost?"

Mags gave her a shrewd look. "How 'bout you do me a favor and take me with you so my pal doesn't say no. And I get the tickets all sorted out. What do you say?"

It was an easier favor than the others that had crossed Vivian's path in the last few days. "You've got a deal."

"Peachy." Mags grinned, lifting her glass in another toast. "Now, any idea why that handsome bartender of yours is looking daggers in this direction?"

"Because my break is long past done," Vivian said, closing the notebook and tucking it under her arm to return to Leo. "Where should we meet you tomorrow night?"

"We?" Mags frowned. "How many tickets do you need?"

"Let's say three, if you can?" Vivian said. "One for each of us, plus I'll bring a fella?"

"Oh sure, that'll be fine. How about you and your fella swing by my parents' house tomorrow night, around nine? Just pull over across the street and flash your lights twice so I know it's you."

"Will do." Vivian stood, stretching out her back. "Thanks, Mags. You're a swell girl."

"I sure am," Mags said cheerfully, already scanning the crowd for her next partner. "And Viv? You'll want to wear something grand. Folks go all out at these things."

———

Bruiser George didn't turn up until half an hour before last call. The band was winding down, giving anyone who wanted it a chance to find a new friend and persuade them onto the floor before the night ended. Dancers were pressed cheek to cheek, bare necks and arms glowing with perspiration while their tired feet slid along the floor. Vivian was gathering half-empty glasses from a table when she spotted George across the room. For a moment, in spite of the sweet love song that filled the air, Vivian tasted bile in the back of her throat.

She hadn't realized, until that moment, that she was so afraid of him.

But she wouldn't let him see it. When he caught her eye over the heads of the dancers, Vivian didn't look away. If a dog was trained to attack, they'd only jump faster if they could smell your fear. He raised his brows in a silent question, and Vivian jerked her chin, pointing to his left. Leo had just spotted him from a table by the dance floor, where he'd been nursing a gin cocktail so he wouldn't stand out too much while he waited.

With any luck, now that she didn't need to ask for Hattie's help, Leo would hand over the letter and that would be the end of it. Vivian waited until she was sure they had seen each other, then turned away.

That was when she spotted Honor by the dance floor. She'd been busy with a couple that Vivian thought she recognized, which probably meant they were people who got their photos in the society pages from time to time. But they were heading to the dance floor, and Honor was standing with narrow eyes and tense shoulders, watching Bruiser George make his way down the stairs and toward Leo.

Vivian stopped next to Honor. "He's not here to make trouble."

Honor didn't jump; she didn't let herself show that kind of surprise. But Vivian saw the quick movement of her eyes, darting toward Vivian to see who had spoken, before she turned. Vivian frowned. It had been gone almost too quickly to see, but for a moment, she had looked stricken—maybe even guilty. It was an expression she'd never seen on Honor's face before.

"Oh?" Honor asked, cutting her eyes back to where Leo and George were chatting, bodies turned just enough away from the crowd that it was almost impossible to spot the moment that the letter changed hands unless you knew what you were looking for.

"I owed his boss a favor, remember?" Vivian said, hoping she had imagined that flash of guilt. "Leo's making a delivery for me so I don't have to deal with him."

Honor nodded, her face as impassive as though the news meant nothing to her. She was already turning away, as quickly as if she couldn't wait to put distance between them.

Vivian took a step back, stung. She had come over as a favor, so Honor wouldn't worry about Bruiser George's presence at the club that night. She might as well have saved herself the effort. She was about to storm off when Honor turned to look directly at her for the first time. "Are you okay?"

Her concern sounded genuine, and it made an achy knot clench inside Vivian's chest. She wanted to tell Honor what had been happening. But she was too proud for that. "I'm fine. Why wouldn't I be?"

"As long as you're not—" Honor's hand rose; for a moment, it looked as though she would brush her fingers against Vivian's cheek, or maybe smooth back the dark curtain of hair that had fallen in front of her ear. Vivian tensed, too caught by surprise to pull away. But Honor noticed the flinch and dropped her hand.

Vivian sighed, tired of things feeling so strained between them. Desperate to think of something to say, she started with the first thing that came to mind. "Hey, any chance you know a thing or two about the Ham—"

But Honor was already walking away. "You're supposed to be working," she called over her shoulder. "And so am I."

The heat of the dance hall couldn't stop the chill that slithered its way down Vivian's spine. For a moment, as Honor had turned away, Vivian had seen that same stricken look flash across her face.

Vivian watched her go, trying not to remember Hattie Wilson's taunting smile in the back seat of the car. Instead, she took a deep breath and headed toward the bar. She had a shift to finish. And then she had to ask if she could borrow a dress.

TWENTY-ONE

Three Days Left

When Vivian saw the first address on her list of deliveries, she had to bite the inside of her cheek against a long string of angry language that would have gotten her fired on the spot. But she was too tired, and too agitated, to keep her face as impassive, and Miss Ethel pounced.

"Is something amiss, Miss Kelly?" she said, too sweetly. "Do the customers whose purchases put clothes on your back and food on your table not meet your standards?"

Once, it would have taken all Vivian's self-control to keep the sarcasm out of her own reply. But dealing with Miss Ethel was an old habit now; there was no point in arguing back. And, looking at that address, she had bigger things to worry about than Miss Ethel's ugly moods. "No, ma'am," she said. "I'm very grateful for Mrs. Wilson's business. And the others as well, of course."

Miss Ethel sniffed. "I should hope so. Now get along. You have two other deliveries first. Mrs. Wilson wants you at eleven o'clock."

Vivian gritted her teeth. She needed her work for Miss Ethel. But another summons from Mrs. Wilson was almost enough to make her quit.

Vivian didn't owe her anything, not anymore. Hattie Wilson might have been cold and ruthless, but even she wouldn't claim things weren't square between them.

Unless Vivian had done something wrong. Maybe she'd stolen the wrong letter. Maybe George hadn't delivered it. One way or another, a summons from Hattie Wilson meant the woman wanted something. And Vivian dreaded finding out what that was.

———•—•———

The maid who led her upstairs looked uncomfortable as she paused outside a room Vivian had never been to before. It wasn't Hattie's office or the parlor where she'd waited during her previous visits. Vivian's nervousness grew.

"Mrs. Wilson says you're to wait in here," the maid whispered, her hand on the doorknob. "And that you're not to disturb her or her guest. She'll come for her fitting when she's ready."

"What does that mean?" Vivian demanded, but she too spoke in a whisper. She knew better than to disobey a woman like Hattie Wilson in her own house. She wondered briefly about Hattie's staff. Did they know what kind of woman they were working for? Or did they fool themselves into believing she was just a wealthy young mother like any other, a widow whose main concerns were her son, her sister, and her social life?

"Mrs. Wilson will be with you when she's ready," the maid repeated, opening the door and putting a finger to her lips.

The little sitting room was barely more than a hall between other spaces. The only window was small and high, and the stiff furniture looked as if it had been put there just to get it out of the way. But at least there were two chairs, and a table between them where Vivian could put down the box she was carrying and rest her aching arms. The delivery for Mrs. Wilson was small, but the other two that morning had been evening gowns. Hauling the oversized boxes across so many city blocks had left her shaking with exhaustion.

Three out of the four walls had doors. The one she had come through closed silently behind her. One was closed. And the third was cracked open, just enough that she could hear voices from the other side. Vivian sighed as she sank into one of the chairs. Why tell her to come at eleven just to make her wait?

Vivian dropped her head into her hands. She didn't want to find out what sort of game she was being dragged into now. And she didn't want to sit silently, in a cold, uncomfortable room, waiting for two women who weren't counting down their last days of freedom to finish whatever gossip was entertaining them for the day.

Occupied with her unhappy thoughts, it took Vivian several minutes to realize she recognized both voices, not just Mrs. Wilson's.

She'd only heard the second voice twice before. But so many details from the day Huxley Buchanan was killed, and the awful days since, had stuck in her memory whether she wanted them or not. His wife's voice was one.

"I don't know what I'm going to do without him," Evangeline Buchanan said between hiccups. Vivian was surprised by how genuinely upset the woman sounded.

"And to think you married him in the first place just for your son's sake," Hattie Wilson replied. It was the gentlest Vivian had ever heard her sound. Did the icy Mrs. Wilson actually care?

No, it had to be an act. Otherwise, why make sure Vivian was there to overhear?

"I wanted what was best for Corny, of course," Mrs. Buchanan said. She sniffled, and there was a loud sound of a nose being blown into a handkerchief. "What mother doesn't? But Huxley . . ." She sniffed again and sighed. "I have so many regrets, now. I never truly gave our marriage a chance."

"Yes, an affair does rather distance one from one's husband, does it not?" The sympathy in Hattie's voice took on an amused edge.

"What did . . . How did . . ." Vivian could hear the panic in Mrs. Buchanan's voice. "What do you mean?"

"Dear, don't fret. You know I say it without judgment. Such things happen. Who is the man, by the way?"

Mrs. Buchanan's voice was stiff as she replied. "If you do not know more, Henrietta, I am certainly not going to share."

"Why, Aunt Evangeline, you know I am only concerned for your well-being," Hattie Wilson said, her voice gentle once more. "I only wish to be certain that he is discreet, whoever he is. Imagine how damning the rumors would be if word got out. Why, some people might even have the gall to suggest one of you was responsible for Uncle Huxley's death."

Vivian's heart sped up. If Mrs. Buchanan had been having an affair, maybe her husband hadn't been killed over a matter of business at all. Maybe it had been a matter of passion.

"Well, we could not have been. We were . . ." Evangeline Buchanan hiccupped back a sob. "We were together that morning."

Vivian's hopes came crashing back to earth. If that was true, it made all too much sense why Mrs. Buchanan had refused to tell the cops where she was. Was there any way to prove it?

"And oh, Henrietta." Mrs. Buchanan was still talking, words coming out in a confessional torrent, as if now that she'd started she couldn't stop. "Henrietta, you've no idea how I regret it. The whole thing, but that morning . . . If I had been at home, perhaps nothing would have happened. He would not have been alone with that girl . . . And now Huxley is gone, and I . . . I think I could have fallen in love with him if we'd had more time. If I had given us more of a chance . . ."

"I am certain you could have," Hattie said. Vivian wondered if

Mrs. Buchanan could hear the amused undercurrent to her words. "It must have been a terrible shock to discover how he left things in his will."

That prompted a sad little laugh from Mrs. Buchanan. "His death was the shock. But I wasn't . . . I knew how he was leaving things. I tried to persuade him so many times to change his mind, to leave more to me and not his bastard, but he was adamant." Her voice dropped into a whimper. "What am I supposed to do now?"

"It's not so hard to be a widow," Mrs. Wilson said. Vivian could hear the smile in her voice.

Apparently, Mrs. Buchanan could too. "Maybe for someone like you, Henrietta. You have your whole life still ahead of you, and plenty of money with which to live it. But am I to find a third man to marry? At my age? Dear God, the prospect is terrifying."

"Don't sell yourself short, Evangeline. You're a beautiful woman still. And not yet that old. Uncle Huxley was hardly the only man north of fifty in New York looking for a wife."

Mrs. Buchanan sniffed. "At least he remembered Corny somewhat. That's a comfort to a mother. They did get on so well, you know. They shared a drink together nearly every night."

Nearly every night. Vivian's mind had begun to wander, but it latched onto those words like an alley cat pouncing. What better way to gradually poison someone than to share a nightly drink? And if Corny Buchanan had tried one way to get rid of his stepfather, but grown impatient with waiting . . .

The medical examiner had been right. The police weren't looking into the poison at all, or, if they were, they were keeping it under wraps. Mrs. Buchanan would never have mentioned such a thing otherwise.

"Your idea, I presume?" Hattie asked. "Poor Corny would never have thought of something so sociable on his own."

"It was good for them to get to know each other," Mrs. Buchanan said defensively. Vivian could hear the sound of a chair being pushed back, small things being gathered. "If you mean to be comforting, Henrietta, you are falling far short of the mark."

"I often do, unfortunately," Hattie said without much remorse. It sounded like she, too, was standing. "A defect of my character, whatever my intentions. But I am sorry for you, Evangeline. It's plain you aren't happy to have him gone."

"Why would I be happy?" Mrs. Buchanan demanded through a sob. "Really, Henrietta, I don't understand you sometimes."

"I'll see you at the funeral," Hattie said. Vivian thought she could hear a pleased edge to her voice. "My sympathies, once again," she added, accompanied by the sound of Mrs. Buchanan stalking out of the room. She shut the door so firmly behind her that the window in the room where Vivian sat rattled.

A moment later, the door between the two rooms swung open. Vivian sprang to her feet. But Mrs. Wilson only gave her a brief look before turning away. "You may come in now."

They were in a beautiful sitting room, the ladies' parlor, Vivian had once heard the Wilsons' housekeeper call it. It had new paper on the walls since the last time Vivian had been there, a modern, geometric pattern of angles and lines. Her feet sank into the plush carpeting as she walked, and the velvet curtains that framed the windows were so thick and long that they puddled on the floor. Vivian felt sorry for the maids whose job it was to keep them clean. Every bookcase was filled with books—modern novels, the kind Vivian might actually like to read if she ever had the time for that sort of thing.

Hattie settled into one of the thickly upholstered couches with a sigh, the index finger of one hand tapping against her cheek as she surveyed Vivian.

Vivian set the delivery box on the table. She wanted to sit down, too, but she didn't. She didn't know what game Mrs. Wilson was playing, but she didn't want to risk making her mad.

"Well?" Hattie asked at last. "Are you going to say thank you?"

"For what?" Vivian asked, her voice tight. "For showing me how likely it is that I'll be arrested for murder? If she knew she wasn't going to inherit much of anything, she had good reasons *not* to want him dead. That doesn't help me."

Hattie shrugged. "Well, I didn't know what she was going to say," she replied, not sounding concerned at all.

"Unless you think she had some other reason to want him gone?" Vivian asked, eyes narrowing. Mrs. Buchanan might have encouraged her husband and son to have nightly drinks because she was the one slipping poison into Huxley Buchanan's glass. But that only made sense if she had something to gain from his death.

Mrs. Wilson shrugged again. "No, not a woman like Evangeline. All she wanted out of that marriage was better prospects for her son and a more secure life for herself. She got both, and a decent enough husband into the bargain. She's lost most of that with his death."

"Rokesby got something out of it," Vivian pointed out. "Shares in the business, right? Same as you."

Hattie's eyes glittered behind her lashes. "Ten percent interest," she said, her lips pursing in irritation. "Not much of anything at all, in the grand scheme of how these things work. But that's a matter for the future," she added, looking past the walls of the room they were in for a moment. Vivian had the sense that Hattie could see that future, that she had a plan for it. The thought made her shiver.

Hattie's gaze snapped back. "But we were discussing the present moment, I believe." She raised her eyebrows, waiting.

Vivian gritted her teeth. "Thank you," she ground out.

"You're welcome. And now, I believe—"

"I owe you another favor?" Vivian snapped, knowing it was unwise to interrupt but not stopping herself in time. "I thought I was here to make a delivery."

Hattie glanced at the box on the table. "Which I do appreciate. But

I'm not one to waste an opportunity. And . . ." She smiled. "It never hurts to have a girl like you in my debt."

———•———

H ere, I thought the red one would look best on you."
Vivian took the slinky dress from Bea, running her fingers appreciatively across the silk before she folded it carefully and wrapped it in brown paper. "Thanks a million, Bea."

"Happy to help." Bea was smiling, but she looked nervous. "And it's okay if you make an alteration or two. Gotta look swell tonight, right?"

"That's the goal," Vivian agreed, though her mind was a thousand miles away when she said it. The lodge ball was in just a few hours. And hopefully, hopefully, she'd be able to find out what Corny Rokesby was up to, what he had been up to the morning his stepfather had died.

Because if it hadn't been him, and if it hadn't been Huxley Buchanan's wife or business partners who wanted him dead . . .

"Bea," Vivian asked before she could stop herself. "You've known Honor for a long time now, yeah?"

"Sure," Bea said, sounding wary. One hand traced absent circles over the rough wood of the table where they sat, and she didn't quite meet Vivian's eyes. "Ever since I started working at the Nightingale."

"Do you think she could kill someone?" The words came out barely louder than a whisper. The silence in the room was painful. It was the closest they had ever come to the night neither of them wanted to talk about. Vivian stared at her friend, and Bea stared at her hands.

"I think anyone could," she said, lifting her eyes at last. "You or me. Florence." She swallowed. "Honor. But we'd need a damn good reason to do it."

Vivian nodded as she gathered up her package. "Thanks again for the dress," she said, her voice hoarse. "I'll let you know how it goes."

Bea tried to smile and failed. "Good luck."

181

TWENTY-TWO

H oly moly, Viv, don't you look smashing," Mags said, giving Vivian's borrowed gown a look up and down. Vivian, feeling self-conscious, resisted the urge to touch the rhinestones at her ears or the feathered headband that was pinned across her forehead. Mags gave Leo an equally approving glance, smiling sideways at him as she slid into the cab's back seat. "I've seen you around, I think, from time to time? Making puppy eyes at Viv and wowing on the dance floor. I always thought you looked like a swell time."

Leo, dressed to the nines in what Vivian was sure was a custom-made suit and matching hat, gave her a wink. "I am, sweetheart."

Mags laughed. "Lordy lord, I'm guessing you have your hands full with this one, don't you?" she said, rolling her eyes at Vivian. Vivian couldn't tell what she was wearing, but it couldn't be a gown—it was short enough to be hidden under an elegant little coat. Mags leaned forward to give the cabdriver the address for their destination.

Vivian frowned as Mags flopped back against the seat with a happy sigh. "I thought the place was in Harlem?"

"It is," Mags said, practically bouncing in her seat with excitement. "But we're heading somewhere else, first, to change and meet up with our ride for the evening."

Vivian stared at her in confusion. "Change?"

———•——

Mags strode up to the front of the pretty brownstone and leaned on the buzzer. The houses were only three stories tall in this part of the city, and slender rather than hulking, but the glimpse of elegant furnishings and soaring ceilings that Vivian could see through the bow window still shouted the wealth of whoever lived there. She tugged nervously at the shoulders of her borrowed gown—she'd had time for a few alterations, so at least it fit well—wondering who exactly Mags was taking them to meet. She only relaxed a little when Leo took her hand and squeezed it.

But when the door swung open, Vivian found herself staring at a familiar, sandy-haired face. "Jimmy?" she demanded, too stunned to be polite.

Pretty Jimmy Allen beamed at them. "God almighty, doll, you look smashing," he said, echoing Mags's compliment without knowing it. He gestured broadly to welcome them inside. "Come on in. I take it Mags didn't tell you who got your tickets, then?"

"No, she didn't," Vivian said, hovering awkwardly in the hall as Jimmy closed the door behind them.

"Didn't want you to cut out the middleman," Mags laughed, pausing only to plant a quick kiss in the air next to Jimmy's cheek before she snatched up a black bag that was waiting in the hall for her and clattered up the stairs.

Vivian had found out months ago that Jimmy and Mags both belonged to the part of New York that had houses on the Upper East Side, mansions on Long Island, and old family businesses funded by even older money. But she'd never seen him outside the Nightingale, where distinctions like that didn't matter so much. Even once she had become part of the staff instead of a customer, Jimmy had still always treated her like a pal, dragging her onto the floor when she was available to kick up her heels for the Charleston, or treating her to a cocktail on her nights off. Unlike most of his friends, though, Jimmy never tried to get frisky with her or any of the girls he danced with. Vivian knew why—he had once described himself to her, only a little coyly, as *not the marrying type*. But even in the underground world of the Nightingale, he always seemed to prefer to keep his private life private, away from the eyes of any friends or neighbors who might cross his path.

Even the trust of a shared secret, though, was not quite enough to set her at ease as he ushered her into his small but opulent sitting room, where light danced off a crystal chandelier. Vivian was almost afraid to sit down, but Leo, always at ease no matter where he found himself, was already happily accepting the offer of a drink and a seat.

"And what's your name, tall-dark-and-handsome?" Jimmy asked as he poured their cocktails. He wore a beautiful brocade robe—was it silk?—over loose trousers, and Vivian couldn't say for certain whether he had a shirt on under it. Was he not coming with them? "Or are we skipping those kinds of formalities tonight?"

"Leo," he replied easily, lifting his glass in a small toast. "Thanks for arranging things."

"My pleasure," Jimmy said, handing a drink to Vivian as well, as she perched uneasily on the edge of a wingback chair. "I'm just glad Mags found someone to keep an eye on her tonight. She got plenty pouty when I first said I wouldn't take her along."

"Why wouldn't you?" Vivian asked, taking a sip. The liquor was top-shelf, but she didn't want to get tipsy. Not when she was going to need to keep her eyes and ears open all night.

Jimmy gave a secretive smile, shrugging one shoulder. "I don't think there's any harm in her getting out to enjoy herself. But a girl like her in a place like that could find trouble just as easy as she might find fun. And I can't spend my whole night keeping an eye on her."

"Well, we'll be able to do that," Leo said, crossing one ankle over the opposite knee and leaning back in his chair. "Or, more likely, I will. Viv's got her own business to take care of."

"So I heard. Corny Rokesby, is it?" Jimmy said, giving Vivian an assessing glance. "Never tell me you've got a sweet spot for an odd duck like him?"

"Not likely," Vivian said. Even though she wasn't going to drink it, she was glad the glass of liquor gave her something to do with her hands. "Do double exes mean anything to you?"

"Exes like the letter?" Jimmy frowned, then shook his head. "Should they?"

"No reason they should. But they mean something to Rokesby, and I'm hoping to find out what."

"Viv . . ." Jimmy hesitated, glancing down at his own glass. When he looked up, his normal, easygoing expression was gone. "What do you know about the lodge balls?"

"You mean the masquerade portion of it?" Vivian asked, as carefully as he had.

Jimmy nodded. "That. And . . ." He glanced hesitantly at Leo, as though not sure how to phrase what he wanted to say.

Vivian could guess, though. "And from what I've heard, seems like there's plenty of men and women taking the opportunity for what you might call personal business, right? Business of the romantic kind that maybe they can't pursue in other places?"

Jimmy nodded again, still looking wary. "And I know that *you,* Viv . . . well, I've seen the way certain dance hall owners look at you. Or looked at you, in the past," he added quickly, nodding politely at Leo. "So I know you're not . . . we've got a few things in common, yeah? You get it."

She did. And she knew why Jimmy didn't want to just say that he was a fella who liked other fellas, and that Corny Rokesby might be too. People like him—like her—had to be careful what they said, and who they said it to. And Jimmy didn't know Leo.

"He gets it too," Vivian said quietly, nodding toward Leo. "We're not looking to spoil anyone's fun, Jimmy. Or tell anyone who might care what that fun is. We just want to know . . ." She paused, considering how much to share. "You heard his stepdad died?"

A different sort of wariness crept over Jimmy's face. "I heard. I heard it wasn't exactly what you'd call natural causes. But what has that got to do with you?"

"I wish it had nothing to do with me," Vivian said, the words coming out brittle. "It does, but it's a whole mess to explain. Rokesby had something going on the day Buchanan died, and he has that same something going on tonight. I need to know what it is."

"Okay." Jimmy let out a huff of air. "That sounds . . . I can live with that, if that's all it is. Otherwise the night ends here and now, pal. I'm not on board with prying into that part of anyone's personal life."

"Me neither," Vivian said, her face feeling hot. Preferences like theirs weren't the sort of thing people discussed openly—it was too uncertain, too much potential for danger if the wrong person overheard. The fact that Jimmy had brought it up, even if they were both still mostly talking around it, showed how serious he was.

"And I'm not saying that's what Rokesby's there for," Jimmy said quickly. "I've got no idea what the fella gets up to, or what those, what did you call 'ems? Double exes might be. But I had to lay out some ground rules."

"Sure thing," Vivian said, taking a large gulp of her cocktail before she remembered that she hadn't meant to drink more of it. Clearing her throat, she asked, to change the subject, "Why did Mags run off when we got here?"

"Oh that." Jimmy stood, smiling once more. "She wanted to change for the party. Which I need to do, too. So. Make yourselves at home." He gestured broadly around the room. "We'll be back down soon."

Vivian watched the door close behind him, then took a deep breath. Setting her glass down, she moved to the sofa where Leo was sitting, sliding across it until she could bump her shoulder up against his. "You okay, tall-dark-and-handsome?" she asked playfully. He had started looking serious before Jimmy left the room, and it worried her.

It took a moment for him to answer. "She still looks at you that way, you know."

Vivian didn't have to ask who he meant. But when she pictured Honor looking at her, she didn't see the heat or the yearning that used to spark between them. She saw the almost guilty look that Honor had tried to hide from her. "No, she doesn't."

"Viv, I'm not an idiot," Leo said, standing so he could turn and look at her. Vivian felt cold without the warmth of him pressed against her, and she wrapped her arms around herself protectively. "I know—I know the two of you were close. I asked you about it almost the first day we met, remember?"

Vivian wanted to argue that they had never been close. Honor had always put up walls between them, and Vivian hadn't been much better herself. But she had a feeling that saying as much to Leo wouldn't help just then. "You did," she said cautiously. "But you're the one I'm here with, right?"

"Right, sure, but . . ." Leo let out a frustrated sigh. "But do you want to be?"

Vivian stared at him. "What the hell does that mean?"

"I saw you two last night, Viv," he growled. "When I finished handing off that letter to Bruiser George. You two were looking pretty cozy. Like you were in a world of your own."

"We weren't . . . what?" Vivian stared at him. There had been nothing cozy about her chat with Honor last night. "Why are you starting a fight now?"

"I'm just telling you what I saw."

"No, you're not," Vivian snapped. "You couldn't have because that wasn't what was happening at all. You want to start a fight, just like you wanted to start a fight with George two nights ago."

"That's not—"

"And you know what I think?" Vivian interrupted him, just barely remembering to keep her voice low. "I think it's because the person you *want* to fight with is your uncle, and you can't do that."

"You don't know a damn thing about my uncle," Leo snapped.

"You think I don't?" Vivian felt hot and cold all over, and she wasn't sure whether it was anger or something else. "You think I've got no idea what it's like to have a family that doesn't want you? You could walk out that door right now, and I wouldn't be surprised one bit. It would just be business as usual because everyone—"

She clamped her mouth shut so tightly that it hurt, horrified by what she had been about to say. *Everyone leaves.* Whether it was true or not, it sure felt like it some days. She stared at Leo, her hands balled into fists by her sides. She was shaking, and she didn't care if he saw it. "He's a bastard, Leo. You've always known he's a bastard. So don't go taking it out on me. I've got plenty else to worry about right now."

A muscle jumped in Leo's temple. "I'm not going to walk out," he said at last.

"Good." Vivian eyed the glass that she had set down and, before she could think better of it, downed the rest of it in one gulp.

"Nothing's going to happen to you, Viv," he added, his voice growing gentler at last, the Leo that was always there when she needed it. He reached for her hand, and she let him take it, let him pull her to her feet. But even the warmth of his palm, the rough feel of the calluses on his fingers, couldn't soothe her this time. She felt like she was going to jump out of her skin. "I won't let it, no matter what he says."

"I've only got two days left after tonight, Leo," she said, her voice coming out hoarse. "If we don't turn up anything on Rokesby, I don't know what to do next."

"We'll find something," Leo said, pulling her close enough that he could wrap his arms around her and rest his chin on the top of her head. Vivian let him. It wasn't an apology, but as raw as they were both feeling, it was probably as good as she could hope for. "I promise. We're going to find out who did it."

She wanted to tell him not to make promises. She wanted to tell him that she was getting scared. She wanted him to admit they might run out of time, so she wouldn't feel so alone in her growing fear.

Instead, she wrapped her arms around his waist and buried her face against his shirtfront, filling her mind with the smell of starch and wintergreen and the spice of his cologne, pretending that she believed him.

"Yeah," she whispered. They were headed somewhere known for the hundreds of secrets that were kept behind its walls. All they had to do was find out what Cornelius Rokesby's were. "We will."

———•———

Mags returned first, strutting down the staircase to join them in the hall. Vivian stared, not bothering to hide her surprise. Mags wore a tailored men's evening suit, jacket left open over a three-button vest so she could stick one hand casually in her pocket. A slim black tie circled under the collar of a white shirt so crisply ironed that Vivian could smell the starch, and her brown curls were stuffed underneath a top hat. Just above her upper lip, she had drawn a thin curl of a mustache.

"Well?" she asked, leaning one hand against the banister and grinning at them. "What do you think?"

"Don't you look handsome," Vivian said, finding her voice at last. Handsome wasn't quite the right word—it was impossible for bubbly

Mags to look anything but cute, no matter what she wore. But she smiled broadly, clearly pleased with the compliment.

"I thought so too!" she said eagerly, bounding down the last few steps. "I figured, when in Rome, right? Or when heading to Rome." She laughed. "Golly, I had no idea men's clothes were so comfortable. Though it's a bit odd to be so buttoned up," she added, sliding one finger inside the collar and tugging a little. "But I'm sure I'll get used to it."

Before Vivian could respond further, a throat cleared with a delicate *hmm* from the top of the stairs. They all glanced up, including Mags, to see the elegant woman smiling coyly at them as she glided down the stairs.

Her gown—pure silk, Vivian could tell even from a distance, by the way it slid around her hips and legs—was so fashionable it had probably been made just that month. Pearls draped around her neck and down her stylish, boyish figure. Her bobbed hair was wavy and blond, held back by a netted cap that sparkled in the electric light of the hall's chandelier as she reached the bottom of the stairs, and a white-and-black fur stole was tossed almost carelessly over one shoulder.

The glamorous woman smiled Jimmy's smile. "Am I all in order?" she asked, giving her hair a delicate fluff.

"You look sensational," Mags said, grinning as she held out her arm. "Shall we?"

Vivian tried not to stare as they all climbed into the car that waited for them outside. In the face of all that glamour, she felt awkward in her borrowed dress and dancing shoes with worn heels. She fingered the edge of her coat as they settled into their seats, touching the hem that she had mended just last week and hoping no one had noticed the repair. She'd leave her coat in the car, she decided, when they got to the lodge. Better to be cold than look ragged.

"I'm guessing you won't be going by Jimmy tonight?" Leo asked.

"You may call me Annabel Lee tonight," Jimmy—Annabel—said. Her voice had changed along with the rest of her appearance, into something softer and richer, but still with the husky edge of a man's deepness.

"Bit of a risky name," Leo pointed out as the car jolted into motion. Vivian glanced out the window, watching the city streets slide by like a dream. "That poem doesn't end too happily."

"You're a fan of Poe, then?" Annabel sounded delighted. "My, you are full of surprises, tall-dark-and-handsome."

"Blegh," Mags said, making a face with her tongue pointing out. "Too stuffy. Don't you two read anything modern?"

Vivian, feeling more awkward than ever, shrank back into her seat, wishing she knew what they were talking about. Maybe she should ask to borrow some of Bea's books of poems. But who had time to read that stuff?

Before she could feel too left out, though, Annabel turned to her, leaning forward even though there was clearly no one around to hear them. "Now that you can't get away, Vivian, I'm going to need some gossip. What is going on with your Danny-boy recently? He's mellowed in a way I can't quite put my finger on . . ."

Vivian laughed, suddenly feeling less out of place. This she could handle. "You haven't heard? He got married."

"What?" Mags, who had been enjoying slouching in her seat, trouser-clad legs stuck out in front of her and knees propped wide, bolted upright. She looked horrified. "No! Why is everyone always getting married? That's when you stop having fun!"

The other three laughed. "Not everyone is fresh out of school, sweetheart," Leo said with a grin. "There are people, you know, who think settling down with someone special *is* fun."

He didn't look at Vivian as he said it; she didn't know whether she was relieved or hurt.

Mags made another face. "But that sounds so boring . . ."

As the gossip carried them north to Harlem, Vivian pushed Leo and their fight and thoughts of the future out of her head. She had plenty to worry about in the present before she needed to think about what came next.

At last, they joined a stream of cars all converging on a single building, nearly a full block long and built of cream-colored stone, its windows blazing with light and music pouring from the door every time it opened to admit someone. As their progress slowed to a crawl, Mags pressed her face against the window, taking in the spectacle of hundreds—were there already thousands?—of glamorous men and women. Vivian, after a moment of hesitation, slid across the seat to peer out too. Her heart was hammering against her chest as she scanned the people, wondering if Corny Rokesby would, in fact, be there tonight.

At last, their car reached the front of the line. As a uniformed attendant reached for the door, Annabel smiled. "Welcome, friends, to the famous Rockland Palace and the Hamilton Lodge Ball." She turned toward the door, then paused, glancing back at them all, her brows raised. "Try not to get in too much trouble. Or if you do, don't tell anyone you came with me."

"Wait, it just occurred to me," Mags piped up as the door swung open. "Do I need a new name for the night?"

———————

Vivian had thought, after years of dancing and working at the Nightingale, that there wasn't much in New York's nightlife that could surprise or overwhelm her.

The Hamilton Lodge Ball proved her wrong. After presenting their tickets at the door, they were surrounded by a sea of people, the sound of the crowd filling the high ceilings and wide halls, competing with the music that flowed from the ballroom. Overhead, spectators peered down from dozens of boxes, watching the dancers and the mingling crowds alike.

"Too bad we don't have a box," Mags said, sounding breathless as Leo spotted a bar and led them toward it. "Maybe next time we can get a reservation for one?" she added hopefully. "It's murderously hot down here."

Annabel raised her brows. "Next time?" Mags just grinned in response and accepted the cocktail that Leo handed her.

"Cheers, friends," he said after he finished handing their drinks around, and they all raised their glasses, though their eyes were almost immediately drawn back to the crowd. It was well worth watching, ball gowns and frock coats as much on display as slinky evening dresses and sharply tailored jackets. There were people dressed as biblical virgins, Greek gods and goddesses, and more than one shepherdess with dozens of flounces on their skirts. Some women were dressed as if they were about to perform a burlesque striptease on the vaudeville stage. Vivian stared at all of them, drinking in the beautiful, scandalous clothes.

The band played a smooth rendition of "Yes, Sir, That's My Baby." But the dancers weren't as good as the ones at the Nightingale. The dancing, clearly, was there to give partygoers something to do, but it wasn't the point of the evening.

The point was to see and be seen. To be part of the crowd. And— for more than half the people there—to take the anything-goes opportunity to be whoever they wanted.

"Golly, those folks have slow feet," Mags said, eyeing the dancers as critically as Vivian had done a moment before. She gave Leo a look from the corner of her eye. "What do you say we go for a spin?"

He glanced at Vivian. "I don't know how much attention we want to be drawing tonight," he said slowly.

"Oh, come on, be a sport," Mags begged. "Look, there's lots of fellas dancing with other fellas out there, it won't draw any attention at all."

That made him laugh. "I meant the dancing, kid, not your outfit," he said, shaking his head. "I think Viv wanted to keep a lower profile tonight."

"Well, that works out just fine then, doesn't it?" Mags pointed out. "We'll go make a scene on the dance floor, and Viv can do . . ." She shrugged. "Whatever she's going to do. Let's shake a leg. *Please?*"

"Go ahead," Vivian said, taking Leo's drink from him and nudging him with her shoulder. Someone needed to keep an eye on Mags—that had been the deal. And Vivian couldn't look for Rokesby if she was babysitting all night. "I'll meet you back here in . . . maybe an hour?" She didn't have a watch, but there was a hulking, sonorous grandfather clock in the hall that she'd heard booming a few minutes before.

Leo still looked uncomfortable, but at last he nodded. "You'll be okay without me?"

"Just peachy," Vivian said. "You get out there and show 'em how it's done."

Mags laughed with delight, handing over her glass as well and grabbing Leo's arm.

Vivian took a sip of her drink as she watched them go. Everywhere she looked was packed with people. And even though the Grand United Order of Odd Fellows, the Hamilton Lodge fraternity, was a Black organization, the ballroom was awash in faces of every color. Everyone flirted openly with whoever they wanted to, whether men, women, or those who couldn't quite be pinned down as either. No one batted an eye at even the most outrageous outfits. Absolutely no one was hiding their liquor.

And why would they bother? If the police raided a place like this, they were as likely to arrest attendees for indecency as imbibing, so the partygoers might as well enjoy themselves.

Besides, there were too many people to round up. Vivian downed the rest of her drink recklessly. She was probably safer here than she'd ever been at the Nightingale. The thought made her heartbeat speed up with excitement before it stuttered back to reality.

She wasn't safe anywhere. Not really. And she needed to keep her eyes open and her mind sharp if she was going to find out what she needed to know.

She pulled her thoughts back to earth as Annabel beckoned for her to follow. They approached a group of women, some dressed with modern flair like Annabel, a few in old-fashioned ball gowns. As Annabel exchanged air kisses and pleasantries, Vivian's eyes went to the beadwork on the women's gowns. She had spent too many hours making dresses not to think about how long each panel would have taken to complete. It wasn't until she lifted her eyes that she realized several of the women wore wigs and, in spite of perfectly rouged cheekbones and long, smoky eyelashes, likely lived their everyday lives as men.

"Corny Rokesby?" one of them was just repeating. Vivian's attention snapped back to the conversation. "He's here. I do believe I saw him about half an hour ago over there"—she gestured vaguely toward one of the back halls—"talking with some scowly little man in a checked suit that I didn't know at all. Terrible suit. Terrible hair," she added with a throaty laugh. "All gone on the top, though he'd combed quite a lot over from the sides in an attempt to hide it."

"Absolutely appalling for Corny to be here tonight, you know," another added, her silk fan moving briskly in a losing battle against the heat. "Did you know his stepfather died just a few days ago?"

"No, I hadn't heard!" another exclaimed. "What happened?"

"Oh darling, it's even worse than that," the first woman said, clearly relishing every word. "He didn't die. He was *murdered*."

"I thought that was just a rumor . . ."

As they traded gossip, Annabel introduced her as simply "My friend Miss Vivian," and the others accepted that with no questions. That wasn't surprising—Vivian was used to the Nightingale, where most folks shared little about themselves beyond a name and an occasional hint of what their daytime lives might look like. She smiled at them but kept her mouth shut as she sipped her drink and listened.

Someone mentioned Buchanan's bastard daughter, speculating about who she might be and what she would do with his money. The others were less interested in the daughter than in how Mrs. Buchanan had reacted.

"She hasn't been seen since it happened," one woman said with obvious relish. "Can you imagine being the man who turned his wife out into the street after his death?"

"Oh, but didn't she just marry him for his money anyway?" another said dismissively. "She wanted her useless son to join his firm, because the good Lord knows Corny Rokesby wouldn't make anything of himself unless he was forced to. Would *you* reward that with any kind of real inheritance?"

"Mm, and we're all models for making something of ourselves, dear," Annabel said with a roll of her eyes while the others laughed.

"Are you including yourself in that statement?" one of them asked.

"Oh, absolutely," Annabel said, smiling playfully. "I'm useless as they come, except on the dance floor."

The conversation drifted away from Buchanan's death, and Vivian started to feel lightheaded from the heat and the smoky air. After a minute, Annabel caught her eye and gestured delicately toward the bar, making graceful excuses as she ushered Vivian away.

"Thank you for that," Vivian said quietly once their conversation would be lost in the noise of the crowd around the bar.

"I hope you can find him, sweetheart," Annabel said, setting her glass aside. "And now, I'm off to enjoy my evening, which means you and your handsome fella need to keep an eye on Mags, as we discussed. She's exactly the sort of bright young thing who could get herself in a heap of trouble without even realizing it."

"But you're not worried about me?" Vivian asked, one corner of her mouth kicking up self-deprecatingly. "Is that because I'm not young enough or not bright enough?"

"It's because you know how the world works, doll. And Mags is still figuring it out." Annabel gave her hair a fluff and blew Vivian a kiss. "See you around?"

"See you around."

Vivian took a deep breath once she was on her own, resisting the urge to sink back into the woodwork. The air was heavy with cigarette smoke and the scent of perfume. From where she stood, she could just see the grandfather clock, though its noise was lost, and she thought it was just after eleven o'clock. Early in the night by some standards, but time was ticking away, and she didn't want to waste any of it.

She headed in the direction of the hallway where Corny Rokesby had been spotted. Vivian wished she had thought to ask if he had been wearing a costume. But she was glad for the crowd as she wove her way through on quickstep-light feet. No one noticed her. No one would remember her.

She left the front doors behind; whatever *XX* was, she didn't think it would be happening in the entrance hall. Instead, she found the stairs and wandered up, trying to stay near groups of people so she didn't stand out. The second floor was crowded, especially near the boxes that overlooked the ballroom. The third floor, though, was nearly empty; there was no view of the downstairs from there, and the halls were narrower, with smaller rooms and few open spaces for guests to mingle. Vivian could guess that, as the night wore on, they would be the preferred spot for partygoers to sneak off for a bit of necking or petting—or whatever else they wanted to get up to. But the evening hadn't grown quite that naughty yet.

She moved carefully and quickly, listening for the sound of voices. But the few people she did run into up there didn't seem to be looking for anything except a bit of quiet or privacy.

She hurried back downstairs, tagging along with a group of costumed partygoers as they made their way toward the ballroom. She hadn't seen him on any of the floors . . . could Rokesby be meeting with someone in one of the boxes?

The band had just struck up a brassy Charleston when she arrived. On the other side of the room, she saw Mags abandoning her drink to drag Leo back onto the floor. Vivian craned her neck to see into the boxes, wondering if she would be able to recognize Rokesby from that distance if he was in one of them.

"Ready to dust off your shoes, gorgeous?"

Vivian turned to find a stranger, his brown hair turning handsomely gray around the temples, eyeing her with heavy-lidded appreciation. When she looked at him, he gave her a slow smile that she could guess was an invitation to more than a dance. "You look like someone who loves to move fast."

"I like it just fine on the dance floor," she said, her voice light but firm. If Corny Rokesby was in one of the boxes, the best way to spot him would be from the dance floor, though the song might be too fast to get more than a quick look at each of them. But she had no intention of spending the rest of her night escaping a fella who thought a dance entitled him to something more. "But I'm not interested in anything else, and I've got a mean right hook when I need it."

To her relief, the man laughed instead of getting offended. "I believe it, pretty girl. Dancing it is." He smiled as he offered his hand. "I'm awful fun at that too."

His grip on her hand was light but firm, the hold of a confident lead. Vivian couldn't help smiling back. "I believe it," she said, echoing him. He laughed and pulled her hip to hip. A moment later they were off.

He hadn't been lying; he was a fun dancer. He swung her across the floor with confidence, leaving plenty of space for her to add her own flair to their movement. They wove their way through the other dancers with wild kicks and stomps, splitting apart, mirroring each other, meeting up again only for him to spin her in the opposite direction with a light touch to her hip, her elbow, her back. With each movement, Vivian tossed her head back, eyeing the people in the boxes.

If Annabel's friend had spotted Rokesby so easily in the hallway, she suspected he wasn't wearing a costume. So she let her eyes sweep past the elaborately dressed royals and sailors. She spotted a few men in suits, but one of them had a beard. Another was busy necking with someone in an elaborate white wig at least half a foot high.

But that didn't mean it wasn't Rokesby. *XX* was as likely to be an affair he was having as it was anything else. Vivian tried to spot the couple again as her partner caught her around the waist to spin them in a tight circle, their steps slowing gradually as the music wound its way through the final bars of the song. If it was, that would mean he had been with someone the day Buchanan died, and if she could figure out who—

Vivian forgot what she was thinking as her partner slowed them to a stop. She ended facing the far side of the ballroom and a short gentleman in a loudly patterned checked suit, the sides of his hair combed over the bald spot on top. He had just extracted himself from a conversation, and she could see the scowl on his face from across the room.

"I was right about those fast feet of yours, pretty girl," her partner was just murmuring as the applause died down and the band launched into a foxtrot. "What do you say we go for another—"

"Wish I could," Vivian said quickly. "But I'm meeting some friends. Maybe another time?" She flashed him a smile as she slipped out of his encircling arm. It *had* been a fun dance, but she had other things to think about.

The little man in the checked suit was hurrying around the edge of the ballroom; Vivian expected him to head toward the main doors. But instead, he went toward one of the alcoves that were tucked along the walls. Most of them held chairs where dancers could rest their feet, watch the crowd, and steal a private moment or two. The one that the scowling man was heading toward was empty except for a silk screen, beautifully painted with birds and blossoming tree branches. Vivian, still trailing yards behind him, frowned in surprise as the man ducked around the edge of the screen and disappeared.

She stopped at the edge of the alcove, waiting for him to come out. When he didn't, Vivian glanced around the room, wondering if anyone else had noticed his disappearance. But no one was watching; they were all too busy with their own business for the night.

Vivian waited a moment, wondering if she dared. But if he was the man who had been talking with Rokesby earlier, that was something to go on when currently she had nothing else. Gritting her teeth, she walked into the alcove and ducked around the screen.

The space behind it was deeper than she had expected, and there was a door at the end of it. When Vivian inched it open a crack, there was light coming up, and a staircase leading down. The building had a damn basement, she realized. Why hadn't she thought of that before?

She could hear faint voices from the bottom of the stairs, almost drowned out by the music from behind her. There was more than one person down there.

Vivian hesitated only a moment. Should she find Leo and tell him where she was going? If she got into trouble, it would be good for someone to know where she had gone.

But that might take too long. What if someone locked the door? What if the people down there left before she got back? What if Mags got too interested and decided to crash whatever private party was happening?

She didn't want to just stand there, waiting for someone to find her. If she went down there and needed an excuse for appearing, she could always pretend to be a drunk partygoer who had found her way into the basement by accident. It wasn't an unlikely story. She had gotten herself out of difficult jams before.

Vivian started down the steps, closing the door behind her.

There were electric lights in the stairwell—not too bright, but enough that she could see where she was going, even with the door closed. The noise of the ballroom grew more distant as she went down, the murmur of voices becoming louder. They weren't angry voices, she was relieved to hear. And there were men and women both, which meant she hopefully wouldn't be too out of place.

There was another door at the bottom of the staircase. Before she could talk herself out of it or think through all the things that could go wrong, Vivian turned the knob.

The voices were louder here, but the room was almost completely empty. It was also smaller than she expected, a passageway more than anything else. Opposite her was a doorway with a red velvet curtain pulled across it. The voices came from the other side, a polite murmur. Between her and whoever was on the other side stood a man in a black suit.

He watched her as she let the door fall closed behind her, his face impassive, not moving or saying anything. Just waiting. Vivian's eyes darted from one end of the room to the other before settling back on him. Beside him stood a table shaped like a very short column with a black lacquered box on top.

Vivian swallowed, then decided that there was nothing to be lost by being friendly. "Hi," she said, giving the man a big smile.

Was she imagining the little flicker of a smile around the corners of his mouth in response? God, she hoped not. "Good evening, madam," the man replied gravely, giving her a slow, deliberate nod.

Another beat of silence. Vivian resisted the urge to bounce up and down on her heels. "Well?" she said at last, gesturing toward the curtain behind him. "Are you going to let me in?"

This time there was no smile. Instead, a frown appeared between his brows. "I believe madam has forgotten to give her passphrase," he said, speaking with a deliberate pace that Vivian recognized. She had used it often enough herself with customers who'd had one drink too many and were having trouble following directions from the people trying to stop them from barging into the wrong washroom.

Passphrase. "Of course," Vivian said, while her stomach churned with panic. "My passphrase. Golly, they're hard to remember after a few glasses of champagne, aren't they?"

"I can imagine they would be," the man said. He was still firmly planted between her and whatever was happening behind that curtain.

She gave him another bright smile. "Don't you think that, just this once, you could—"

"As always, madam, rules are rules," he said, shaking his head. He gestured toward the door behind her. "Perhaps tonight you should—"

"Wait," Vivian said quickly, cutting him off. If this was Corny Rokesby's *XX,* there was no way she was giving up now. "I remember it, I promise."

XX. Each *XX* entry in his appointment book had something written next to it.

"It was . . ."

Are those poems next to them? Mags had asked. Not poems, but . . .

Vivian cleared her throat. "Violet," she said slowly, watching the man as she spoke. His shoulders, which had been stiff and pulled up, as though he were preparing for something unpleasant, were relaxing once more. She wanted to shout with triumph, but she kept a disarming smile pasted across her face while she tried to picture the words Rokesby had written. "Charmer. Snakebite . . ."

Damn it, what was the last one?

"Gin."

This time, she was sure she hadn't imagined the smile as he stepped over to the column-shaped table. Flicking open the top of the box with a single finger, he pulled out a white half-mask, black ribbons dangling from its sides, the whole thing sparkling with glass beads. He held it out to her with a little bow.

Vivian took it, trying to hold back the urge to laugh. What was this baloney? But hiding her face from whoever was on the other side of that curtain probably wasn't the worst idea in the world. As she tied it across her face, the man stepped aside and gestured toward the velvet curtain. "Enjoy your evening, madam."

"Thanks so much!" she said brightly, giving him a little wave, which he returned with a bemused nod. She pulled the velvet curtain back just enough that she could step past it.

The first room had been smaller than she expected. This one was larger, though half of it was still left in shadow. There were three small, round tables set up in the middle of the room, though only a few people sat at them. A handful of other men and women hovered near the chairs or around the edges of the room, some chatting, others silent. Though they were all dressed for the party upstairs, none of them were wearing costumes, other than half-masks like the one she had been given.

Vivian had the feeling that this gathering, whatever it was, was the real reason each of them had found their way to the lodge ball that night.

Two women in skimpy, spangled outfits with feathers in their hair were moving through the room with trays, offering the guests glasses of champagne. Everyone she saw accepted, some of them toasting each other with the familiarity of old acquaintances. Or maybe rivals— their smiles weren't exactly friendly. Others tossed back their drinks with grim determination or sipped them slowly, leaning back in their chairs as they surveyed their surroundings.

Vivian didn't much want another drink herself; she'd had plenty upstairs already and getting fuzzy-headed didn't sound like such a good idea when she still didn't know what was going on.

But she didn't want to stand out either. When the waitress came to her, Vivian accepted a glass, lifting it to her lips and taking the smallest sip possible as she tried to look around without being too obvious.

The people were well worth looking at, even with their masks on. Every tie and handkerchief there was silk; every gown was beaded or fringed, and to her eye, clearly hand-sewn. The weight of money was thick in the air. As her gaze moved around the room, Vivian suddenly realized why.

Each table had a clear glass box set in its center. All the boxes were locked with small, heavy padlocks. And clearly visible inside each were three unopened packs of cards and two trays of ivory dice.

Gambling. *XX* was code for gambling—exclusive and, she could guess from the wealth on display, very high-stakes gambling. Vivian didn't know whether to laugh or run for the door. She had no experience with cards or craps and knew she couldn't bluff her way through a single game. But she didn't want to leave before . . .

Vivian turned slowly, still hiding behind her champagne, to eye the rest of the guests. There. He was slouching in one corner, his masked face turned away from the room as he talked with one of the other gamblers. But she recognized those bright red curls and the way he tapped his fingers against his thigh in a fidgety, anxious rhythm. She hoped, for his sake, that he didn't do that while he was gambling.

If he was here tonight, that probably meant that the day his stepfather was murdered, he was busy losing money at the craps table. Or maybe winning it at poker. Either way, he couldn't have been doing that and killing Buchanan at the same time.

But maybe he had lost early and headed home. Someone had been sticking arsenic in Buchanan's drinks, after all, and who better than the stepson who lived with him? Maybe Rokesby had been content to wait for his inheritance until he had stumbled home that day, broke and desperate, and wanted to hurry things up. Or maybe Buchanan had found out about the gambling, and they had gotten into a fight—

Vivian was so busy thinking through all the ways that Rokesby might still be guilty that it took her a moment to notice the scowly man in the checked suit. He was stationed at the opposite wall, the only one there not wearing a mask, watching the room with a greasy, narrow-eyed gaze. And as that gaze found her, he frowned.

Vivian's stomach clenched. He had been talking to Rokesby upstairs, which meant the masks were to protect their identities from each other. The scowling man must know who everyone was.

He would know that she didn't belong.

Vivian kept her gaze moving around the room, turning slowly away from the man in the checked suit, not wanting him to realize that she had seen him watching her. Her fingers tightened around the stem of her glass. She wasn't that far from the door. It would be easy enough to slip out, and—

"Hello again, pretty girl."

Vivian started, spilling champagne over her fingers, as the suave voice spoke right near her ear. Spinning around, she found herself facing her partner from the Charleston upstairs, the wings of gray hair at his temples looking like an elegant extension of his own mask. He grinned at her and took the hand holding the champagne in his own.

"Dear, dear," he murmured. "Let's not have that go to waste." Before she could protest, he had lifted her hand to his mouth and kissed away the drops of champagne.

Vivian, hot all over, pulled it away as soon as she could without spilling more. "I told you I was only interested in a dance," she said coldly, though she kept her voice low enough that no one else in the room would hear.

He only laughed, releasing her without complaint. "Well, pretty girl, clearly you're interested in more than that," he said, gesturing around the room. "If I had known we were heading to the same place, I would have offered to escort you down. But . . ." He looked her over once more. "I don't think I've seen you at one of these before?" There was a curious lilt to his voice, and she saw his brows rise behind his mask as he waited for a response.

He was a regular, then. Which meant he'd know whether Rokesby had been at the last one or not. Vivian gave him a flirting smile while she tried to remember what she had read in Rokesby's appointment book. "My pal would have gotten me into the one on the fifteenth, but it's harder to slip away in the daytime, isn't it? At least, for a girl like me." She gave him an unsubtle look up and down while she took another sip of champagne. "I imagine a fella like you has a lot more say in how you spend your days."

He laughed again. "True enough, I suppose. Though now I'm curious who among our fellow players got to know you before I did."

It was the opening she was waiting for. Vivian tilted her head toward Corny Rokesby. "My fire-haired friend over there."

"Mr. Red?" The man glanced at Corny, looking surprised. "I bet he's glad you weren't there after all. No man likes to have a pretty girl see him lose that badly."

Vivian's heart thumped painfully against her ribs. If Corny had lost money . . . "He never could get his fidgets under control," she guessed, trying to sound as if she already knew what she was talking about.

"Gives the game away every time," the man agreed, winking as he raised his glass. "Here's to a better night, for you at least, your first time joining us."

Vivian clinked her glass against his and, since it would have been rude not to, took a gulp, dismayed to see that there wasn't much left. She hadn't meant to drink so much. But she'd be slipping away soon—no good could come of being there when the actual gambling started. "I bet he couldn't wait to get out of there," she said, wondering how much time Corny would have needed to get back to the house. "I know I would have."

"Maybe, but they're dead serious when they say that no one can leave until the gameplay is done. He had to stay until the end, just like the rest of us." He laughed. "Don't want anyone ratting us out to get their money back, after all."

Vivian froze. "Oh. Yes. I mean no, we don't want that," she said, not sure what she was saying but hoping her surprise wasn't written all over her face. If they didn't allow anyone to leave . . . did that mean once the game started? Or once they walked into the room?

"And that game went on for half the damn day. I probably could have bought a new company with what I lost on that last hand," the man was saying, apparently happy to take the chance to brag and not noticing that she was barely paying attention anymore. He winked at her. "If you get out early, don't feel too bad. Come sit on my lap and I'll keep you entertained."

"Golly, what an offer, mister," Vivian said, hoping he thought her breathlessness was meant to be flirtatious. But her eyes were fixed on the door.

A new man had just walked into the room, and this one didn't wear a mask either. His suit fit so perfectly it looked like it might have grown on him, and he was flanked by two men whose smart jackets did little to soften their menacing posture.

Vivian swallowed. Judging by the confident way the new man looked around the room, the muscle flanking him, and the quick, nervous way that the man in the checked suit hurried to his side, this was the man in charge. It took all her willpower not to bolt for the door that instant. Would she still be able to slip away?

"Ah, it looks like our host is coming to greet his newest victim," the man said, giving her a friendly nudge with his shoulder. "I'll give you your privacy, of course, but come find me after." He winked again. "Like I said, I'm a good time, on *and* off the dance floor."

"Sure thing," Vivian said faintly, forcing herself to smile as she watched him walk away. She wanted to grab his hand and make him stay with her. But just because a fella could hold his own in a Charleston didn't mean he was trustworthy. She remembered the feel of his mouth on her fingers as he licked away the drops of champagne and shivered. She could handle herself without that just fine.

"Good evening, madam."

The host had reached her. To her relief, only the man in the checked suit was with him; his bruisers still stood a few paces back, though they were watching her as well. The host smiled, but it was clear to her that it was a show, put on for the benefit of the other players. Up close, his smile was cold, and it didn't reach his eyes.

"Evening," Vivian said, hoping her smile was more convincing than his. "Hell of a shindig you throw down here."

His nod could hardly be called that, a bare dip of his chin. His eyes didn't leave hers. "I'm glad you approve. But my associate tells me—" He gestured toward the man in the checked suit—"that perhaps we were not expecting you to join us this evening. I'm certain we have not yet received your deposit." Behind his back, she saw two of his fingers move. At the gesture, one of his muscled escorts peeled away from the wall he was propping up and began ambling in their direction. The host smiled at her once more, and it was even colder this time. "May I ask who invited you to our little soiree?"

Vivian shifted so that her weight was forward on her toes. "Do you want his real name?" she asked, her voice as light as if he were an old friend asking her for a dance. She kept her eyes away from where the waitress was making her rounds with the champagne again, getting closer and closer to them.

The host raised his brows, looking bemused, as though her apparent lack of discomfort puzzled him. He gestured at her with one hand. "If you please."

"Sure thing, mister. I know you know the fella," she added, glancing at the man in the checked suit, who looked surprised at being addressed directly. Vivian leaned forward conspiratorially. "My friend Corny Rokesby."

The host frowned. "Mr. Rokesby?"

"Of course," Vivian said, smiling brightly. "He's sitting right over there."

They all turned to look in the direction she was pointing. The moment they did, Vivian stepped back, sticking one foot into the path of the waitress. The woman stumbled, and Vivian helped her along, sending the tray of glasses and a half-full bottle of champagne flying toward the men. There was the sound of glass shattering, shrieking from the waitress and several guests, bellows from the men—but Vivian hadn't

waited for any of it. She was already plunging through the velvet curtain and dashing toward the steps, ignoring the shout of the man who
had handed her the mask.

It didn't occur to her, until the moment her hand was on the knob,
that they might have locked the door behind them. She would have
sobbed in relief when the door swung open, but she didn't have time.
She yanked it shut behind her, already taking the steps toward the ballroom two at a time. The door at the top was unlocked too. She could
hear shouts and pounding feet from below before they were drowned
out by the clamor of five hundred conversations, all happening at once
to the sound of a jazzy, brassy quickstep.

Vivian slammed the door behind her, tearing off her mask and
tossing it on the ground before she dashed around the silk screen and
plunged back into the crowd.

TWENTY-THREE

Vivian pushed her way toward the dance floor, trying to find her friends. Were Mags and Leo still dancing? No, they had said they would meet at the bar in an hour. How long had she been gone?

She changed direction, then froze. In front of her, she could see the two bruisers from downstairs blocking the door back toward the bar and staircase while they scanned the crowd, clearly looking for her. Vivian tried to melt back into the crowd, searching for another exit.

She had reached the edge of the dance floor without realizing it. And she could see another door on the other side. Looking around quickly, Vivian grabbed the hand of the first unpartnered person she saw, a lanky boy dressed as some kind of creature with furry trousers and horns on top of his head, wearing nothing but a vest over his otherwise bare chest.

Vivian didn't even bother to ask what his costume was supposed to be. "Fancy a spin?" she asked, a little breathlessly, trying not to look back over her shoulder. The more she looked at them, the more likely they were to spot her. They knew what she was wearing, even if they hadn't seen her face. And she didn't want them seeing what she looked like without her mask.

"With you, doll? Absolutely," the boy said, grinning as he slid his arms around her. "How fast should we go?"

"Fast as you like," Vivian said. The band had just started a Baltimore, and the line of the dance should carry them around the floor toward the other door. The back of her neck prickled with nerves, and she could feel her body flushing hot then cold, over and over.

The boy chatted as they danced, but she would barely have been able to hear him over the noise of the crowd, even if she hadn't been straining her ears for the sound of someone spotting her. She nodded when he spoke and laughed when he smiled, barely even noticing when he pulled her too close so he could hold her body against his bare chest.

As they neared the far side of the ballroom, he lowered his mouth toward her ear and dropped his voice. "What do you say we slip out for a bit and get to know each other better? I'm sure we can find—"

"There she is!"

The voice carried over the noise of the band and the dancers, landing on Vivian's ears like a siren. Glancing over her shoulder, she saw the two burly men pushing their way through the crowd, trying to circle around the dance floor to cut her off.

She slid out of her partner's arms, leaving him with a quick, "Thanks for the dance," as she ran for the door. She didn't look back to see if the two men were following; the shouts of irritation and a few yelps of pain told her they were still in pursuit.

The door at this end of the ballroom was tucked into a corner, and still closed instead of wide open like the ones at the other end. Vivian flung it open anyway and discovered a staircase heading up; she hesitated, but there wasn't much choice. She kicked the door closed behind her and dashed up, praying it would open up somewhere she could hide.

It was longer than she expected, with a landing and a turn but no door at what she thought was the second floor. There was nothing for it but to keep climbing; she could hear the men's curses as they came through the door and discovered the staircase themselves. A moment later, the clomp of their feet echoed up after her.

Vivian took the steps two at a time and was panting by the time she reached the top of the stairs and threw open the door there. She slammed that one behind her as well, cursing frantically when she discovered it didn't lock. She whipped her head around, trying to get her bearings in the few seconds she had to make a decision.

She was at the end of an empty hallway, stacked with extra chairs and lined with old photos of the Odd Fellows through the years. There were doors opening off the hall, but if she went in one of those and the men followed, she'd be trapped.

The footsteps were pounding up the stairs behind her; her time was up. Vivian ran toward the end of the hall. Maybe it would end somewhere crowded so she wouldn't be alone when the men caught up to her.

Her luck wasn't in. Around a turn in the hall, she found herself dashing toward an open gallery, carpeted in a deep burgundy and scattered with marble pillars, a spot where guests could mingle with drinks or spill over into extra dancing space when the downstairs filled up. At the moment, it was empty; the party hadn't yet made its way up to the third floor. But across the gallery, she could see the stairs heading down. And the second floor, she knew, was crowded with people.

Vivian risked a glance over her shoulder. And then her feet met nothing, and she was tumbling through the air.

It was only a moment before she caught her balance; the hallway had ended in three steps down to the gallery. Vivian bit back a yell as she landed on one foot and felt her ankle buckle beneath her. She gasped as she grabbed at a pillar to haul herself up.

She managed a few more steps, but a jolt of pain shot up her leg. Whimpering, Vivian ducked behind a pillar, trying to breathe quietly even though she was panting with fear. Her ankle throbbed, and she could feel sweat dripping down her back. But everything was still and quiet, and she let herself hope that she had shaken them off.

Vivian craned her neck just far enough that one eye could peer out from behind the column. Then she pulled back quickly; the two men in dark suits, one with an enormous mustache and the other with shoulders like a mountain, had just reached the three steps where she had fallen. Her breath stuttered through her chest, and she pressed her face against the marble, praying the chill of the stone would help her think.

There had to be somewhere she could go to get away from them. Could she find Leo if she made her way back down? He and Mags were almost certainly still dancing or drinking, but he'd be watching for her. Could they sneak out and find a cab before . . .

Laughter filled the gallery suddenly, a dozen voices talking over each other in a cheerful, drunken babble that made Vivian jump, then press herself more tightly against the pillar, hoping she hadn't given away her hiding place. A crowd of women tumbled up the stairs, gossiping about the dancers and complaining about sore feet, more than one stumbling and tipsy while their friends kept them upright.

"I thought there was a washroom up here?" one of them called, the others chiming in helpfully and pointing in multiple directions before they finally decided they had climbed one floor too far and needed to turn around.

The small crowd flowed around Vivian without noticing that someone was hiding there. She took a deep breath and waited until she was surrounded. When she was sandwiched between a medieval ball gown and a pirate queen, she stepped away from her hiding place and joined them.

She wanted to look back and see if either of the men had noticed, but she couldn't risk it. There were no shouts or running feet, and she told herself that was a good sign. But for all she knew, they were still following, just waiting for an opportunity when fewer people were around.

Vivian was swept down the steps, trying not to stumble on her injured ankle, and back into the heat and noise of the party. She let herself be carried along into the washroom, where the women scattered to fix their lipstick and powder, adjust their costumes or wigs, or disappear into the back room to take care of personal business. Several simply threw themselves onto the upholstered benches, resting their feet while they chatted and sighed and wondered cheerfully about who would get into different kinds of fun trouble downstairs.

Vivian stood with her back against one wall, still shaking too hard to move. She couldn't stay in the washroom all night. She didn't think those men would spend much longer looking for her—she couldn't be worth that much effort, could she? She was just some unknown girl who wandered into their game and pulled a runner without causing any real trouble. But what if the man she'd been talking to told them she'd been asking questions? What if they were outside the door, waiting to grab her the moment she tried to leave?

"Oh, sorry!"

One of the women stumbled into Vivian as she tried to fix the ribbons on her shoe while hopping on one foot. Vivian grabbed her arm to steady her, and several of her friends laughed and yelled at her to sit down before she broke her neck. As they helped her into a seat, one turned to thank Vivian, then frowned.

"You all right there, sugar?" she asked, sounding genuinely concerned. She was wearing a men's suit, a walking stick in one hand. Her blond hair was cut so short it could only barely be called a bob, and she wore not only deep red lipstick and mascara but had lined her eyes strikingly with kohl powder. "You look a little green around the gills. Too much gin?"

"No. Sorry." Vivian shook her head, shrinking farther against the wall, her mind still outside with the men who might or might not be there. "I didn't mean to crash your party."

Her statement was met with a chorus of protests as the whole group turned to see who had wandered in with them. Seeing so many strange faces turned toward her put Vivian on guard—what if one of them turned her in? But at least she wasn't alone, cowering behind a pillar and praying two bully-boys didn't drag her downstairs for questioning or worse.

She took a shuddering breath. "Any chance some of you could help a girl out? I gotta get back downstairs to find my pals, but I . . . I need to make sure no one sees me do it."

"What happened?"

"Hell, are the cops here? Are we being raided?"

"Don't be dumb, they never show up to these—"

"Did you steal something?"

The chorus of voices was overwhelming. But they weren't sending her packing, at least not right away. Vivian tried to decide who to answer first. Her ankle throbbed, and she wished she hadn't had that drink downstairs, no matter how much she had needed to blend in.

"It's a fella, isn't it?" the blonde asked, cutting through the clamor of her friends' questions. Her mouth twisted as though she had tasted something sour. Her walking stick rested, point down, on the floor, and she spun it from the top with quick, deliberate flicks of her fingers in between her words. "You're hiding from him."

Vivian swallowed, not even trying to hide her nervousness. "Yeah." Her voice came out in more of a whisper than she intended.

There was a murmur from the others, but the blonde, who was clearly the ringleader, gestured them into silence. She gave Vivian a considering look. "Someone you know, or someone who decided to give you a bit of trouble?"

"Second one," Vivian said, feeling less shaky in the face of what she hoped was sympathy. "He and one of his pals . . . Well, I was trying to shake them, so I tagged along with all of you. I don't know if I fooled 'em or not, but . . ."

A wild thought was forming in her head. Almost no one in the room of gamblers could have seen her face, could they? The two men chasing her would have seen her dress, and maybe remembered what her hair looked like. But beyond that, they'd have a hard time finding a single girl in a place like this.

If they didn't have an easy way to recognize her anymore, she could disappear into the crowd and get far away from the lodge ball.

The women were still chattering in low voices, trying to decide whether someone should peek out the door or venture toward the stairs to see if someone was waiting.

"But even if we don't see someone, that doesn't mean the coast is clear," one pointed out. "They could be just waiting for her to come downstairs." A murmur of agreement went among her friends, and Vivian cleared her throat.

"Well, here's the lucky thing," she said, as all the faces turned toward her. "They don't really know me. They just . . . I got a bad feeling, you know? So I tried to leave, and they didn't like that." She was relieved to see heads nodding around the room. "One of them tried to grab me, so I ran, and he and his pal came after me."

"Lord almighty," the blonde muttered. "Don't they have better things to do with their time than chase a girl who's clearly not interested?"

"You'd think," Vivian said, letting them hear the shakiness in her voice. "But since I don't know how good a look they got at me . . . I think, if one of you could switch clothes with me . . ." She trailed off, glancing hopefully around the room.

There was a painful moment of silence, and Vivian wondered if she'd made a terrible mistake. The blonde eyed her consideringly, and Vivian held her breath. She knew exactly who in the room she needed to convince.

Finally, the blonde turned toward her friends. "All right, girls. Who wants some new glad rags for the night?"

An eager, approving babble of voices began chiming in with suggestions about who was the right size for the swap. "It's a shame you already bobbed your hair," one said, shaking her head in disappointment. Vivian wasn't sure if she should be offended or not until the girl added, "If it were long, we could have chopped it all off for you, and they'd never recognize you then!"

"Leila," the blonde said at last. "I think you're probably closest in size to our new friend here. What did you say your name was, sugar?"

"Vivian," she replied, then bit her lip, wondering if she should have given them a fake name. But who were they going to tell?

"Vivian. All right. You and Leila swap."

"I guess that makes the most sense," Leila sighed, but she was smiling. "Easier to get home without a hassle in your getup, anyway. It's a pretty dress. Though I was feeling all kinds of eye-catching in this one!"

Leila had golden-red curls pinned up around her head like a crown, topped with a spangled and feathered cap. Her costume was a stunning confection of silk and gauze, shimmering with so many rhinestones and glass pearls that Vivian's fingers ached with the thought of sewing them all into place.

And it only covered about a third of Leila's body.

Vivian nodded, hoping that her eyes weren't as wide as they felt and trying not to look shocked. Judging by the giggles around the room, she wasn't succeeding.

She had never been half-naked in public before, and she wasn't looking forward to the thought of the attention she could get, strutting through the lodge in an outfit that a vaudeville dancer would wear on stage. But they were right: there was almost no chance that the men from the gambling ring would recognize her in that getup. And they'd never look twice at Leila, with her bright hair, even if they did notice that her dress was the same color as they one they were looking for.

Vivian nodded. "There's a tie in the back," she said, gesturing over her shoulders. "Will someone help me with that?"

The blonde had chosen well; the burlesque costume fit Vivian like a glove. Her dress—she'd have to pay Bea back for it, but there was no way around that—was a little too short on Leila. But it wasn't bad enough that anyone would notice.

Vivian stared at herself in the mirror. She had never thought of herself as prudish, but now she had to resist the urge to cross her arms across her midsection. She didn't even want to think about how much would be exposed when she walked and the silk panels of the skirt fluttered around her legs.

But she barely recognized herself in the costume, especially when the pirate queen, who was taller than the rest—he had shed his hat and wig for the moment and introduced himself as Archie—helped her pin Leila's feathered cap on top of her hair. That meant the people searching for her—God, she hoped they weren't still searching for her—probably wouldn't recognize her either.

"There you go, sweetheart," Archie said, smoothing down her bob with expert fingers before settling his own hair and hat back in place. "You look smashing."

"I feel naked," Vivian whispered, blushing, which made Archie laugh.

"All right," the blonde said, gathering her troops. "We're all heading down, and we'll just hope that whoever's trying to cause trouble for our new friend gets thrown off the scent by so many beautiful girls all together."

Vivian felt wobbly with nerves, but she knew how to put on a good show. As they left the washroom, she looped her arm through Archie's, walking as carefully as she could on her injured ankle. She began asking him about his costume and how the masquerade winners were judged, a wide, dazzling smile on her face.

They reached the first floor before she spotted the two men. They were lurking near the staircase, watching both the stairs and the doors.

She was only a few feet away when she felt their eyes on her. Vivian didn't look at them, laughing loudly as Archie and another girl described the ball gown one of last year's winners had worn. Her skin was crawling, and she wondered if her ankle would give up completely if she had to run again. The one with the mustache took half a step toward her.

But his eyes weren't on her face. They were traveling over her exposed midsection and her pearl-draped hips. Vivian felt a hysterical laugh bouncing around in her chest. Half of her wanted to shrink away from his leer. But the smarter part of her leaned into the spectacle, swaying her hips deliberately so the panels of silk shifted and whispered against her stocking-clad legs, and the rhinestones scattered over her body sparkled under the electric lights of the chandeliers. When his eyes traveled up to her face, catching hers for a moment, she winked and blew him a kiss.

Mustache's eyes lit up, and for a moment Vivian wondered if she'd made a mistake. But he was still leering, and he took another half step toward her before a jab from his friend's elbow caught his attention. He winced, turning away to glare at Hulking Shoulders as the two began whispering heatedly, their survey of the room growing more lackluster with every sweep of their heads.

"—stay here or tell him she's long gone?" she heard Mustache grumble, rubbing at his ribs where his friend's massive elbow had hit him.

Vivian didn't wait to find out what they'd decide. She was shaking with relief as she was swept out of their sight and into the ballroom, where the girls scattered, heading to the dance floor or to the bar.

Vivian caught the blonde's eye. "Thank you," she whispered.

"You okay from here? Or you think you'll need an armed guard for the rest of the night?" the blonde asked. "Looked like pretty rough types."

Vivian shook her head. "They looked right past me," she said, barely able to believe it.

Leila, who was holding the blonde's arm, laughed. "Well, not right past you," she said. "I think right *at* you is more accurate."

Vivian felt herself blushing, and the heat in her face only grew as the blonde looked her over once more. "Can't blame them," she said with a wry grin before sliding her arm around Leila's waist. "Come on, love. That dance floor is calling our names."

"And how," Leila agreed. "Enjoy your new duds!" she said over her shoulder as they disappeared into the crowd.

"All right, doll," Archie said, giving her arm a squeeze. "You need help finding your people?"

Vivian wanted to beg him to stay with her. But she didn't know him, and he didn't owe her anything, and she could see that he was already looking longingly after his own friends. She shook her head. "I'm good from here. Thanks for the offer, though."

"We gotta stick together when the fellas get nasty," he said with a wink. "Good luck out there. You find your friends and get out of here while the getting's still good, yeah?"

"Absolutely," Vivian said, meaning it. She returned his wave as he swanned off into the crowd, then took a careful step. Her ankle was sore, but the sharp pain had mellowed. She needed to get off it soon, but if she sat down, she wouldn't have the energy to get up again. So she began a slow circuit of the room, trying not to limp as she headed in the direction of the bar. It was hard to blend into the crowd in Leila's costume; no one batted an eye, but plenty of folks looked her up and down, and a few started to move toward her. Vivian changed direction more than once, dodging between clumps of people as she scanned the room for familiar faces.

She didn't see anyone from downstairs, and she hoped that meant they had given up on finding her. But she was still sweating with nerves. The band was shifting from the hot, frenzied tempo of the last hour into something a little gentler when she finally spotted Leo and Mags, just at the edge of the dance floor, applauding the end of a song.

Vivian hurried over to them, stumbling a little on her sore ankle. They were looking in her direction, but Mags's eyes went right over her. Leo's lingered before he began to turn politely away. Then recognition dawned, and his head snapped back toward her.

"Viv?" he said in disbelief, grabbing Mags's hand and hauling her off the dance floor while she protested. "Sweetheart, what . . ." He didn't even pretend that he wasn't looking her up and down with open, heated appreciation. "Not that I'm complaining, but what happened to your clothes?"

"Good golly, Viv!" Mags exclaimed, though luckily the noise of the people and the music meant her surprise didn't turn any heads. "You look like you joined a burlesque troupe since we seen you last." She looked excited by the thought.

"I'll tell you in a cab," Vivian said, glancing around. "But the night's over. We've gotta head out." When Mags started to protest, Vivian shook her head. "Right now."

Leo, to her relief, didn't stop to ask questions, just put an arm around each of their waists and led them toward the door. On the way, he spotted a coat someone had hung over a chair, and he slowed long enough to snag it with one hand and drape it over Vivian's shoulders.

When she protested, he pressed a single finger against her lips. "As much as I'm enjoying the view, I don't think you should be strolling down the street in that getup."

"But it's stealing," Vivian hissed.

He pulled it around her like a cloak. "Not the worst thing I've done in my life. Come on." He frowned at her. "Are you limping?"

"Turned my ankle a little," Vivian said, shaking her head. "Doesn't matter. Let's just get out of here."

It might have taken them an hour to reach the door, or maybe it was only a few seconds. Before Vivian was quite sure how it happened, they were back on 155th Street, where people were still arriving, laughing and smoking and clamoring to get into the party. Leo led them through it all, sliding up to a cab that three men had just left and ushering Vivian and Mags in without missing a beat. Vivian was still catching her breath as she slid across the back seat.

Mags leaned forward to give the cabbie Jimmy's address. "I have to change, but he gave me a key and said his housekeeper would make sure I got home, sweet man," she explained, settling back against the seat with a long, noisy exhalation. "Golly, my little puppies are tired. But wasn't that fun? Should we go back next time? Viv, why didn't you want to stay? You could've had any dance partner you wanted in that skimpy little thing!"

"Not sure I like the sound of that," Leo muttered.

"Can I borrow it for the next ball, do you think?" Mags added eagerly.

After the last panicked hour of her life, the question felt so absurd that Vivian began laughing. Between gasps, she told them what she could—with the cabbie still up front, likely listening to everything they were saying, she didn't want to say too much. But she could tell them about stumbling into a private party and the host who had taken exception to her being there. Mags's eyes grew wide as she described running from the two bruisers, and Leo whistled appreciatively as she explained about swapping clothes with another girl.

"One of them looked right at me and didn't say a thing," she finished. There were tears in her eyes, and she wasn't sure which emotion they were from. She still couldn't believe she had gotten away with it.

"And then I found you and, well, I decided I'd better not stick around and see if they wised up. Better to hightail it out of there with all my rhinestones intact."

There was more she needed to tell Leo, but that could wait. It had to, with the cabbie up there. And it had to because she didn't want to think about it. Not yet. Maybe not ever. As she spoke, one of his hands slid under the hem of the coat, his fingers stroking her thigh. She shivered, from the heat of his touch and from the comfort of being there, being safe, with him.

"Holy moly," Mags exclaimed with wide eyes as the cab stopped in front of Jimmy's sleek brownstone. "I can't wait to go back next time."

"Might be without us," Leo said with a wry glance at Vivian. "Sounds like poor Viv had a lot of excitement for one night."

"Shame," Mags said, sliding across the seat. "Well, maybe I can find someone else to take me. Night!"

They waited until she disappeared inside before Leo gave the cabbie Vivian's address. She let him handle it, sagging back against the seat, exhausted as the excitement and panic of the last few hours drained out of her. As they pulled away from the curb, it was hard to believe that the quiet neighborhood around them was in the same world as the Hamilton Lodge Ball. Hard to believe that any of it had happened.

Had any of the last week happened? If she stared at the sky, she could almost convince herself that everything else, every fear and worry and stolen moment of joy, was just a dream.

She wanted, so badly, for all of it to be a dream.

The hum of the cab's motor. The shift of the seat as Leo slid closer. The brush of skin on skin as his hand slipped underneath the coat, turning her toward him so that his mouth could find hers, careless of the driver only a few feet away.

"My brave girl," he breathed against her lips in between kisses, his voice and his hands both shaking. "I should have known you can always handle yourself. But I'll need to hold you close—" His hands slid around to her back, leaving a trail of heat across her bare skin. "Just to be certain that you're safe."

"I don't mind that at all," Vivian whispered back. If he kept kissing her, she could tell herself he was right, that she could handle whatever came her way. She could tell herself she was safe, and she always would be.

If he kept touching her, she could keep pretending that nothing else was real.

Vivian usually had rules for herself. She didn't drink more than she could handle. She didn't let her neighbors see her coming and going from the Nightingale. She didn't get carried away with men or women.

Rules were important when you needed to stay in control to survive.

But if nothing was real, then her rules didn't matter. She barely let Leo go so that he could pay the cabbie and she could unlock the door to her building. They stumbled upstairs, Vivian thankful that this year there was only one flight between her and the privacy of a locked door. She fumbled with her keys while Leo's hands found their way once more under the stolen coat she was still wearing.

"Come here," he growled as soon as the door was shut and locked behind them.

Vivian, still giddy with relief, shivered as the fabric of his suit jacket slid against her skin. She didn't object as he pushed the coat down her arms and let it fall to the floor while his mouth found hers again. It took barely a heartbeat for his kisses to go from teasing to something more serious, and Vivian gasped as he bent to scoop her up in his arms.

"We should probably get you off that ankle," he suggested.

"Probably," Vivian whispered, before letting out a squeak as he tossed her on the bed. She sat up immediately, though, pulling him to her as soon as he shed his own coat and yanked his arms out of his suspenders. She tried to kiss him again, but he slipped away from her mouth to press taunting, nibbling kisses against her neck and the bare expanse of her shoulders.

"I like this outfit," she gasped, her head falling back. Something was wrong, she knew—something she needed to tell him. But she didn't want to think about anything except the weight of his body against hers.

"I do too," he said with a laugh, one hand sliding behind her back so he could ease her down onto the bed.

A jolt like an electric shock shot through Vivian, and her mind stuttered, wondering if she should put a stop to things before they got carried away. But maybe, just this once—

"You didn't tell me what you found out," Leo murmured against her collarbone. "What was Rokesby up to? Have we got him?"

The question hit her like a slap, sending her dizzy thoughts tumbling to the ground. The heat racing through her body was suddenly gone, chased away by cold fear and the awful truth that the night hadn't gotten her any closer to answers. The weight of Leo's body, so exciting a moment before, suddenly felt like it was suffocating her. She put her hands against his chest and pushed him away from her.

As soon as she did, Leo sat back on his heels, his frown as worried as it was confused. "What's wrong? Did I hurt you or—"

"No," she said, her voice hoarse as she scooted away from him.

"Viv—"

She turned away, feeling suddenly too vulnerable. She hated being afraid, hated the creeping sense of dread that was taking over, hated that the whole night had been a dangerous waste. She was too exposed again, the cold air shivering against every inch of bare skin, and she yanked the blanket off the bed to wrap it around her shoulders.

"Viv—"

She felt his hand on her arm, and she stood up abruptly, wincing as her bad ankle throbbed under the sudden weight. But even that couldn't pull her back to him.

"We've got nothing," she said, her voice catching. Swallowing against the knot that had tightened in her throat, Vivian took a shaking breath and tried again. "Double exes means gambling. That's what the private party was. And Rokesby was in a game when Buchanan died. It couldn't have been him."

"Well, maybe he . . ." She could hear the desperation in Leo's voice, could picture him trying to come up with something, anything, that would convince her not to worry. "He could have still been the one with the poison. You said they might have been different people."

"Maybe, but I'm not being accused of poisoning anyone." Vivian's hands shook where they clasped the blanket against her chest. She didn't turn to look at him. "And I can't prove it either way. I've got nothing."

The silence behind her felt like another person in the room with them. At last, she heard the bed creak as Leo shifted his weight to stand. She waited for the feel of a hand on her shoulder, an arm around her waist, not sure whether she wanted the touch or if she would pull away again. But he didn't come toward her.

"Well, then, we'll keep looking, right?"

He didn't say that they were nearly out of time. He didn't mention Honor Huxley.

Vivian didn't either. "Why don't you head to the washroom while I get changed?" she said instead, turning around, still clutching the blanket closed with both hands. "I'll get a bed made up on the floor for you."

For a moment, she thought he would protest, that he would pull her into his arms and hold her close enough to feel the thump of his heart against her own. She stared at him with wide eyes, silently hoping that he would come to her. If he did, she could lean on him again. She could let him convince her, at least for one more night, that everything would be okay.

"Leo." Her voice came out barely above a whisper as she reached for him.

But he was already turning away and didn't see. "Sure thing, sweetheart," he said hoarsely. "Back in a jiff."

By the time he came back, locking the door behind him, Vivian was curled up in bed, the covers pulled high enough that he wouldn't be able to see her face. She listened to the sounds of him moving around in the near-dark, settling at last on the floor next to the bed, where she'd laid out a pillow and quilt for him.

"Night, Leo," she whispered.

"Night," she heard him sigh.

She could feel tears burning against the back of her eyes, but she didn't cry. Vivian had rules, and she didn't believe in crying.

TWENTY-FOUR

Two Days Left

Vivian tried to slip out for work the next morning without waking Leo up. But he lifted his head when she tripped over the burlesque costume, which she had left in an unhappy pile next to her bed after yanking it off the night before.

"Why are you up already?" he asked, yawning. "Isn't it Saturday?"

"Working deliveries today," she said softly, hoping he'd just go back to sleep. She wasn't in the mood for company. With one foot, she shoved the beautiful tangle of silk and spangles under her bed. "You should go back to sleep."

"Nah, I'll get home then," he said through another yawn, rubbing his eyes as he sat up, then dragged himself to his feet. "If you're headed to the washroom, bring back some water? I'm going to keel over without coffee."

He made enough for both of them, and Vivian nodded her thanks when he handed her a mug. But she didn't say anything, and he didn't either.

That was good. She didn't want to talk about what happened between them the night before. It hadn't been a fight. It had been . . . She didn't know what to call it, or which one of them it had come from. But the careful way they were watching each other this morning felt like stepping on a puddle that should have been frozen over, only to feel cracks growing beneath her feet. If she moved, if he spoke, she didn't know if they would stop or spread, and she didn't want to risk finding out.

She wanted to believe that, whatever it was, they'd fix it once the Buchanan mess was sorted out. But after last night, after realizing Rokesby couldn't be the one they were looking for, it was getting harder to convince herself that it would get sorted out at all. She wondered if Leo was realizing the same thing.

Vivian rinsed out their mugs and left them in the basin. "I've gotta get to work."

Leo nodded, scooping up his coat and hat. He was still in his suit from the night before, still smelling of smoke and gin and cologne. "Lead the way."

The streetcar he needed was on her way to Miss Ethel's; it made sense for them to walk together. The silence hung between them as they walked, and Vivian didn't want to be the one to break it. But she couldn't help glancing at his face, only to find him stealing anxious looks at her too. Their eyes collided, and he looked quickly away. For a moment, Vivian felt so alone that she couldn't breathe. She wanted to turn away and leave him there. Instead, she took a deep breath and reached for his hand.

She could feel the way he tensed, and she thought he would pull away. But then his fingers relaxed, sliding between hers as they stopped next to the streetcar platform. Vivian wanted to close her eyes, to sink against him, to convince herself that she didn't have to be alone.

That was when she saw the man in the blue suit leaning against a lamppost across the street. He was holding a newspaper, his head tilted down as if he was reading. But even from that distance, Vivian could feel the weight of his stare.

She had seen him before. She had seen him nearly every day that week.

In spite of the sunny morning, Vivian felt cold, a prickle of uneasy comprehension slithering down her spine. Her fingers tightened on Leo's. "He's been following me."

Leo frowned. "What? Who's been——" He saw where she was looking and glanced over his shoulder, then cursed, turning so that his body blocked her from the man's view.

Vivian dropped his hand and stepped around him so she could see the man again. She stared at him openly, coldly enough that he stopped pretending to read his paper and stared right back at her. He tipped his hat, and even from that distance, she could feel the mockery in the gesture. Vivian clenched her jaw, anger suddenly replacing the uneasiness. "He's a cop, isn't he? The commissioner is having me followed." When she glanced back at Leo, he didn't look surprised. She sucked in a breath. "You knew."

He glanced at the man, then nodded. "I guessed, at least. He'd want to make sure you didn't skip town."

"And you didn't say anything?" Vivian demanded.

He sighed, and she could see a muscle clench in his own jaw. "What would the point have been, Viv?" he asked, his voice coming out bitter. "What should I have done, asked him to stop? Promise him you weren't going anywhere and he should believe me because we're family? He'd just get angry, and nothing's worth that."

Vivian stared at him. "Nothing?"

Leo winced. "That's not what I meant," he said through gritted teeth.

They stared at each other without speaking. It was only a moment, but it felt like a lifetime. Vivian could feel the cracks in the ice growing. "You could have told me," she said at last. She didn't know if she was being unreasonable or not, but the thought of someone following her for days, watching where she went and who she talked to, seeing Leo stay with her each night and leave in the morning . . . She felt ill.

"Well, next time I will," Leo said, giving her a smile that looked like too much work.

She knew it was supposed to be a joke, but Vivian didn't laugh. Instead, she glared over his shoulder once more at the plainclothes cop. "And I'll tell him where he can stick his watching me," she ground out.

"Viv, you go talk to that fella, you'll only make more trouble. It's just a few more days—"

"Not him," Vivian said, breathing heavily. She felt as if she'd been running, even though they hadn't moved in minutes. "Your uncle."

"No."

She turned to stare at him. "No?" She wasn't surprised that he didn't like the idea. But she was outraged that he thought he could tell her what to do.

"It's a bad idea, and you know it," he said, dropping his voice. He glanced around, looking uneasy, and stepped closer to her. "He's not my uncle. He's made that clear. And you showing up to yell at him will just . . . it's going to make things worse."

"I'm not just going to waltz in there and throw a fit," Vivian said, stung. "What about the arsenic? What about the fella Buchanan was meeting with? There's things that don't add up, and your lawyer friend said the best way to help myself was to give them someone else to suspect. We can at least try to do that, right?"

"Vivian." Her name came out like a sigh. "They're probably already looking at those things. Which means they'll find something, right? There's still time."

"Not that much," Vivian said, shaking her head. "And that Levinsky said—"

"You can stick it out a few more days, can't you?" he asked, reaching for her hand without letting her finish. "We stay away from him, and then it'll all be over and done."

"Don't." She couldn't tell if he was just trying to distract her or if he really believed it, but she had seen the panic in his eyes when she mentioned his uncle. She wanted to push him away, to make him say which scared him more: the thought of losing her or the thought of angering the family that didn't want him anyway. She took a deep breath, shivering as the wind picked up, the sky growing dim as a mass of clouds hid the sun from view. "I'm not just going to sit around waiting. I have to do something."

"Of course we'll do something. Nothing's gonna happen to you, okay?"

"You don't *know* that," she said sharply, pulling back. The cold air caught her breath, bitter in her throat and her lungs, and there was nothing sweet words or gentle touches could do to change that. "Don't keep pretending like this isn't real. It's happening."

"I know that, Viv—"

"Then act like it!" Her voice was nearly a shout, and she glanced around nervously, wrapping her arms around her own body as though she could protect herself from the curious stares directed her way. More quietly, she added, "I'm so scared I can't think straight, and you're talking like there's nothing to worry about at all."

"I won't *let* there be anything to worry about," he insisted, his voice gentle again as he pulled her into his arms. Vivian let him, her body still stiff and distant. All she could think about was the cop across the street watching them. "I won't let anything happen to you. We'll figure it out, just . . ." He sighed. "Don't go talk to the commissioner, okay? Trust me, it's better you don't get him thinking about you any more than he already is. We'll just focus on finding out what we can." He pressed his lips against her temple. "We'll turn up something, okay?"

"Yeah," Vivian said softly. "We'll turn up something."

She waited at the streetcar stop until Leo was out of sight, then waited a few more minutes just to be sure. As soon as she was confident that he was gone, she took a deep breath and headed across the street. The cop in the blue suit tucked his paper under his arm, watching her through narrow eyes as she walked up to him.

"Having a nice morning, pal?" she asked. She wanted to sound unconcerned, but her hands were shaking, and she was pretty sure her voice was too.

The cop looked her over. He was younger than she expected, with hair slicked back under his hat and the smell of starch clinging to him. But he didn't look like a kid who was brand new on the job. "Not too bad," he said. "You heading home now? You could always invite me in for a cup of coffee if you are. It'd be the neighborly thing to do."

"Shame we aren't neighbors, then," Vivian said through a too-sweet smile. "You're not the only one working today, so you can look forward to running your feet off after me. Or . . ."

He only waited a few seconds before he demanded, "Or?"

"Or you tell me where I can find your boss on a Saturday morning."

He snorted. "Not likely, kid. He doesn't want to talk to you."

"But I want to talk to him," Vivian said softly. She didn't have time for games. Not anymore. "I already know where he lives."

The cop raised his brows. "I hope that wasn't a threat."

"I'm not that dumb," Vivian said. "I'm just letting you know that I'm heading there either way. So you can go with me and make sure I get to see him, nice and quiet, or I go anyway and make a big scene trying to get in. I can guess which he'd prefer."

The cop gave her a considering look, and Vivian held her breath, wondering if he would just get annoyed and arrest her right there. But at last he nodded. "Whistle us up a cab, then, kid. We should be able to catch him before he's done with his coffee."

———•———

Miss Kelly."

The commissioner was indeed having his coffee, at the desk in his office while he read through the morning paper. Apparently, he worked on Saturdays too. Vivian rubbed her palms nervously against her skirt, then clasped them in front of her.

"To what do I owe the dubious pleasure?"

The cop in the blue suit hadn't come in with her. Vivian couldn't blame him for that. The commissioner terrified her, too. But she was already in his office, doing exactly what Leo had told her not to do. She took the seat across from him without being invited and leaned forward, her hands palm down on the surface of the desk.

"I want to know why you won't just leave me alone. If you've looked into Buchanan's life at all, you know I never met him before. You've got nothing to connect me to him aside from bad timing."

"It seems that way, yes," the commissioner agreed, taking a sip from his coffee.

The agreement, stated so simply and quickly, caught Vivian off guard. For a moment she just stared at him, not remembering what she had planned to say next. "If you know it wasn't me, then why do you still have your guys following me?" she demanded at last.

The commissioner sighed, leaning back in his chair and steepling his fingers in front of him. "Dear girl, it's not that simple. My position is precarious, like that of any other man who's attained some measure of power in this city. Mr. Buchanan's death was violent, and ugly, and now it's not just the press clamoring for a good story. The public want answers. The politicians who control who sits here"—he tapped the arms of his chair—"want answers. It's my job to make people in this city feel *safe*. Which means that, in this instance, it's my job to give them what they demand."

"Don't they demand that you not blame people for crimes they didn't do?"

"And can you prove you did not commit this one?"

Vivian gritted her teeth. She had no proof, any more than he did, and they both knew it. "You could prove that someone *else* did it," she said, struggling to keep her voice calm.

He turned a page of his paper, already looking bored. "Unfortunately, those inquiries have turned up only dead ends. So whether I think you're telling the truth or not won't, in the end, matter. Within a few days, I will be required to produce a killer. And at the moment, you are the most satisfying suspect available."

"But what about the other fella?" Vivian demanded, darting to her feet without really realizing what she was doing. "The one who met with Buchanan that day? Isn't he more likely to have snuffed Buchanan than someone like me?"

The commissioner sighed; he almost sounded like he was disappointed in her. "Young lady, if you continue to make up stories, it won't go well for you in court."

Vivian stared at him. "Make up . . . What are you talking about? I was sitting right there when the maid came and . . ." She trailed off as he watched her impassively. "You have no idea who he was, do you? Did you even *try* to find him?"

He sighed again, then took another drink of his coffee. The gesture made Vivian think of Buchanan, chatty and a little tipsy, drinking his own coffee as he worried about her being warm enough outside. She bit her cheek hard, forcing the memories to stop there. She didn't want to picture what had come next.

The commissioner, if he noticed her distress, didn't comment on it. Instead, he shook his head. His voice, when he spoke again, was sharp. "We looked into your story. It was easy enough to disprove. None of the servants came to summon Buchanan for a business meeting, because no one called at the house during that time." He took in her disbelief without a flicker of change in his own expression. "I can't guess what a girl like you might know about a trial, though I imagine you know a criminal or two." His lip curled a little as he spoke. "But, as I said, making up stories will not help your case when you're sitting in front of a jury. I suggest you abandon that line of misdirection."

"It's not . . ." Vivian's breathing was coming faster. "It's not misdirection. A maid came and told him . . . and he walked out . . ." Maybe Leo had been right, and she shouldn't have come. "Who told you no one came to the house? Whoever it was, they were *lying*."

"Are you claiming that everyone in that house is a liar?" His brows rose. "Because they all told the exact same story. You were the only person who arrived from the time Mrs. Buchanan and her son departed until the police got there."

"That's not true," Vivian insisted with a whimper, but he was already standing, clearly done with her.

"Your week is almost up, Miss Kelly, so I will no doubt see you in two days. In the meantime, say your good-byes to whoever you must. That sister of yours, perhaps. Or that girl who sings in illegal places." His smile was cold. "For now, I will have my office to myself again. Or must I summon one of my men to take you out?"

Vivian took a step backward. Her whole body was shaking. She wanted to shake him, too. She wanted to say something that would make him feel as lost as she felt. She wanted to run as far away from the city as she could.

But he had mentioned Florence, and now he was talking about Bea too. She knew the reminder wasn't an accident.

"I'll go," she said, staring directly at him. She wouldn't let him see her afraid. "But it's not over. Not yet."

He didn't even notice; he was already leaning back in his chair, shaking the pages of his newspaper to smooth them out. "Tell yourself whatever you like," he said, not looking up. "It won't make a difference to me."

———·———

When she reached the street, she stopped, her feet drifting into stillness almost on their own. She stared around her at the city waking up, knowing she needed to get to work but not able, yet, to make herself move. Across the street, she could see her shadow in the blue suit waiting. Apparently, he had wanted to be far away from the commissioner when she stormed into his office.

If no one had come to the house . . . it didn't make sense. Someone had to be lying. The meeting had happened, otherwise Buchanan would never have left the sitting room. Surely they could see that?

But at the same time, part of Vivian wanted it to be true. If no one but her had come to the house, it meant Honor couldn't have been there. She couldn't have killed her father. She couldn't be letting Vivian take the fall.

Vivian so badly wanted that to be true.

"What are you doing here?"

Vivian jumped, her hands rising into defensive fists as she spun around. The voice hadn't been familiar, but the face was. Levinsky stood next to her, clearly just arriving for work in uniform and with what looked like a lunch pail in his hand.

Across the street, she saw the cop in the blue suit stand up—he had been leaning against the wall of a bakery—then settle back down when he realized she was talking with another cop.

"Levinsky," she said, slowly lowering her fists. Vivian didn't bother to keep the bile from her voice or her expression. "Coming to have a word with that nasty piece of work you call a boss? Maybe he'll tell you to arrest a church full of nuns. I bet you'd do it, too. Whatever he says, doesn't matter if anyone's guilty. Isn't that right?"

He didn't interrupt until she was done. "Guessing you were here for a chat with the commissioner, then?" he asked. Vivian, still breathing heavily, jerked her chin in a quick nod. Levinsky grimaced. "Not the nicest way to start the day."

"No," Vivian bit off. "It wasn't."

"You don't sound like you're having a great week."

Vivian wanted to yell at him. But his tone was so wry and sympathetic, it deflated the anger she was trying to hold on to. "I guess you could say I'm not," she said, with a laugh that had tears in it. She had no reason to trust him, and every reason not to. But he'd seemed genuine enough at the Nightingale, and she wanted to believe what he'd said about trying to help people. God knew she needed help.

"How much do you know about my case?" she asked slowly, watching

Levinsky's face. "You heard what I told the cops who arrested me, about someone meeting with Buchanan?"

"Oh, that," he said, nodding. To her relief, he still looked sympathetic. "And the servants said no one did."

"Commissioner called me a liar," Vivian said, her hands clenching into fists once more. "And I guess it looks that way. But I'm not. Which means someone else is."

"And you want me to do something about it?" he guessed. She couldn't tell, from the way he asked the question, what he thought of that idea.

Vivian met his eyes steadily, though her stomach was turning over. She'd never asked a cop for help before. "You said you cared about helping people. I'm people. And something here doesn't add up. If one of his business partners is hiding something, or paid off the servants . . ."

Levinsky sighed, taking off his hat to run his fingers through his hair. There were dark circles under his eyes. Vivian remembered what he'd said about his new baby at home. "Couldn't have been the partners," he said, settling the hat back on his head and letting out a slow breath. Before Vivian could protest, he tugged her into a shadowed corner between two buildings. "I told you the one, Whitcomb, he was at the office, right? Well, we talked to Mr. Morris's servants. Apparently, they don't like him much, so they were happy to spill the beans on him. He was at home that morning. With his mistress. Couldn't have been him either."

Morris. Vivian had forgotten the names of Buchanan's partners until that moment. And she was willing to bet that Hattie Wilson's Mr. Morris, and his scandalous letter, weren't unrelated.

His scandalous letter that was signed *E.*

"Can I give you a tip?" she asked slowly, glancing around to make sure no one was close enough to overhear. Levinsky nodded warily. "Go back to talk to his servants again. And take a picture of Mrs. Buchanan with you."

His eyebrows climbed up his forehead. "What makes you think—"

"I hear things," Vivian said. "Can you find out? If it was her, she couldn't have been the one to do it either. But maybe one of the partners hired someone, or one of Buchanan's servants knows . . . Someone was there that morning."

Levinsky nodded at last. "All right, I can look into it." One corner of his mouth lifted in a grim smile. "And I can pay special attention to that lousy stepson of his. My gut says there's something fishy about that one."

Vivian bit her lip, trying to decide how much to share. But Levinsky noticed the gesture, small though it was. "What else do you know?" he demanded. When Vivian hesitated, he scowled at her. "If you want my help, you don't hold out on me."

She couldn't really argue with that. "He's got his secrets, and he lied about that appointment book for sure. But he couldn't have been there when Buchanan died." She gave him a brief rundown of Corny Rokesby's gambling.

"So he did need money," Levinsky said, looking thoughtful when she was done.

"Yeah, but didn't you hear me?" Vivian said impatiently. "He couldn't have stabbed the poor bastard."

"There's that." Levinsky frowned, then nodded and gave her a little push toward the street. "All right, get going. I've got my own day to suffer through, and I know where to find you if I learn anything. Just keep your head down, okay? Don't make trouble you don't need to."

"Sure thing," Vivian agreed, not meaning a word of it. She didn't have time to keep her head down. "I gotta go to work anyway."

Levinsky gave her a skeptical look, but he didn't call her a liar to her face. She was grateful for that. Once in a day was enough.

She turned her steps toward Miss Ethel's shop, glancing over her shoulder just in time to see her shadow in the blue suit fall into step, half a block behind her.

TWENTY-FIVE

When she finally got home, after three deliveries that didn't even get her any tips for working on a Saturday, there was someone waiting for her.

Vivian nearly turned around and fled when she saw her door sitting open. She had given the cop shadowing her the slip on her last delivery, heading out the back door instead of the front just for spite, just to prove she could. But now she almost wished he was downstairs, someone she could call on for help.

Then Florence poked her head out the door.

Vivian nearly sagged against the wall with relief. "Flo! What are you doing here?"

"Waiting for you." Florence looked her over critically as she ushered Vivian into the room. "Were you working? You look dead tired."

"Saturday deliveries is all. I'm fine," Vivian said, yawning in spite of her protests. "You know how it goes." She gave Florence her own up-and-down look. "Should you be walking around by yourself?"

"I didn't stop being a competent human being just because I got pregnant," Florence said, her cheeks pink with annoyance. "I know how to ride a few miles on the streetcar, thanks."

The surge of affection that Vivian felt for her sister in that moment made her throat tight. It was a relief to have Florence snap at her over something so ordinary and dumb, instead of tiptoeing around her feelings looking worried. "I love you, Flo," she said suddenly, pulling her into a hug.

Florence looked startled. But as soon as her surprise passed, she hugged Vivian back. "I love you too, even if you do drive me crazy," she said, her own voice sounding choked.

"Did you just come by to say hi?" Vivian asked, finally letting her go.

"No, something at the restaurant arrived for you. Well, it's got both our names on it. But I figured we should open it together."

Vivian frowned as she took the letter, wondering who would be writing her in the first place. There was no return address. She glanced up at Florence. "Hasn't been a lot of good news in my life lately."

Florence shrugged as she lowered herself into a chair, wincing. Vivian wanted to ask if her hip was bothering her again but managed to hold back the question. "Maybe not, but you'll keep wondering about it if you don't open it," she pointed out. "Might as well get it over with."

She was right, of course. Vivian made a face, then ripped the envelope open.

Dear Miss Kelly,

After a good deal of time going through our records from 1904, one of my assistants found an entry I believe to be for a Mrs. Mae Kelly, who died of pneumonia that winter. Her body was scheduled for burial on Hart Island but was claimed in February. There is no record of the name of the claimant. When this happens, it can be generally assumed the claimant couldn't prove a relationship to the deceased and that money changed hands. However, the record did include an address, which I've enclosed. I hope this information can prove useful to you. I'm sure we will be in touch in the future.

Sincerely yours,
CN

"What is it?" Florence asked, looking worried.

Silently, Vivian handed the letter over.

Florence read it through with a frown on her face that gradually turned into disbelief. Vivian watched her read it again, then a third time, going very still as her eyes darted over the paper. At last, she raised her head. "What did . . . Who sent this?"

"The medical examiner at Bellevue," Vivian said, not sure whether she wanted to laugh or cry. Of course this came now, when she might not be around to see it through. Of course. "I owe him another favor now, I guess, fat lot of good it'll do him."

"But this means . . ." Florence stared back at the letter. "We weren't wrong. Someone did care about her. And you think it was . . ." She swallowed. "Do you think it was our father?"

"Hard to tell without a name," Vivian said cynically, trying to ignore the ache of longing in her stomach. "You can decide what to do with it, I guess. I might . . ." She swallowed. "I might not be around to decide."

Florence had been staring at the letter once more. At that, though, her head snapped up. "Don't say that," she insisted, half rising, one hand braced on the table to steady herself, her voice growing shrill. "Of course you will be."

Vivian reached for her sister's hand. "My week's almost gone."

"No." Florence's grip tightened, and Vivian could see the tears spring up into her eyes. "But you said you could . . . Aren't there any other suspects?"

"I'm trying," Vivian said quietly. "I'll keep trying until they haul me away. But—"

"I won't accept that," Florence snapped, shaking her head. "Not when we just found—" She broke off, staring at the letter in her hand, then back at her sister. "And the baby's coming, you have to be here for that."

"Flo." Vivian's voice cracked. "Don't do this. Don't make it harder, please? Let's just . . ." She pressed her fingers against her eyes. "Let's just be here together, okay? That's all I need right now. Please."

She could hear Florence take a shuddering breath. "Okay," she said quietly. Vivian lowered her hands in time to see Florence look down at the letter in her hand. "What do you think I should do with it?" she asked, her voice very small.

The question made Vivian unexpectedly angry. "Nothing," she said fiercely. "Throw it away. You don't need them, whoever they are. You have a family now, and it's one that wants you. Whoever it was, we're nothing to him, and he's nothing to us."

"But maybe we could be something."

The thought was so painful that Vivian would have torn the letter to pieces if she'd been the one holding it. "Do whatever you want, then," she said, her voice hoarse from holding back everything she didn't want to say. "I don't think it's going to matter much to me."

The brittle silence that followed made her regret the words as soon as they were out of her mouth. She wanted to take them back. But she was so tired of pretending.

"Come on," Florence said gently, standing and holding out her hand. "I need to run a few errands before I head back downtown. Keep me company?"

Vivian took a deep breath. "Yes," she said, pushing herself out of her chair. Planning could wait. She and Florence didn't have many days left together. "I'd like that."

The cop in the blue suit was waiting for her when she got home at last, leaning against the front of the building and scowling at everyone who went past. A cigarette that was nearly gone hung from his fingers.

He didn't bother to straighten as she stopped in front of him. Vivian lifted her chin, daring him to say anything, and his lip curled as he stared at her. "Suppose you think you did something clever there," he said.

"Not really, no," Vivian said. "I didn't need to be clever. You weren't trying very hard."

He glared at her, and out of the corner of her eye, she saw one of his hands clench into a fist. It hadn't been a smart thing to say, but the reckless feeling inside her was back. Her breath came faster. What was one more bad decision in a day full of them?

But he only snorted, in irritation or laughter, she couldn't tell. He tossed down his cigarette, grinding it out with his heel before immediately lighting another. "Anything else today, kid?"

"Not 'til tonight," Vivian said. She gestured at the cigarette in his hand. "Got an extra in there?"

The cop raised his eyebrows at her, but he didn't give her a lecture on girls who smoked. She was already heading toward a bad end, and they both knew it. He lit one for her and handed it over. For a moment, they both smoked in silence.

"Well," Vivian said at last. She turned her face up toward the warmth of the sun and wished she could stay like that forever. "We've gotta eat. How about you treat me to a late lunch?"

This time his brows nearly disappeared under the brim of his hat. But almost immediately, he started laughing. "Sure, little girl. Why not? Like you said, we gotta eat." Still chuckling, he shook his head, tossing his second cigarette down. "There's a chop suey joint a few blocks east of here."

"Sounds swell," Vivian said. "What's your name, by the way?"

"Edison."

"Nice to meet you, I guess." Vivian gave him half a smile; they both knew she didn't mean it. "Let's shake a leg, then. I want to get a nap in before I head out tonight."

He chuckled again. "Plenty of time to sleep in prison, little girl."

Vivian took one more drag from her own cigarette before sending it to join his on the pavement, two fallen stars ground out with the heel of her shoe. "I guess there will be," she said. One more day. She wasn't going to give up. Not yet. Not until she'd run out of time completely. "Lead the way, Mr. Edison."

TWENTY-SIX

Saturday wasn't one of Vivian's shifts at the Nightingale. But she still put on her dancing shoes and her lipstick at nine o'clock. The wild feeling was still buzzing inside her, and she knew she couldn't sit at home. She needed to be with people. She needed to dance, and flirt, and pretend her time there could last forever.

And she needed to talk to Bea. She had one last idea to try.

She didn't arrive until after the night had started. When he saw her, the doorman started to swing the door open but stopped, frowning, with his eyes on Edison, who lurked a few steps behind her. He didn't say anything—he rarely opened his mouth if he didn't have to—but she could see his broad shoulders tense as he eyed the plainclothes cop and waited. Vivian didn't know whether the bruiser recognized him, or if he just recognized trouble when he saw it. Either way, he didn't look pleased.

"I'll dance 'til last call," Edison said easily, his own smile knife-edged. Vivian didn't like him any better after spending time with him.

Vivian wasn't surprised that he knew the club's password; he'd been there before, after all. But that didn't mean she liked it.

"He's part of the deal tonight," Vivian said when the doorman gave her a questioning look. "Don't worry, I won't stop you from throwing him out if he causes trouble."

"I've got a job anyway," Edison said, shrugging. "Precinct chief wants me to collect the milk money from your boss."

"You handle yourself, then," Vivian said dismissively as they went in. The hall was carpeted, and at the end of it, thick velvet curtains hung over the doorway. The heavy fabric swallowed up the sound of their footsteps. "And don't bother me."

"Just don't try to give me the slip again," Edison warned, stretching out one arm to block her way.

Vivian regarded him coolly. "It's not my job to make yours easy," she said, ducking under his arm before he could stop her and pushing through the curtains. She didn't wait for him to follow.

She didn't pause at the top of the steps as she usually did, either, to take in the Nightingale in full swing. She didn't want Edison to think she was giving him time to catch up.

Bea was on the bandstand, laughing in between verses as the trumpet player stood for a solo. Danny was behind the bar, leaning on his elbows to talk to a rowdy-looking trio of baby vamps in bright lipstick and brighter spangles.

Vivian didn't see anyone else she knew, but she didn't spend much time looking. Instead, she hurried down the steps and made a beeline for the dance floor. It took barely a moment for her to snag a partner, and only another moment until she was in his arms. When the song was done, she let him buy her a drink, ignoring the look Danny gave her from the other end of the bar, and then she was back on the floor with another partner for a Charleston, a quickstep, anything that would let her lose herself in music and heat and feet moving too fast for her to think.

She didn't stop until the band slowed the tempo for a waltz and she felt a gentle hand on her arm. Vivian stiffened but didn't turn around. She recognized that touch, the scent of vanilla and whiskey and spice that came with it.

"Danny's worried about you, pet," a soft voice murmured in her ear. "He thinks you're looking for trouble."

"And what do you think?" Vivian asked, glancing over her shoulder.

Honor was watching her carefully. "I think you want to escape, and this is the closest you can get," she said quietly. "I can't really blame you for that."

"Funny," Vivian said, her voice shaking as she turned around. Reality was catching up with her again, whether she wanted it to or not. "I've got plenty I can blame you for just now."

Honor flinched, and for a moment they stared at each other silently. Then she held out her hand. "Let's escape together, just for a little while."

Vivian didn't move, her eyes on Honor's outstretched hand. She knew she should say no. But she was still feeling reckless. What was one more bad decision? She took Honor's hand. "I know you love a waltz," she said. She wanted to sound flippant, but her voice caught on the words.

"I do," Honor said, and her voice was hoarse too. "Particularly with you."

Vivian swallowed. "Then we should probably steal one more before we run out of time."

Honor flinched again, and for a moment Vivian thought she would pull away. But she pulled Vivian toward her instead. Honor's lead was light and easy to follow, as always. She slid through the music like silk and poetry, holding her loosely and not too close, though Vivian couldn't say whether that was for Honor's sake or her own. Vivian closed her eyes, the wild feeling melting away until, for the briefest moment, there was only honesty between them.

"Will you miss me?" she asked softly as the final bars of the waltz drew to an end. There was a breathless silence, then the band launched into a Baltimore and dancers scrambled for new partners. No singer, this time: Bea was on a break, so the brass could be as loud as they wanted. But Vivian barely heard any of it. She expected Honor to push back against the question, to insist that everything would be all right.

But Honor had never been one to ignore reality, even when it hurt. She raised her hand to brush the backs of her fingers against Vivian's cheek. "Every day, pet," she whispered. "I will miss you every day."

It ached to hear her say it, but it was a relief, to know that someone else saw the world that she saw and wasn't afraid to admit it. Honor might lie, but she didn't pretend.

Vivian took a deep breath and stepped away. "Thanks for the waltz," she said, just loudly enough to be heard over the music. "But I can't spend all night on the dance floor. I've got a few cards left to play."

Honor's hand had fallen back to her side; she nodded without pro-test. "Good luck, Vivian," she said, just as softly. She sounded as if she meant it.

Vivian was about to turn away but paused. "He was nice to me," she added. "Your dad, I mean." Once, she might have said it as part of a plan, something to get a rise from Honor. But tonight, she was still thinking of her conversation with Florence. She'd have wanted to know, if it had been her father. She'd have wanted to know anything about him at all. "He was worried that I wouldn't be warm enough doing my deliveries on foot. And . . ." She had forgotten, until that moment. "He mentioned you. Said he had a daughter who was a bit of a hellion. Said that if he'd been a better father, he'd have known that daughter more."

Honor had closed her eyes when Vivian mentioned her father, as if she was in pain. "Thank you," she said, nodding as she slowly opened them. "I'm glad to know that about him."

Vivian nodded, left with nothing else to say, or maybe too much to say to begin. She turned away without speaking again.

She'd wanted to lose herself on the dance floor for as long as possible. But Honor had broken that spell, and now it was time to find Bea.

Her friend was in the dressing room, shoes kicked off while she lay down on one of the room's small sofas, her long legs bent at the knees and the hem of her dress bunching around her thighs. Her eyes were closed, but they opened with a snap as Vivian entered. When she saw who it was, she scrambled into a seated position.

"Viv!" She started to say something else, then yawned. "How are you? I tried to come by today, but you weren't there. Did you . . . You don't look like you're jumping for joy over there. Did you not go to the lodge ball after all?"

"Jesus, Mary, and Joseph, that already feels so long ago." Vivian dropped onto the sofa next to Bea, letting her head fall back as she closed her eyes. "We went. Thanks for the dress, by the way. It didn't . . ." She winced. "It didn't make it back with me. So I owe you for that, too."

"It didn't—" Bea was staring at her when she opened her eyes. "What does that mean? Viv, what happened?"

Her eyes grew wide as Vivian talked, quickly and quietly, knowing they could be interrupted at any moment. Her summons from Mrs. Wilson, the ball, the gambling, her panicked run through the lodge. She didn't stop there, barreling on through confronting the commissioner, her growing dread as she realized that neither the wife nor stepson could have been the one to stab Buchanan.

"Leo's going to show up at some point tonight, and he's going to be mad as all hell when he finds out I went to talk to his uncle," Vivian added, dropping her head back again.

"Who cares?" Bea said fiercely. "You've got more important things to worry about."

"I know, but—" Vivian opened her eyes. Bea was one of the only people she would let see her afraid. "It ended up being useless anyway. And I don't want things to end with him angry at me over something useless."

"Who says anything is going to end?" Bea demanded.

Vivian's stomach clenched. She knew her friend meant well. But she needed people to stop pretending that everything was fine, to stop telling her she was wrong to be scared.

Vivian took a breath. "Bea, I've only got one more day. Assuming the commissioner doesn't change his mind and haul me in early. Things could be ending pretty damn soon."

"And you're going to use that day," Bea said, giving her a small shove. "You don't know that it was useless. That Levinsky fella said he was going to look for whoever it was that showed up to talk to Buchanan, yeah? Maybe he'll convince someone to start talking—"

"Bea." Vivian shook her head, laughing a little. "It's a hell of a day when you're telling me a cop is going to solve my problems."

"Well, maybe this'll be the time it happens!" Bea said as she stood. Stretching out her shoulders, she headed to her dressing table. "Come on," she added, meeting Vivian's eyes in the mirror as she bent forward to examine her makeup. "You can't give up, Viv."

"I never said I was giving up," Vivian said, sitting forward. She'd realized earlier, over her silent lunch with that cop Edison, that she'd missed something important. "That's why I'm here. I need to ask you something."

"Shoot," Bea said, reaching for her lipstick.

"The commissioner said that no one on the staff will admit that someone came by that morning, right?" Vivian said, her words coming quickly. "But I know at least one person saw him. I *know* one of the maids came to tell Buchanan that someone was waiting for him because I saw her. If I can talk to her . . ."

She didn't need to finish. Bea spun around, her lipstick clattering to the table unnoticed. "God, that's so simple. Of course you should talk to her. Did you get her name?"

"No," Vivian said, grimacing. "I know it wasn't Lena because she showed me in first. The one who came to get him was older. She was probably in her fifties, maybe coming up on sixty. And most folks don't stick out that kind of work that long, right?"

"Viv—"

"So I'm betting she was the only one that age in that house, other than maybe the housekeeper. I mean, it's hard to say how old she was for sure, because work like that'll wear you out fast. But if we can—"

"*Viv.*"

Vivian broke off. Bea was staring at her. "What is it?"

"There's no one that age working in that house."

For a moment, Vivian's mind went blank. "That doesn't make any sense," she said, shaking her head. "Are you sure?"

"I'm sure. Half the people barely look old enough to be out of school. There's no one north of forty except the housekeeper."

For a moment, nothing felt real, as though Vivian was floating when she expected to be standing on solid ground. "But I *saw* her."

"She must have quit," Bea said slowly. "Remember, they kept losing people? They hired me so fast because someone *else* had quit the day before. It must have been her."

Vivian let out a breath. "Do you think she left because her boss was killed?" she asked slowly. "Or because . . ."

"Or because she'd seen whoever it was and wanted to get out of there," Bea said, her voice barely above a whisper. "Jesus." She'd picked up her lighter from the dressing table without seeming to notice what she was doing, flicking it open and closed with nervous energy.

Vivian rubbed at her temples. She needed a drink or a dance. She needed something to go her way, just one thing, anything, would be enough. "Bea, I think I need—" She broke off as Bea yawned so big that it made her hands shake, the lighter nearly falling from her fingers. Vivian frowned. "Are *you* okay? You look dead on your feet."

Bea gave her a dirty look. "Gee, thanks," she said, but her sarcasm was undercut by another yawn. She shook her head. "It's just the working two jobs, is all. I think I'm going to quit tomorrow. Mama needs me home with the kids more than we need the extra dough." Glancing at the lighter in her hands, she let out a gusty sigh and turned to search for her cigarette case.

Vivian hesitated. But if ever there was a time to ask for a selfish favor, this was it. "Can you wait one more day? I need to get back into that house."

Bea met Vivian's eyes in the mirror, looking wary. "What for?"

"Because they'll have records, right? People keep that sort of thing about who works for them. And I know she did work there. So maybe I can find, I don't know." Vivian shrugged, feeling overwhelmed. She'd been so certain talking to the maid was the key to getting herself off the hook. Now, she was worried that tracking her down would lead to even more trouble. But she had to try. Didn't she? "Maybe it'll say where she lives, or where else she's worked? Something. Anything."

"Viv, it was already a big risk sneaking you in there once," Bea said. She was still and serious now, no more fidgeting with her lighter or lipstick. "We got lucky that time. The odds of us getting lucky again . . ." She shook her head. "If you get caught, they'll take that as proof you're guilty. And I'll probably be headed for the lockup right along with you."

"I know," Vivian said, not looking away. She knew it was a risk. And Bea knew why she was asking. There was nothing else to say. She waited for her friend's decision, sweat trickling down her spine even though her hands were cold.

At last Bea sighed and flicked open her cigarette case. Pulling one out, she lit it and took a drag. Vivian could see her hands shaking. "All right," she said, very quickly, as though agreeing before she talked herself out of it. "The funeral's tomorrow, so most folks'll be out of the house for the morning. Be at the back door at nine o'clock. We should have time to search for . . ." She shrugged, blowing out a stream of smoke. "For whatever we can get our hands on."

Vivian let out the breath she had been holding. "Thank you."

"Just don't get caught," Bea said, grabbing the ashtray to stub her cigarette out. "I really don't want to end up in the slammer."

"Me neither," Vivian said with a trembling laugh as Bea headed for the door.

She paused, one hand on the knob, and sighed. "It'll be okay. We'll be in and out, just like last time, yeah?"

"In and out," Vivian agreed, nodding. "Now get back on that bandstand or Mr. Smith'll be having kittens."

That made Bea smile. "I'd pay to see that, cool customer like him. Come on. Get yourself a drink. You look like you need it."

She did need it. And she needed it even more once she saw who was waiting for her at the bar, pacing back and forth while Danny cast grumpy looks in his direction and the other customers gave him plenty of space. As soon as he caught sight of her, Leo fell still, one hand braced on the bar, the other a fist crumpling the brim of his hat.

"I told you not to talk to him," he said as soon as she was close enough. His voice was quiet, but his anger was clear.

Vivian sighed, sinking down onto the stool. "How'd you find out?"

"He *told* me," Leo bit off. "I had a job for him today, and he had the cop I was working with bring me in after just so he could go off at me. And he's a treat when he's angry, let me tell you. My favorite part was him saying that if I couldn't get my girl under control, he'd have to remind me who mattered in this city, because it's sure as hell not people like us."

Vivian sighed again. "I'm sorry I made things rough for you."

"Viv, you idiot, it's not me I'm worried about," Leo snapped. He looked like an alley cat, bristling and ready for a fight. "He gets angry enough, he takes it out on you, or—"

"He's already planning to arrest me, Leo. I've got a day left of freedom. One. Day." She bit the words off, bitterly glad to see him flinch. "What did I have to lose?"

"Or maybe he gets angry enough, and he comes after my dad," Leo said, his voice starting to rise. "Or my dad's friends, or our old neighbors down on Bowery. Did you even stop to think of that?"

"I don't want to fight, Leo," she said, feeling suddenly tired. She would have kept her voice to a whisper, but no one would be able to hear them over the band anyway. She propped one elbow on the bar and leaned her head into her hand. "Can we just let it go? Please?"

"Just let it go?" he said, pushing at his own temples with his fingertips. Neither of them wanted to look at the other. "Viv, you told me you wouldn't—"

"I never said I wouldn't," Vivian pointed out. When he opened his mouth to argue, she sighed. "What did you expect me to do?"

The fight went out of him, like a Coney Island balloon deflating at the end of the day. He dropped onto the stool next to her. "Okay." He blew out a breath. "Okay. You're right. Let's just—" He broke off suddenly, his eyes fixed on something over her shoulder.

Vivian, suddenly nervous about what he'd been about to say, would have demanded that he finish. But Leo wasn't paying attention anymore.

"Levinsky," he said slowly, climbing to his feet. The Leo she'd been fighting with a moment before was suddenly gone. This one was wary. "What brings you by tonight?"

Vivian spun around on her stool, her own heart speeding up. He couldn't be there to—

No. He was alone, dressed in a regular suit. Vivian glanced around, wondering where Edison had got to and if he was curious why another cop was there, especially since he'd seen them talking to each other just that morning. But she couldn't spot him, though she didn't doubt he was there somewhere. After she'd given him the slip that afternoon, there was no way he'd be taking his eyes off her now. She turned back to Levinsky.

He fidgeted with his hat as he glanced between them, then around the room, as though making sure no one was close enough to overhear.

Plenty of people were, but with the night in full swing and the band close by, no one was going to bother trying to listen in. Still, he took a step closer.

"Not here to talk to you, actually," he said, nodding to Leo before turning to Vivian. "I thought I'd find you here. I wanted to tell you that I followed your tip. You were right about Mrs. Buchanan. She was with Morris that morning."

Vivian let out a shaking breath. One more person was in the clear, and it wasn't her. "Anything else?" she asked, hoping she didn't sound as desperate as she felt.

"Well, I went back to Buchanan's house, like I said I would."

"And?" Vivian asked hopefully.

Slowly, Levinsky shook his head. "I talked to everyone in the house. No one would say a word about a visitor that day," he said, grimacing. "Which might mean that whoever it was, they know better than to stick their nose in his business. Or . . ." He trailed off.

Vivian took a deep breath. "Or?"

"Or you didn't hear what you thought you heard. You said you fell asleep, right?" He shrugged. "Maybe you dreamed some of it."

"I didn't," Vivian said fiercely.

"Then whoever it was, it's someone the folks in that house don't want to talk about." He shrugged again. "Either way, I came up empty-handed. I'm sorry I—"

"Good evening, friend."

The smooth voice, polite and firm and sharp with warning, made them all jump. Vivian shivered. It was the second time Honor had surprised her that night.

The Nightingale's owner was leaning against the bar, looking Levinsky up and down. She smiled at him, but it didn't reach her eyes. "I don't think I've seen you around here before. And your colleague"—she tilted her head toward the other end of the bar, where Edison sat, watching them all—"already collected the milk money for the week. You're welcome as a customer, of course. But you don't seem to be drinking or dancing. So I'm curious what I can do for you this evening?"

Vivian didn't know whether Honor had spotted the cop on her own—it was the sort of skill someone in her line of work learned—or whether Danny had remembered him and sent for her. But Levinsky clearly hadn't expected to be noticed so fast. He took a step back, then straightened his shoulders and stepped forward again, clearing his throat.

"You're the daughter," he said, without bothering to explain whose daughter he meant. He didn't need to. "Honor Huxley."

"I am," Honor said, just loud enough to be heard over the band. "Does that matter?"

"It might," Levinsky said, placing his hat on the bar and resting one hand on it. He glanced pointedly at Vivian before he turned back to Honor. But for the life of her, Vivian couldn't figure out what he was trying to tell her. "Got time to answer a few questions?"

Honor's chin pulled back, her gaze growing harder. Vivian felt a chill snaking down her spine. What was going on? "Depends on what the questions are, Mister . . . ?"

He gave her a considering look. "Levinsky," he said at last. "Your father left you a substantial inheritance, and that after what I understand was a lifetime of pretty thorough neglect." He shifted his weight as he spoke, his fidgeting done, his stance suddenly more aggressive. It was directed at Honor, Vivian was sure, a reminder that while they were in her domain, he was in control outside these walls.

"That doesn't sound like a question to me," Honor said, her voice giving away none of her thoughts. A muscle jumped in Levinsky's jaw. "And I've already discussed my inheritance with a few of your colleagues."

"That's right," Levinsky said, pulling a notebook out of the inside pocket of his jacket. He flicked through several pages. "And you told them . . . Here it is. You told them that you hadn't spoken to your father in years and were unaware that he'd changed his will. Is that correct?"

"That's what I told them, yes," Honor said, her voice even more expressionless than it had been a moment before. She was still leaning against the bar, a picture of casual poise. But she had gone very still, aside from her eyes, which cut so quickly toward Vivian and back to the cop in front of her that Vivian almost thought she had imagined the look.

The chill spread through Vivian's chest. She didn't remember Honor's exact words, the night they had discussed her father. But she knew Honor had told her, with no uncertainty, that she had known about her inheritance.

There could be a good reason she had lied to the cops. Maybe she had misspoken. Maybe she had wanted to avoid trouble with Buchanan's wife and stepson. Maybe she had just wanted to keep the cops from poking and prying into her business, into the Nightingale, into all the people who depended on her work and her protection. Maybe—

Levinsky wasn't done. "I talked to a few other people who were in the room when your father's will was read."

"You can call him Mr. Buchanan to me," Honor said with the barest hint of a smile. "He wasn't much of a father." She gestured at his notebook. "As I'm sure you've noted in there."

"So it seems. But in that case—" Levinsky's voice grew sharper. "Why did they think you didn't seem too surprised by how he'd left things?"

Honor lifted her brows. "Being surprised and showing surprise are two different things. I imagine you have to keep a pretty tight rein on things in your line of work. It's the same in mine."

"Hm." Levinsky narrowed his eyes. "So you were surprised?"

"That's what I said."

"Did you?" he asked. But he didn't wait for an answer before continuing. "You must have some theory, then, as to why he did that, after half a lifetime of pretending his bastard children didn't exist."

If she was offended, Honor didn't show it. "I do, which, again, your colleagues have already asked me about." She tilted her head to one side, her expression growing a little mocking. "Didn't they share their notes with you?"

Vivian could tell what she was doing, making him dance in circles, making him defensive and uncomfortable. She bit her lip, torn between loyalty and suspicion and hoping no one could see the conflict on her face.

She didn't want to tell Levinsky that Honor was lying. Her fingers clenched around the seat of her stool. People like her didn't rat each other out. But she wanted, so badly, to know why Honor had done it.

"You've built quite a business here, Ms. Huxley," Levinsky said, leaning pointedly on the title. "In certain circles, you might even be considered a powerful woman. The sort that ordinary folks need to watch their step around."

Vivian's hands clenched tighter, the wooden edge of the stool painful against her palms. She had known what he was getting at. She just hadn't wanted to admit it to herself.

"I'm flattered you think so," Honor replied, standing up straight at last. "But I'm just an ordinary businesswoman."

"Far from ordinary," Levinsky said dryly, looking her up and down. It was clear he didn't mean it as a compliment.

"But still a businesswoman, which means I don't have time to sit around chatting, pleasant though this conversation has been." This time, Honor didn't bother to hide her sarcasm. "Some of us have work to do."

"How much do you have to pay each week to keep this place open?" Levinsky asked as she started to leave. "Must be a pretty penny."

"You can check the numbers next time you're the one sent to collect," Honor said, not bothering to turn back. "Have a drink on me, Mr. Levinsky. And then get out. I don't need you messing with my customers tonight. Or my staff."

Levinsky glanced at Vivian and Leo once they were alone. "How good a liar is she?" he asked, flipping his notebook closed and tucking it back into his jacket.

The best, Vivian wanted to admit. "I don't know," she said out loud.

Levinsky sighed. "Well, she's sticking to her story, if nothing else. Let me know if you turn up anything about her, though," he added. "She's damned suspicious, as far as I can tell, even if no one else at the station seems to think so."

"I don't know that I have much time left to keep an eye on anyone," Vivian said, choking a bit on the words. She wanted to go after Honor. But she felt glued to her seat. She didn't look at Leo, but she could feel his eyes on her.

"Well, do what you can." Levinsky replaced his hat on his head. He nodded at them. "See you around."

They were silent once he was gone, but Vivian could feel Leo's eyes on her.

"Viv—" he began.

She cut him off. "I have to go. I'll be right back."

"Don't do this to yourself. She won't—"

Vivian wasn't listening, already off her stool and heading for the back stairs and Honor's office. She didn't even make it that far.

Honor was at the bottom of the stairs, in deep discussion with Benny and Saul, while she pulled on her coat. When she saw Vivian, she paused, meeting her eyes. Then she kept going, settling her coat and retrieving the hat that Benny was holding out to her.

"Got it?" she asked.

"Crystal clear, boss," Benny said, nodding. Saul gave her a small salute, two fingers at his temple.

Honor dismissed them both with a flick of her fingers, then turned toward the back door, the one that led into the alley and the tangle of streets that would take her away from the Nightingale.

"Where are you going?" Vivian demanded, grabbing Honor's wrist before she could reach the door.

"I have a few things to do tonight," Honor replied, her voice cold as she pulled her arm away. "That a problem for you?"

"I thought you had a business to run?" Vivian said recklessly. "That's what you told that cop, wasn't it?"

"Danny's here," Honor said, her red lips pressed together in a tight line. For a moment, she looked like she wanted to say something else. Then she shook her head. "He knows how to look after things. And Benny and Saul will make sure there's no trouble."

"Honor—" Vivian hated the way her voice cracked on the word.

Honor didn't look at her. "Time for me to go, pet."

"Honor."

But she was out the back door and gone. Vivian didn't follow after her.

When she returned to the dance hall, Leo was still sitting at the bar. He looked relieved when she reappeared, though his relief faded into worry as he watched her. She stopped next to him, bracing her hands on the bar as she took a deep breath.

Take me away, Vivian wanted to tell him. "Dance with me," she said out loud, trying to give him a smile. "I could use a distraction."

"Sure thing. Give me just a minute." He looked relieved by the simple, normal request, standing and giving her a wink before he headed for the bandstand.

Vivian turned back to the bar, watching without really seeing as Danny, halfway down the room, shook up a couple of gin cocktails while bending his ear toward Saul, who was muttering something too quiet to be heard by anyone else. Danny nodded, pouring out the drinks as Saul disappeared. He must have felt her eyes on him, though, because once he was done, he wiped his hands and came to lean on the bar across from her. "What is it, kitten?"

The gentle question made Vivian want to cry. She swallowed back the urge. She had one more day. A lot could happen in a day.

"Danny-boy, what's Honor been up to recently?" she asked instead. "This week. It seems like she hasn't been around much, some days. She been busy?"

He didn't ask why she wanted to know, though she could tell from his expression that he was curious. Vivian held her breath, wondering if he would answer. Danny and Honor were a team. They were always on each other's side, more than anyone else in the Nightingale.

Would he tell her if he knew? There was Florence now, and God knew her heart would break if anything happened to her little sister. But would loving Florence be enough to outweigh what he owed Honor?

"She's been busy, for sure," he said slowly. "Out, some nights. I've been in charge here a lot." He shrugged. "Had to do inventory myself most days. She's been hard to pin down."

"What about last Monday? Was she around for inventory then?" Vivian asked. She could barely get the words out. She desperately wanted an answer. And she didn't want it at all.

Danny frowned, running the cloth over the bar slowly. "I don't know," he said at last. When he looked up at her, Vivian knew he understood what the question really meant. It made her heart want to break, that he was answering her at all. Florence had won out. "I don't think she was, though."

Vivian felt like she couldn't breathe. Why hadn't she thought to ask him before?

Because she hadn't wanted to believe it, ever since that conversation in the car with Hattie Wilson. She still didn't want to. She was still sure there had to be another explanation, anything else. Anything that meant Honor hadn't lied to her, hadn't set her up, hadn't been willing to let her take the fall.

A touch on her shoulder made her jump to her feet, every nerve on edge. She spun around to find Leo standing there. Up on the bandstand, they had just slid into the opening bars of "Charleston Charlie," fast and fun. Around them, couples were heading toward the floor.

"I thought you might like a fast one," Leo said, glancing between her and Danny. "Everything okay?"

Danny opened his mouth to reply, but Vivian got there first. "Everything's peachy," she said, tucking the pain in her chest down as far as she could. If all she thought about was the music, she didn't have to admit that her heart felt like it was breaking. "That's exactly what I want right now."

Leo looked like he wanted to ask more, and she could feel him looking past her at Danny. But she didn't give him a chance, grabbing his hand and hauling him toward the dance floor.

TWENTY-SEVEN

One Day Left

Vivian waited across the street, hovering at the edge of the park where a small crowd of children were chasing pigeons under the trees. The shrieking, darting bodies provided plenty of distraction in case anyone looked out of the house's windows.

Vivian shed her coat while she waited. Spring had finally come to the city, all at once, in a breath of warm air that made her think of sweaty days hauling deliveries uptown and sultry nights spinning through the arms of strangers and friends. She didn't let herself wonder if she would see those days and nights. She just turned her face up toward the sun and tried to ignore the ache like homesickness that was taking root in her chest.

Edison's replacement had been waiting across the street that morning when she snuck out, dodging through crowds at the streetcar stop to give him the slip. Leo hadn't been with her. After a string of nights spent sleeping on her floor, he hadn't come home with her after last call. He had a job, he'd whispered, pressing a kiss against her forehead.

He'd see her tomorrow, and everything would be okay, don't worry. Don't worry. We don't need to worry.

At last, Vivian saw the car pull away from behind the house, catching the glimpse of a pale face behind veils of black netting, a tall figure staring stoically ahead. She waited until they were followed by an exodus of servants from the tradesmen's entrance, most of them wearing black armbands, though she doubted they were heading to the funeral. She wouldn't have, if she were in their place and granted a rare morning off.

Bea opened the back door as soon as she saw Vivian slip down the alley. She had a black armband too, its stitches quick and sloppy. Vivian wondered which maid had been responsible for making them, squeezing the rapid sewing in between her other duties.

She hadn't let herself realize, until that moment, that she'd have to enter Buchanan's study again. But as soon as she was in the doorway, the memory of that day hit her like a punch to the gut. The feel of blood slipping against her hands as she turned him over. His blank eyes staring past her, his mouth fallen open as though he were just about to speak.

Bea was behind her, holding the door open and watching down the hall to make sure no one was coming. Vivian shuddered, taking a step back, scrubbing her hands against her dress as though she needed to clean them of blood once more. "I can't," she whispered.

"You can," Bea said mercilessly. "You have to. Or you have to give up and get out."

"Bea," Vivian whimpered. "This is where he died."

"You have to," Bea said again. But her hands were gentle as she placed one between Vivian's shoulder blades and gave her a push. "A memory can't hurt you."

Vivian wasn't so sure about that. But she forced her feet to carry her forward anyway. And then she stopped in the middle of the room, not sure where to begin.

"His papers are over here," Bea said, half closing the door behind them and crossing to the cabinet behind the desk. "I looked earlier, while everyone else was getting Mrs. Buchanan and her son out the door. I didn't see anything about people who worked for them, but I didn't have much time to look then. I can help you go through them now."

Vivian had to swallow back the knot in her throat. "I don't deserve you."

"No, you don't," Bea agreed, her smile strained. "I'm as grand as they come. Now, stop wasting time. You take the drawers on the right."

They worked in silence. The half-closed door meant no one would see them kneeling behind the desk if they were walking down the hall, but it also let them hear if anyone was coming. Luckily, there was silence.

The drawers Vivian was going through contained mostly letters, notes about business or missives from friends, a note from Corny Rokesby that had apparently accompanied a bottle of gin. Seeing that made the lump come back into Vivian's throat. What must that gift have meant to Buchanan, who had lost both his own sons, if he had kept the note?

But there was nothing about servants, not letters of reference or notes checking previous employment. Nothing.

"Any luck on your end?" Vivian whispered.

Bea shook her head. "Not yet," she whispered back. "But I've still got some more to go through. Just give me a minute."

Vivian swallowed. Every minute felt precious, and she didn't want to give up any of them. But she nodded anyway; there was nothing else to do. She was about to put her whole stack of papers back in their drawer when the letters at the bottom of the pile caught her eye. They were clearly older than the others, the ink faded in some spots, the paper torn in others. She pulled one out, curious. When she unfolded it, a playbill for a vaudeville show tumbled into her lap.

My Handsome Huxley, the letter began, *what fun we had last night.*

And it went on from there in a way that made Vivian's cheeks grow hot. It was signed *M., who will always be Your Diamond.* She glanced at the playbill, which declared that the show would feature *The Magnificent Margaret Diamond,* with a sketch of a woman in a costume even skimpier than the one that had let Vivian escape from the lodge ball.

She glanced at the date on the letter, a suspicion growing in the back of her mind. She flipped through the rest of the love letters, all from *M.,* until she found what she was looking for.

Huxley my darling, why won't you write back? I know I promised never to call at your house, but I'm growing worried. The doctor says he suspects twins . . .

Vivian sat back on her heels. She would never have suspected that Honor's mother had been a vaudeville actress.

In fact, she'd never suspected much of anything when it came to Honor's mother. Honor had said her mother caught influenza and never recovered, and Vivian had assumed that meant she was dead. But what if she wasn't?

What if she was still alive and in Brooklyn? If anyone would know how Honor really felt about her father, whether she could have been the one to end his life, it would be her mother. Wouldn't it?

Vivian flipped through the letters, looking for the most recent one. She might not be able to find the maid. But if she could find an address for Honor's mother, maybe she could get something like an answer. Maybe she could find out, one way or another, if Hattie and Levinsky and probably Leo too were right. Maybe—

Her hands shook as she pulled out the most recent letter.

Huxley, you bastard. You sweet-talking, snake oil bastard. You're never going to write, are you?

This one had an address. But it was dated more than twenty years ago.

Apparently, Huxley Buchanan had cared about his onetime lover enough to keep her letters. But he hadn't cared enough to reach out again, even after he brought his daughter back into his life.

Or maybe she really was dead. There was no way to know without asking Honor. And even if Vivian could bring herself to do that, could she trust anything Honor told her?

"What in God's name are you doing in here?"

Vivian's helpless rage drew to a sharp point of panic as she spun toward the door, where the housekeeper stood, one hand on the door, the other trembling where it held a poker in front of her. She stared at Vivian with wide eyes. "What do you think you—Dear God." She broke off, taking a step back. "You're the girl who—You can't be here! How did you get in this room? How did you get in this *house*?"

Vivian shoved the letter into her pocket without thinking, just in case she needed both hands free. "I walked right in," she said reck-lessly, her breath coming too fast.

Bea was still kneeling behind the desk. Vivian didn't glance down, but she could feel her friend's trembling. Bea hadn't been wrong when she said she could end up in jail if she was caught sneaking someone into the house—particularly the girl suspected of murdering someone in that very room. For the moment, Bea was hidden from the house-keeper's view. But she wouldn't be for long.

Vivian took a step around the desk. The housekeeper stumbled back, lifting the wavering poker higher. "Don't you go anywhere," she said, her voice shaking as badly as her hands. "You stay right there while I telephone the—"

"The police?" Vivian broke in. "I wouldn't risk that if I was you."

"Stop talking," the housekeeper snapped.

Vivian shrugged. "All right, lady. You do what you want. It's your funeral, though."

"Are you threatening me?"

"Not hardly," Vivian said. "I'm helping you out. It's no picnic having the cops after you. I wouldn't want you to go through that."

"Why would I . . ." The housekeeper stared at her. "Why would they . . . You don't mean to imply they'll think *I* let you in? What nonsense."

Vivian took another careful step forward. The housekeeper didn't look like the sort of woman who knew her way around a fight. But she had a weapon in her hands, and Vivian didn't. "It'll make them plenty suspicious, is all I'm saying," she said, trying to sound as certain as possible. "They've gotta be wondering about that poison, after all."

The housekeeper's face went white. "What do you mean?"

"They didn't ask you about that?" Vivian said. She'd have thought the police would question at least some of the staff about the arsenic.

"Of course they did, but that has nothing to do with—How do you know about that?"

Vivian was pleased to see the housekeeper looking uneasy. She had intended to put the woman off balance, chase her away so Bea could slip out unseen. But seeing the thoughts flickering across her face, Vivian had another idea. "Look, they think I stabbed him, right? I didn't, but they think so. But when would I have had a chance to poison him? That has to be someone who lived here, right?"

"Right . . ." The housekeeper said slowly, frowning, as though she had momentarily forgotten her distrust and was simply trying to follow Vivian's logic.

"And who better than a servant? If the cops see that I got in the house and was sneaking around when only you were here . . ." She trailed off, giving the woman a sympathetic smile as she shrugged. "You see, I'm just trying to save you a trip down to the station."

"What . . . what nonsense," the housekeeper said faintly, but her heart wasn't in it. The poker was down by her side, and Vivian could see her shaking. It was almost enough to make Vivian feel bad. But she pushed that thought aside. She had other things to worry about.

Vivian took another step forward. "Look, you met me before," she said, giving her best wide-eyed, innocent expression. "Do I seem like

I could kill someone? Let alone a fella like Mr. Buchanan? He was twice my size. And you know I'd never come around here before, so how could I have anything to do with the poison?"

The housekeeper frowned. "But then what are you doing here now?"

"Look, I get it, no one wants to talk to the cops about whoever it was that came to meet with Buchanan that day."

"No one did—"

"I said I get it," Vivian interrupted, then, seeing the expression on the housekeeper's face, nodded. "Okay, maybe you actually don't know. I believe you. But someone saw him. I know that maid had to, because she came to get him. He wouldn't have gone to his office just because I told him to, right? He wouldn't have had any reason to."

"I guess . . . I guess that could make sense," the housekeeper said slowly.

"All I want is to talk to her. She was older, fifties maybe. And she quit right after. You know who I'm talking about?"

The silence that hung in the room was painful. Vivian wished Bea was by her side, but she kept her eyes straight forward.

"Her name was Maggie Chambers," the housekeeper said at last. "I can't tell you much more than that, I'd only hired her a week before and we've been through so many maids in the last two months."

Vivian let out a relieved breath. "But you have some kind of record on her, right? An address, maybe, or a reference that she came with when she applied for the job? That's all I'm here for. I just want to talk to her."

She waited, barely breathing, to see what the housekeeper would decide.

"If I give you her reference, I want you to get out of here," the housekeeper said, her voice and her eyes both flinty. "And you don't come back. I don't need you throwing around that kind of talk about poison. And I sure as hell don't want Mrs. Buchanan finding you here."

"Fair deal," Vivian said, nodding. "Just do me one other favor?"

The housekeeper's eyes narrowed. "What?"

"Put down the poker?"

"I don't think so." The housekeeper hefted it once more. "I keep my hands on this until you're back in the street. Where you belong."

Vivian clenched her jaw, but it was far from the worst thing that had been said about her, even to her face. She could let the insults pass. "Lead the way, then. I promise not to get too close."

They were on the landing of the main staircase when Vivian risked a glance back up toward the hallway. She was just in time to see the top of Bea's head disappearing around the corner and out of sight.

Vivian let out a silent breath. At least that was one less thing to worry about. She hurried to catch up with the housekeeper.

The housekeeper's office was downstairs, just off the kitchen. The housekeeper made her wait in the hall. Vivian shifted from foot to foot nervously, glancing up and down the hall. She hadn't seen a telephone in there before the door closed. But what if the plan was just to leave her there in the hall until everyone else came back? She'd be arrested for sure, and then—

She jumped half a foot in the air when the door opened suddenly and the housekeeper reappeared, her cheeks bright with nervous color and an envelope in her hand.

"Maggie's position before this one was in a shop," she said, speaking very quickly, as though eager to be done with the conversation. "She assured me she'd had previous experience as a maid, and she seemed competent enough. But I imagine you'll have better luck at a shop anyway than you would at someone's home."

"Thank you," Vivian said as she slid the letter of reference out of its envelope. "I'll—" She broke off as her eyes caught on the address at the top of the stationery. "Where's the real one?"

"What?" The housekeeper scowled at her. "I just gave it to you, stupid girl."

"Me, the stupid one?" Vivian demanded. "That's the address for Howard's on Seventh. It's a store for men's hats, and a hell of a ritzy one at that. Not this"—she thrust the letter forward and shook it— "ladies' toiletries and cosmetics baloney. Did you even check the reference before you hired her?"

"I told you, it was a busy week," the housekeeper snapped. "And I'm doing you a favor here. Don't you go making trouble over it."

Vivian felt like the bottom had dropped out of her stomach. She had been so close. There had to be something else. "But it's a fake," she insisted.

"I gave you what I had," the housekeeper said, starting to sound angry now as well as nervous. "Take it or not, I don't care. Now beat it, or I really will call the police."

Vivian felt like she couldn't breathe. She wanted to find Bea and tell her what had happened. To sit down and cry until she didn't have any tears left. To run away and not stop running until she was somewhere no one knew her, and to hell with what that would mean for the people she left behind.

Instead, she folded the reference letter very carefully, her hands shaking, and slipped it into her pocket next to the crumpled letter from Honor's mother. Then she turned and walked out of the house without a word.

Around her, people carried on with their lives, no rest for New York, even on a Sunday. Vivian pushed through the crowds without seeing them, and eventually her feet carried her home.

She closed the door behind her, finally alone again, and took both letters out of her pocket. She set aside the one from Honor's mother and stared at the reference for Maggie Chambers.

It was a fake, no question there. But it wasn't nothing. It proved Maggie Chambers was real, that she had been there. And it proved she had lied. That had to matter.

Her week was up tomorrow. But she could take the letter with her.

She could force them to look at it. What had that lawyer, Dubinski, said? She just needed to give them someone else to suspect. Maybe Maggie Chambers was protecting whoever had met with Buchanan. Hell, maybe she had offed him herself, though Vivian had a hard time picturing that tired woman having a reason to kill someone. But she clearly mattered.

She'd prove it to them tomorrow. And then, no matter what happened, she'd know she had done all she could.

But just in case . . .

Vivian shoved both the letters under her pillow and turned back to the door.

Just in case it didn't work, she knew there was only one place she wanted to be now.

TWENTY-EIGHT

Mrs. Chin handed her a tray once more, along with strict instructions to see that her sister ate at least the broth. Vivian's hands shook as she went upstairs. Florence might've thought she'd been the one doing the mothering between them, but Vivian had always looked after her sister. Vivian had wanted to give her a life that made her happy, even if it meant doing things Florence wouldn't have approved of if she'd known about them. At least Florence had that now. She had a family.

She had someone to look after her, even if Vivian was gone.

Florence was sitting in the middle of the room folding laundry when Vivian knocked. "Hey, Flo," she said softly, poking her head around the edge of the door. "You up to a visit?"

Florence looked up. Her eyes were shadowed, from fatigue or worry or probably both. But she smiled at her sister. "Are you supposed to make me eat again?"

"Can you?" Vivian asked. "How are you feeling?" She didn't say why she was there. She would, eventually. But for the moment, she just wanted everything to feel normal between them, to talk about Miss Ethel or the baby or anything but the clock that had finally run out.

"Like a whale," Florence said, shaking her head. "And it's only going to get worse from here. Put that down and help me with the laundry? I can't eat until we clear some space."

The basket was full of baby clothes, carefully mended from all the children who had worn them before, and freshly washed. Vivian knelt next to her sister and pulled out a handful. She closed her eyes, trying to picture her sister as a mother. That wasn't hard.

But when she tried to picture Danny as a father, all she could see was him behind the bar of the Nightingale. And Honor was there, as always, standing beside him.

She pushed the image out of her head quickly. She couldn't let herself think of Honor right now. Swallowing, she buried her nose in the pile of laundry, trying to chase the hurt away.

"I made a decision about the letter," Florence said, one hand on the small of her back as she rose and carried a neat stack of little blankets to the chest of drawers she and Danny shared. Two of its drawers had been cleared out. One was already full of diapers, pins, and rags. The other was empty, waiting for the impossibly tiny clothes in the wash basket to be folded and tucked away. "From the medical examiner. I sent a response last night."

"To him?" Vivian asked, frowning. But as soon as she looked up, she knew what Florence meant. "To the address. To our . . . to whoever it was that buried our mother."

"Yes."

Vivian's hands clenched around the handful of laundry she had pulled from the basket. Her throat felt too tight to say anything.

"You didn't want me to," Florence said as she lowered herself back to the floor, settling close to Vivian. It wasn't a question. "You meant it when you said I should throw it away. Why?"

Vivian stared at the baby clothes in her lap. For a moment, the words felt tangled up in her throat, and she wasn't sure she'd be able to get them out. "I don't know. If he is our dad . . . he's already let us down, hasn't he? Who's to say he won't do it again?"

"He might," Florence agreed. "It's a risk, letting people into your life."

"Exactly. It's just more people to hurt you, right?" Vivian glanced up at her sister. "And more people to miss."

"But there's also a chance that it's more people to love you," Florence pointed out, running her hands over a little cotton gown to smooth it out before folding it into a tidy square. "You've spent your whole life wishing for more people to love you, Vivi, and looking for people that you could love back."

Vivian wanted to look away. It made her furious sometimes, how well Florence knew her, how well she had always known her, even when they had been so hurt by each other that they felt like strangers. It left an ache like homesickness inside her. And it soothed the ache at the same time, knowing that Florence was always there, even when they were apart.

That wouldn't change, would it? Not with distance, not with Danny. Not with the new baby. Not even with the walls of a prison or worse between them. Florence had always known who she was. She had always known how desperately Vivian wanted someone to show her she was worth loving.

But now . . .

"What is it, Vivi?" Florence asked gently, scooting close enough that their shoulders pressed together. "I've always been the one who wanted to leave well enough alone. You always insisted on looking for more. Why not now?"

Vivian couldn't look at her sister. "I don't know which would be worse," she whispered. "If whoever it is didn't want us, and I wasn't with you to share the hurt. Or . . ." She swallowed. Could she admit something so awful?

"Or they do, and you aren't there to share that either."

Vivian nodded miserably. Florence always knew her, even the parts she wanted to hide.

Florence turned suddenly, pulling Vivian into a tight hug in spite of the lump of her belly bulging between them. Vivian clung to her just as fiercely, her face buried against her sister's shoulder. "I always worried it would be your nights out, dancing and drinking and all the rest of it, that would lead to this kind of trouble," Florence whispered. Vivian could hear the tears in her voice. "I never thought it would be dressmaking that—" She broke off with a rough, shuddering breath. "Goddamn it, Vivi," she whispered.

"Language, Flo," Vivian gasped, not sure whether she wanted to laugh or cry.

"Don't," Florence insisted fiercely. "I'm your big sister. I'm supposed to fix this. I'm supposed to keep you safe."

"It's not your fault," Vivian whispered. It was someone's fault, but it sure as hell wasn't Florence's. And she wouldn't let her sister say good-bye thinking she should have done something more. Vivian held her more tightly. "It's no one's fault."

"It's—"

The gentle tap on the door made them both jump, but it was just Danny, hesitant as he closed the door behind him. "It's getting late," he said softly. "And I have to head to work soon. What's the plan, girls?"

Vivian frowned, glancing between him and Florence. "The plan?"

"I said I was supposed to keep you safe, and I'm going to," Florence said in a fierce whisper. "There has to be something, right?" She looked to Danny.

"You don't expect us to just let you get hauled away, do you?" he asked, crossing his arms and scowling at Vivian. "We can hide you, or maybe get you out of town. I'm sure Leo knows someone who—"

"Don't you dare," Vivian said sharply.

"But—"

"Don't you *dare,*" she repeated, pulling out of her sister's arms. "You remember how this works, right? Florence could be in danger if I disappear. I'm not risking that."

"And what if I don't care?" Florence demanded.

"Maybe you don't for your own sake." Vivian tilted her head toward Danny. "But he does. And you've got more than just you to be thinking of right now."

Florence clenched her hands into fists, as though they wanted to pull protectively around her belly and she wouldn't let them. "But you're already here," she whispered, her voice breaking. "And I can't let you go."

"It's all right, Flo," Vivian said gently, wanting it to be true. But even if it wasn't, she needed Florence to believe it, or at least pretend to believe it, long enough to keep her safe. "It'll be okay. You'll be okay. Just promise me you won't do anything to risk yourself or the baby."

"But—"

"Promise me." She had spent so long trying to set them both free. Florence had made it. Vivian wasn't going to let her give that up. "Please."

There were tears in Florence's eyes as she nodded. "I promise," she whispered.

Vivian looked at Danny, her voice catching as she asked, "You'll make sure of it, right?"

"Always," he said, nodding. The smile he gave her was sad. "Are you coming, Viv?"

"Where?"

"To the Nightingale, of course. Don't you want to say good-bye? Just. You know. Just in case."

More than anything, she wanted to say. Vivian wondered if her chest had finally cracked open, if both of them could see every selfish, longing heartbeat inside her. But she couldn't. Not tonight. She glanced at her sister. "But—"

Florence turned her face up toward Danny. "You'll make sure she's safe?"

"For as long as I can," Danny said, laying his hand on her shoulder. When she reached up to press hers against it, so tightly that Vivian could see white around her knuckles, he took her fingers in his and brought them to his lips, then bent to kiss her mouth, so softly, so sweetly, that Vivian had to look away.

A moment later, she felt Danny nudge her arm. "Come on, kitten. Get your glad rags on and meet me downstairs." He gave her a smile. "When the party might end, you can't waste a moment, right?"

"But—" Vivian tried to call after him, but he was already out the door. Vivian wiped her eyes before any tears could fall and give her away. She turned back to her sister. "I'm not going anywhere, Flo. I'm staying right here with you."

But Florence shook her head. "Go home, Vivi. And I don't mean that miserable little room where you sleep." Her smile was like heartbreak as she laid her palm against Vivian's cheek. "I mean your real home."

Vivian dragged in a breath, leaning into her sister's hand. "Thank you," she whispered.

Florence had always known her, even the parts she wanted to hide.

TWENTY-NINE

Vivian couldn't see the stars that night. The city lights were too bright, the dingy clouds too thick. But inside, Danny would pour her a drink, and champagne stars would fizz inside the glass. They'd dance like the couples on the floor, the people who found their way there hoping to escape something.

The band was just getting started, Mr. Smith counting them in on a syncopated rhythm, Bea catching it and starting out quiet, her voice growing louder and bolder until the brass joined, swinging in fast and hot while the dancers tumbled onto the floor.

Vivian took a deep breath. This corner of the world would go on, night after night, even if she wasn't there. But if she was going to go, she sure as hell wasn't going quietly.

She caught the hand of the first person going past.

"Hey, fella," she said, her smile wide and dazzling while her heart ached. "Want to make a scene on the dance floor?"

THIRTY

B y midnight, Vivian thought she must have danced with nearly everyone in the Nightingale. The ankle that she had twisted at the lodge ball throbbed, but she ignored it. It didn't hurt bad enough to stop her. Not tonight.

She could have sworn Bea was singing just for her, all her favorites filling the air. She danced with men and with women. She laughed and flirted and poured her heart out into the night, wanting to leave part of herself there forever.

But she kept an eye on the door too. She hadn't seen Leo all day, and he hadn't answered when she'd telephoned his place from the Chins' restaurant. She told herself he was avoiding her—partly because that was better than worrying that something had happened to him, and partly because she couldn't help wondering if it was true.

It wasn't until the first soft notes of a waltz floated down from the bandstand, Bea humming the melody into the microphone in a melancholy counterpoint to the piano, that Vivian realized who else she hadn't seen yet.

On a night like this, Honor would usually be working the crowd: glad-handing the wealthy visitors, watching anyone likely to make trouble, checking in with Mr. Smith on the bandstand. She kept the moods up, the customers smiling, the right people happy with cash or favors or just showing that they were important.

And tonight, she was gone. Instead of being behind the bar, Danny was drifting through the crowd in her place.

Vivian shook her head at her most recent partner, who was trying to coax her back onto the floor for the waltz. "You're sweet to ask, but this sappy stuff is too tame for me," she said, patting his cheek, trying to sound like she didn't have a care in the world. "Come find me for the quickstep." She blew him a kiss and ducked into the crowd before he could protest, making a beeline for Danny.

He saw her coming, but he kept a friendly smile on his face. He shook another hand and slapped another back, then gestured for one of the waitresses to bring a round of drinks to the well-dressed table of dancers resting their feet during the waltz. Only when they were settled, laughing and chatting, did he step away.

"Tearing a path through them, Viv," he said softly. "You're going to leave some broken hearts behind you tonight."

"Where's Honor?" she demanded. Her voice shook, but she held his eyes, refusing to let him look away.

He didn't, but the sympathy in his expression was almost worse. "I don't know. Hux said I'd be doing her normal rounds tonight. She had things to take care of."

"What kind of things?" Vivian forced herself to ask. "And don't pretend you don't know, Danny. She tells you everything."

"Not everything," he said. "Not tonight. Go back to dancing, Vivian. Don't waste—" He broke off, staring toward the bar. "Goddamn," he whispered. "Does he even know who he's serving?"

Vivian turned to see where Danny was looking, and she grabbed his arm without thinking, feeling cold all over.

The commissioner finished talking to the bartender, who was nodding pleasantly at him like he would any other customer. When they finished, the commissioner walked calmly over to a table in the corner. Two young men were already sitting there, but one steely look and a few quiet words sent them stumbling over each other to find somewhere else to be. The commissioner settled in to wait for his drink.

Danny cursed softly and thoroughly. "Why'd Hux pick tonight, of all nights, to have other business to deal with?" Vivian, her hand still on his arm, could feel the tension humming through him. Danny glanced at her. "Either we're about to get raided, or you're about to get arrested."

"Neither." Both of them jumped at the quiet voice behind them. Leo gave them a crooked smile that had none of his usual confidence. "That's the good news," he added, reaching out to slide Vivian's hand off Danny's arm. "Sorry I'm late."

"What's the bad news, then?" she asked.

His grip tightened. "I'm sorry, Viv. God knows we tried. When he called me in, I thought maybe I could still—" He broke off, but it didn't matter. He didn't need to finish. "I'm sorry," he whispered again. "He's waiting for you."

When Vivian looked back at the commissioner, he was watching her. Someone had delivered his order; two glasses now sat on the table in front of him. He raised just one finger and motioned her forward.

"You should head back to the bar, Danny-boy," Vivian said, giving him a nudge with her shoulder. "Don't go looking for trouble if he's not going to make it."

"I told Florence I'd keep you safe," he protested.

"She'll understand."

He hesitated, but at last he nodded. "Don't leave without saying good-bye?"

"If I can."

Vivian watched him head back toward the bar, falling in with a group of customers there, loose-limbed and smiling as if he didn't have a care in the world. She wasn't the only liar in the Nightingale that night.

"Do you want to talk to him alone?" Leo asked once Danny was gone.

"No," Vivian replied. She wanted to say yes, wanted him to believe that she wasn't afraid. But she was tired of pretending with him. "Stay with me."

Leo's hand tightened on hers again, and it took her a moment to realize that it wasn't a gesture meant to comfort her. He didn't want to go. Whatever had happened between him and his uncle that day, he wanted to be as far away from the man as possible, even if it meant leaving her alone.

"Never mind," she said, after a beat of silence that felt like a lifetime. She wanted to cry at the thought of walking up to that table by herself. Instead, she gave him a smile. "I can handle him by myself."

He let out a breath as he pulled his hand away from hers. "You can. You'll be fine." She didn't know if he was trying to convince her or himself. "Thanks, Viv."

Vivian had never felt so fiercely, painfully alone as she did crossing the room to the commissioner's table.

He sighed when she stopped in front of him. "I was beginning to get impatient," he said, and the pleasantness in his voice made Vivian shudder. "Sit down, please."

Reluctantly, she took the seat across from him, and he slid the second drink he had ordered to her. "My treat," he said, lifting his own glass in a toast. "To your health."

"That's a bit rich, if you're here to arrest me," Vivian said, but she took a sip of the drink anyway. It was top-shelf. Of course it was.

The commissioner laughed. "I didn't say how long that health would continue," he said, and Vivian hoped she didn't look as ill as she felt. "But you can calm down. You're bristling like a cat, you know, and there's no reason to. Not yet. I'm just here with a message."

"From who?"

He raised his brows. "From myself, of course. I don't run errands for other people."

"Why bother coming then?" Vivian asked. Her own voice was shockingly calm to her ears. If she didn't know better, she'd think they were old friends. "Why not have one of my shadows say whatever needs saying?"

The commissioner raised his brows at her. "Do you have a shadow tonight?"

Vivian stared coolly back at him. "I guess I just assumed you put some new guy on me after I gave the other one the slip. Hope he didn't get in too much trouble," she added, not meaning a word of it.

The commissioner shook his head. His expression could have almost been called a smile. "You were good practice for them. My boys get too complacent sometimes. And some of them aren't used to playing by your sort of rules." He took a drink. "Lovely stuff, that. My compliments to your employer. But to answer your question, young lady, you don't have a shadow. I'm not a cruel man, you see. I thought you might like one final night to yourself. I came here in person to say so."

Vivian had been counting down the days, but his words still felt like a fist to the gut. For a moment, she couldn't breathe. For a moment, she wondered if she'd ever breathe again.

"One final night," she repeated softly.

"Indeed." He smiled. "Enjoy it. Tomorrow I'll expect you at my office at nine o'clock in the morning."

"And if I'm not there?" Vivian asked, still speaking quietly. If she raised her voice at all, she wasn't sure what would come out.

The commissioner didn't blink. "Then at nine thirty, I'll send someone to arrest your sister. I'm sure I can find a good reason. At ten o'clock, I'll find that husband of hers—it's so easy to have the Chinese tossed out of the country, you know. And then at ten thirty . . ." That small smile hovering around his mouth again. "Well, Mr. Green and I have already discussed what happens next."

"I'll be there," Vivian said, her voice shaking. She thought of Maggie Chambers and the letter under her pillow. "But don't count me out. Not yet. I might have a thing or two that throws a wrench in your plans."

He raised his brows. "Do you think that makes a difference to me?"

Vivian pressed her lips together, trying to ignore the cold, tight feeling inside her chest, and met his eyes. "Doesn't mean I won't try."

"If you like. I hope you understand, it's nothing personal, young lady." The commissioner stood and retrieved his hat. "I'll expect you at nine o'clock tomorrow morning."

Vivian stared after him as he walked toward the stairs, two plain-clothes cops that she hadn't noticed before falling in beside the commissioner as he strode toward the door. Or maybe they were his personal muscle. It didn't matter. Did anything?

"Viv!"

It took Vivian a moment to realize where the shout was coming from. Bea was shoving her way through the crowd. Up on the bandstand, the bass and the trumpet were improvising a quick, lively duet while the other musicians took a breather. Bea's eyes were wide as she ducked around dancing couples.

"Was that—" She stared after the commissioner's retreating back, then looked at Vivian with hopeful eyes. "He's walking away. That's good news, right? He's—"

"He's expecting me in nine hours," Vivian said, closing her eyes against the stricken look in Bea's.

"But . . . but there's something we can do, right? God, there has to be something we can do. If they arrest you for murder, you aren't walking out of that jail again."

"I know," Vivian said softly.

"There will barely even be a *trial*. Do you know what they do to murderers in this city?"

"I know."

"We have to—"

"Bea." Vivian shook her head. "That's it. I've got my orders."

"But—" Bea trailed off, and they stared at each other silently. "What can I do?" she whispered at last.

"Throw me a party, pal," Vivian said. "Keep singing everything I love. I'm not giving up. But if I'm saying good-bye, I want to do it in style." She nodded toward the bandstand. "Mr. Smith wants you back."

When Leo met her in the middle of the dance floor, he was silent, and he didn't want to meet her eyes. But Vivian held out her hands anyway.

At last, he took them and pulled her close. "How long do you want to stay?"

His hand on her back was warm, but she felt icy cold. "I'll dance 'til last call," she whispered.

She'd lose herself in the music one more time. And then she'd face what came next.

THIRTY-ONE

Five Hours Left

The sun was only a few hours from rising when Vivian hopped off the streetcar, Leo at her side. The streetlights were pools of molten gold, but all they lit up was piles of slush and trash and empty streets.

Vivian didn't care. Leo took her hand without speaking, and she let him, though hers were too numb to really feel his touch. The night was cool, but she was colder, a chill that had started in her chest when the commissioner left and slowly spread through her body.

She stared at every ugly, unloved building that they passed as if she were seeing them for the first time. She wished she thought they were beautiful. Shouldn't she be seeing everything with new eyes as she climbed the steps toward her home? Shouldn't she be thinking kind, loving thoughts about the people sleeping on the other side of each door?

Will Freeman, who threw his windows open to share music with the world. His snoring was clear as she went past his door. Mrs. Gonzales's youngest was teething again, and she could hear angry, screeching whimpers drifting down the stairs. Mrs. Thomas could never sleep through the night after years of waking up with one baby after the other. She'd be on the third-floor landing, the window thrown open while she smoked, the only time of day she could be alone. Mr. Brown whimpered behind his door, the sound of a man who'd had too much to drink or not enough, anger and hopelessness spilling out of him and into the world.

They weren't beautiful. They were angry and difficult and hopeful, in spite of everything. They were kind and infuriating. They were alive, and real, and free.

Vivian stumbled on her bad ankle at the top of the steps, her legs worn out and her mind fuzzy. But it was still sharp enough to recognize the person standing in front of her door, black jacket hanging over crossed arms, hat casting shadows over half her face so that Vivian couldn't see her expression.

"Honor," Vivian whispered. "What are you doing here?"

THIRTY-TWO

Honor glanced at Leo, still standing at Vivian's side. "I came to talk to you, pet," she said quietly. "I wanted to see how you are."

"How I am? I hope you mean you came to say good-bye. You owe me that much, at least." Vivian took a step forward. Maybe they could be honest with each other at last. "Maybe you could also tell me why. I'm turning myself in, I don't have a choice there. So maybe it doesn't matter anymore, not really. But I know that you—" Vivian broke off, caught off guard by the flood of words. Honor was staring at her, unreadable as ever. Why had Vivian ever thought she might care?

"Did you hate him that much?" she asked.

Honor shook her head. "I never hated him."

Vivian hauled in a shuddering breath. "It's me you hate, then?" she whispered, her voice breaking.

There were tears in Honor's eyes. That didn't make sense. Honor, of all people, never cried. "Vivian, I could never—" She stopped, looking at Leo. He hadn't said a word, but Honor still hesitated. "You're right, it doesn't matter anymore." Slowly, deliberately, she shook out her jacket and shrugged it back on. This late at night, with her hat perched on top of her pinned-up hair, anyone walking past her on the street would probably see a stylish young man. Honor moved through the world however she wanted.

She walked away whenever she wanted.

She settled her coat, then gave Vivian a small nod. "I won't bother you anymore, Vivian." She paused. "And, I know it won't make a difference, but I am so—"

It took Vivian a moment to realize she wasn't going to finish her sentence. "What?" she demanded. "You're so what?"

Honor stared at her without speaking, and Vivian couldn't even begin to guess what she was thinking. "Well, there it is. We all have hard choices to make," she said softly, almost as if she was speaking to herself. She took a deep breath. "I have some business to take care of that can't wait. So, good-bye, Vivian."

"Honor."

"I'm glad you won't be alone tonight," she added, glancing at Leo again before she turned away and headed for the stairs.

"Honor."

And once again, she was gone.

Vivian turned away from the quick, determined sound of Honor's feet on the stairs. Her whole body ached with exhaustion, the fight that had carried her through the week suddenly gone out of her. She wanted to lie down and sleep for the few hours she had left. Maybe, just maybe, she could do that without dreaming.

"Come on," she sighed to Leo, fishing her keys out of her bag. "Let's—"

Her hand froze even as she reached for the door. She didn't need her keys. It was already open a single, careless inch. Vivian stared at it, not moving. Then—

"God*damn* it."

"Viv?" Leo sounded alarmed. "What happened?"

"She can pick locks," Vivian said, her voice shaking. She shoved the door all the way open. "Don't you remember? Honor can pick locks. Goddamn it."

"What did she want?"

"I don't know," Vivian said, staring around wildly as Leo closed the door behind them. "There wasn't—"

She broke off. There was. Of course there was. Vivian walked straight to her bed and yanked the pillow aside. Both the letter from Honor's mother and the reference for Maggie Chambers were gone.

How had she known? Or had she just wondered what Vivian might have found and searched, just in case? The letter Vivian could understand; if she had found something her mother had written, she'd have snatched it up too. But what about the reference?

Honor knew Maggie Chambers. That had to be it. The maid, whoever she was, had been in on the plan the whole time.

"What is it?" Leo asked. "Did she take something?"

Vivian jumped, spinning around to stare at him. Had it even been a minute since Honor had left? There was still time to catch her if they hurried.

"Where are you going?"

Vivian was already at the top of the steps. "I'm going to follow her. Are you coming or not?"

Even in the dim hall light, she could see the muscles clench in his jaw. "Yeah," he sighed. "I'm coming."

Vivian didn't bother to keep her steps quiet as they ran downstairs and back out into the night. Her ankle ached, but it was a distant pain, drowned under waves of anger and adrenaline. The city was still dark, but it wasn't quiet. Somewhere across the river, she could hear a factory bell clanging, its sound louder in the quiet, clear air as it dragged the next round of workers into their shift.

Vivian was breathing hard as she turned, looking up and down the street. Had Honor disappeared?

"There," Leo murmured, pointing, a figure in a suit and hat disappearing around the dim corner at the end of the street.

They turned the corner just in time to keep her in sight, Vivian grim and determined, Leo's reluctance almost a physical presence beside her. Two blocks. Three. Five blocks heading east. Vivian wanted to run after her, to grab her and shake her and demand answers. But she knew better than that. They hung back enough that if she turned, they could duck out of sight.

"What did she take?"

"Letters," Vivian said. Quietly, she told him what she had found that day.

"How do you think she knew they were there?" Leo asked when she fell silent. He grabbed her hand to keep her from stepping in an oil-slick puddle.

"I don't think she did," Vivian replied. She'd had enough time to think it over as they dodged through the city streets. Ahead of them, Honor turned south. "I think she got a little bit lucky. She must have decided to check my place. She had to know it was worth looking because . . . because she knows me." She swallowed back a lump in her throat as she said it. If Honor didn't know her so well, it wouldn't hurt so much. "She had to know I was looking for whatever I could."

"So she is mixed up in it," Leo said quietly.

Vivian nodded. "Whoever that maid really is, Honor knows her. She wouldn't have taken that reference, otherwise."

"She's the person who was meeting with Buchanan that morning."

"Maybe." It made too much sense not to think it. But it still didn't feel quite right. "Whatever it is, maybe we're about to find out."

Leo didn't say anything in response. They were coming to a busier part of the city, where restaurants served sleepy customers through the night. It was easier to blend in here. It would also be easier to lose Honor. They began to move more quickly. Ahead of them, Honor disappeared around another corner. When they finally reached it, she was half a block ahead, just climbing into a cab.

In a moment she'd be gone from sight. Vivian stared around wildly. There were three more cabs on this street, drivers snoozing at the wheels, waiting for any final fares as the last revelers of the night stumbled home. She didn't have any money with her, but that didn't stop her from banging on the window of the first cab to wake the driver up. Paying the fare was a problem for the future. She couldn't risk Honor getting too far ahead. Vivian yanked the door open and slid in, scooting all the way over so Leo could follow her.

"We're going the same place as your pal up there," she said, a little out of breath and hoping he couldn't hear it. Or maybe he'd think they were on the run and drive even faster.

The cabdriver gave her a skeptical look as Leo slammed the door shut behind them. "What's the address?" he said gruffly.

"No idea," Vivian replied, trying to sound cheerful and harmless. "You know how it goes. We're just supposed to follow them. Better hurry."

She held her breath, thinking for a moment that he would refuse. But then he shrugged. "Fare's a fare," he said gruffly, and pulled into the street.

"Are you sure it's worth it?" Leo asked, one leg bouncing anxiously.

"I need that letter," Vivian whispered, staring straight ahead, her eyes locked on Honor's cab, worried their driver would miss a turn or lose sight of it.

"Looks like they're going over the East River Bridge," the cabbie said gruffly. "Still want me to follow?"

"Yeah. Yes. Thanks, mister."

Leo didn't say anything else as they drove over the impossibly long suspension bridge and turned into Brooklyn. Vivian started to feel lightheaded. She had read the letters. This was where Honor had grown up.

"Pull over here," Leo told their driver quietly when Honor's cab began to slow down. Vivian glanced at him; he gave her a brief, tight smile as he pulled a small roll of cash from his pocket and peeled off a few bills. He held them out. "Twice that, plus whatever the fare is, if you stick around, yeah? We might need to scram in a hurry."

The cabbie took the cash—he'd have been crazy not to—but he scowled at them as he did it. "I ain't sticking around for anything not on the up-and-up," he said. "First sign of trouble, I'm off."

"We're not here for trouble," Leo said, handing over another bill. "I just don't want my gal to ruin her dancing shoes hoofing it back over that bridge."

The cabbie snorted. "Sure, pal. Whatever you say. I'll stay 'til I have a good reason to go, how 'bout that?"

"Works for us," Leo said. "See you in a bit."

Vivian was already heading down the street, not wanting to lose sight of Honor, on foot now and turning into a narrow alleyway. The street on the other side could barely be called that, hemmed in by buildings like teetering children's blocks. The cabs certainly wouldn't have fit down there.

Honor headed toward one of them. Laundry that someone had forgotten to bring in still fluttered from lines between its windows. A woman sat on the front stoop smoking, a blanket wrapped around her shoulders. Inside, a dog barked, then broke off with a yelp and a whimper.

Vivian stopped in the shadow of a building. If Honor was meeting someone inside there, they'd have to figure out how to sneak in. Maybe if they—

"Should I have been expecting you tonight?" The woman on the stoop blew out a long stream of smoke and leaned back on one hand, looking up at Honor.

"It's morning," Honor said quietly, stopping on the pavement without climbing the steps. "Sun'll be up in a couple hours."

"Not here it won't," the woman said, gesturing at the buildings that surrounded her. "Takes longer for it to make its way over this horizon. Though maybe you've been gone too long to remember that."

She leaned forward as she spoke, and the light from a flickering streetlamp stuttered across her. Vivian grabbed Leo's hand. She hadn't been able to catch more than a glimpse of the maid's face that day—Maggie Chambers had been too careful to keep her head down. But Vivian recognized the sandy-gray hair, the hoarse voice.

Honor had known exactly where to find her. In Brooklyn. Did that mean—

"Don't act like you're neglected," Honor growled. "I'm here every week. You're the one who's refused to move."

"I like it here," the woman said. She chuckled, but the sound was lost in a fit of coughing. "But you don't, so what brings you by?"

Honor pulled a paper from her pocket and held it out. Even from this distance, Vivian could see that her hands were shaking. "You said it wasn't you."

Maggie held her hand out for the paper, and her face twisted into a grimace as she read. She looked back up. "Well, and you clearly didn't believe me. You knew I'd done it, or you wouldn't have been trying so damn hard to get me to leave town this week. Nothing's changed."

"Nothing's changed? If the cops had seen this—"

"But they didn't," Maggie snapped. "And they're not going to, right?" Deliberately, she ripped the paper in half. Vivian couldn't stop the whimpered gasp that escaped her. Honor started forward, one hand outstretched, but Maggie ripped it again, and again, then shoved the pieces into the pocket of her housedress. "They're not going to," she repeated.

Honor let her hand fall. "And Maggie Chambers?" she asked. "You just went ahead and used your real name? What if he'd recognized it? What if he'd recognized *you*?"

"He never bothered to learn my real name, the bastard. I was Margaret Diamond to him. And as far as recognizing me . . ." Maggie snorted, gesturing angrily toward herself. "Even if he did bother to look closely at one of his maids, would *this* make him think of the pretty dancer he used to know?"

A roaring sound filled Vivian's head. It felt so real that she flinched, cowering back against the wall.

Maggie was still talking. "Especially with a little makeup on. I haven't lost that knack, even after all these years, so don't talk to me like I'm stupid, Honor."

"Like you're stupid?" Honor demanded. "Like you're *stupid*? After what you did, *that's* your biggest worry?" Her voice cracked, and when she spoke again, she sounded small and lost. "You told me it wasn't you, Ma."

"Did you believe me?"

"No." Honor's voice was bleak.

"Oh, baby girl." Maggie stood, shaking her way through another bout of coughing. Her bluster faded away as she came down the steps to wrap her arms around her daughter. "He doesn't deserve this from you. He's the reason your life has been so hard. He's the reason we lost Stella. This way, he's finally taking care of you like he always should have. All I did was make the world a fairer place."

"All you did—" Honor pulled away. "Can you hear yourself talking, Ma?"

Maggie glared at her. "Don't pretend like your hands are so clean, my girl. I know what sort of work you do. So don't get all high and mighty and act like you're better than me. We're the exact same kind of trash, you and me, and we do what we need to so we can survive."

"This is different," Honor said, her voice so quiet that Vivian could barely hear it. "And you know it is."

For a moment, neither of them spoke. Vivian could have sworn the whole city had gone silent around them, waiting.

"What are you going to do, then?" Maggie asked, before she was interrupted by another hacking cough that shook her whole body.

She grabbed the railing and slowly lowered herself back onto the steps. When she spoke again, her voice was weaker. "I'm your *mother,* Honor."

"And he was my father."

"And he didn't give a damn about you!" Maggie yelled, coughing again. "I was there every goddamn day, when you were hungry or sick or getting into trouble. I was there when Stella—" She broke off and took a deep, shaking breath. "I was there. I didn't owe him anything, and neither do you," she said, her voice small and sad.

"It's not just him—" Honor started to say, but her mother began coughing again. Honor abandoned her protests and knelt next to her, wrapping an arm around her shoulders. She closed her eyes, pressing her forehead against her mother's.

"It's just you and me, right, baby girl?" Maggie Chambers said, cupping a hand around her daughter's cheek. "We're all we have left." Neither of them moved.

"Come on, Ma," Honor said at last. "Let's get you inside."

"I don't need you to tell me . . ."

Vivian couldn't listen to any more. She turned, walking so quickly that she was nearly running, and then she was running, pushing her way blindly through the alley, until she burst onto the quiet Brooklyn street, gasping for air almost as badly as Maggie Chambers had.

She wanted to blame Honor. She wanted to hate her—but oh, she couldn't make herself do it. She understood too well.

What if it had been her and Florence? Could she have turned on the only family she still had in the world, the one person who had never left her when everyone else had?

Vivian lifted her face toward the cloud-bruised sky, letting the cold air dry the tears that wanted to fall. She and Honor had always been too much alike.

"Viv, are you okay?" Leo's touch on her arm made her jump, but she didn't pull away. "That was . . . was that really . . ."

"She was the maid," Vivian said. "The one who told him—" She laughed bitterly. "So all the other servants who said no one else came to the house that day were telling the truth. It was her the whole time."

"She ripped it up," Leo muttered. "That was your proof, and she's just going to throw it in the trash."

Vivian pressed her hands against her temples. "I can try—I can still tell him tomorrow, right? The commissioner. I can tell him about Maggie Chambers . . ." She was pacing back and forth across the pavement, she realized, her steps jerky and frantic. She stared at Leo. "Will he do anything about it if I have no proof?"

Slowly, Leo shook his head. "I don't think he'd have done anything even with proof."

"But maybe someone will," Vivian said, wrapping her arms around herself. "A cop, a lawyer, someone . . ."

"Maybe," Leo said, but his heart wasn't in it.

"And if they don't . . ." Vivian's voice cracked. "I guess at least I got my answers."

Leo pulled her roughly to him, and Vivian laid her head against his chest, shivering. "Are you cold?" he asked. "We need to get you inside."

She was cold. She was numb all over, her ankle throbbing, her heart knotted inside her chest. "Take me home," she whispered.

He did. The cabbie hadn't left, but Vivian was barely paying enough attention to be relieved. She was silent through the ride, staring out at the city that had always been her home, watching tall buildings and dark windows flickering past. The window was icy against her cheek. On the seat between them, she reached for Leo's hand. He jerked it away, but a moment later it was back, and his fingers curled tightly around hers.

The ride back might have taken five minutes or five hours. None of it felt real. If it hadn't been for those two sensations—the chill of the glass, the warmth of his hand—she might have believed that everything around her was only a dream.

She had her answers. And she was out of time.

She didn't let go of Leo's hand while he paid the cabbie or while they climbed the stairs to her cramped, ugly little home. She hadn't stopped to lock the door when they left, and soon enough they were inside. She dropped his hand to close the door behind them, then turned, her back against it, her palms pressed against the wood. "Leo," she said softly.

He didn't seem to know what to do with himself, fidgeting with his hat as he paced from one side of the room to the other, spinning it in anxious circles until he lost his grip and it tumbled to the floor.

"Leo," she said again.

He stopped in front of her, breathing too fast, and finally looked at her. "What are you going to do?" he whispered.

There had been ice holding the pieces of her together, but that whisper cracked it. She grabbed his coat and yanked him to her, needing the feel of his mouth, his body, anything to remind her that for a few hours more she was still herself, still alive, still free.

For a moment, his weight pressed her against the door, and then his hands were at her hips. It was only a few steps from the door to the bed; he lifted her easily and tumbled them both onto it. She sat up so she could push his jacket away, but instead she clung to it, her breath coming in shuddering gasps.

"Leo, you gotta help me," she begged. It hadn't seemed real, until that moment, like something from a film instead of her life. She hadn't believed that she would have to go to that station in the morning. "You can get me out of town, right? I can head for Chicago or—"

"I can't, Viv," he said, his voice cracking. There were tears in his eyes, the only time she had ever seen him cry. The pads of his fingers pressed against her skull, her cheeks, as though he was afraid she would disappear in front of him. "You know what he said. He'll come after my father. I can't . . ." He pressed his forehead against hers, and he was shaking. "Please don't ask me to choose."

"I won't," she whispered, her eyes closed. "I won't, I'm sorry. I couldn't go anyway. Florence and . . ." She gasped back a sob that wanted to escape. She wouldn't cry. She wouldn't. "I'm just so scared, Leo. I'm so scared. I can't . . ."

His mouth caught hers as her words trailed off, and she could taste salt on both their lips. She kissed him back, fingers going to his waistband to yank at his shirt, frantic as they slipped underneath.

Leo's hands, normally so smooth and sure of themselves, were clumsy as they fumbled at the buttons down the back of her dress. Vivian drew away just long enough for him to pull it over her head, her own fingers greedy at the buttons of his shirt. She was cold, so cold, she would never be anything but cold again, but his skin was warm and she sank against him as he tugged his own shirt off and threw it aside.

His weight on top of her as he kicked his trousers away, his mouth against her skin, his fingers tracing a path down her body that made her shudder. None of her rules mattered anymore. She buried her face against the curve of his shoulder, and her fingers dug into his sides, hungry and desperate as she pulled him to her.

If she could only get close enough, maybe, somehow, she could disappear into him. And then no matter who came looking, they would never find her again.

THIRTY-THREE

Leo fell asleep after, but Vivian stayed awake, watching the dawn light creep through her window and across the floor and listening to the world outside her walls slowly coming to life. It was warm under the quilt, and she could hear the quiet huff of his breath. But Leo had pulled away in his sleep.

It didn't hurt as much as she thought it would. There were times for holding on tightly to whatever you could, but they both knew this wasn't one of them. Vivian slipped out of the bed without waking him and dressed silently. She had perfected the skill back when she and Florence still lived together and she would sneak out, spangles on and shoes in hand, to meet Bea for a night of dancing. Her clothing was more practical this time, skirt and sweater and sensible shoes. But she still carried them, moving across the floor on silent, stockinged feet. She wanted Leo to sleep for as long as he could. It was easier that way.

She hesitated, then tucked enough money into his jacket pocket to pay him back for the cab ride last night. She didn't want things to end with her owing him anything. She left her key on the table next to his hat. He'd know to take it to Danny and Florence.

She paused just by the door, looking around the room one last time. That was when she noticed the quiet change in Leo's breathing, the tense stillness of his shoulders. He was awake and pretending not to be, listening to her go.

Neither of them said anything. It was easier that way, too.

There was nothing left to do except take a deep breath and start walking.

———— ·· ————

"Wait here."

The station was busy, even in the morning. Vivian could hear the rowdy clamoring of the drunks who had been arrested the night before, the grumpy bustle of the officers going about their work. The sergeant held a door open, gesturing impatiently for her to go in.

The room was a little box, with a table and chairs and nothing else. Just looking at it made her skin crawl, made her want to run in the opposite direction. She had fast feet. Maybe she could make it out the front door before they caught her.

Vivian hauled in a breath and walked through the door. Very carefully, she took a seat. The door clicked shut behind her. She didn't think of anything, not Florence or Leo or the memory of Honor with her forehead pressed against her mother's. She couldn't let herself.

She didn't know how long she waited before the door opened.

"Miss Kelly."

She jumped to her feet, wincing as she landed on her bad ankle and knocking over her chair as she did. The commissioner gave her an impatient look, and Vivian pressed her lips into a tight line to keep them from trembling.

"I'm glad to hear that you were more than punctual this morning," he said, pushing the door farther open. "Follow me."

Vivian wanted to ask where she was going. They hadn't taken her name or her information at the front desk, nothing that struck her as a normal arrest. What did that mean? She kept her mouth shut, afraid of what would come out if she opened it, but she was shaking as she followed him down the hall.

It ended in a closed door, where the cop Levinsky waited like a guard. "Anything from her?" the commissioner asked, sounding bored.

"No, sir," Levinsky replied, his eyes darting to Vivian as he opened the door. "Just as you left her."

The commissioner gestured impatiently, and she followed him into the room, still unsure what was going on. The room was another ugly box, though it had a table set with a steaming coffeepot in one corner and a line of chairs facing the wall opposite the door. That wall was made entirely of glass, a window into a room like the first one Vivian had been in.

On the other side of the window sat Maggie Chambers.

Vivian stumbled back a step, her breath catching. Levinsky, who had followed them in, caught her arm before she tripped.

"Please control yourself," the commissioner said impatiently. "It's a transparent mirror. We can see through from this side, but she can't see us."

"Who . . ." Vivian swallowed. "What . . ." She didn't know how to finish, or even what she wanted to ask.

"I believe you know Honor Huxley, Huxley Buchanan's daughter?" the commissioner said dryly. It wasn't really a question, but Vivian nodded anyway. "It seems the woman in there is her mother, which of course means she was once Mr. Buchanan's mistress. Miss Huxley has provided us with papers—somewhat damaged, but still informative— proving that her mother took a job as a maid in Mr. Buchanan's home, with the intention of causing him harm."

Honor had . . .

Vivian couldn't tell if she was still breathing or not. She pulled away from Levinsky, feeling lightheaded, and took a step toward the glass. Honor had turned her mother in.

"It seems she was the one who killed him," the commissioner continued, still sounding bored. "Do you recognize her from your visit to the Buchanan household that day?"

Vivian stared through the glass. She could see glimpses of the beauty Maggie Chambers must have been when she was young, but poverty and anger and illness had done their work. Sullen lines cut deep channels across her face, and her papery skin hung loosely around her neck and chin. But she still sat with the ramrod-straight poise of a dancer, and she glared at the mirror, as if she knew someone was behind there, watching her, before a familiar hacking cough made her double over, wheezing.

"Miss Kelly?" the commissioner asked impatiently. "You said a maid came to get Mr. Buchanan for a meeting with an individual who, apparently, did not exist. Was she that maid?"

And underneath it all, Vivian could see the shape of Honor's own face. There were the high cheekbones, the smoothly arched brows, the lips that always smiled like they had a secret. She didn't speak. How could she take the last part of Honor's family away from her?

The commissioner sighed, motioning for Levinsky to bring him a cup of coffee. "You might as well know that Miss Chambers—she has been going by Mrs. Huxley for some years, but she was never married—has already confessed to the murder of Mr. Buchanan. It seems she blamed him for the death of her second daughter, which occurred some years ago."

Vivian turned toward him sharply, not bothering to hide her surprise. If Maggie had already confessed . . . But what if he was lying to her?

"As we would like to put this matter behind us, your corroboration will be appreciated. Was Miss Chambers the maid you saw that day, who lured Mr. Buchanan away with this fictitious meeting?"

The commissioner took a sip of his coffee while he waited for her answer. In the moment that his eyes were off her, Vivian flicked a glance toward Levinsky, hovering behind his shoulder. Levinsky nodded, just once, but it was enough. God knew how it had happened, but she trusted him.

The commissioner was telling the truth.

"Yes," Vivian said, barely able to find her voice. "Miss Chambers was the maid who came to get Mr. Buchanan that day."

"Excellent. Thank you, Miss Kelly." The commissioner downed the rest of the coffee in a single gulp and handed the cup back to Levinsky. "I appreciate your help in clearing up this misunderstanding," he added as he strode from the room.

"Misunderstanding?" Vivian demanded, following him. "Do you have any idea what kind of hell this week has been? Or how it felt when you showed up last night and—"

"No." The commissioner stopped in front of his office door, waiting for Levinsky to open it for him. "Nor do I care. Just be thankful and get out. I have better things to do with my day than stand around arguing with ungrateful girls."

He pulled the door firmly shut behind him. Vivian stared after him, then rounded on Levinsky, who was still watching her.

"That's it?" she demanded. "After all that, it's just done?"

"That's it." He shrugged. "You can leave."

"But . . ." Vivian wanted to go, more than anything else in the world. But she didn't trust any of it. She swallowed, glancing back over her shoulder to the room they had just left. "What will happen to her?"

"The maid?" Levinsky looked surprised by the question. "She'll have a trial, same as you would have. Press'll love it. Lotta dirt in this one."

"I'll bet," Vivian said faintly. "I guess . . ."

So many times in the last few days, she had felt like she was in the middle of a dream, hoping she would wake up and find that her only worries were paying rent and keeping the new boys at the Nightingale from getting too fresh.

But now that it had happened, she didn't know what to do with herself.

"I guess I'll go home," she said.

———•—

She thought about splurging on a cab ride home to celebrate. But she didn't really feel like celebrating yet. Not until she could see Honor, face-to-face, and find out what had changed in those dawn hours. Not until she could demand an explanation for everything she'd been through in the last seven days.

And anyway, she hadn't brought any money with her to the station, not trusting that it would make its way back to Florence after they booked her. She didn't even have a nickel for the subway.

So she walked. The sky had been bright and sunny when she was too dazed to appreciate it. Now there were clouds and a sullen drizzle beginning to fall. Soon, her hat and shoes would be soaked through. She didn't care.

Vivian dodged through the crowds that thronged the sidewalks, around piles of trash and puddles. The smell of something cooking made her stomach growl; she hadn't been able to eat anything that morning.

Coffee, she decided as she pounded on the front door of her building and waited for someone to open it, unable to get in on her own without her keys. She wasn't great at keeping food around, but she had coffee tucked in a cabinet. She'd start with that. And then—

"What's the matter with you?" Mr. Brown growled as he yanked the building's creaky front door open and scowled at her. "Ain't you got no respect for folks who might be sleeping?"

"It's coming up on noon," Vivian pointed out. But even his angry face, violet circles under his eyes and cheeks crisscrossed with a drunk's red veins, was a welcome sight. She pressed a kiss against his cheek and slipped past him. "Thanks for letting me in."

"You been drinking, girl?" he called after her.

She hadn't felt the rain when she was outside, too caught up in her own thoughts. But she was shivering by the time she made it to her front door, hoping that Leo hadn't bothered to lock it when he left. She let out a sigh of relief when it swung open.

He stood in the middle of the room, dressed and ready to leave, hat already on his head. But he wasn't moving, just staring down at the key she had left on the table.

Vivian let the door swing shut behind her, and the crash made Leo jump. He spun around, his hand going to the back of his waistband, before it fell away.

"Vivian."

"Hey, Leo."

The silence stretched between them as they stared at each other. Neither of them knew what to say.

"You're shivering," Leo said at last.

"I—yes." Vivian glanced down, then wrapped her arms around herself. "It's raining out. And I didn't have any money with me for the subway."

"What are . . . What happened? Why aren't you . . ." He pulled off his hat and ran a hand through his hair.

"They let me go," Vivian said, her thoughts tumbling over themselves. How could she explain what Honor had done? "She was there already. Maggie Chambers. She'd already confessed, and your uncle told me I could go." She swallowed, then repeated in a small voice, "They let me go."

"Goddamn, Viv, I thought—I can't believe—" He let his hands fall to his sides. "You left without saying good-bye."

"What would the point have been?" Vivian asked. His arms should have been around her, she should have been reaching for him. They should have been giddy with relief. But neither of them moved. "You could have said something, too."

"What would the point have been?" His voice cracked as he echoed her. "What happened? Why'd they let you go?"

"Honor." Vivian sounded bewildered even to her own ears. "Maggie had already confessed when I got there. Honor turned her in. Even though it means she'll lose . . ." She was crying, she realized. "She said she wouldn't help, and after last night I knew—I think I'd have done the same if it had been me, I can't blame her for—But she knew what would happen to me, Leo, she knew and she didn't say a word, and it *hurts*—And then God knows why, but she changed her mind and—"

Then Leo did cross the distance between them, his arms going around her, holding her so close that she could feel his heart pounding against her chest. He didn't say anything while she sobbed into his jacket.

When she pulled away at last, he offered her a handkerchief, and Vivian choked out a laugh at the boring, everyday gesture. She wiped her cheeks.

"Sorry," she said, shaking her head. "I'm all a mess. I don't even know what to do with myself now."

"You don't have to apologize," Leo said, brushing her hair off her face with gentle fingers. "It's been a hell of a week. Sometimes, I guess, that's just how it goes."

There was an edge to his voice, something quiet and resigned, and she saw it in his eyes, too, when she looked up at him. He gave her a sad smile as he shrugged. They both knew he wasn't just talking about her tears.

"You should probably go talk to her, right?" he suggested, tucking the handkerchief back into his pocket. "She owes you an explanation."

"Yeah," Vivian agreed. "One hell of an explanation. Do you . . ." She bit her lip, then carefully asked, "Do you want to come?"

"Do you want me to?"

Vivian wanted to say yes, for his sake. But she shook her head. "That's probably a talk we should have alone."

Leo let out a slow breath and nodded. "Seems fair. Why don't you go see if there's any hot water in the washroom? And when you're done, I'll head downstairs and whistle up a cab?"

"Thanks," Vivian said quietly. "I'd appreciate that."

He shrugged. "Feels like the least I can do."

She caught his hand when he would have stepped past her, holding it tightly until he turned to look at her. "You okay, Leo?"

"Yeah," he said at last. "Like I said, it's been a hell of a week. But I'll be fine." For a moment, she thought he would kiss her. But he only squeezed her hand in return. "You will be too, Viv. I promise."

———·———

The Nightingale's front door was locked when she finally made it there. It was a long time until business hours, but Vivian knew that this was when Danny was usually taking deliveries and doing inventory. She headed down to the cellar door.

But the newest bartender was the one there unloading crates, helped—or, more likely, supervised—by Benny. "Where's Danny?" she demanded from the doorway, suddenly worried.

Benny had clearly heard her coming; he nodded but kept his focus on his work, shoulders straining against his shirt as he hefted two crates at the same time. But the bartender jumped, knocking one of the shelves and nearly sending several bottles toppling to the floor.

"Careful," Vivian said, grabbing his arm. "Everything okay?"

"Everything except you nearly giving me a heart attack," he grumbled. "Danny's at home, far as I know. Why?"

Of course. Of course Danny would be home with Florence today. Vivian swallowed. She needed to go see her sister. But first, Honor.

"Just curious, is all," she said. "I'm looking for Honor, is she around?"

"Haven't seen her," the bartender grumbled.

Benny, though, frowned as he set down his crates. He rubbed his palms together as he straightened up. "Saw her going upstairs when I arrived. She didn't . . ." He picked up a crowbar and began to lever the crate open so the bartender could unload bottles of gin. When he spoke again, it sounded as though he was choosing his words carefully. "She looked like she had something on her mind. Dunno if she wants to be interrupted."

"Thanks, Benny." Vivian didn't much care what Honor wanted just then, but she wasn't dumb enough to say that out loud. "I'll take my chances." About to head upstairs, she paused, glancing into the crate of gin. "There's only twelve bottles in there."

That earned her another scowl from the bartender. "So?"

"Usually they send fifteen," she said a little impatiently. "You should check it with Honor."

He shrugged. "They might've just changed their shipment size. Happens all the time."

"Sure. But if they did it without telling her, and she still paid for fifteen, she'll want to have words with the fella."

"I thought I was the one doing inventory here," he grumbled, but Vivian was already gone. She didn't have time to stick around and soothe his ego.

She paused at the top of the steps, closing the door behind her and taking in the quiet dance hall. Most of the lights were off, and the rooms were silent and empty, as though they were holding their breath.

The stairs were dark, and Honor's office was locked. But the second door on the landing was open. Vivian closed it behind her and climbed slowly to the third floor, taking in the transformation from the Nightingale to Honor's home. There were new prints on the wall since the last time she'd been there. A pair of shoes, still wet from the rain, left by the closed door.

Vivian took a deep breath and knocked. "It's me," she called softly.

The Honor that opened the door wasn't one she had ever seen before. She was used to Honor in control, white shirts starched and trousers pressed. She had seen Honor hinting at seduction, barefoot and taunting, wrapped in a silk robe and likely nothing else. Makeup and hair always perfect, lips curving in a scarlet smile that was her defense against the world.

The Honor that opened the door had no defenses. She looked as if she hadn't changed or slept in over a day. Her suspenders hung down around her hips, the collar of her shirt sagging open at her throat, her feet bare. Her hair was only half up, like she'd begun removing pins but forgotten what she was doing, most of her curls spilling down her back. Her eyes were red and her cheeks pale. It was the most human Vivian had ever seen her.

"They let you go," Honor said, staring at her.

"They did." Vivian had to remember to breathe. "Are you going to let me in?"

Honor stepped back and opened the door further, letting Vivian walk past her into the little sitting room. There was a glass of liquor sitting on the table, but it looked like it had been poured and forgotten. There was a plate of breakfast, but that hadn't been touched either.

Honor closed the door behind them. The only thing Vivian could read in her expression was wariness. She walked toward the table. "Do you want to—"

"I followed you last night," Vivian interrupted. Better to say it all at once, so they both knew where they stood.

Slowly, Honor turned back toward Vivian, lips pressed together as though she were in pain. "Then you know."

"I know," Vivian agreed. The air between them was so tense an electric current might have been running through it. "What will happen to her?"

Honor shrugged. "A trial maybe? I don't know. They told me she confessed, so maybe not. Maybe just . . ." She swallowed and looked away. "I'm trying not to think about it."

"You might . . ." Vivian cleared her throat, remembering what Levinsky had said. "You might try talking to your father's wife. It'll be all over the papers if it becomes public. Some journalist will spin it as a tragic love story, revenge tale, something like that. She'd probably hate that. Mrs. Buchanan, I mean. She'll want to keep it quiet. You might be able to cut some kind of deal with her."

Honor shook her head. "You always were a smart girl."

"Why did you do it?" Vivian whispered, taking a step forward, then another. She could see Honor's chest rising and falling with her breath, the beat of her pulse in the hollow of her collarbone. "You kept quiet all week. You tried to convince her to leave town. And then, all of a sudden, you changed your mind. *Why?*"

"Because." Honor's voice cracked on the word. She was always so cool, careful and controlled and impossible to read. Now she was none of that. She cupped Vivian's face in her hands, and they were close enough to each other that Vivian could see tears in her eyes. "For most of my life, it was her and me and Stella against the world. And then Stella died, and she was all I had left. I thought it would hurt too much to lose her. But it would hurt far, far worse if I lost you."

Vivian took a step back, away from the gentle, hopeful touch, and smacked Honor across the face. Honor reeled backward, grabbing the back of the chair to catch her balance. When she looked up, her eyes were snapping with anger.

Vivian didn't care. "You knew," she ground out. "You saw what I was going through, and you knew the whole time she had done it. And you said *nothing*."

"I didn't know for certain."

"You knew." Vivian stared at Honor, not giving her the chance to look away.

At last, Honor nodded. Her shoulders slumped, the fury and fight gone out of her. "I knew. And I kept my mouth shut."

"You should have *told* me," Vivian said, knowing Honor could hear the hurt in her voice.

"Told you what? That my mother was a killer? That I was choosing her anyway?" Honor's cheek was red where Vivian had struck it. "I knew she didn't deserve it. But I still did."

"Why did you, then?"

Honor shrugged helplessly. "She's my mother. Why did you just tell me how to help her, after everything we put you through?"

The sound that escaped Vivian might have been a laugh if it hadn't been so bitter. "I guess mothers are tricky things for me, too," she said. "I don't know if they break your heart worse when they're around or when they're gone. But God knows I don't want to be the reason you lose yours."

"And would it be another betrayal if I took your advice?" Honor asked, touching her cheek gently with her fingertips, as though checking how badly she was hurt. She didn't look away, though.

Slowly, Vivian shook her head. "I don't think it would be, no."

"And . . ." Honor hesitated, taking half a step forward. But she stopped herself, her hands tightening on the chairback once more. "Are we—"

"Don't," Vivian warned her. "You don't have the right to ask me that yet."

"That's fair," Honor said softly. "Do you know when I'll see you again?"

"I'll be around."

"Vivian."

She'd been turning for the door, but she stopped.

"I'd do it again, pet," Honor whispered. "Even if you decide you hate me from here on out. Even if I have to live every day of my life without you in it. I'd choose you all over again. Every time."

"Well." Vivian took a deep breath. "That's a start, I guess." She met Honor's eyes. "It doesn't fix it. But it's a start."

THIRTY-FOUR

Florence cried when she saw Vivian standing in the doorway, though she tried to pretend she was just feeling weepy because of her pregnancy.

"You're not very convincing," Vivian laughed, holding her sister close.

"Shut up," Florence sniffed, pulling away just far enough that she could look at Vivian's face. "How?" she asked simply.

Danny had been sitting with Florence when Vivian arrived. But after pressing a quick kiss to his wife's head and giving Vivian a hug, he made himself scarce. Vivian was glad, both that she could have her sister to herself and that she didn't have to explain for him. He knew Honor better than almost anyone—except, perhaps, Vivian realized, for her. But Honor hadn't told him about her mother, and Vivian didn't know whether she should or not.

"They caught the woman who did it," she said simply, steering her sister back toward her chair. "She was working as a maid in his house, but they had a . . ." She hesitated. "A romantic history together. They had a child who didn't survive. She blamed him."

It was all true, and it left so much out.

"My God, could they have cut things any closer?" Florence gasped, half laughing and half crying. "I'm sorry, I'm dragging you around, but I don't want to let go of your hand. I don't want you to disappear on me."

"I'm not going anywhere," Vivian murmured, leaning her head against her sister's, temple to temple. They sat like that until there was a knock at the door and Danny's cousin Lucky poked his head in.

"Auntie sent me with a treat," he said. "Hey, Viv. Good to see you're not in prison."

She tried to laugh at that, though her stomach twisted into knots. "Thanks." Part of her still half believed that she would wake up tomorrow and discover she was there after all. "Pinch me," she whispered to Florence while Lucky handed over a plate of buns fresh from the kitchen.

Florence waved to Lucky as the door closed behind him. "Why?"

"I want to make sure this is real." Vivian stared around the tiny, pretty room, curtains fluttering at the window, a much-patched quilt spread across the bed. Florence in her rocking chair, the only furniture she had brought with her into her new life. The rain still fell outside, an irregular beat like the intro to a jazz number. "It feels like a dream."

She yelped as Florence pinched her arm. "It's real," Florence whispered, running her hand gently over the sore spot she had just made. "Danny kept telling me it would be all right, and I didn't believe him."

"He was saying that just to make you feel better, you know," Vivian pointed out.

Florence laughed and took one of the buns from the plate. "I know. But he was still right. And now I have everything I need again."

Vivian dragged a breath past the lump in her throat. Florence's certainty, that she was loved and all would be well, rubbed at the tender places in Vivian's heart, the places that wished she had that certainty herself. "Flo, you love Danny, right?"

"Of course I do," Florence said, frowning at her.

"Well," Vivian said slowly, not sure she wanted to say it but pushing herself through the question anyway. "What if you love someone, but the person you love does something unforgivable?"

Florence looked surprised by the question, but there was a small smile tugging at the corners of her mouth. "There's no 'if' about it. They *will* do something unforgivable. It's what people do."

"What happens then? Just hope that one day, they'll make it up to you?"

"No. They can't." Florence shook her head. "There's no making it right. That's what it means for it to be unforgivable."

"But—"

"Vivi." Florence took her hand. "Sometimes forgiveness is a gift you choose to give, even though a person could never possibly earn it, because you love them. Because *they* are forgivable, even if whatever they did isn't."

"That sounds . . ." Vivian shook her head. "Really damn hard."

"It is." Florence smiled. "It's one of the hardest things in the world. But if you can't do it, you're going to go through life alone. Because everyone you meet, everyone you love, at some point will do something unforgivable. We're human. We can't avoid it."

"And what if you don't know whether you love them enough to do it?"

"Well . . ." Florence winced, one hand going to the side of her swollen belly. Without being asked, Vivian fetched a stool from the corner so Florence could prop her feet up. "That's the first thing you've got to figure out, then. Some people deserve that kind of love from you. Others don't. Sometimes hard things bring you together, and sometimes they push you apart. And sometimes it's no one's fault which it ends up being. It's just the way life goes." Still rubbing her belly with one hand, she stretched sideways to retrieve the mending basket from the floor. "Any chance of you telling me who we're talking about?"

Vivian was silent, biting her lower lip as she looked away from her sister's probing gaze. Her eyes fell on the basket, and before she knew it, she was laughing. "Oh hell," she gasped. "I just remembered. I didn't tell Miss Ethel I wouldn't be at work today."

She felt tears pricking against the back of her eyelids once more as she hiccupped her way through her giggles. Florence, who had been threading her needle, set her things down. She levered herself out of the chair once more and went to sit on the bed. "Hand," she ordered, holding out her own.

Vivian, unsure what was about to happen, took it, only hesitating a little. Florence frowned for a moment, as though she were listening to something no one else could hear.

"There," she murmured, and placed the palm of Vivian's hand against her belly.

The movement caught Vivian off guard, and she nearly snatched her hand back from the series of fluttering kicks. "Flo," she said, staring at her sister. "That's the baby."

It felt like a stupid thing to say, but her sister only smiled in response. "Sure is."

"Holy moly," Vivian muttered, staring wide-eyed at her hand as the kicks disappeared for a moment, then resumed in a sudden flurry. "Does it hurt?"

Florence laughed. "I wouldn't say it's comfortable," she admitted. "But I don't mind. Taking care of someone who needs you isn't always a comfortable thing."

The kicks disappeared. "That felt a little pointed," Vivian said, giving her sister a wry look.

Florence's smile didn't waver. "It was." She patted the bed next to her. "Come here."

Vivian hesitated only a moment before sliding in next to her sister.

Their legs stretched toward the footboard, feet tangled up with each other, and Florence eased her arm under Vivian's shoulders, guiding her sister's head to her shoulder.

They didn't say anything. At last, Vivian rolled over, curling into a ball as she pressed her face against her sister's side, and cried.

Florence didn't let go.

———–·—

She had to go eventually. Florence needed to rest, and Vivian wanted to try to keep her job, since she'd still need to pay rent and all the rest of it. But she took her time about leaving, packing away the mending and making sure Florence was settled.

"Flo . . ." Vivian paused in the doorway. Her curiosity got the best of her, as it always did. "It wasn't Danny who did something unforgivable, was it?" She hesitated, but she was pretty sure she already knew the answer. "It was me."

Florence, already lying in bed, smiled without opening her eyes. "Time for you to get to work, Vivi. I'll see you tomorrow." More softly, she added, "I'm so, so glad I get to say that."

Vivian swallowed down the lump in her throat. "Me too," she whispered. "God, me too."

———–·—

It took Miss Ethel a full thirty minutes to get through her lecture on how girls who wanted to keep their jobs should learn to use a telephone, even when they had emergencies in their family. At last, though, she sighed and grudgingly admitted that, since she did have customers waiting on deliveries, Vivian could at least work that day.

"But we'll see what happens tomorrow!" she snapped as she shoved three boxes across the counter. "I've got my eye on you."

She made it through two deliveries before she saw the address on the final box; when she did, her heart plummeted into her stomach. It was another delivery for Mrs. Morris.

Vivian's hands trembled as she knocked on the door. What if that same maid—what had her name been?—answered? What if the Morrises were on the lookout for a thief and suddenly remembered, when Mrs. Morris saw her again, that she had been there that day?

No, that wouldn't happen, Vivian reassured herself as the housekeeper—not the maid, thank God—led her upstairs. Mr. Morris couldn't have told his wife, or anyone, that his erotic letter from another woman had gone missing. She didn't need to—

"You've got a hell of a lot of nerve, coming in here like this."

The gruff, angry voice made Vivian jump, tense and alert as a feral alley cat who had just smelled a strange dog in her territory. The housekeeper sighed. "He always forgets to close the door," she murmured. "This way, please."

The shout hadn't been directed at her. But Vivian's heart was still racing as the housekeeper led her past the open door of what she could guess was Mr. Morris's office. He was pacing across the room, his face an angry purple. A woman sat calmly across from him.

"Perhaps you would like to close the door before we continue our discussion?" the woman asked.

Vivian stumbled over her own feet even as the door slammed shut. She knew that voice.

Mrs. Morris was in her sitting room again, alone this time. "Did I hear Mr. Morris shouting?" she grumbled to the housekeeper.

"Another meeting, ma'am," the housekeeper said, going to draw the curtains and adjust the tilt of the mirror in the corner. "He's closed the door now, I believe."

"He always forgets," Mrs. Morris said, shaking her head. "Oh, lovely, this must be my new tea gown?"

Vivian's mind stumbled to keep up as Mrs. Morris chatted through her fitting. There was one spot on the back that needed to be taken in, though it didn't require more than a few stitches. She hurried through the rest of the appointment, shifting her weight impatiently from side to side while Mrs. Morris tried on the dress once more. At last she pronounced it perfect, and Vivian could throw her things into her bag and say a polite good-bye. She hurried down the stairs, afraid that she would be too late.

She almost was. The black car was parked out front, the woman from Mr. Morris's office just about to climb in.

Vivian took a deep breath. "Mrs. Wilson!"

Hattie Wilson paused, her only sign of surprise, then turned very slowly, a pleasant smile on her face. "Miss Kelly. What a happy coincidence. It seems you're not in jail."

"I'm not," Vivian agreed, breathing heavily as she stopped next to the car, hoping she wasn't making a huge mistake. But she had to know if she was right. "You're blackmailing him."

Hattie tilted her head toward the car. "In you go."

Vivian only hesitated a moment before obeying. The driver—not one she recognized this time—slammed the door closed behind them. A moment later, the car pulled smoothly away from the curb.

Mrs. Wilson watched her, giving nothing away. "Well?" she asked.

"Imports are a useful line of business these days," Vivian said pointedly. "What did he sign over to you?"

Hattie raised her brows. "His share in the company. He'll still hold the seat on the board nominally, of course, but he'll vote as I say. I can be very persuasive, even when I don't have blackmail material. When I do have it . . ." She lifted her shoulder in a pretty little shrug. "I'd have liked to fold the business completely into Wilson Enterprises. Unfortunately, that puts me at a square fifty percent. Which is exactly equal to Mr. Whitcomb and Mr. Rokesby."

"Can't find anything on them?" Vivian asked, her heart pounding as she thought of Corny Rokesby's drinks with his stepfather.

"Mr. Whitcomb is distressingly upstanding, or at least as upstanding as anyone is these days, and Corny refuses to sell me his shares. Sadly, you can't blackmail a young man like him. What am I going to threaten him with, exposing that he drinks? Everyone does."

"He also gambles."

"A relatively common vice, all things considered," Hattie said, shaking her head. "Still, I'm fairly satisfied with how things have progressed and what I do have control of. And who knows what I might discover in the future? Now." Her voice grew a little harder, though her smile didn't disappear. "Did you need something other than the chance to tell me you finally put two and two together?"

"I owe you, right?" Vivian said, thinking quickly. "What if I can tell you something you don't already know? About Mr. Morris?"

Hattie's brows rose. "Depends on what it is."

"You wanted to know who Evangeline Buchanan was having an affair with." Vivian took a deep breath. "She's the *E* in that letter you had me steal from Mr. Morris."

Hattie Wilson's lips parted, then slowly curved into a smile. "Hmm. That is interesting," she said, sounding amused. "Where did you come across such a curious tidbit, Miss Kelly?"

"Like you've said, I'm a resourceful girl." Vivian watched her carefully. "So are we square?"

That made Mrs. Wilson smile again. "For the moment, Miss Kelly, I believe we are. Now, did you need anything else? Or should I have Peter drop you off at your squalid little home?"

"The squalid home, please," Vivian said, carefully keeping a smile on her own face. "Thanks so much for the chat."

———·———

can't believe you're working tonight," Bea said, standing aside so Vivian could borrow her dressing table mirror to fix her lipstick. "After everything that happened."

"Where else would I be?" Vivian asked, shaking her head and running her fingers through her hair to smooth it down. The back of her bob tickled her neck. She'd need to get it trimmed soon. "All my favorite people are here. Except Florence, but she's probably already asleep. Apparently, it's tiring to grow a baby."

Bea snorted. "You're not nearly as calm as you're pretending, so quit trying to fool me."

"I can never fool you," Vivian said, setting down her lipstick and meeting her friend's eyes in the mirror. "I'd never even try."

Bea rolled her eyes. She had never been the type of girl who got sentimental. From her, an eye roll was as good as a hug. "All your favorite people, one that you're avoiding, and one that you're not sure if you want to kiss or punch?"

Vivian didn't need to ask who the last two were. "What would you do if you were me?"

"Oh, no, ma'am," Bea said, shaking her head as she bent to tie her shoes. "I don't go in for that messy nonsense. I've got my fella, and he's got his job that's completely separate from here, and that's the way I like it. You keep your romantic troubles to yourself."

"Bea," Vivian protested, laughing in spite of herself.

To her surprise, Bea gave her shoulders a quick squeeze. "I was gonna miss you something fierce," she whispered.

Vivian didn't try to hold her when she stepped back, though she wanted to. "I should hope so," she said, which made Bea roll her eyes again. "Come on, time for you to go wow 'em."

It was crowded and rowdy on the dance floor that night, and at times people were stacked around the bar three and four deep. Vivian eyed the new bartender each time she went to collect another round of drinks, wondering cynically if he would last.

"Can you make something without gin? I can't stand the stuff."

The eager request caught Vivian's attention as she went to drop off her tray and start her first break, though she wasn't sure why. Did she recognize the person talking?

But it was a girl she had never seen before, smiling hopefully at Danny, who clapped a hand to his heart and pretended to be shocked. "Won't drink our gin?" he teased her. "What is the world coming to when I can't serve a pretty doll my signature fizz?"

She giggled. "Is that all you know how to make?" she teased him back. "They told me you could shake up anything."

"Oh, well, in that case." Danny leaned his elbows on the bar and grinned at her. "You look more like a whiskey girl to me. Am I right?"

And that part caught her attention too. Gin and whiskey, she realized.

She hadn't really had time to care about who was poisoning Huxley Buchanan because she wasn't being accused of poisoning him. But it had to be someone around him more than Maggie Chambers had been. Someone like a wife who convinced him and his stepson to share a drink every night. Or a stepson who did what his mother told him.

She set her tray down slowly, staring at Danny and the girl while they continued to banter, Danny barely needing to watch his hands while he mixed her drink.

Some people didn't like gin cocktails.

Corny Rokesby had been one of them.

"Viv?"

The quiet voice interrupted her train of thought, and Vivian turned to find Leo standing near her, spinning his hat on the bar with one hand while he eyed her uneasily. "Wasn't sure if I'd find you here or not," he said.

Vivian swallowed. "You okay?" she asked, not sure what else to say.

For some reason, that made him smile. "I'm doing swell," he said, stepping closer to give her shoulder a gentle bump. "You?"

"Running my feet off," she said. It felt easier to talk about work than anything else. "Lotta troublemakers here tonight."

She gave him a glance that pretended to be stern, and his smile grew. It felt good to tease him again. But it was almost too light, as if both of them were playing a role, not sure exactly what the other expected.

"Well." Leo ran a hand through his hair. "If you have a break coming up soon, can I take you for a spin?"

Vivian almost said no. But he was smiling at her, and for a moment it felt like when they had first met, when he had been nothing but a charming stranger with fast feet and a killer smile. When everything between them had been all possibility and no history.

"I'm on a break now," she said softly. "If you're free."

It was a foxtrot—not one of her favorites, but simple to fall into. They still moved like they had the first time they'd danced together, like they'd been dancing forever. It was easy to glide across the floor in each other's arms.

And it hurt, because the distance was still there. He wasn't a charming stranger. Being with him, being held by him, was comforting. But it was also a reminder of everything hard that had happened, everything she didn't want to think about and he didn't want to discuss. Vivian didn't know if that was the sort of thing time could heal, if they would be able to forgive each other for the way they hadn't been able to weather the storm together.

Sometimes hard things bring you together, Florence had said. *And sometimes they push you apart. And sometimes it's no one's fault which it ends up being.*

When the dance ended, Vivian didn't pull away. Leo held her close, and she rested her head against his shoulder. Neither of them spoke for a long time. The other dancers moved around them, and if they complained, Vivian didn't hear it.

"Thanks, Leo," she said at last. "For trying. For everything."

He hooked a finger under her chin and lifted it, bending to brush a single, sweet kiss against her lips. "Anytime, Viv," he said softly. "We're pals, yeah?"

"Always." Her smile trembled, but she nodded. "Always."

He held her until it was time for her to return to work. And then he found another partner and got back out on the dance floor. Because Vivian and Leo had that in common, too. When they were dancing, the rest of the world didn't exist.

———

When her next break rolled around, Honor found her in the alley behind the Nightingale, sitting on a pile of old crates in comfortable silence with Bea while they passed a cigarette back and forth. In the distance, they could hear music, and Bea hummed along, occasionally singing the lyrics under her breath. Vivian tipped her head back, staring at the way the moon edged the clouds with silver. The night air smelled of trash and worse, and the chill of it made her throat ache, but she didn't care. It still felt glorious.

They hadn't left the door open behind them; the city was too quiet tonight, and they knew better than to risk the sounds of a party spilling out into the street where any curious cop passing by might hear it. So when the door opened, they turned immediately, a burst of sound and light spilling over them and briefly making the walls of the alley glow gold.

Honor, silhouetted in the doorway, surveyed them for a moment before letting the door fall closed behind her. "Great set tonight, Bluebird," she said. "That fella I saw lurking around the bandstand wasn't scouting new talent, was he?"

"I wish," Bea said, shaking her head. "Just a little puppy dog looking all hopeful. I told him the bank's closed and sent him packing. I don't think he'll make any trouble over it."

"You let me know if he does, and I'll have Benny or Saul give him a talking-to. Can't let anyone mess with our songbird." Honor was back to her usual self. But she still hesitated before she turned to Vivian. "I hear I have you to thank for catching a problem with our gin order."

Vivian ground out the cigarette against the wall behind her. "I don't think that new fella's going to cut it behind the bar."

Honor sighed. "They never do, do they? No one can keep up with our Danny-boy."

"He hits on all sixes, that's for sure." Bea hopped down from the crates and stretched, though she glanced between Honor and Vivian warily while she did. She knew what had happened by now. "Time for me to get back on the bandstand. You coming, Viv?"

"In a minute," Vivian said, not moving. She didn't think Honor had come out just to talk about the gin. "Go knock 'em dead, Bluebird."

The silence stretched through the alley after Bea was gone, chased by a cold breeze and the sound of two cats fighting in the distance.

"Guess I owe you a drink, for that catch," Honor said at last.

"I don't need a drink," Vivian said softly, standing as well, though she kept her distance. "But I could use your help with something."

"Depends on what it is."

Trust Honor not to agree without laying out terms, even now. It almost made Vivian want to laugh. "A letter. I need help writing a letter that I'm going to convince a lousy fella to sign. And it needs to be airtight. I figure you'd be good at that sort of thing." She took a deep breath. "And like you said. You owe me." They both knew she wasn't talking about the booze order.

"That's true." Honor gave her a considering look. "All right, pet. Come inside, and let's see what we can do."

THIRTY-FIVE

This time, when Bea let her in at the back door of the Buchanans' house, she didn't slink from hall to hall or peer around corners. She walked straight to Huxley Buchanan's study, Bea at her side. Vivian knew where she had left the letters, and she suspected that no one had done anything about them in the last two days.

She kept her head down in the room itself, though. Those memories were still too raw. And she had liked Huxley Buchanan in the few minutes she had known him, in spite of everything she had learned about him since.

"Is it there?" Bea asked from the doorway, where she was keeping an eye on the hall.

Vivian could hear a few voices in the distance, but none of them sounded like they were coming near. She didn't waste any time, though. Kneeling behind the desk, she let out a relieved breath when she found the drawer of letters still untouched. It made part of her simmer with anger—had the cops bothered to look through his things at all?—but there wasn't time for that.

It didn't take her more than a minute to find what she was looking for. Vivian read it through twice, eyes flicking rapidly back and forth, to make sure she had remembered it correctly. The letters from Honor's mother were there, too. She hesitated a moment, then pocketed those as well. There was no telling what Mrs. Buchanan or Corny would do if they found them. And if it was her mother, she'd have wanted to keep them. Honor could decide what to do with them herself.

Then she stood and walked to the sideboard, examining the different bottles, uncorking the cut-glass decanters and sniffing their contents.

Smiling, grimly satisfied, she joined Bea at the doorway. "Ready?"

Bea's lips kicked up at the corners. "Feels like a good day to quit this damn job."

"You're wasted here, anyway," Vivian agreed. "The only place you belong is on stage. Where do you think he is?"

"Still in bed, the lazy owl," Bea said, shaking her head. "But that probably works even better for you, doesn't it?"

They didn't bother knocking when they reached Corny Rokesby's bedroom, just walked right in. He was sitting up in bed, still in his pajamas, his red hair a mess around his head while he yawned his way through a cup of coffee. When they walked in, he jumped, then cursed loudly as it splashed all over his lap.

"Goddamn," he yelped. "What the hell do you think you're doing? Who are—" He broke off, his eyes narrowing as he recognized Vivian. "You."

"Me," she said, smiling as Bea closed the door behind them. "Hi again, Mr. Rokesby. Late night gambling? Or were you out with the Gold Coast Boys again?" She tossed his appointment book onto the bed as she spoke.

He glanced at it; when he looked back at her, his eyes were snapping with rage. "You know I could report you for stealing, don't you, you stupid bird?"

"You could," Vivian agreed calmly. Behind her, she heard the click of Bea turning the key in the lock. Rokesby started to look nervous. "But trust me, I'm doing you a favor when I say you don't want to have anyone else in on this conversation."

"And why is that?" he asked, crossing his arms and drawing himself up, even as he was still sitting in bed with a lap full of hot coffee.

"Because I doubt you want them to know that you were poisoning your stepfather."

He threw himself out of bed, scattering the remainder of his breakfast tray across the coverlet. "Get out," he ordered, his voice rising to a squeak.

"Really?" Bea said, her voice dripping with sarcasm. "You didn't want to play it any cooler than that?"

"And you! You're fired!"

"You think she'd want to stay and work for you?" Vivian demanded. "Fella who gets his stepfather to have a drink with him each night, pretending like he wants to be friends. And the whole time he's just making sure he drinks a little arsenic every day, just waiting for him to get sicker and sicker."

"That's applesauce," Rokesby said, but she could see his hands shaking. "That's slander."

"And it sure is suspicious, don't you think, that the bottle of gin you gave him has somehow vanished from the sideboard in his study, just when the police might have needed to check it for arsenic?" Vivian continued relentlessly. "And he'd have known that you didn't like gin, so he wouldn't blink an eye that you didn't want to share it with him." She shook her head, turning to Bea. "Guess he thought he'd be getting more in the will. Bad bet, that one."

"Must have been a shock when it was read out," Bea agreed.

"You can't prove anything," Rokesby said defiantly. "Not that there's anything to prove. But like you said, the bottle of gin is gone. So." He crossed his arms, looking satisfied.

"Hmm. Not sure about that." Vivian glanced down at the letter, as though reading through it again. "I know a medical examiner who'd be happy to share some information about arsenic poisoning. And this letter your stepdad kept about your gift sure looks suspicious when it's paired with that missing bottle."

"That's still not enough to take to the police," Rokesby said, but he sounded less sure of himself.

"I never said I was going to the police."

Something in her voice finally got through to him; he paled and took a step backward, stumbling into his nightstand and having to catch his balance against the bedpost. "Then what . . ."

Vivian smiled as she handed Bea the letter. "It's so much worse, isn't it, to think what people would say if they found out? The speculation. The whispers. Maybe even a column on it in the paper. They wouldn't use your name, but everyone would know who they meant." She paused. "Just imagine what your mother would think. Your friends. His business partners."

His eyes darted around the room, as if looking for an escape. At last, he swallowed visibly and turned back to her. "What do you want?"

Vivian pulled out the letter Honor had helped write. "I want you to sign this."

"And then you'll give that back to me?" he asked, gesturing toward the paper Bea held.

Vivian laughed at him. "No, I'll hang on to that. But as long as you hold up your end of things, I can promise you it won't see the light of day."

"And why should I trust you?"

Her voice grew hard. "Because unlike you, I'm not a murderer."

"I didn't kill him," Rokesby protested. "They caught—" He broke off as she raised her brows at him. She could see his jaw clench, but he nodded. "All right. What am I signing?"

———•———

Are you sure this is how you want to use it?" Bea asked once they were outside, leaving the Buchanan house behind as quickly as possible. "You know she's dangerous."

"I know." Vivian held her hat on her head as they dodged across the street, ignoring the angry honking of a cab. "But I think it'll be worth it." She didn't say it would be safe. They both knew there was no way to predict that.

Bea didn't look happy about it, but she nodded. "Well, I hope you don't mind if I hightail it home instead of coming with you."

"Smart of you," Vivian agreed. Before Bea could take off, though, Vivian caught her arm. "Thank you. For everything. For taking that job and . . ." She shrugged helplessly. "I owe you."

"You've done the same," Bea said quietly. "Or close enough, anyway. Things are square between us, Viv." She pursed her lips, then added wryly, "Except that you still owe me a dress."

That made Vivian laugh. "I'll sew you a new one myself," she promised. "See you tonight."

She didn't have far to go once Bea left. Fifth Avenue was crowded with mansions and, after a year of deliveries, she knew her way around them.

No one blinked an eye at her when she said she was checking on an order. Vivian waited in the kitchen, feeling like the letter in her pocket would burn a hole straight through her coat. Her fingers tapped an anxious beat against one thigh until a maid finally motioned for her to follow.

Hattie Wilson was seated behind her desk, reading through a stack of papers. But she laid them aside, elbows on the desk and her chin resting lightly on her fingers, as she regarded Vivian. "Thank you, Annie," she said to the maid. "You may go. Close the door."

Vivian tried not to shiver as the latch clicked. She didn't think she needed to be afraid. But it was impossible not to be unnerved by that steely gaze, framed by Hattie's doll-like face.

"I hope you're not here to be a nuisance, Miss Kelly," Hattie said at last. "I'd hate to have to ruin the lovely turn your week has taken."

"Actually, I'm here to make your week a whole lot better too," Vivian said. The flicker of interest in Hattie's face felt immensely satisfying. Vivian pulled out the letter Corny Rokesby had signed and laid it on the desk.

Hattie gave her a considering look, lips pursing slightly as she took her time picking up the paper, making it clear that she was still the one in control. But her cool demeanor cracked, just for a moment, when she picked up the letter and read through it. Her lips parted slightly, and a slow smile spread across her face.

When she looked up at last, though, Vivian could see satisfaction and wariness warring in her expression. "Corny Rokesby is signing his shares and his seat on the board over to me."

"He is," Vivian agreed, taking a seat at last, pleased when Mrs. Wilson didn't protest.

"Explain."

Vivian shrugged. "I found out a little something about Mr. Rokesby this week, something he doesn't want to become public. So long as I'm hanging on to the proof, you get his share in the company. Which means you've got yourself sixty percent of a helpful little import business." She smiled. "Are you going to say thank you?"

"I might," Hattie said. She held out her hand. "I assume you have this proof on you? I'd like to see it."

"I'm sure you would," Vivian said, not moving. "But that'll stay between me and Mr. Rokesby. Call it insurance."

"Smart girl." Hattie's smile grew thoughtful as she read through the letter again. "I don't see your name on here, Miss Kelly. Why is that? Surely you'd have preferred to have the shares signed over to you."

Vivian snorted. "I live in the real world, thanks. No one would buy it, and I don't need cops sniffing around trying to figure out what the game is. But no one will blink an eye at you. At least not too much." She stood. "You're welcome."

Hattie set the paper down, resting her hands flat on the desk on either side of it. She was watching Vivian with more wariness, more respect, than she ever had before. "Why?" she asked. "Why help me out?"

"Because." Vivian went to the mirror that stood in one corner. She took her time smoothing down her hair and settling her hat at just the right angle before turning back to Mrs. Wilson. She smiled. "This time you'll be the one who owes me a favor. And I'll collect when I'm good and ready."

———

You made it out in one piece," Honor murmured when she found Vivian that night, waiting at the bar for Danny to hand her a tray of drinks. "It was a hell of a risk to take, you know."

Vivian shrugged. "She'd have been an idiot not to accept, even if she doesn't like owing me."

"I meant going to see Rokesby," Honor said, leaning one elbow on the bar. To most people there, she would have looked perfectly at ease. But Vivian could see the wariness in her expression, as though she expected to be told to take a hike at any moment. "There was no way to know how he would react, and you spent enough time tangling with the cops this week. I'd have thought . . ." She hesitated, then took a deep breath. "I wish you hadn't chanced it again so soon."

It had been a risk. But she'd been determined to take it, determined, at last, to be the one in control. She hadn't explained any of that to Honor, just told her what she needed and waited. Honor hadn't hesitated before agreeing.

"Why'd you help me, then?" Vivian asked, genuinely curious.

For a moment, she thought Honor wouldn't answer. "Because you asked me to. And if I want you to trust me again, that means I start by trusting you," Honor said at last. "Because I'm sorry. I know it's not enough. But for what it's worth, I'm sorry."

"It's not like you got out of this unhurt either," Vivian said, watching her hands as she ran one finger along the edge of the bar. "I do know that. Your mother . . ."

"It's not the same," Honor said. "I've got a lot of work to do to earn your forgiveness. This was as good a place as any to start."

Vivian picked up her tray, newly filled and ready to be taken to a rowdy table of college boys. The cocktail glasses shivered against each other, though the sound of them was lost in the music, and she turned to look Honor full in the face at last. "You can't," she said.

Honor's chin moved, the barest flinch. She was good at hiding how she was feeling. But Vivian saw it. She wondered what Honor had been like as a child. Occasionally criminal, she had said. But that had been about what she did, not who she was.

Had Honor also spent years dreaming of a family that would want her, find her, take her away from the life she hated? Did she also watch everyone around her, waiting for the moment when they would leave and she would be alone again, fending for herself?

Vivian took a deep breath. "But I might decide to forgive you anyway," she said as she turned away. "One day. Maybe. No promises, though."

When Vivian made it back to the bar, Honor was gone. She closed her eyes and leaned against it, reminding herself that she was safe. That she'd wake up in the morning and would still be safe. It was hard to believe, but she was getting there.

"Vivian!"

She opened her eyes when she heard Danny hollering her name, expecting to be handed another round of drinks. Instead, he was grinning at her, holding out a towel. "We could use an extra set of hands back here. Up for it, kitten? Nightingale needs you!"

Vivian glanced around. They really were in the weeds tonight, and the new bartender was barely keeping up. Regulars and strangers alike were crowding at the bar, and they shouted jokes and encouragement at her while Danny waited expectantly.

Vivian felt a giddy laugh rising in her chest. She was getting there, and she was home.

"You know me," she said, smiling at the crowd. "I'm always up for a challenge."

AUTHOR'S NOTE

Though interracial marriage was frowned on, and often illegal, in the 1920s, only some parts of the country had laws against it. In New York, it would have been legal for Florence and Danny to marry. Because Chinese immigration was so limited (and Chinese women, in general, were not permitted to emigrate to the United States) it was not uncommon for women from poor Irish or Italian immigrant families to marry Chinese husbands. Even when interracial marriage was legal, however, it was still a complex decision for the men and women involved. Chinese residents were at a high risk of deportation, and women who married outside their race could lose their U.S. citizenship.

While Chinese immigration was highly restricted in the 1920s, there were workarounds, most of them having to do with labor and economics. Danny and his family take advantage of one of these: if you owned a restaurant, you could sponsor family members to emigrate and work for you, though these arrangements were supposed to be temporary. The research of Beth Lew-Williams and Heather Lee are both excellent starting points for learning more about Chinese immigration in the United States.

Though a drag ball might seem like a modern invention, the Hamilton Lodge Balls were real events that took place yearly at the Rockland Palace Dance Hall in Harlem. They were a cornerstone of queer nightlife culture in the 1920s and 1930s, but they'd been around since 1869. (Though as far as I know, there were no illegal gambling rings camped out in the basement.)

These annual events were known officially as Masquerade and Civic Balls, and the masquerade portion of the night was a major part of their appeal. Members of the LGBTQ community traveled from around the country to participate, and newspapers reported on the costumes of the winners, often announcing them by name.

The New York Age noted in 1930 that, "Scores of males of pronounced effeminiate [*sic*] traits gracefully disported themselves in beautiful evening gowns. They might have been mistaken anywhere for fascinating shebas." Female partygoers also were welcome to attend in drag, and many newspapers described masqueraders as being part of "the third sex."

But the Hamilton Lodge Balls weren't just a gathering for the queer community. They became a major event in the New York social scene for people from a wide cross section of classes, sexual orientations, and races. In 1927, a writer for *The New York Age* wrote that "Color prejudice was thrown to the winds" as people of all races mingled together. In 1926, an estimated 1,500 people attended. By 1933, that number had grown to 6,000, and the police and fire officials had to be present to maintain order. I'm indebted to the excellent research done through Queer Music Heritage, as well as many other scholars in the queer community, for compiling resources on the history of the Hamilton Lodge and its masquerade balls.

Curious readers may have noted the odd story that Vivian and Mags discuss about party guests being knocked out by ingesting, rather than inhaling, chloroform. This was based on a real poisoning case in the early twentieth century, in which a party host spiked his guests' drinks with chloroform and robbed them of $3,000 while they were unconscious. For more about poison crimes in the Jazz Age, I highly recommend Deborah Blum's *The Poisoner's Handbook: Murder and the Birth of Forensic Medicine in Jazz Age New York*.

Finally, though Vivian gifts Bea a copy of Countee Cullen's book of poetry, *Color,* it was published later in 1925 than this book takes place. Cullen was a brilliant star of the Harlem Renaissance, and his poetry is well worth seeking out if you've never read it.

ACKNOWLEDGMENTS

To Nettie Finn, it was a privilege to work together, and I will always be grateful for everything you did to bring the Nightingale to life.

To Hannah O'Grady, for your excitement about taking on this project and your insights in the final stretch.

To Whitney Ross, I've said it before and I'll happily say it a million more times: I'm so lucky to have you in my corner.

To Allison Ziegler, Sara LaCotti, Hector DeJean, Christina MacDonald, and the entire team at Minotaur and St. Martin's Press, for all the work that goes on behind the scenes to bring a book to life.

To the librarians, archivists, and historians who have put so many maps, fashion plates, songs, restaurant menus, cookbooks, magazines, newspaper articles, and other documents online. You have my eternal thanks.

To the booksellers and librarians, especially Flannery, Chelsea, and Sarah, who have been endlessly enthusiastic about getting these books into readers' hands.

Acknowledgments

To everyone at Bright Eyes, especially Reagan.

To Neena and Gemma, for endless listening and encouragement. To Genevieve, Becky, and Shannon, for inspiring me with your own writing. To Mike and Kelsey, for giving me my favorite spot to write every summer. And to Josh, Steph, Ross, Ben, Diana, Jen, and Beau, for being the best weirdos around.

To my kids, for their patience and flexibility (at least when it counts).

To Brian, for absolutely everything.

To you, reading these words, I wouldn't be here without you. Thank you.

ABOUT THE AUTHOR

Leah O'Connell

Katharine Schellman is a former actor and one-time political consultant. These days, she writes the Nightingale Mysteries and the Lily Adler Mysteries, which reviewers have praised as "worthy of Agatha Christie or Rex Stout" (*Library Journal*, starred review). Katharine is a graduate of the College of William & Mary, and lives and writes in the mountains of Virginia in the company of her husband, children, and the many houseplants she keeps accidentally murdering. You can learn more about her at www.katharineschellman.com.